MOSCOW TRAFFIC

JULIETTE M. ENGEL, MD

A Novel

Published by:
Trine Day LLC
PO Box 577
Walterville, OR 97489
1-800-556-2012
www.TrineDay.com
trineday@icloud.com

Library of Congress Control Number: 2023949584

Engel, Juliette M.
Moscow Traffic—1st ed.
p. cm.
Epub (ISBN-13) 978-1-63424-441-1
Print (ISBN-13) 978-1-63424-440-4
1. Fiction. 2. Thriller. I. Title

First Edition
10 9 8 7 6 5 4 3 2 1

Printed in the USA
Distribution to the Trade by:
Independent Publishers Group (IPG)
814 North Franklin Street
Chicago, Illinois 60610
312.337.0747
www.ipgbook.com

The road to the truth is a good story.
                                        – Old Russian saying

TABLE OF CONTENTS

Chapter One

THE BOOK OF MIRACLES

Kurzan Monastery, Russia, Anno Domini 1355

The following letter from Bishop Rostovsky Voronov to his lifelong friend and patron Prince Yaroslav the Redeemer was written in the waning hours of the Year of our Lord, 1355.

Greetings Dear Patron Prince,

Winter is upon us and I fear it will be my last. Frost creeps up the path and ice clogs the well. The fever that seized me in autumn has progressed. I can scarce draw breath without fits of coughing that leave me bloodless. I waste away, yet I am driven to put onto paper my memories and to share with you the unembellished truth about the miracle at Kurzan.

As you know, each year in August I have taken to the Moscow River with my clerics for a pilgrimage to St. Kirill's—five days by ship each way and an arduous journey for a young man, let alone an old one. Last summer was no exception. Three longboats were loaded with supplies and clerics. We added two bowmen for each boat as protection against the heathen Balts. Pagan tribes are known to attack and kill clerics who attempt their conversion from the old ways of human sacrifice.

Downriver, the voyage was swift and effortless. My sermon to the congregation at St. Kirill's was well received and I spent a week among pleasant company. Time and age weighed heavily on my bones by the time we started our voyage back to Moscow.

The return upstream was laborious. Oarsmen strained against the current, often forced to wend their way by means of pools, backwashes and eddies. At night, we camped on shore — lulled into slumber by the roar of the river so loud that hummed through my bones until my teeth rattled.

At dawn, the camp rose to morning prayers and I woke each day wearier than the day before. I prayed to the Holy Mother for the strength to make the journey home to the cloisters. At breakfast, I revived a little over my bowl of herbs and kasha. Youthful voices wafted through the mist on all sides followed by the scraping of longboats as oarsmen slid them over the riverbank to the water. The vitality of natural life surrounded me—the scent of pine, wisps of pollen blowing like snow across the dark sand, the chattering of startled birds.

I sat in the prow nestled in furs. The river current ran swift and deep, but the surface was smooth — mirroring white clouds and waterfowl. The naked arms of the oarsmen, their laughter and malty breath gave comfort. I have reached the age when observing youth awakens pride, not envy. They sang the lusty ballads of the river and paid no mind to the old relic perched in the bow.

> Volga, Volga, swift and wide
> A tender virgin for my bride...

Time passed and my thoughts drifted. I stared down at my hands, marveling at the pale, bony claws that have replaced them. These were once a powerful woodsman's hands, callused and brown with cord-like veins. Those hands knew the softness of a woman and were clasped in prayer upon the hour of her soul's departure. I loved and lost her, then joined the cloister at Smolensk. There they became the delicate instruments of a cleric, the brown flesh fading to white. The warmth of a woman's skin was replaced by the stiff purity of parchment awaiting the stroke of my pen. Now, behold the gnarled arthritic talons of an old bishop who longs for a warm bath and soft feather bed.

South of Rolnik where the river narrows, the chanting was replaced by grunts and ponderous breathing. Muscles strained; jaws clenched. Men heaved and sweated against the treachery of the river. At first, I urged them homeward but by late afternoon, seeing that Moscow could not be reached before sunset, I ordered the boats to stop on a sandy shore. We would rest and continue our travels at daybreak.

The oarsmen beached the boats. Servants caught fish to stew with our few remaining vegetables while the clerics erected my tent. The young ones were sent into the forest to gather pine needles for my bed. After stew and evening prayers, our party lay down to sleep — I in my tent, the men on blankets spread over the sand. The bowmen stood watch in the moonlight.

I was soon lulled into slumber by the force of the river. Its vibrations thundered through the soft ground and shook my spirit free. I became a crane flying high above the river. Sunlight glistened on my white wings. Below, a pale corpse floated in the water, pathetic in its nakedness. Its white beard and hair drifted in a halo around the withered face. The outstretched arms had claws for hands.

My wings lifted me skyward, away from that portent of approaching death. I raised my head and stared into the brightness of the sun. At first, the light was glorious. It washed the sky in burnished gold. But as I stared, I smelled scorching flesh and my eyes boiled in their sockets. I was encased in white fire, my wings aflame. I tumbled and fell.

Startled, I awoke — or did I? My tent chamber was filled with light. It shone through the linen walls and surrounded my bed.

"Fire, fire!" I struggled to rise to my feet and shake sleep from my brain. My heart pounded and I gasped for breath.

When I could stand, I hobbled to the tent opening with the aid of my staff. "Fire, fire!" the words stuck in my throat. There was no fire. The longboats were beached undisturbed on the shore. The campfire had burnt out as had the torches. Even the guards were asleep. I could see every detail because the encampment was awash in light — yet the forest and the river beyond lay in darkness.

I gathered my wits and discerned that the source of light was a single point suspended in mid-air. Curiosity made me venture away from the tent to investigate. I discovered a glowing, rose-colored bridge that extended across the great expanse of the river and disappeared into dense forest on the opposite shore.

I approached the bridge with a warm wind at my back that seemed to lift me. My steps grew lighter. My spine straightened. Staff in hand, I mounted the bridge which hovered a few fingerbreadths above the surface of the river. Wherever an eddy or whirlpool splashed the bridge, sparks hissed and snapped like wet, green wood on a campfire.

At first, I was afraid of falling but the wind encouraged me. Crossing myself and praying, I floated across the bridge at surprising speed. My dear prince, what visions raced through my mind while the songs of angels whispered around my ears. The past, the present, and perhaps the future of mankind swirled before me. Secrets were revealed. They appeared and vanished before my mortal brain could capture them.

On the far side, the light delivered me to a circle of ancient kedr trees. It was the kind of place where the pagan Balts sacrifice to their goddess Zemyna. Justice is swift and cruel for those heathens. Their rituals are soaked in the blood of sinners. Had I been drawn to this place by pagan sorcery? Were there savages lying in ambush, ready to slit my throat? The wind grew stronger, nudging me forward. Branches bowed and groaned overhead as if whipped by my fear.

"Come into my house..." I heard those words and the wind ceased. It was so quiet that I perceived my labored breathing and beating heart. Was this sudden silence, the stillness in the air, witchcraft? I crossed myself and kissed my crucifix. Then I drew on the full armor of God as instructed by Saint Paul. I called up a legion of guardian angels and stepped into the circle.

There I beheld the greatest miracle granted to any mortal man. Before me, in her beauty and simplicity, the Holy Virgin stood with her gown and golden hair blowing about her although there was not a breath of wind. Her feet were bare against the forest floor.

I fell to my knees in fear and trembling to kiss the hem of her gown, but she took my hands and drew me up until I gazed into her eyes. In them, I saw the world aflame. Churches and villages burned. The faithful were driven from their homes. I tried to withdraw from the terrifying scenes, not knowing if they were future or past, but she held me close.

"Come, penitent…" This time her eyes revealed a place of eternal peace — a cloister behind high walls devoted to healing, a great church of white stone with blue domes and golden stars surrounded by fields of wheat, orchards of apple and pear trees.

"Take me home," she whispered in a voice like the wind. I knew that I had been chosen to rescue the Virgin from this pagan place and to build her a house, a great monastery where she would be safe for all time.

"Yes," I said, bowing and crossing myself. "In the name of the Holy Trinity, I pledge my word."

When I looked up, she had disappeared. Where she had stood, an icon swayed from the branch of a kedr tree. The delicate face of the Holy Virgin glowed upon it in every perfect detail. I saw enfolded in her arms, with His face pressed against her cheek, the Holy Child. I understood at once that this icon had been the source of my vision and of the miraculous bridge that had drawn me to this pagan place. It became my anointed task to rescue the Virgin and build a home for her and Baby Jesus.

I fell to my knees, weeping and praying, thanking God for sending an old man such a precious task late in his life. I prayed until the chattering of birds heralded sunrise. Exhausted, I took the icon from its branch and clutched it to my breast. Once again, I mounted the bridge and crossed the span of light at great speed. On reaching the encampment, I threw myself on my bed and slept like the dead.

Next morning, all was in readiness for departure when the clerics came to wake me. They helped me to my feet and discovered two things: My staff was missing, and in the bed next to me lay a rough-hewn slab of oak, about one-cubit square. I trembled and struggled for words, feeling weak in my knees.

"What is it?" they asked, pointing to the icon.

"It's the Holy Virgin," I said, crossing myself. I held it up for them to behold. But the beautiful faces of the Virgin and Child were gone. In their place there were crude renderings in reddish-brown pigment.

"Isn't that the pagan goddess Zemyna? The one the Balts sacrifice children to?" asked the clerics, drawing back in fear. "Is it painted in blood?"

What an old fool I must have looked with my mouth gaping open and even more the fool when tears came to my eyes. I told them the story of the miraculous bridge and finding the icon in the forest. "It is the Holy Virgin and Baby Jesus. The Holy Mother came to me and begged me to save them from the pagans. 'Take me home,' She said. We must build Her a church here and now."

Their eyes were wide, first with astonishment, then with disbelief. At the end of my telling, they thought me either mad or possessed. There was doubt on every face. I had one chance to prove the rightness of my mind.

I pointed to the far side of the river where my staff must still lay and commanded that they row me across. On the far shore, I ordered the servants to search the woods for the staff. After about one hour, I heard shouts from the trees. They had found the staff where I had left it in the circle of kedr trees.

I knew what must be done. I took a woodsman's axe from my servant and began the work of building a church for the Virgin. The others joined me in my work. Soon, a search party that had set out from Moscow when we did not return to the cloister arrived and went to work.

By afternoon, the woods were filled with believers who heard of the miracle and came to offer their devotions to the Holy Virgin and their labors to construction of Her house. By evening, we had built a small church near the bank of the Kurzan River. When all were gathered for prayers, I placed the Virgin inside, blessed the church and decreed that upon that site a great monastery should be constructed, declaring the name of the monastery to be Kurzan.

With the blessing of the Metropolit of Moscow, the icon was consecrated and named the Virgin of Kurzan. Under his instruction, it was transformed into a work of art by the finest icon painters who made the long journey from Sergeev Possad.

First, they soaked the wood in brine to clean it of blood and dried it in the sun. Then they painted the surface with exquisitely rendered faces of the Virgin Mary and Infant Jesus exactly as I had seen them on the night of my vision. Master artisans applied layers of gold leaf until the halos gleamed. The finished work was encased in a mantle of hammered silver, inset with uncut gemstones. It was installed in the newly constructed Church of the Kurzan Goddess by the Metropolit Nikolaev himself.

A second miracle occurred when the angry Balts, who had besieged us steadily since the taking of their icon, came out of the forest en masse waving their weapons and demanding the return of their holy relic. Instead of fighting them, we opened the gates of Kurzan and invited them into the Church of the Kurzan Goddess. At the sight of their goddess's new beauty and the birth of an infant son named Jesus, they dropped to their knees and asked to be baptized. They became devout Christians and remain so to this day.

At the time of this writing, more than a year has passed. I am surrounded by the bustling new monastery and the enthusiastic hymns of young brothers who have come to worship and serve. A village settlement called Kolomeno has grown up around the monastery walls. The new refectory houses pilgrims who come from the far reaches of Rus to seek healing from the Virgin of Kurzan. They are generous in their gratitude.

The Balts have settled in the village. They tend the gardens and livestock. They are enthusiastic farmers and have planted an orchard from here to the river. In a few years, hectares of apple trees will bear profitable fruit. Merchant Jews have settled among them and built a bakery and metalworks.

In spring, once the ground thaws, the bellmakers will come to cast a great bell. Kurzan Monastery will acquire a commanding voice and join the Golden Ring of monasteries encircling Moscow.

Sadly, for me, I will not live to hear it. The brilliance of autumn has faded. Winter has come to rap on windows and rattle doors. Soon the soul of one old bishop will depart like a wisp of smoke up the chimney to join the white cranes flying to Our Lord Jesus Christ in Heaven.

Every morning at dawn my clerics carry me into the Church of the Kurzan Goddess where I pray before the Virgin of Kurzan. I am nearly weightless now, more spirit than living flesh. My dry bones crumble within me, yet the Virgin has granted me life beyond what is natural so that I might finish this task for her. I am grateful that it is nearly done.

Know, my Prince, that I die a happy man, content that the Virgin of Kurzan is safe in her place of sanctuary. But I confess to you, and only to you as my oldest, dearest friend, that sometimes when I look upon her splendor, I feel ill at ease as if she mocks me a little. I am ashamed to admit it, but I wonder if something pagan remains in her, soaked into the wood like blood.

I will say nothing about my doubts. They die with me. The people adore their icon. The pilgrims who arrive from far and wide bring steady revenue to the monastery and the village where they pay for bread and board. They come to pray for healing and the Virgin of Kurzan does not disappoint them. The Holy Mother grants miracles every day that are entered into our Book of Miracles.

Now, I must bid you farewell and pray to our Lord Jesus to deliver our souls from infidels and sinners. I am your devoted Servant on earth and in heaven,

Roskovsky Borisovich Voronov
Bishop of Kurzan
1355

And so began the Book of Miracles that was kept in Kurzan Monastery through fires, famine, floods, invasions and plagues for 573 years.

It ended in 1928 and became another story.

Chapter Two

THE MYSTERY

Seattle Washington, October 4, 1997

D r. Peter Stone fumbled for the telephone. "Hello?"

"She's dead!"

"What?" Peter bolted up in bed. "Baba? Is that you?"

"My girl, she's dead."

"Caroline? Dead?" He switched on the light. "What happened? What are you talking about?"

"I'm telling you, Peter. The Russians killed her." The old woman wailed. "In Moscow."

"That can't be right. She's in New York." He picked up the clock: Four-thirty. "Who told you this?"

"Some federal agent called. I can't bear it."

"Where are you? Are you in New York?" He pulled on his pants and struggled with his shirt, phone tucked between chin and shoulder.

"I'm at home. Her coffin will be at Sea-Tac in half an hour. Come get me."

"I'll be there in ten minutes."

He raced his red Jeep Cherokee over rain-slicked streets, ignoring the downpour. He had not seen Caroline since the night she stormed out of their houseboat nearly one month ago. He had expected her to come back after a cooling-off day at Baba's like she usually did and was surprised when she had flown to New York City. *But we'd worked it all out on the phone, hadn't we?* She said that she wanted time on her own to work on her singing career. He had agreed to wait. Besides, he could take advantage of her absence to finish his paper on sociopathy in post-Soviet Russia for the *Journal of Forensic Psychology*. He had often longed for quiet when she practiced scales and vocal exercises in their living room, rehearsing operatic roles until he also knew them by heart.

But now their little houseboat on Lake Union was too quiet. He missed her music and light-hearted chatter. His work as chief medical resident on the locked psychiatric ward of Harborview Hospital left him emotionally drained each day. Coming home to the silence had become an ache in his chest. *Russia? Impossible. She's coming home at the end of this week.*

The Jeep's tires squealed around corners and through stop signs. He skidded to a stop in front of Baba's weathered bungalow atop Blue Ridge. Caroline's childhood home was the last of the old fishermen's cottages that had once perched in a brightly painted row along the bluff. The view of downtown Seattle was spectacular, but the sandstone cliffs were steadily eroded by the tides of Puget Sound. All but one of the cottages had succumbed to wind and waves and fallen into the sea.

Baba waited at the gate. Before Peter could get out of the car to help her, she climbed inside. Drenched and shivering with rain-slicked hair, she looked even older and smaller than when he had seen her the week before.

"Thank God you've come. I was afraid you might be on call at Harborview." She clasped his hands with cold fingers strong as talons. "I cannot face this alone."

"You aren't alone. We'll get this sorted out together," Peter said more calmly than he felt. The old lady looked ready to fly to pieces. He pulled an Army blanket from the back seat and wrapped it around her shoulders. "Can you tell me what Caroline was doing in Moscow?"

"Singing in some Russian opera—*Ivan Susanin*, I think. Yes, she had starring role for opening night at Pushkin Theater."

"Why didn't she tell me? Why didn't *you* tell me?" Peter had a dozen questions, but he checked his rising frustration. There was no point in upsetting Baba more than she already was. He needed to be strong, to stay centered and get the facts. Maybe she had misheard or misunderstood. She was elderly and her English was far from perfect.

Baba shrank down in the seat and pulled the blanket around her. "She wanted to succeed on her own. She said you would understand. Do you understand? I'm not sure that I do."

Peter shrugged. He didn't have an answer. He put the Jeep in gear and sped through sleeping Seattle—downhill across the Fremont Bridge to Western Avenue and onto the Alaskan Way Viaduct at thirty over the limit. The road rolled out in front of them in a straight line that ran to infinity.

"It is my fault," said Baba. "She deserved better than me—a real family instead of a silly old babushka who lives in the past, the Russian past."

"That's not true. You gave her music and taught her to sing." Peter squeezed her arm through the blanket, willing warmth into her trembling limbs.

"I taught her nothing—a few vocal scales and how to play piano. She progressed far beyond what I could give her. She is going to be great star… or she was…" Baba's voice faltered and they sank into silence until she spoke again. "The City of Seattle will condemn my house soon. I might as well die before they tear it down or it slides into the Ship Canal and becomes risk to navigation. What will become of my roses?"

Peter sped up more, recalling the winter nights in the cozy parlor when Baba played the piano and Caroline sang. Outside, Seattle might be a modern city of swiftly moving traffic, factories, trade, and ships which gazed ever westward toward the markets of Asia. But inside the cottage, they were cosseted in another, quieter world — a timeless memorial to aristocratic old Russia.

"I should have told Caroline the truth about the Russian Revolution and Civil War, but it was too terrible to speak of. Sometimes she caught me going through old photographs and asked about my family. I make up a little something, an innocent fairy tale that brings the dead to life for a few moments." Baba sighed. "Maybe I do wrong. I want her to be American with happy past. I hoped she would settle down with you, Peter—to raise a family and never experience such ugliness as I have seen."

Peter slowed as they turned into the entrance of Sea-Tac International Airport. Baba pointed. "Drive to last hangar on Cargo Road. See the lights?"

They parked and he followed her onto the tarmac wishing that he had brought an umbrella. Halogen lights illumined sheets of rain. A cargo lift drove out of the open hangar. Men in hard hats and yellow vests darted between dry places.

"I hear a plane." Baba clung to his arm.

The whine of turbines heralded the approach of a Boeing 737. The jet's nose loomed through the mist followed by flashing red lights, wings, and shrieking engines. The plane rolled to a halt. The engines cut. A mobile lift maneuvered into place while cargo doors lowered from the plane's belly. Wind gusted. Rain poured from Peter's hair into his eyes. He wrapped his arms around Baba to cover her with his coat.

Her knees gave way at the sight of a long box sliding onto the platform. "No, no…" she moaned. "My baby, my little girl." Peter held her tight. His mind detached, as if the rain pounding the sleek coffin was a scene from a movie that he could switch off at will.

The box lowered. Baba struggled against him. "Let go, let me go." When it was close to the level of the tarmac, she broke free.

"Baba stop," he shouted, startled by her ferocity.

She pushed past the ground crew who drew back in surprise. With a howl of grief, she hurled herself on top of the coffin. A crack rent the air. The lid split in two pieces that clattered onto the tarmac. Baba disappeared inside the box.

The scene froze except for the rain. No sound came from the coffin. The crewmen stared at it open-mouthed, then they turned to Peter. He stepped forward and peered over the rim. Baba lay face down inside. The coffin was empty save for a layer of sand.

He lifted her gently and brushed the grains from her face.

She dug her fingernails into his coat, arched her back, and screamed: "My baby—where is she?!"

Chapter Three

THE CRIME

Seattle, October 4, 1997

Peter eased off the I-5 freeway onto James Street, then turned right up First Hill to Harborview County Hospital. He had called ahead and arranged for his colleagues in the emergency room to meet the Jeep with a wheelchair. He wanted to admit Baba for observation and she was too exhausted to argue. His next stop was a meeting with the King County Executive, Lex Frasier. Lex had been his friend and a fellow rugby player since university. He needed answers and if anyone had them, or could get them, it would be Lex.

The King County Courthouse was also on James Street but down-hill and to the south in a part of Seattle that once was good, then bad, but verged on good again. It was one of his least favorite buildings—an ugly gray cinder block box with a few oddly proportioned stone columns stacked around the entry. Peter parked in an overpriced lot, turned up his collar against the rain and joined a brigade of county employees in berets, fedoras, and baseballs caps.

He cleared security and entered the lobby. At this time of day, the high-vaulted vestibule was packed with freshly scrubbed lawyers, hair still wet from post-workout showers at the Washington Athletic Club, toting briefcases or towing banker's boxes strapped to cheap suitcase dollies. They looked refreshed and eager in contrast to their clients who hovered close-by in rumpled clothes, menaced by the oppressive staleness of the King County hall of justice.

The elevator door opened and Peter was pushed to the back of the lift. He nodded to some of the attorneys that he knew. He'd had his moments in the courthouse that left him with little patience for a criminal justice system that flooded his county psychiatric unit with non-committable criminals who had obvious psychiatric problems but refused voluntary treatment.

As a result, the locked unit was crowded to bursting, understaffed and barely under control. Most of the patients had been there many times before. Half of those were true psychotics, lost in a world that could neither confine them nor set them free. The others were hardened thugs who knew how to game the system. Any idealism that Peter once had was long gone by the time he exited the elevator and walked down the fluorescent-lit hallway to Lex Frasier's fourth floor office.

"Hello Dr. Stone," chirped Miss Underhill. "Help yourself to coffee. It's Starbucks." Lex Frasier's secretary had outlived many generations of County Executives and been cheerful ever since Peter could remember. "Mr. Frasier is with Police Chief Blandings. They're retrieving some files for your meeting. Have a seat."

Peter poured a mug, letting the warm brew revive him. A visitor from upstate New York once joked that Seattle was the only place in the world where people could talk for twenty minutes about coffee. He leaned against the windowsill and gazed down on the wet street imagining Caroline's blond head in the crowd that hurried down Second Avenue toward the Pike Place Market. She had always been out in front someplace.

"Peter!" Lex boomed from the doorway. "I knew you'd turn up." The affable, mustachioed giant in tweeds swept into the waiting room with Chief Blandings, a small wiry man. "Come into my office. Bring your coffee."

They sat around a glass-topped conference table littered with notepads, paper clips and pens. While the Chief of Police organized his papers, Lex and Peter exchanged some ritual chitchat for the chief's sake. Neither wanted to reveal their personal relationship with Caroline. They would let him say his piece and leave. Yes, it was true, the expansion plans for the Harborview Psych Unit had been quashed again by the City Council. No money. Just an expanding volume of psychotic criminals ping-ponging around a system that denied their existence until it tripped over one of them in the search for a serial killer or hard-core pedophile.

After a minute of shuffling, Blandings stacked his papers and looked up expectantly. Lex nodded and tamped tobacco into his pipe, "Fill him in, Chief. Dr. Stone needs to understand the politics."

"Are you sure he should hear this?" asked Blandings. "Can we count on his discretion?"

"Peter is our consultant on Russian criminology. He speaks and reads the language fluently. I don't, do you?"

"Fine, fine." Blandings grimaced, showing yellowed teeth. He was lean, fit and had a raptor stare that he turned on Peter. "To say that we have an awkward situation on our hands is an understatement. We aren't even certain that a crime has been committed but whatever happened, everyone from the mayor to the governor wants this Caroline Luke thing cleaned up yesterday. We're in the middle of negotiating the first Pacific Rim Alliance Treaty – the PRAT."

"To put this in context," said Lex, "the City of Seattle stands to make millions when this trade agreement is signed."

"That's right. We can't let a scandal with Russia muddy the waters," said Blandings. "If you want your new loony bin at Harborview, you better hope the Russkies, the Japs and the Chinese will think Seattle truly is the Emerald City. This Luke case has to be handled quickly, quietly and on the down-low. We can't let that old Russian grandmother of hers stir up trouble with the press." Blandings slid a file folder in front of Peter. "This is everything we have so far. Most of it is in Russian." He looked at his watch, pushed back his chair, and stood up. "I've got to go greet the Chinese delegation at the Edgewater. I'll leave you two ruggers to work out the details." The door closed behind him.

"Sorry about the chief," said Lex. "He's under a lot of pressure and yes, he is a sonofabitch. Brusque seems to work for him."

"Damn the politics, Lex. I need answers." Peter opened the file. His adrenaline rush was fading. The wet cold had soaked into his bones leaving him feeling sluggish and sad.

"I'm sure you do. We all do." Lex lit his pipe. "Take a look at those documents. You're the only one that can read them."

"Did she really go to Moscow?" Peter inquired as he thumbed through papers typed in Cyrillic. "The coffin was empty, weighted with sand. It wasn't even real, just a papier-mâché box, a stage prop that fell apart in the rain. Maybe she didn't leave the country."

"I'm afraid she did. The State Department confirmed it." Frasier tossed Peter a brown envelope. "Customs sent this over a few minutes ago. It's her passport. It came with the coffin. What's in the folder?"

Peter scanned the papers. "Here is a Death Certificate from a Dr. Krimsky. This one is an Affidavit of Death from the Moscow City Morgue. The next one is in English—a Confirmation of Death and Citizenship by the American Embassy. So, where the hell is Caroline?"

Lex opened another envelope. "And here's one in English, too—a $5000 invoice from American Airlines for transporting a coffin from Moscow to New York and Seattle."

"When did you learn about this?"

"Our office was notified by the State Department this morning, same time as the grandmother." Lex's face softened. "How is the old lady? What does Caroline call her? Baba? Raised her, didn't she?"

"That's right. Caroline didn't know her parents." Peter frowned, remembering how the elderly woman had collapsed in his arms like a broken bird. "She's strong but in shock. I admitted her to Harborview. We'll keep a close eye on her there."

"God bless the old girl." Lex sighed.

Peter picked up Caroline's passport. Flicking it open to her smiling photo, he recalled the day it was taken. She had washed her thigh-length hair for the picture, blown it dry, and braided it into a thick rope of gold.

"It's just a passport photo," he had teased her. "Why the fuss?"

"Every first impression is important," she laughed. "You never know who you'll meet, even in the passport line."

Remembering her laugh brought the ache back to Peter's heart. He rubbed his chest. "These Russian papers look legit," he said. "I've seen the same stamps on other cases coming through Harborview. The Russian Notary stamps can be faked. I wouldn't put too much faith in them without confirmation." He pushed the file back to Lex. "There's nothing phony about her passport. Something terrible has happened. You need to call Interpol."

"No can do." Lex shook his head. "The first thing I did this morning was contact the Moscow police. They are not aware of any crimes. Until they give me something to act on, some indication that she's in trouble, my hands are tied."

"What do you mean 'if'? Of course, she's in trouble." Peter sat up, revived by a flash of anger. "We're talking about Caroline, for God's sake. You know exactly what kind of trouble she can get into."

Lex nodded. They had both fallen in love watching her sing sultry ballads at the Blue Moon Tavern in a beige minidress that made her look naked under her veil of hair. It had all seemed sexy and fun when they were university students. "So, what was your girl doing on her own in Moscow?" he asked.

"I didn't know she was there." Peter grimaced, annoyed at how lame that sounded. "We'd had a fight and she stormed out like she does whenever we argue. She goes to Baba's. They eat popcorn and watch old Russian movies and she comes back the next day as if nothing's happened. When she didn't come home, I called Baba and found out that she'd gone to New York."

15

"Did you talk to her there?"

"Of course. She was doing auditions and looking for an agent. I paid her hotel bill and she promised to be back home this week. The first I heard anything about Russia was this morning from Baba." Peter rubbed his face. "I should have gone to New York with her."

"Why didn't you?"

"At first, I didn't want to take the time away from work. Later, when I changed my mind, she didn't want me to come. She said she needed to be on her own. I gave her space because that's what she asked for."

"Sometimes I just don't get you," said Lex shaking his head. "You're a thirty-two-year-old MD and a senior fellow in criminal psychology. You speak five languages. Hell, you speak Russian like a native. You're the chief resident on the biggest, scariest psych unit in the Northwest, but Caroline has you stretched over a barrel."

"I admit that I've never understood her ambition," said Peter. "And just to be clear, I didn't go into forensic psychology because I'm well adjusted," he added. "Few people do. But that's beside the point." He shivered as the magnitude of his loss sank in. "We've got to find her. Maybe she's hurt or lost. What if she's been trafficked?"

"An empty box, some dubious Russian documents and a passport aren't enough to request an international investigation that might throw a wrench in the PRAT negotiations," said Lex. "That's why I asked Blandings to fill you in on the politics."

"You're saying there's nothing we can do?"

"There are strict protocols that I'm obliged to follow in this situation." His old friend's face cracked a sly grin. "However, there are no such constraints on you. You have worked with the police enough to know at least something about police procedure but you are not part of the department. You speak Russian and can get around Moscow on your own."

"I'll bring her back myself." Peter perked up, energized by the plan. "Great idea."

"I hoped you'd say that," said Lex. "You can leave tonight. There's an Aeroflot flight from Sea-Tac at eight p.m."

"I'd better get organized." Peter checked his watch—seven-thirty a.m. He could still make it to Harborview Hospital in time for morning psych rounds. "What about work? I'm the attending physician on the locked ward this month."

"No problem. Governor Dan will call your boss and free you up for a few days. We've already discussed it and he agreed. As I understand it, you and he go back a ways. Grad school, wasn't it? You and Caroline and Dan Evans doing that summer in Russia with the Jackson School of International Studies?"

"Five years ago—an immersion Russian language course." Peter frowned at the memory of grimy streets and toilets that made his eyes water from the ammonia fumes. "It would help if I knew why she went. Baba said something about starring in an opera?"

"She's right. The police commander faxed me this." Lex slid him a copy of a playbill for opening night at the Pushkin Theater of Opera and Ballet in Moscow. It announced the international debut of American soprano Caroline Luke singing the lead role of Antonida, the virgin bride, in Glinka's opera *Ivan Susanin*.

"Starring in Russia's National Opera," Peter's eyebrows went up. "This is a career maker. Of course, she went. Why didn't she tell me?"

"That I do not know." Lex shrugged and pointed to the date. "The opening was three nights ago. According to the American Embassy, she was a big hit. Everyone loved her—then poof, she vanished in the middle of the cast party, costume and all. A few hours later, the embassy representative was called to the city morgue. He supposedly identified her body. Then the morgue sealed up the coffin and shipped her body home—except that they didn't. You know the rest same as me."

"Will the American Embassy in Moscow help me? They're the ones who claim she was in the morgue." Peter skimmed through the documents. "This is signed by George Tanner, American Citizens Services."

"Not much joy there. According to them, Caroline Luke is dead and they see no reason to look for her. You'll have to convince them otherwise. Besides, they don't do anything quickly. Everything goes through channels and more channels and since you're not a cop, you don't pull any weight. You're better off just finding her and handling this privately—and quietly." Lex tossed him Caroline's passport. "Take this with you. The embassy will need to issue her a new passport before she comes home. Somebody punched a hole in this one."

"I'm sure she's all right." Peter tried to sound optimistic as he stood up to leave. "She's very resourceful."

Lex squeezed Peter's shoulder. "I'll make copies of all these and send them to Harborview with the rest of the documents as soon as I get clearance from Olympia."

"What about a contact in Moscow? I'll need to liaison with the police, won't I?"

"I do have some joy in that department." He handed Peter a fax cover sheet with an address and telephone number for Commander Alexander Golokov of the Moscow Militia. "This commander is a forensic psychology buff. He's read your papers on sociopathy and even asked for you as our consultant. He's willing to keep this unofficial as long as we keep it out of the international press." Lex rolled his eyes. "Worse luck for us, Caroline made a lot of friends in the media and they've spread the story of her disappearance around Russia. It's just a matter of time before the *Seattle Times* catches up and the State Department steps in."

"And Chief Blandings has a seizure."

"Bring her home before that happens and we'll all be happy." He tapped Golokov's name. "You'll meet with this gentleman first thing. He has offered to take care of your visa through the Russian Consulate in Seattle and arrange for you to stay in Caroline's apartment. She lived with a family named Pavlov. Maybe they know something. You can snoop around, talk to the host family and the neighbors, but Commander Golokov is your liaison. Keep him in the loop."

"Thanks, Lex. Looks like you've had a busy night."

"I'm here every morning by four a.m. Time zones are a bitch," said Lex. He patted Peter's back. "Caroline's a special girl. Bring her home."

Peter stared at the fax. Snapshots of the dingy Russian capitol scrolled through his memory. He had hated Moscow with its grimy, rundown buildings, pervasive smell of sweat, diesel, and cabbage, the merciless poverty and dirt. No one had a cellphone. People barely had landlines. Only the cities were fully electrified and had indoor toilets. Caroline had loved every bit of it—even the scratchy little towels at the Rossiya Hotel that gave him a rash. He'd sworn never to return.

"Wait. There's more," said Lex. "I don't know what to make of this." He handed Peter another faxed page. The Russian heading indicated an official police file, but it consisted of several lines of Cyrillic poetry. Someone had hand-printed the question, "KURZAN?" at the top.

Peter stared at the unfamiliar word. "What does it mean? Kurzan?"

"How should I know?" Lex shrugged. "Now buck up and get going. I'll help you however I can but remember what Blandings said—quick, quiet and on the down-low."

He pushed Peter into the hallway, stalked back to his office and slammed the door.

Chapter Four

THE PSYCHOLOGIST

P eter climbed the back stairs from the Harborview Hospital parking garage two at a time and let himself into the High Security Psychiatric Unit with his keycard. He managed to slip unseen into his office, leaving the overhead lights off. He wanted to clean up and stifle his wild imaginings before psych rounds.

He brushed his teeth and shaved by the light over the office sink, then did his best to comb his short, sandy-blond hair. In the closet, he found a clean, starched white coat embroidered with his coded number. He pulled it on over his damp clothes. No one who worked on the locked ward used their real names around patients. He was Dr. 174. Ready for the day, he switched on his lights. There was nothing he could do about the fact that he wasn't wearing socks.

There was a knock on the door. His senior resident, Dr. Sarah Pickford, must have been waiting outside. She put her head in. "I heard you're taking emergency leave." She set a steaming dark blue mug on his desk and peered over her reading glasses at his bare ankles. "You look like you could use some coffee."

"I've got to leave town for a few days." Peter took a sip, grateful for the heat. "Can you cover for me?"

"Sure. What about your research?"

"That can wait until I get back," he said. "I'll be gone less than a week."

"No problem. Just update me on your active cases after rounds."

"Thanks," he said, but she didn't leave. "What is it, Sarah?" he asked.

"Did something happen to Caroline? I mean—is Caroline all right? I saw that her grandmother was admitted to the Cardiac Care Unit." She put up her hands and shrugged. "Sorry, none of my business but you look kind of sad."

"I'll fill you in when I get back. I promise. Can you keep an eye on Baba for me? Don't let them send her home too soon."

"I'll take good care of her." Sarah turned to leave, stopping at the door. "Where are you going?"

"Russia." He said it before his brain was engaged and wished he hadn't. "Let's keep that between you and me."

"Russia?" Sarah whistled softly and closed the door behind her.

Peter sat in his ergonomic chair and switched on the closed-circuit television network. Overhead monitors scrolled to life revealing a hive of activity behind each of the locked doors that comprised the ward. Patients were eating breakfast, using the toilet, taking their meds, struggling against restraints. Even at this early hour, the unit teemed with disordered life—the by-product of dysfunctional minds considered too dangerous to be set loose in Seattle.

For Peter, Harborview's psych unit was a safe world where chaos was conquerable. Madness could be restrained, medicated, and controlled. Psychosis was subdued and brought to heel. Via the monitors and through his glass walls, he could anonymously observe and supervise every corner of the ward.

He used a code to open his desk. He put in his rucksack and removed the current patient files that he would update and turn over to Sarah, stacking them neatly on the desktop—the only movable items on the expanse of clean, brushed steel. The rest of his office furnishings were minimalist and monochromatic—a gray metal bookcase, two utilitarian black chairs bolted to the floor and a cheap, oversized, black and white photograph of Mount Rainier reproduced on canvas and epoxied to the back wall.

No glass, no throwable or breakable items that could be used as weapons were allowed on the ward. No personal photographs were kept where patients might see them—no smiling kids, lovers or pets. No one received personal mail or displayed their names on degrees. Pens and pencils were locked in drawers when not in use. The rules were strictly enforced. Many of these patients were dangerous psychopaths who would not be locked inside for long. Those who were not imprisoned or deported would soon be back on the streets disrupting life and commerce in downtown Seattle.

At 8:30, he joined his colleagues for rounds. They started at the bed of a tattooed, bearded man who struggled against full-body restraints and cursed them in an unknown language. Then they moved through the locked rooms, reviewing each case. Peter usually led the discussions. Today he barely listened while Sarah described the violent psychotics and criminal sociopaths who had been admitted overnight. He glanced frequently at the wall clock, thinking of Caroline. Was she wandering through Moscow alone? Maybe she had met strangers who bought her fried potatoes in a workmen's café. Maybe she was hitching a ride in a gypsy cab. She had done those things before.

He recalled how she lectured him on their trip to Russia when he tried to warn her to be cautious around strangers. "There's no point in traveling if you're afraid of foreigners," she'd said, striding across Red Square in short khaki shorts with a backpack that thrust her breasts against a sleeveless white tank top. She was suntanned and braless. Peter had lumbered along beside her like an oversized guardian angel, frowning at the men who stared at his nearly naked girlfriend. She was free to be her careless self as long as he was along to protect her. Would she be so brazen on her own?

After psych rounds, he called Aeroflot and booked his ticket. Then he met with staff, completed his charts and signed the open cases over to Sarah. In late afternoon, Lex couriered the documents from Olympia along with his Russian visa. Peter packed them in his rucksack and took the elevator to the Cardiac Care Unit to look in on Baba. She had been sedated and was snoring softly. He checked her electrocardiogram and read the chart—no complications thus far. She was tougher than she looked. He left her a note with Lex's phone number to inform her that he was on his way to Moscow.

He exited Harborview by way of the Emergency Room. A few trauma patients lay on gurneys, tended by interns and med students. X-ray techs rolled a portable fluoroscope from one trauma suite to the next. He checked the triage board for pending psych cases. There weren't any—just a minor car wreck, a drug overdose, and a non-life-threatening shooting. Psych patients, the real crazies, came much later. By midnight they would fill the halls with their threats and incoherent mutterings.

The senior trauma staff were seated at the nurses' station doing justice to a box of glazed buttermilk donuts, their weekly treat from Ching's Bakery in nearby Chinatown. They beckoned for Peter to join them, but he had no appetite for donuts or banter. He gave a friendly wave and headed for the emergency exit. No need to mention Russia to this crowd. He would be back before they realized he was gone.

Driving home to his houseboat on Lake Union, he imagined his colleagues closing ranks behind him—washing away his footprints like a tide.

He packed and showered, cutting it short when Aeroflot called to inform him that his ticket was waiting at the KLM desk at SeaTac. He pulled on a sweater and jeans and thought about the last time he had flown to Russia. He and Caroline had begun packing weeks in advance. Now, he barely had time to throw a few clothes into a carry-on.

When his bag stood ready by the door with his yellow North Face parka draped over the top, he surveyed the living room. Even in absentia, Caroline dominated the space. A profusion of brightly colored scarves, handbags, and costume jewelry hung from every doorknob and picture frame. Her scent, China Rain, lingered on the furniture. Disorderly stacks of sheet music and opera librettos cluttered the baby grand piano and spilled onto the floor. He hadn't cleaned since she left. He wouldn't touch anything until she returned.

He poured a tumbler of scotch and carried it to his desk, an oasis of masculinity in the midst of Caroline's girlish exuberance. He kept the dark wood surface clean and uncluttered except for his computer monitor. He laid out his passport, visa, and Lex's files, wondering once again what the handwritten word "KURZAN?" on the fax from Commander Golokov meant.

He connected his dial-up modem and searched the internet, eventually finding a Cyrillic reference to a 14th century Russian Orthodox monastery. Kurzan had been one of the ancient Golden Ring of monasteries that formed a circle around Moscow, each one a day's journey by foot from the Kremlin. It had been looted and burned by the CHEKA, precursor to the KGB, in 1928 and subsequently converted into a prison for boys. *What could Kurzan have to do with Caroline?*

He moved on to the Cyrillic poem on the fax. He and Caroline had studied the Russian poets as part of their summer at Moscow State University. "You can't understand the soul of a people without studying their poetry," Caroline gushed in class after reciting *Requiem* by Anna Akhmatova, her favorite poet, with a dramatic flourish. "Russian language is lyrical, musical—perfect for poetry. Much more so than English. Reading it aloud is like singing."

Peter had been less enthusiastic about poetry in general. He turned his attention to the poem on the fax and read it aloud, trying to make it sing. It had a crude musicality in the Russian language, more like rap music than art. He translated it into English, looking for clues as why it had been sent by the Moscow police:

> *There are no shadows to my face,*
> *Only sharp angles without resistance.*
> *You are the broken mirror of my reflection*
> *In a thousand shards of silvered glass—*
> *You expose my empty soul.*

22

I am your dancing bear.
I howl, I cry, but no one answers.
I whirl and twirl,
The wildest in this wilderness.

It was signed UZI. The name was familiar. Peter had done some reading on this folk-poet/gangster, whom he considered a notable case study of the new breed of post-Soviet sociopath. More than a few of those had wandered into Washington State since perestroika and wound up in Harborview en route to deportation. There had been a painter and some musicians among them—charming but lethal men. The Soviet Union had produced more than its share of artistic criminals.

He had also read a recent article in the *New York Times* that described UZI as the "Russian people's poet of the Twentieth Century." UZI's clumsy but heartfelt attempts at poetry had drawn quite a following among disenfranchised youth in Russia who set them to rap music and sang them in the Metro station tunnels where the acoustics were remarkably good. Another article in *Time* Magazine alluded to rumors that UZI was the mastermind behind a new and powerful Russian mafia group. There were whispers that he donated large amounts of money to the arts. There were no pictures of the man and he had never appeared on television.

Did UZI have something to do with Caroline's disappearance? Is that why Commander Golokov included the poem? A poet would attract Caroline, but not a gangster. She abhorred violence. His face flushed at the thought of another man touching her and he struggled to keep a cool head. He was trained to stifle his emotions, to remain professional, clinical, and detached in stressful situations. It wasn't working.

He tried to order his thoughts by re-arranging the documents evenly across the surface of the desk. He recalled how Caroline loved to disrupt his compulsive neatness. She would wait until he was deep in concentration working on his thesis, then stretch out across his meticulously organized papers. No matter how annoyed he was at the interruption, his anger sublimated to passion when she would laugh and let her robe fall open.

In spite of her distractions, he completed his MD degree with honors and was well on his way to his PhD. "I told you so," she'd said. "Sex is good for the mind. It flushes out the rusty bits." He stared at the Cyrillic documents but saw only the post-coital sheen of sweat on her porcelain skin.

"Come back to me," he said aloud, unwilling to consider the possibility that she might not.

The wind gusted. A squall churned the lake and rattled the houseboat windows. Seattle was earning its nickname Rain City. Waves lapped below the floorboards, reminding him of stormy winter weekends when he and Caroline drove aboard the Winslow Ferry in her little Volkswagen and sailed across Puget Sound to the Olympic Peninsula. They would buy a box of warm Norwegian pastries in Poulsbo, then spend the next two nights in an oversized feather bed at the Seafarers Hotel in Port Townsend eating *krumkake* with their fingers and making love on the sugary crumbs, oblivious to the winds that howled off the Strait of Juan de Fuca.

"I'm going to sing at every great opera house in the world," she would boast, her head on his shoulder, her hair a golden fan across his chest. "I'm going to be famous."

"Of course, you are."

"I'm going to make you very proud of me," she would say. "You'll see."

"I already am proud," he'd reply stroking her cheek. Did he believe in her vast ambitions? Or was that what she needed to hear so that she'd open herself to him? It hadn't mattered—not then. He loved her whether she was famous or not. Looking back, he should have appreciated the breadth of her determination.

He drained his glass. Next to the bottle of scotch a clear paperweight caught the light. He ran his fingers over the smooth Plexiglas in which the eye of a white peacock feather was embedded. He picked it up and let it warm in his hand. He had been eight years old when his father pressed that feather into his hand at their final parting. Years later, he encased the feather in plexiglass and took it with him to university. Now he dropped it into the pocket of his parka—a remnant of the past that he carried with him to other worlds.

The squall subsided and the howl of wind was swallowed by empty silence. It was time to go. Peter collected the documents and packed them in his flight bag. He turned off his computer and stared at the place on the sofa where Caroline had lounged in her pink bathrobe with her hair tousled, her cheeks flushed from sex and wine. He had just stoked a fire in the woodstove and opened their second bottle of 1982 Bordeaux when she spoiled it by asking: "Can we talk?"

She had been trying to start a conversation about her opera career for days. "Of course," he replied and sat beside her, unable to put her off any longer.

"I've outgrown Seattle and that's a good thing," she said with forced cheerfulness. "It's time for me to go to New York and sign with an international agent. Everyone says I'm ready for the major opera houses. They audition in New York at the Baldwin Hotel."

He recognized that she was serious from the set of her jaw. "How long do you need to be there?" he asked.

"At least six months, maybe more." She took his hands. "I want you to take some leave and come with me. It'll be an adventure for us both."

He should have kissed her and said, "It will take some planning, but of course I'll come." Instead he went blank and skimmed along the razor's edge of a past he would do anything to avoid. In the time before Seattle and Wenatchee, before Stone Farm and the death of his father, there was the specter of New York City where he was born. How could he explain to the woman he loved that every molecule in his body was repulsed by that cursed place?

She pushed harder. "I'm nearly twenty-five years old. If I wait much longer, I'll be too old for romantic leads. I need to audition while I'm in my prime."

"I can't leave the psych unit in the middle of my chief residency. I might lose my job."

"No, you won't," she countered. "Everyone takes leave for professional enrichment. You can see patients at Bellevue Hospital. They have all kinds of crazy people there. They would love to have a multi-lingual forensic psychologist like you for a few months. It will be good for your research." She advanced. "Come on, Peter. We're young and in love. Let's enjoy ourselves in the Big Apple."

"You're not being logical," he countered. "There is a lot to consider."

"Like what?" Her cheeks reddened. "I stayed in Seattle for your MD and your fellowship. Now I want you to come to New York while I launch my career. What is illogical about that? Once I am an established soloist, I'll start earning good money. We can start a family."

"I can't go to New York—period." He felt cornered and defensive. "I just can't explain it to you right now."

"This isn't like you, Peter. What's wrong? You're sweating."

"I'm not even sure that I want you to go off singing in exotic places all over the world." He countered with the truth. "I love you the way you are. I'm happy with us the way we are. I don't want anything to change."

"Nothing has changed. I've always said that I would graduate from Cornish and go on to an international career in opera. Well, the time has come to launch myself onto the stage. At twenty-five, it's now or never." She gazed past him, staring out the window at a future he couldn't see. "I need sponsors, financial backing—a wealthy patron or two who believe in me and will donate to theaters to support my work and get me started. I'll never find that in provincial Seattle."

"I can support us. I won't be a resident forever."

"You don't understand. I need to hire an agent, do publicity and market myself. I have to have the right clothes and a few pieces of real jewelry. All of that is expensive. You've seen me lose roles that were perfect for me because there's no money backing me up." She balled her fists in frustration. "Without patronage, the cards are stacked against me. That means that I have to work harder and go to New York." She looked up at him with eyes that pierced his heart. "Well? Are you coming?"

At that moment, he should have taken her in his arms and admitted that her request was not unreasonable. A few months at Bellevue Hospital would be a great enhancement to his education. And as to finding a patron, she needn't worry on that front. He had a trust fund, the Petrosyan Fund, that he'd never mentioned to her because he didn't use it himself. It was something he'd inherited from his father. All he needed to do was pick up the phone and call Daniel Karlov, the trustee, to find out what was in it.

Instead, he froze at the memory of his father's rasping voice and his parting words: "It's blood money, criminal money. Forget you ever heard of the Petrosyan Fund. It's killing me. It never bought anyone happiness."

Peter looked in Caroline's eager eyes. "No," he said. "I'm not coming."

Her face fell, her jaw slackened in disbelief. Then anger flushed her cheeks a deeper red and tears welled in her eyes. He tried to hold her. "It's complicated. I can explain," he said, but she shook herself free and ran barefoot into the rain.

****

Peter drove his Jeep to Sea-Tac Airport for the second time that day and parked in the overnight Dollar lot. He collected his Aeroflot ticket and Russian Visa at the KLM desk and boarded the train for the International S Terminal.

An hour later, his giant Aeroflot Ilyushin rumbled down the runway for the eleven-hour flight to Moscow. There were empty seats on either side of him, so he should be able to stretch out and sleep. The last time he had flown Aeroflot, the University of Washington charter had been full. Barefoot grad students from the Jackson School of International Studies wandered the aisles sharing trail mix and cheap wine.

Caroline sat cross-legged on the seat beside him with *Land of the Firebird* open on her lap. She chattered away in her perfect though slightly old-fashioned Russian entertaining him with little-known facts: "Did you know that Empress Elizabeth invented the rollercoaster? Did you know that Peter the Great was six feet eight inches tall?" They had just celebrated the end of finals with a week of camping at Shi Shi Beach on the wild Pacific coast. She had an all-over tan and smelled of summer.

The memory faded. Passengers in other rows had wrapped themselves in blankets and slept. The stewardess brought him a pillow, but Peter didn't want to sleep. He wanted to roll back the clock to happier times. His mind drifted to Shi Shi again and the vision of Caroline at the end of the seven-mile rainforest trail from Lake Ozette.

"It's the Pacific Ocean!" She pointed to the mist-shrouded shoreline. She threw off her backpack and leapt gracefully over driftwood logs to the wide, sandy beach. At the water's edge, she unloosed her hair, letting it blow wildly as she sang Brunhilda's aria, the Valkyrie throwing herself into the flames. Her operatic soprano rose above the wail of wind and waves as she splashed through the riptide. "The immolation scene," she shouted, "from *Götterdämmerung.*"

By the time he reached the tideline carrying his pack and hers, she had transformed into Norma, the druid priestess. He followed her, laughing until his sides ached. She sang "Casta Diva" to the misshapen boulders that hovered offshore. Shi Shi's hunch-backed stone giants watched her from the mist.

Once the tent was assembled and the campfire burned brightly, she pushed him to the sand, and mounted him. Her pale face and breasts rose above him in the firelight. Her golden hair fell over her shoulders, brushing his face. She moved slowly at first, building his tension until finally she pounded against him howling like a she-wolf. He was caught in the frenzy of motion, pain, and passion. He flipped her over and fell into her universe.

"Shi Shi is where heaven meets earth," she sighed afterward, lighting a joint. He added driftwood to the fire and wrapped an unzipped sleeping bag around them both. Moonlight had banished the stars. The air was crisp, spiced with ozone.

"You are a goddess," he whispered, tucking a strand of hair behind her ear. "How can you love a boring *tabula rasa* like me?"

"You're not a blank slate. There's no such thing." She looked askance. "No matter what you've convinced yourself of, you descend from generations of people—each with a story. They are always with you in your soul. Don't you want to know where they came from? How they got here? Your father was Russian, wasn't he?"

Later, while she slept, he tucked her in and left the tent. He walked down to the water and let the breakers lap his feet and ankles, burying them in sand, pulling him out to the moonlit sea.

Aboard the Ilyushin jet, Peter turned out the overhead light, and wrapped himself in his North Face parka, determined to sleep for the rest of the long flight. The smell of Russian cigarettes lingered in the plane's upholstery even though smoking had been banned for a year. He remembered Caroline sniffing her seatback. "Yum," she laughed, "Russian incense."

He understood why Caroline wanted to know who she was. Her great-grandparents were White Russian aristocrats. Her father died before she was born, and her mother's name had been kept secret since Baba adopted her.

Peter had barely known his parents either. His father died when he was eight. His mother, always distant, was living with her latest husband in Florida and rarely communicated.

He felt in his pocket for the plexiglass paperweight, his only link to Denis, his Russian-born father. He rubbed the smooth surface with his thumb and recalled the night when Denis had placed the white feather in his hand. He had been awakened earlier by his mother, Ruby Mae, shrilling in her deep South accent, "I'm a peacock, Denis, not a god-damn duck."

"You are a peacock, darling," cooed his father. "It gives me great pleasure to see such an exotic bird in my apple orchard." There was a slight Russian accent to his father's speech. His mother, Ruby Mae, was pure Alabama.

"You don't get it. I hate this place—this ridiculous Stone Farm. I was a big star when you married me."

"Yes, my love. You were the Peacock of the Bellagio, the crown jewel of Las Vegas."

They paused and Peter imagined his parents lighting cigarettes. He smelled the memory of smoke. Ruby Mae said, "Why don't you take some of your old man's money—that Petrosyan Fund? Take me and the kid back to New York. Buy us a decent house in the Hamptons."

"I've already explained to you why. The Petrosyan Fund is criminal money. I can't accept it anymore." Denis wheezed. "Please, my precious," he gasped. "Get me some water."

"Get your own water. I'm not your maid," she snapped. "I'm not staying here another night. I hate this place."

"Stop shouting, you'll wake the boy. Some water…please."

Peter heard her opening and closing drawers while his father coughed. He ran to the kitchen and filled a glass. He brought it to his father. Denis drank. "Thank you, son." He pulled Peter into bed with him. They watched his mother stuff evening gowns and underwear into open suitcases. "She doesn't understand. It's Russian blood money. I won't touch it ever again."

"Money is money." Ruby Mae slammed the closet door. "You can write me a big fat check now or in court. I'm taking the kid." Peter lay on his father's chest, frightened by the rasp of his breathing and the fevered heat of his body through the damp nightshirt. His mother rummaged in his bedroom, returning with another suitcase. "Get dressed. We're leaving."

Peter clung to his father. "Daddy's sick," he cried.

"Your daddy's sick all right—sick in the head. He makes me live in this dump when he's worth millions. Your daddy was a Wall Street banker when I married him. He was an important man in New York, a rich man." She jerked Peter's arm.

To his horror, Denis's grip weakened. Peter burst into tears. "Don't cry, son. You'll be all right," he said. "I've given you a great gift. From now on, your life is a clean slate—a *tabula rasa*. You're an American, a fresh new boy who sprouted from this land like one of my apple trees." Peter didn't feel like a fresh new boy.

"Look," Denis forced a smile. He picked something off the bedclothes— the eye of a white peacock feather. "Your mother must have dropped it." He took Peter's hand and pressed it against his palm. "Forget about me. Forget you ever heard of the Petrosyan Fund. It's filthy money that never bought anyone happiness. Go live a happy life. Never look back."

Peter had clutched the feather all the way from Wenatchee to Seattle. There were sequins and little white pearls glued to it. He picked those off and threw them out the car window somewhere in the Cascade Mountains. From then on, he did his best to become that fresh, new boy—a tabula rasa. "Never look back" became his credo.

Now, in his twilight sleep, the jet engines droned. Dreams flashed through his mind like doors bursting open, then slamming shut before he could see who stood at the end of a long, paneled hallway before a blazing fire in a castle in New York City.

Chapter Five

PETROSYAN KAMINSKY

New York City, October 5, 1997

As Peter slept, his Aeroflot Ilyushin jet traced an arc over Canada to Greenland on the Great Circle route to Moscow. It flew far north of New York City and the penthouse on the 35th floor of Petrosyan Towers where an old man lit a Cuban cigar and poured himself a snifter of Courvoisier. Petrosyan Kaminsky then settled into his overstuffed chair before a warming fire. He swirled the amber liquid and savored the prize on his mantelpiece. After seventy years of searching, Russia's oldest and most revered icon, the Virgin of Kurzan, was finally his.

"Here's to you, old girl." He raised his glass to the shabby, two-foot square slab of curved oak coddled in the glow of a spotlight. "I'm afraid that you are looking poorly these days." The silver mantle of the centuries-old icon was missing, the wooden surface scuffed and faded, and the faces of Mother and Child barely discernable. Ironically, the damage made the icon more valuable at auction.

Petrosyan had arranged for a quick private sale before the Russian government caught wind of the theft of its national treasure. Arthur Wellington, Sotheby's Curator of Russian Art, would arrive in the morning with an armed escort to pick up the icon and Petrosyan's collection of related historical documents. Buyers were lined up from Beijing to Riyadh, ready to bid millions for the last of the great Russian icons.

Petrosyan sipped more cognac. "Tonight, it's just you and me," he said. "Let's have some music—Tchaikovsky, I think." Using the console in the arm of his chair, he selected a string quartet. As the music played, he squinted up at the smudged faces and reminisced on his childhood—something he loathed.

He and his older brother, Ephraim, had grown up poor in a two-room log house on the Jewish side of Kolomeno Settlement. Everyone was poor in that Russian village nestled in the shadow of Kurzan Monastery, even his father the doctor. Long winter nights were spent by the fire listening to Granny tell stories about the ruthless pagan goddesses who ruled the northern forests before the Jews and Christians came—Lilith … Baba Yaga … Mati Syra. The goddess Zemyna was the local favorite—a temperamental, fickle creature who could cure illness, or, if she chose, inflict cruel vengeance. The specter of Zemyna painted in the blood of sinners still served as a warning to unruly children who wouldn't mind their elders.

"Where is Zemyna now?" Petrosyan asked his grandmother.

"She's locked inside the monastery in the Church of the Kurzan Goddess," said Granny. "She's been there for nearly six hundred years. They've renamed her the Virgin of Kurzan."

"Can we go see her?"

"Of course not. You can't just walk into the church and have a look."

"Why not?"

"Because for one thing, we are Jews," said Papa, puffing on his pipe. "She is a Christian goddess now."

"We want to see her." The boys were insistent. "Please."

"Then you'll have to wait until next summer." Mama peered over her knitting. "They bring her out of the church in August for the summer processional."

"Just climb the old oak and wait for her to go by," said Granny. "The Bishop of Kurzan carries the goddess through the woods for all to see."

"Why do they do that?" asked Ephraim.

"They take her back to the circle of kedr trees where the heathens worshipped," said Father. "The icon was found there hanging in a tree."

The boys exchanged skeptical glances. "Why go back to a pagan place?"

"Don't look for logic. It's a religious tradition that has gone on for centuries," said Mama. "We have our feasts and holidays at the synagogue and the Christians have theirs. One must always be respectful."

"Now off to bed with the two of you." Father tapped his pipe on the hearth. "It's time to sleep."

The boys climbed the ladder to their bed on a shelf above the stove. Whispered plans were finally hushed by their father when he blew out the last candle.

****

Now the elderly Petrosyan addressed the relic on his mantelpiece. "So, what do you think of my humble home?" He gestured broadly, taking in the 17th Century oak paneling of the drawing room. He'd had his penthouse shipped stone by stone from the Lapukhin Castle on Vestogo Island. The interiors were taken from every part of the Russian Empire.

31

Thanks to his business arrangement with Comrade Joe Stalin, he'd had his pick of the best.

A premonition shivered through him. He pulled a rug up over his knees. The fire snapped and flared, setting his nerves on edge. He eyed the icon suspiciously. *What are you up to?*

He jumped when the telephone rang. It was his agent in Seattle. "Sorry to call so late, sir," said the private investigator. "I'm at Sea-Tac Airport. Your grandson just picked up a ticket at KLM and took the subway out to the S-gates. By the time I got through security there were flights boarding to Paris, Dubai, Hong Kong, and Moscow. He could be on any one of them."

Petrosyan sat up. "Pray to God it's not Moscow. Give me the access code for Aeroflot. I'll check that one. You look at the other flights." He switched on his computer. It booted slowly, displaying a blue screen with a spinning wheel. Exasperated, he rose from his chair and shuffled to the window. It calmed him to look out over Manhattan. He poured another brandy and willed his breathing to slow. *I knew this was too easy.*

Heat burned the back of his neck. He rubbed it and turned to glare at the Virgin of Kurzan. A few flecks of gold leaf glinted in her halo. He hadn't noticed those before. Had the eyes changed color, or was it a trick of the light? They seemed more prominent. *Calm down.*

"I'm not afraid of you. You are nothing but a block of wood," he said defiantly, lighting another cigar. Emboldened by the icon's lack of reaction and the cognac, he taunted: "In a few days, you'll be locked in some dark vault in Riyadh with the rest of your kind." He tapped an oversized leather portfolio. "With these old parchments, this provenance, your *Book of Miracles*, I'll clear twenty million."

He gave the computer a kick. It didn't boot any faster. *If Pyotor is on that plane, he needs protection. I need a plan.* Petrosyan had vast resources at his disposal. His success as an art smuggler had made him one of the wealthiest men in New York and he thought nothing of hiring mercenaries throughout the world to move people and other forms of contraband. But who could he trust in Moscow to protect his grandson? There weren't many that he could rely on in that swamp of corruption. He brightened when he remembered the Chechens, two police lieutenants from Grozny in southern Russia—Ruslan Amiroev and his cousin, Ahmed Kadyrov. He was tempted to pick up the phone and call them but paused. First, he should have his facts straight. Maybe Pyotor was on his way to Paris.

Finally, the computer chirped. An Aeroflot login appeared on-screen. He entered the in-flight code and password. While he waited for the data to populate, he clicked open a desktop folder labeled "Peter Stone." Images of a sandy-haired young man with a pleasingly round Slavic face appeared. He zoomed in. "Hello, Pyotor." The boy had been born Pyotor Kaminsky, but Denis, his father, had anglicized the name to Peter Stone when the boy was four years old.

It had taken Petrosyan two years to track his son's family to Stone Farm in eastern Washington. After Denis's death, he'd transferred the Petrosyan Fund into Peter's name. When Petrosyan's older brother and business partner Ephraim had been shot with the rest of the family in a Moscow purge, he added their money to the fund and appointed his attorney, Daniel Karlov, as trustee.

Petrosyan had written long letters to Peter over the years that explained all this, but never sent them. They were kept by Karlov to be given to the boy the moment he inquired about the origins of the fund, or about his family. He never did. He grew up working a variety of jobs to fund his education and purchase his little houseboat.

The fund was now worth several hundred million dollars. Pyotor would know that if he read the monthly statements that Karlov sent.

"Why haven't you contacted me?" Petrosyan implored the smiling face on the screen. "Why haven't you asked a single question? What must Denis have told you to turn you against me?"

The old man tapped a few more keys and opened photographs of a couple on the deck of the houseboat—Peter and a graceful blonde with a waist-length ponytail. The happy domestic scenes had been photographed over the past five years.

He'd investigated Caroline Luke the moment she moved into the houseboat. On paper, she was an excellent match, the great-granddaughter of Count Lukhinov of Ostankino and the great grandniece of St. Ossipov of Soliviki. Pyotor looked happy and well cared for. At least he did until she walked out on him and went to New York. He'd been looking unkempt and less happy since then.

Petrosyan scowled. *Selfish woman. How dare she abandon Pyotor. She's just as bad as Ruby Mae, that showgirl that Denis married.* His eyes widened with a terrible insight. "Caroline," he said aloud. "That's why Pyotor is flying to Russia. He's chasing after that damn opera singer."

At last, the Aeroflot GPS screen popped on, confirming that the flight from Seattle to Moscow was now over Moose Jaw in northern Canada heading toward Gander. Petrosyan scrolled down the list of passengers. There he was in seat 12B—Peter Stone.

He picked up the phone and dialed the Chechens. Ruslan and Ahmed were the best bodyguards he knew. They were courageous, smart, and loyal. Once they signed onto a job, they saw it through as long as they were paid on time—and they were Muslims, so drunkenness was not a problem. They'd been mujahideen fighters for the CIA in Afghanistan, which meant they could get their hands on the kind of equipment that would give him eyes on Pyotor.

While he paced, listening to the whirs and clicks of his call to Moscow wending its way under the Atlantic Ocean, Petrosyan was certain that the eyes of the icon followed him.

She knows what I've done. I'll have to be more careful.

Chapter Six

TANYA PAVLOVA

Moscow, October 5, 1997

The Ilyushin bounced twice on the runway at Sheremetyevo Airport and settled into a smooth deceleration to the applause of the passengers. Peter collected his carry-on by the rear exit and deplaned down rickety metal steps. Two uniformed police officers waited on the tarmac. "Dr. Stone?"

"You must be from Commander Golokov," Peter replied in Russian.

"The commander sent us to escort you to your accommodations in Kolomeno. Come with us, please."

Peter zipped his parka against the wind and followed the officers to a door marked "Diplomats Only." Inside, his passport was stamped with barely a glance in his bag and they proceeded through a set of glass doors that separated the Customs hall from the pandemonium of the main airport.

The air in the terminal was thick with cigarette smoke and smelled of wet wool. Men in fur hats hawked taxis. Porters rolled carts piled with suitcases and cardboard boxes tied with string. Old women surrounded Peter, holding up handknit Astrakhan scarves for sale. Younger women with doughy thighs raised their skirts and shouted in English, "Hey, American boy! Not expensive." Overhead, a mechanical reader board clacked updates to the lists of departures, arrivals, and delays.

He followed the uniforms outside to the driveway, where a police cruiser idled. Peter was about to lift his bag into the open trunk when he heard his name again.

"Dr. Peter Stone?" He turned to see a slender young woman wrapped in white fur hurrying toward him. Before he could respond, she took his bag and pulled him away from the car with surprising force.

"Good evening," she said breathlessly, pushing him along. She looked eighteen, but her voice was more mature. "I'm Tanya Pavlova. Commander Golokov has arranged for you to stay in Caroline's flat. It belongs to my family. I've come to fetch you."

Peter glanced back at the police car. "But didn't the commander send them?"

She paused and opened her gloved hand to show Peter the heart-shaped diamond earrings he'd given Caroline for her birthday.

"Where did you get those?" he demanded.

"You have to trust me,´ she hissed through clenched teeth. "Your life depends on it." She pressed the earrings into his palm and stepped off the curb.

A Mercedes flashed its headlights and pulled forward. Two men with high cheekbones and an Asian cast to their eyes rode in front. They reminded Peter of Chechen soldiers he had treated at Harborview. She opened the door, but he hesitated. "Are these men friends of yours?" he asked, nodding to the Asian men.

"More like friends of yours," she replied, tossing his bag inside. "I met them when they picked me up for the airport. According to my Grandpa, they are topnotch Chechen bodyguards. The driver is Ruslan Amiroev. The other man is his cousin, Ahmed Kadyrov. Now please, let's go." Tanya attempted to pull Peter into the car after her, but he froze, uncertain of what to do.

"Dr. Stone," called the policeman. "Aren't you coming?" Two more officers climbed out of the cruiser and moved toward him. They seemed out of shape in their ill-fitting uniforms.

He looked down at the jewels in his hand—proof of a connection between Tanya and Caroline. "No thanks," he called to the officer. "I'm going with this young lady. She's prettier than you are." He slid onto the backseat next to Tanya. The Mercedes accelerated away from the curb before he could slam the door.

Tanya lit a Stoli cigarette and offered him one. He declined. She tossed the pack to the men in front. Soon all three Russians were smoking. "They're right behind us," she said. "Go faster."

Peter peered through the rear window. The patrol car was gaining on them, siren wailing, blue lights flashing. The Mercedes sped up, weaving around cars and trucks in a blur of lights and bleating horns. He was about to ask why they were being chased when Tanya crossed her arms and looked him over with a scowl of disapproval. "So, you're the asshole boyfriend."

"What? This is insane." Peter grabbed the hand strap as the car swerved. "I should have gone with the police."

"Those aren't policemen," said Ruslan, the driver, meeting his gaze in the mirror. "They are hired thugs. Their uniforms are ten years out of date. Any Russian would know that."

"And the real police drive Nevas, not Audis," said Ahmed, the other Chechen, who flashed a gold-toothed grin. "You're lucky we showed up."

"What are you talking about?" Peter shook his head in confusion. "They told me that Commander Golokov sent them."

"That may be true," said Ruslan. "But they aren't policemen."

"I just landed from America. Why would anyone want to harm me?"

"Indeed." Tanya glared at him. "So why you are even here?"

"I've come to find Caroline Luke and take her home. Nothing more, nothing less." Horns blared. The Mercedes cut off a tanker truck and fishtailed. "Where is she? How did you get her earrings?"

"If I knew where she was, I would tell you," said Tanya with eerie aplomb. "As for the earrings, she gave them to me."

"I can't believe that," said Peter. "She never took them off. She wouldn't just give them away."

"How would you know? Where were you if you cared for her so much? Why was she here in Moscow alone and unprotected?"

"I'm sorry," said Peter, backing down. "I'm worried about her, that's all. Please tell me what happened."

"Caroline came to Moscow like a starry-eyed child. She landed the lead at the Pushkin Opera on opening night. Quite an honor. She was perfect for the part —beyond perfect. We watched her on television as she became Antonida—the golden-haired, virgin bride. She looked delicious, an irresistible morsel for a bird of prey. Is it any surprise that a vulture tempted her to his lair with promises of fame?"

"What vulture? I wish you'd stop talking in riddles."

"Pay close attention, because there are more." She smirked, warming to his frustration. "Lucky for you, there is an older, more powerful vulture that wants you kept alive. As for the rest of us, we are just little doves trapped in the midst of your raptor family squabbles."

"I don't have any family."

"Maybe not in America. But here you are a complication—a big, ugly threat that will tear innocent lives apart. You should never have come. Whatever happens to us now is your fault."

"I have no idea what you're talking about." Each time Tanya spoke things made even less sense. He opened his hand and stared at the earrings, wishing that they could speak.

"Understand this," Tanya leaned further forward so that only he could hear. "I'm as good as dead for helping you, but I am a woman with a conscience. I can't bear to have both of you on it. That is why I take such a risk."

"Will you at least tell me the vulture's name—this predator that took Caroline so I can find him?" Recalling Commander Golokov's fax with the Cyrillic poem, Peter took a guess: "Is it that gangster UZI? Is he the vulture? Is she with him?" No one answered. A pall of silence fell over the car. The Russians smoked and seemed to forget he was there.

The Mercedes drove into the heart of Moscow, slowing in a traffic jam that curved around the Kremlin wall and eased a bit on Tverskaya Street. The busy sidewalk was lined with flashing neon lights. Loud music blasted. Hawkers shouted at him in English: "Come in, come in—see the pretty girls."

"This is Casino Row. Classy, isn't it?" Tanya pointed with her cigarette at a topless woman who struck erotic poses in the window of the Savoy Club. She glanced over her shoulder. "Looks like we've lost them."

"They'll be back," said the driver. "They know where we're going."

The Mercedes drove south along a bend in the Moscow River, past endless identical apartment blocks of crumbling, rust-stained concrete slab constructions that had been slapped together as temporary housing after the Great Patriotic War and remained fully occupied ever since. Outside the comfort of the heated car, Moscow reminded Peter of an old episode from the *Twilight Zone*—a black and white television drama about the end of the world.

Finally, they stopped at a building indistinguishable from the others. "This is 31 Apple Street—our home." Tanya started to open the car door.

"Wait in the car while I check the lobby," said Ahmed. He drew a black snub-nosed pistol and disappeared into the building, reappearing a minute later and giving a thumbs up. Ruslan escorted Peter and Tanya as far as the entrance. Tanya hurried inside. Peter followed her into a foul-smelling entry painted lime green, and up a short flight of cracked, concrete steps. He caught up with her at the elevator.

"This is our lift," said Tanya, opening the door. He stepped with her into a tiny box that was barely large enough for two people. It wobbled slowly upwards making screeching noises at every floor. Pressed against Tanya in the dark, Peter was reminded of everything he disliked about Russia. She was still smoking, and the elevator smelled like fermented piss.

"I still don't understand why anyone would want me dead?" Peter struggled to take in her words but they made no sense. He broke into a sweat. *Too much smoke. Too little air.*

"Whatever." Tanya snorted with a dismissive wave of her cigarette. "I suggest you figure it out and soon before somebody dies."

The elevator creaked open to a dark corridor with metal bars on the apartment doors. *Like a prison.* He squeezed his fingers around Caroline's earrings, reminding himself that he was here because she had been here. To his relief, an apartment door swung open flooding the hallway with light and the smell of soup. A tall man unlocked the steel grate guarding his apartment and extended his hand in welcome.

"This is my father Yuri Pavlovich Pavlov," said Tanya.

"Welcome to Moscow," said Yuri. "And to our humble home."

"I am very pleased to meet you." Peter shook Yuri's hand.

A scruffy, tail-wagging black dog pushed his way into their midst and sniffed Peter's crotch enthusiastically. "Down, Gogol, sit," said Tanya. The old canine ignored her. She bent down to scratch his ears. "This bad boy is Gogol. He only minds Grandpa." She smiled for the first time. She was pretty when she wasn't scowling. "This is my mother Katya." Tanya indicated an unsmiling, dark-haired woman who wiped her hands on an apron. She nodded, blinking her eyes in the silent Russian greeting that meant "I see you."

"Dinner will be ready in five minutes," said Yuri. "Put your bag in Caroline's flat and wash your hands. Oh, and don't forget—you have an appointment at Petrovka 38 in the morning."

"Petrovka 38?"

"Forgive me." Yuri laughed. "Your Russian is so perfect, I forgot that you are a foreigner. Every Muscovite knows that address. It's the headquarters of the GUVD—the Moscow Militia. Police Commander Golokov is expecting to see you there at ten o'clock sharp."

While the Pavlovs put the final dishes on their expansive table, Tanya took Peter to the apartment next door. It shared a short hallway and the same security gate. She handed him a key-ring with three old-fashioned keys. "This flat belonged to my uncle. We decided to rent it to foreigners when he died. Caroline was our first guest. You are the second."

Peter followed her into a one-room studio with a tiny kitchen. A wardrobe stood open and empty. No feminine knick-knacks graced the dressing table where there should have been a profusion of Caroline's brushes, combs, and ribbons. Peter pulled open drawers searching for any signs of her. *Nothing.* "I don't see her personal stuff. Did she take it with her?"

"Later," said Tanya, pulling him away. "First, come talk to the neighbors. They've been cooking all day, waiting for you to come."

"Cooking? For me?"

"It's what we Russians do in times of peril. We cook, we eat—and talk."

"Peril?"

"Yes, great peril—for Caroline, for you, and for all of us poor doves— just like I said. Do you have wax in your ears?"

In the Pavlov's apartment, Peter was surrounded by elderly neighbors with worried faces and rambling stories. They all spoke at once and he struggled to follow their dialects. He learned that Caroline sometimes spent evenings drinking tea in Mrs. Pandova's kitchen or singing impromptu concerts with Mrs. Karasova on the piano.

"A delightful girl. She knew all the old songs, the ones from our childhood."

"Pre-revolutionary songs. Religious children's songs. And she sang them in the old way," said Mrs. Orlova. "They were outlawed by the Communists. I haven't heard them for years. Wherever did she learn them?"

"Her Russian grandmother taught her to sing," said Peter. "They performed together at the Orthodox Church in Seattle when she was a girl. Then she studied opera at Cornish University. For fun, she sang at a college bar called the Blue Moon. That's where we met."

"How fortunate to have your life enriched by beautiful music." Mrs. Orlova clasped her hands together.

"Yes," said Peter, rubbing his chest. The ache had returned. "I miss it."

"We watched her on television when she sang at the Pushkin," Mrs. Karasova wiped away tears. "So beautiful, so talented—a great future in opera … and then nothing. She never came back to us. It happens in this country. People disappear."

"We light candles for her every day," said Mrs. Pipkinova.

"Oh, stop blubbering, all of you," little Mrs. Pandova raised her voice to a squeak. "If you ask me, that horrible man is to blame—pretending to be a gentleman, driving her to the theater, kissing her hand. He's a real villain, that one." She turned to Tanya, "You know who I'm talking about— what's-his-name, that poet." The other babushkas shushed her.

Peter turned to Tanya, "What man? Who's she talking about?"

"Later," Tanya snapped. "I have to get dressed." She left the room. The lock clicked behind her.

He knocked. "Tanya, wait. We have to talk."

Katya took his arm. "Dinner is ready," she said guiding him to a chair beside the old soldier at the head of the table. "Let me introduce my father-in-law, Colonel Pavel Artyumovich Pavlov," she said. "Please sit. You are our guest of honor." She leaned over Peter to kiss the old soldier on his cheek. "Grandpa's been nearly deaf since the Battle of Stalingrad, so speak up or let him read your lips."

Peter sat down and admired the four rows of medals on Pavel's well-mended black suit. The old man squinted back at him appraisingly, then nodded and blinked without smiling. Tanya reappeared in stiletto-heeled boots, a skimpy dress, and heavy make-up. She tucked her black hair under a white fox hat that matched her coat. No one except Peter seemed surprised by her transformation. She said her goodbyes and headed for the door.

"Tanya, wait." Peter stood to follow, but he was hemmed in by old people in chairs. "I need to talk to you."

"Wait up for me," she called from the hallway. "I'll be back around three."

"Where's she going?" he asked Katya.

"To work," said her mother, dishing cold herring and onions onto his plate while Yuri poured a glass of vodka.

"At this hour? Where does she work?"

"Our Tanya is a journalist," said Yuri. "She works at *Eleven News*."

"Tanya has her own column, "The Culture Column," said Mrs. Karasova. "We are very proud of her."

Yuri said grace over the meal. Food was passed and Peter was handed platters of potato salad, egg salad, tomato and cucumber salad, Russian cheese and several varieties of piroshky, sardines on toast, pickled garlic, and pig's foot in aspic, accompanied by glasses of wine, vodka and warm orange Fanta.

By the start of the second course of roast beef and boiled potatoes, jet lag had him in its clutches. He struggled to stay awake. Everyone at the table had opinions to express, but no one knew anything useful. His mind wandered. What had Tanya meant when she'd said, "I can't have both of you on my conscience"? She was afraid of someone—the vulture, she'd called him. And there were two vultures—and old one and a young one? Had he understood her correctly? Who were they?

He was startled when the old colonel grasped his forearm. "I know who you are," Pavel said.

Peter was taken aback. "I'm Peter Stone."

Pavel shook his head. "No." He tapped Peter on the chest. "I know who you really are." The way the old man said the words made Peter's scalp prickle. "You've come because of Kurzan, haven't you?"

Kurzan? Peter recalled the enigmatic handwritten word on Commander Golokov's fax. "What is it...Kurzan?"

"Not a matter of what it is, but where..." The old man slipped a plate of tongue in aspic under the table for the patient dog. "Gogol and I will take you there tonight."

By nine o'clock Peter was stretched out on the sofa bed in Caroline's apartment with his face pressed into the pillow. He had searched every inch of the tiny studio again and found only the faint scent of her on the pillow. He listened to the Pavlovs in the corridor saying good night to their guests and dozed off until he heard the old man telling Gogol to be patient while he knocked on Peter's door.

Chapter Seven

THE FIREBIRD

Kurzan, October 5, 1997

Peter helped Pavel carry a heavy shopping bag to the elevator. They crowded into the lift with Gogol pressed against their legs. Out on the street, a gust of wind stung Peter's cheeks and dusted the dog's black ruff with snow. At the curb, Pavel tapped on the window of the Chechen's Mercedes. It rolled open with a belch of cigarette smoke.

The old man handed the shopping bag to Ahmed. "Here's dinner and a thermos of tea for you boys." He jerked his head toward Peter, "I'm taking the lad to Kurzan. Anything we should worry about?"

"Not so far, Colonel," said Ruslan. "But shouldn't we drive you?"

"No thanks, I have to walk the dog." He ruffled Gogol's ears. "The old boy has to mark his kingdom."

"I'm walking with you," said Peter.

"We'll drive to Kolomeno Park and wait," said Ahmed. "Just in case."

"Suit yourselves. Just don't throw any matches or cigs out the window." Pavel nodded toward an empty lot on the other side of the road. A sign read "Apple Orchard Business Center—Absolutely No Smoking." "That used to be an orchard. Now it's an underground weapons factory. When the ground freezes, explosive gas gets loose. Things blow up."

The Chechens drove off. Peter followed Pavel and Gogol onto a narrow path between tall buildings. They were greeted by a group of medal-bedecked old veterans who sat under a streetlamp playing chess. Their huge fur hats coated with snow reminded Peter of mushrooms.

"Aren't they cold?" Peter asked.

"They're partisans," said Pavel with a chuckle. "Heroes of the Great Patriotic War. They could live for a month hidden in a snowbank eating nothing but grubs. Men and women like them won the war for Russia." The partisans raised their vodka bottles and saluted. Pavel saluted back. No one was smoking.

Gogol led the way around a corner to a flight of stairs that descended into a pedestrian tunnel under Andropovsky Boulevard. In the long, dimly lit passage, they left behind the fast-moving grind of the city and emerged into a quieter place where pristine snow glowed beneath an orb of moon.

"Kolomeno Park," said Pavel with pride. He pointed out the ancient Gates of Muscovy and the remains of the Baptistry of St. George—all that was left of Peter the Great's wooden palace which had burned two centuries before. "When I was a boy, this park was our village, Kolomeno Settlement. This was all farmland and orchards with the monastery in the center. It was a poor village, but quite beautiful."

"Why are you showing me this?" asked Peter.

"Because this is your story." Pavel poked Peter's chest for emphasis. "And your story begins here at Kurzan."

"What do you mean, my story?" Peter shouted into the old man's ear.

"There's no need to shout," Pavel muttered. "I'm not as deaf as they think—I just don't like to listen. There's someone here that I want you to meet. She can explain better than me."

"Here? At this time of night?"

"She doesn't have a telephone." They walked single file under an abandoned watchtower that tilted precariously toward crumbling brick walls. "This was once a prison for boys. It's been closed for several years now." Peter followed Pavel through a steel gate that hung at an angle from its bottom hinge, and into a courtyard cluttered with rusted rolls of barbed wire and stacks of bricks. Pavel waved his hand toward the only well-lit building. "That's the refectory. My sister, Maria Pavlova, lives there. She will answer your questions. But first, we must climb to the top of the bluff. I want you to understand the big picture."

"Does she know where Caroline is?"

"No."

"Then I don't see what this has to do with me," said Peter.

"Everything, Pyotor. Kurzan has everything to do with you." Pavel rolled his eyes in frustration. "Follow me and mind where you step." He scuttled along a well-trodden path toward a vast brick ruin. Peter had no choice but to follow. "This is the Church of the Kurzan Goddess. The roof is mostly gone and there are no icons left inside, but the old ladies still come—the ones who remember."

Candlelight flickered through holes in the walls. Bent old women in black shawls emerged from the shadows. They pressed in around Peter, offering prayers for kopeks. "Not expensive," they murmured.

He searched his pockets and handed out American coins. The ladies seemed pleased. They drifted away, whispering blessings and crossing themselves. Above their heads, a stone staircase curved to nowhere. Moonlight reflected on five shabby blue domes dotted with tarnished stars.

Beyond the church, they climbed to a ridge overlooking the Moscow River. Brightly lit factories lined the far bank. "When I was a boy, this was all part of Kolomeno Settlement. Our people have lived here since prehistoric times."

Peter paused to gaze at the lights, but Pavel and Gogol were moving again. He followed them through a gap in a crumbling wall into a snowy field. A cement angel rose in the center. Its broken wings, eroded by time and weather, revealed a skeleton of rusted chicken wire. The angel held aloft a long scroll printed with dozens of names…Losha…Sasha…Vova. "These are little boy's names, aren't they?"

"Of course they are. This is a children's cemetery."

"The prison for boys? Is it a mass grave?" asked Peter, but Pavel had vanished into a copse of pines. When Peter caught up again, the old man was bent over, hands on knees, panting.

"This is what you need to see, my boy. This is where you must begin."

Below them stretched a bleached moonscape of such devastation that Peter gasped, "What in the name of God is this place?"

"This is Kurzan Monastery—what's left of it."

Peter made out the outlines of crumbling walls, ruined buildings, broken down equipment, debris and the skeleton of a once great church.

"When I was a boy there were orchards and gardens from Kolomeno Settlement to the riverbank with the monastery in the middle." Pavel straightened, opening his arms. "This was a happy, peaceful settlement. The village kids ran wild all summer. We'd swim in the river and dig for arrowheads—me, my sister Maria and Petrosyan…"

"Petrosyan?" Peter blanched at the familiar name—the same as his mysterious trust fund. But before Pavel could say more, an explosion of rap music shattered the silence. Bright rings of red, orange, and yellow neon encircled a building that had been invisible in the dark. Now it lit the night with flashing spirals that spun from the base to the top—a firebird bursting from the ashes of Kurzan.

"My heart!" The old man grunted and clutched his left arm. Peter caught him when he pitched forward, fighting for breath. "God save us from Moscow Traffic."

Chapter Eight

THE VIRGIN OF KURZAN

New York City, October 5, 1997

A rthur Wellington, Sotheby's Curator of Russian Art, rode the private elevator to the 35th floor of Petrosyan Towers and buzzed the intercom at precisely six A.M.

Petrosyan answered but didn't unlock the door: "Go away, Arthur. I'm keeping the icon for another day."

"Come on, Pet. Open up. At least let me see it." Arthur continued to knock and buzz.

Petrosyan ignored him, retreating to his drawing room and closing the heavy oak doors. The old man had been up all night. When the Chechens finally phoned with news that Pyotor was safe at the Pavlovs' flat, he broke out the vodka to celebrate. He was halfway through a bottle of Krystal Premium when Arthur arrived.

He lowered himself into his chair, closed his eyes and stepped through the mirror of memory to the elegant portico of Kaminsky's Gallery of Fine Russian Art on Fifth Avenue. The year was 1940. Liveried doormen bowed as they opened cast-bronze doors looted from St. Isaac's Cathedral in Petrograd. A string quartet played Tchaikovsky on instruments stolen from the Winter Palace. An actress dressed as Catherine the Great offered crystal flutes of Crimean Champagne to customers who entered the elegant store with forest-green velvet drapes and Turkmen carpets, brass and glass display cases, and salesmen in tuxedoes wearing white cotton gloves.

Those were the days. Joe Stalin loved his dynamite. First the palaces went down, then the monasteries and synagogues. Stalin would have destroyed everything, art and all, if Ephraim hadn't convinced him to let the Kaminsky brothers strip the valuables first and ship them to New York for auction. A monastery the size of Kurzan meant a dozen boxcars filled with treasure.

In turn, Petrosyan and Ephraim sent Stalin more cash than he knew what to do with—completely off the books. Stalin called it the "Party's Gold." His secret black ledgers paid for the Communist Party's ruthless rise to power and funded their Special Tasks Unit—Spetsnaz—who specialized in skinning people alive. Petrosyan saw them do it—once. The man's pitiable screams were enough to convince him that Russia had gone mad. He moved to New York and never returned.

He had pleaded with Ephraim to emigrate with his family, but his brother refused. He was eventually shot with his children and grandchildren in one of the Jewish purges in 1979. Stalin was long dead by then and unable to protect him. After Ephraim's death, there was no more art to sell. Petrosyan had no choice but to close his beloved gallery and diversify into other forms of contraband.

He relocated the business to the top floors of a building on West 67th that became the global headquarters of Kaminsky Enterprises, Inc. Now, from the comfort of his armchair, he kept watch over the ever expanding black-market empire. The days of warehouses filled with confiscated artifacts, icons, statues, and jewelry were over, but there were new varieties of smuggled goods from Russia. They lacked the elegance of stolen gold but were just as profitable. Computers and satellite feeds kept him informed of shipments of Tajik heroin or Moldovan prostitutes arriving in the ports of New York, Singapore and Dubai.

Petrosyan puffed on his cigar and recalled the first smuggled treasure, a gold Fabergé egg, a lovely thing that he bought for kopeks from a starving duchess in Petropavlovsk.

He was just a lad when he'd carried the egg aboard a steamship from St. Petersburg in 1919. On reaching New York, he walked to Tiffany's on lower Broadway. He knew that the manager would refuse to see him. Fine jewelry stores were besieged by Russian refugees frantic to sell—so he set the golden egg on top of one of the glass cases.

When he touched the ruby-studded crown, it sprang open like the petals of a flower. Inside, a mosaic of miniature rubies and emeralds formed a tiny iconostasis covered with icons so small that its perfection could only be appreciated with the aid of a magnifying glass. Each petal of the open flower bore a tiny enameled portrait of Tsar Nicholas II, Empress Alexandra, or one of their five children. When he pulled gently on the Romanov crown, the golden petals snapped shut again and the smooth surface of the egg was restored.

The display drew a crowd of customers and the manager himself who sold the egg for $5000. He gave Petrosyan half and admonished him to come directly to his office the next time he had Fabergé, or its equivalent, to sell.

That afternoon, Petrosyan bought a corrupt Customs agent, rented a warehouse, and still had $50 left over for a new suit. From that point forward, his burgeoning commerce in stolen art brought him riches beyond his wildest imaginings. He was thirty-five when he designed Petrosyan Towers and had his castle installed on top. Life had been good to him and when he died, all that he owned would go to his grandson, Pyotor Kaminsky—the doctor who called himself Peter Stone.

Petrosyan coughed, a deep rasping hack. Mortality hovered around him in the haze of cigar smoke. He felt a draft and pushed a lever on his console to crank up the fire. He closed his eyes and soon was snoring.

"Remember…" said the hot summer wind that swept him back to Kolomeno and a boyhood summer. The air was thick with white tupelo pollen—summer snow—and redolent of cedar. He and his big brother Ephraim were schoolboys of eleven and thirteen. They had spent the afternoon perched in a tall oak at the edge of the forest. The summer processional of the faithful would soon leave the monastery and pass beneath them carrying the Virgin of Kurzan. They waited until dusk, carving their initials in the bark. Suddenly bats swarmed out of the hollow tree, startled to flight by the deep-throated bong of the Kurzan bell. The tiny mammals darkened the sky with fluttering wings,

"It's the processional!" Ephraim pointed. "The icon is coming."

Hundreds of candles and torches bobbed through the trees. The faithful parishioners of Kurzan came marching into view led by chanting monks. Some of the brothers jangled bells, others swung incense burners that perfumed the air. They passed under the oak in their high black hats and black silk cassocks that rustled as they walked. Icons bobbed above their heads on tall crosiers. The Bishop of Kurzan, resplendent in red and gold vestments, carried aloft the holiest of the icons, the Virgin of Kurzan.

From his perch in the tree, Pet looked directly into the eyes of the Virgin and for a moment, he was bewitched. But the processional passed quickly and he was distracted by another beauty. An exuberant head of curling blond hair came within reach. Swinging down, he tugged the pink ribbon that held the mass of curls. Little Maria Pavlova let go a shriek. She jerked backwards bumping into old Sergei Vichislavovich, sending them both tumbling into the forest.

Pet and Ephraim broke into peals of laughter as the other marchers hurried over to help the old man. Maria Pavlova was quickly on her feet — her face flushed with anger and fire in her eyes. The boys were in trouble. Maria could climb a tree faster than they could and would probably beat them up. They dropped from the tree, screeching like monkeys, and scampered off to hide.

"I hate you, Petrosyan Kaminsky," she shouted as he ran away.

"I love you, Maria Pavlova," he called back, running backwards, throwing kisses to the sky.

"Take me home," whispered the wind.

****

Shaking himself awake, Petrosyan glowered at the icon: "Trying your tricks on me, are you? I'm selling you and that's the end of it."

The words were no sooner out of his mouth than the wind that had soothed and cajoled became the roar of a voracious fire. Through the flames, the icon glowed so brightly that only Petrosyan and the Virgin of Kurzan existed.

"Redeem yourself, penitent," the fire raged. Suddenly he floated above Kurzan Monastery at sunrise on a long-ago morning in 1928. Black smoke roiled on the distant horizon spoiling a perfect blue sky. The cathedral at Suzdal Monastery still burned from their pillaging of it the night before. In the forest, Chekist soldiers extinguished their campfires and started motorcycles.

"No—I won't look," Petrosyan squeezed his eyes shut against the vision. "Not this memory."

"Open your eyes or fall. ..." And he fell, tumbling and screaming, stopping only when he looked down and saw his own black Zil town car at the south gate of Kurzan Monastery. He watched himself as a young man of twenty sliding open the car window to discover the Bishop of Kurzan perched on the monastery wall, his right hand raised in blessing over him.

"Stupid priest," he'd muttered. "Doesn't he know what's coming?"

"He should," said Ephraim. "He's seen the rest of the Golden Ring monasteries reduced to rubble." Petrosyan's older brother sat on the seat beside him, drinking vodka from a silver flask. They both wore bespoke Italian suits and handmade shoes. "Suzdal was a rich haul, but we've saved the best for last."

"Indeed, we have. Kurzan is the richest cache."

Ephraim passed him the flask. "The Virgin of Kurzan alone will make us a fortune."

"Then I'm leaving this stinking country and never coming back," said Petrosyan, taking a swig. "You can live in Moscow if you want. I'm going back to New York."

Ephraim frowned. "It's just as well. Mayor Pavlov is still raging about what you did to his daughter, Maria. I heard that he threw the torch into the synagogue. He was aiming to kill you, not Mama and Papa. He's a militia commander now and wants your hide. He'll have it, too, if you don't get out of the country."

Petrosyan glared at the bishop standing above him on the wall. "My life has been ruined by that meddling priest. Why couldn't he let me marry Maria and take her to America?"

"Maria Pavlova—such a pretty, sweet girl. I remember playing in the fields when we were kids." Ephraim lit a Turkish cigarette. "What did her parents do to her when they found out she was pregnant?"

"They shaved her head and forced her to become a nun. The bishop sent her away to a convent somewhere in Siberia where I can't find her. Our child will be born a bastard." Petrosyan grabbed the flask and finished off the vodka.

"Poor girl," said Ephraim. "She'll wind up in a labor camp if she isn't shot. This isn't the time to be pregnant or find religion."

"Good riddance to that damn priest." He checked his pocket watch and stared at the bishop. "Just open the gate, so we can get this over with?"

"They're getting ready." Ephraim pointed to the bell tower where two monks lay on their backs pushing the massive bell back and forth with bare feet, swinging it higher and higher until the hammer struck metal. Any other day, the Kurzan bell would have been answered by a chorus of bells from miles around. But the rest of the churches had been destroyed, their bells toppled and de-tongued. The mighty Kurzan bell rang solo.

Chekist agents in grey uniforms circled the black Zil like a pack of wolves. They loaded guns and pulled boxes of dynamite from the trunk. When the wooden gates swung open, they forced their way in. At first, they were hesitant to enter the Church of the Kurzan Goddess until Petrosyan took the lead and they followed, smashing and pillaging. Ephraim joined him and the brothers approached the niche where the Virgin of Kurzan had dispensed miracles and favors for five centuries. The silver mantle was all that remained in place. The icon was gone.

"Damn them," Petrosyan raged. "They think they can hide something that valuable?"

The Chekists lined up the monks and shot each one who refused to reveal where the Virgin of Kurzan was hidden. They beat the bishop senseless while Petrosyan shouted, "Look at me, you bastard! What have you done to the icon? Where is Maria Pavlova? Speak, man." The bishop's eyes were swollen shut and blood ran from his ears. Petrosyan finally lost all patience and shot him in the head.

By the end of the day, every monk had been killed and their bodies thrown onto a smoking pyre. Even the Chekists had grown weary of slaughter and sprawled in the shade of the orchard. They had looted the monastery, dynamited the bell tower and cut the tongue out of the fallen bell, blown the roof off the Church of the Kurzan Goddess, and set fire to everything that would burn. But the Virgin of Kurzan was not found.

"Burn the village and everyone in it," Petrosyan screamed. "Burn that damn orchard!"

****

The dream shattered and the fragments dissolved. The old man woke with a start. A tidy fire crackled on the grate. He leaned forward and looked around the room for assurance that he had escaped from the past and was safe in his penthouse. He examined his hands to affirm that they were an old man's hands.

Comforted, he narrowed his eyes and glared at the Virgin of Kurzan. "Yes," he said through clenched teeth. "I shot the bishop. I burned Kurzan, Kolomeno, the orchard—all of it."

Chapter Nine

COMMANDER GOLOKOV, GUVD

Moscow, October 6, 1997

In Peter's dream, Caroline curled against him, wrapped in his arms—until Yuri tapped on the door. "Come to breakfast, please." The dream dissolved. Peter woke alone and sweating in the hard, little bed. The apartment was stiflingly hot.

"Give me five minutes," he called out.

Yuri moved down the hall with the yipping dog: "Good boy, Gogol. It's you and me today." The elevator creaked open.

Peter propped himself up and squinted into the daylight streaming through the curtainless glass. He got up and tried to pry open a window, but they were painted shut. He showered, shaved, and dressed, searching the apartment once more for traces of Caroline. Finding nothing, he crossed the hall to Katya's kitchen.

Katya smiled and nodded to a little wooden table. "Sit." She flipped the switch on a noisy grinder that saturated the room with the smell of coffee. "This will be ready in a minute." She spooned black grounds into boiling water.

"How is the colonel this morning?" Peter asked.

"The doctor put Grandpa on bedrest. Yuri is out walking the dog."

"It's a good thing that the Chechens were close by with the car when he collapsed," said Peter.

"Poor old Pavel Artyumovich. He's seventy-five and not as strong as he thinks he is." Katya sighed. "He was a Hero of Stalingrad, you know."

"Can I talk to him?"

"He's sleeping."

"He mentioned the name Petrosyan. Do you know who that is?"

"Speak to Yuri when he gets back." She slid tomatoes and eggs from an iron skillet onto Peter's plate and poured thick black coffee into small cups. Peter was adding sugar when Yuri returned.

"Coffee smells wonderful." Yuri brushed snow from his coat and toweled Gogol's muddy feet. He took a seat across from Peter.

"Pyotor was asking about Grandpa." Katya handed him a plate of eggs.

"My father has a dodgy heart," said Yuri. "He isn't supposed to walk so far in the cold."

"Shouldn't he be in a hospital?"

"You obviously haven't seen our hospitals." Yuri chuckled. "He's better off in his own bed."

"He spoke of his childhood and someone named Petrosyan," said Peter. "Do you know who that is?"

"Are you telling me that you don't know? Really?" Yuri raised his eyebrows as he sipped his coffee. "Well, my father is always the one with a plan. It's best to speak with him."

"When can I?"

"The doctor gave him a shot. He'll sleep until supper," said Yuri.

"Maybe you can tell me why he took me to that strange place…to Kurzan?"

"Ah, you saw the ruins," said Katya. She poured more coffee. "It doesn't look like much now. It was once quite beautiful. Long before my time."

"Kurzan was at the center of life here for centuries," said Yuri. "The monastery was known as the crown jewel of Russia's Golden Ring."

"Then it became some kind of prison?" asked Peter.

"A prison for boys, yes. Terrible, absolutely awful—a curse upon the land." Yuri tucked into his eggs. "Now it's a convent. Pavel's sister, my aunt Maria Pavlova, is the mother superior. She's in charge of restoration, if that's even possible. You saw how destroyed it is."

"He wanted me to meet her. Do you know why?"

"As I said, the colonel has a plan. You'll have to ask him."

"He also said that my story begins at Kurzan. He said he knew all about me. What did he mean?"

Yuri shrugged and sipped his coffee. Peter looked at Katya, but she ignored him. *What aren't they telling me?*

"How can I reach your aunt?" Peter persisted. "I want to talk to her as soon as possible."

"She doesn't have a telephone," said Yuri.

"That's what your father said. I guess I'll have to go there."

"Not now, you don't," said Tanya from the doorway. "It's time to go to Petrovka 38." Her face was scrubbed clean. She wore her white fur coat but with sensible boots and a red beret. "You have an appointment with Commander Golokov in forty minutes. Get your things and I'll show you where to catch the bus to Kolomeno Metro."

Peter pulled on his parka and joined her at the elevator. "We need to talk," he said.

"You didn't wait up for me last night. I knocked at three."

"I didn't wake up—sorry. I was pretty tired after taking care of your grandfather. I had to carry him to the car."

"Why did you make him go to Kurzan? You're a doctor. You should know better."

"He took me there. He wanted me to meet his sister."

"He's too old and it was too cold." They stepped into the elevator. She stared at his chest, avoiding his eyes.

"I still have questions," said Peter.

Tanya shrugged. "You have time to ask one question on the way down. Make it quick."

"Where are Caroline's things?"

"My mother put them away for safe keeping. She believes that Caroline will come back at any moment and everything will be all right."

"What do you think?"

"I don't think it will." The elevator opened. Tanya led him outside. They walked single file down a path through a grove of birch trees. Peter struggled to keep up without slipping. They emerged onto a solid sheet of ice where a dozen people stood in a queue. The No. 256 bus skidded to a stop. "Maybe you'll understand more after meeting Commander Golokov," she said.

"Where are those Chechen lieutenants?" asked Peter, looking around. "Do I still need them?"

"Yes, you need them," she said. "They're where they can see you but GUVD can't see them. It's safer for you that way. Ahmed and Ruslan aren't the only ones watching you." She pressed a plastic coin and some cash into his hand. "Here's a token for the bus and rubles for your Metro ticket. Take the Green Line to Tverskaya and walk a few blocks to Petrovka 38. If you get lost, ask anyone for directions. Everyone knows the way to police headquarters."

Peter climbed onto the bus and turned his attention to not missing the stop for Kolomeno Metro. Ultimately, the entire busload got off there and he was swept down a speeding escalator with a tide of commuters. He bought his ticket and boarded the Green Line train.

He was early, so he decided to get off one stop further at Red Square and walk back the extra blocks along the river. He left the Metro at Teatralnaya Station, exiting into a thriving outdoor market. Snow fell on tables piled with clothing, food, and housewares from China. An old woman sold maps of Moscow from a red-and-white plastic shuttle bag. Peter stopped to buy one. "Welcome to Moscow," she said in elegant English. He paid five dollars for the map—too much, he knew, but she reminded him of Baba.

Boys in bomber jackets offered him watches, caviar, and postcards, shouting, "Not expensive." Peter bought a jar of caviar for his hosts and paid twenty kopeks for a shopping bag from a toothless old man with rows of medals on his chest.

He rounded the corner to Red Square. The onion domes of St. Basil's Cathedral floated over a snow-dusted square so vast it appeared to curve with the earth. Peter consulted his map and crossed to the Moscow River embankment, circling back to Pushkin Square. A few more blocks and he stood before the wrought-iron gate of Petrovka 38.

He handed the sentry his passport. "I have an appointment with Commander Golokov."

Inside the massive building, men and women in gray uniforms milled about in the vaulted lobby. The musty smell of old paper reminded him of the King County Courthouse. He handed his passport and visa to an armed guard who gave it to a uniformed woman in a glass booth. Soon, another stern-faced young woman appeared and said, "Follow me, please."

She led him up a flight of marble steps, through a foyer, and into a high-ceilinged office where a short, chubby officer stepped forward to shake hands. "Dr. Stone, welcome. I am Commander Alexander Golokov. Please sit down." He gestured to a red, plush chair. "I'm glad to see you made it safely. I was worried when you left the airport with Miss Pavlova instead of my officers."

The man was backlit by floor-to-ceiling windows that made it difficult to see his features. Peter blinked in the bright light. He had imagined Commander Golokov to be taller. "Those were your men at the airport?" *Did Tanya lie?*

"I sent them to escort you, but Miss Pavlova spirited you away."

"You know Tanya Pavlova?"

"Of course. She is a journalist—quite popular. She writes the Culture Column." Golokov led Peter to a red leather armchair. "Sit down, please." Peter sank into a springless seat that folded him nearly in half. Golokov turned to the young woman who hovered scowling by the door. "Bring us some tea," he commanded with a flick of his hand. "Now, I have a question for you, Dr. Stone. Who were those men with Tanya—the Asian fellows in the black Mercedes?"

Peter answered cautiously, "Just friends with a car, as far as I know."

"Hmmm...They seemed foreign." Golokov fidgeted. Peter waited for him to make some formal statement about international cooperation. Instead he blurted, "You look very fit. Are you a football player?"

"I played rugby at university and in graduate school—but just on weekends now."

"I imagine that violent physical sport is a good relief from the constraints of the locked psychiatric ward in Seattle," said Golokov. "The pressures of our professions can be severe. There must be release."

"I have to admit that mud, sweat, bruises and a few punches are excellent stress relief," said Peter. He waited for the commander to start the meeting, but he didn't. "Why do you ask?"

"I expected a gray-haired professor with thick glasses—not a handsome young sportsman."

"Is that a problem?"

"Not at all. It's just that you remind me of someone else. The resemblance is unsettling. You could be his brother, but never mind. Let's begin our meeting, shall we?"

This time Peter took the initiative. "The government of Washington State appreciates your attention to this case—or rather, this 'situation.' As you know, I'm here as an informal consultant to the King County Executive, Lex Frasier. He's asked me to determine whether a crime has been committed that requires further action on his part. Barring that, he expects me to find Caroline Luke and escort her back to Seattle without drawing media attention."

"Discretion is generally the best approach." Golokov remained standing. "As I indicated to Mr. Frasier, I offer the full cooperation of the GUVD, but as far as we're concerned, there has been no crime and therefore, no need for law enforcement action."

"What about the coffin?"

Golokov shrugged. "It's of no concern to us that an empty papier-mâché box has arrived in Seattle. It's hardly a police matter."

"Miss Luke's grandmother is in the hospital because of the shock."

"I am sorry to hear that." Golokov frowned. "But as I see these events, an attractive young American woman has gone off with her Russian boyfriend. Maybe that's a crime in Seattle, but it's quite legal in Moscow."

"Her boyfriend?" Peter reined back the rising pitch of his voice. Katya's bitter coffee churned in his stomach. "What do you mean by 'boyfriend'?"

"Miss Luke has been seeing a popular poet known as UZI. Maybe you have heard of him in America?" The room closed in on Peter. Time slowed. He saw every dust mote in the overheated air, every water spot on the mismatched rows of brown wallpaper.

Golokov was still talking. "…one artist drawn to another by shared creative passion, eh? Apparently, they met in New York and he became her sponsor at the Pushkin Theater. He is rich and great artists need financial backing from patrons of the arts. I understand that the beautiful Miss Luke is poor as a mouse but she clearly has other assets. They've become quite the sexy couple around town." Golokov chuckled. "I see nothing in her flirtation that justifies American intervention. If we had evidence of foul play—her corpse, for instance—that would be a different matter. Instead, it looks like nothing more than a steamy romance and a practical joke."

"A joke?" Peter's shock hardened into anger. "She's missing. No one has heard from her for three days. That's not normal. And George Tanner at the American Embassy declared her dead. He claims to have seen her body."

"I wouldn't believe anything that red-headed buffoon Tanner says. Have you met him?" Golokov lit a Stoli and offered one to Peter who shook his head. "What if I were to tell you that Miss Luke was seen two days ago—quite alive."

"Were you following her?"

"We were surveilling UZI. Her presence was incidental."

"Where is she now?"

"I don't know, nor do I care. She is a free person and can do what she pleases as long as she doesn't break the law. My interest is in UZI—his crimes, not his affairs."

"Are you really telling me that Miss Luke and this gangster-poet are lovers? I don't believe it."

"Maybe you should look at these," Golokov handed Peter a folder and watched intently as he leafed through reports by various KGB observers. "You can take this file back to Seattle with you. It should settle things with Mr. Frasier and close this matter."

Peter took a minute to skim through the file. "According to these reports, they were seen together at strip clubs and casinos. Miss Luke abhorred those places. Show me proof that she was there."

"Of course." Golokov handed Peter a black-and-white photograph. "This was taken at the Casino Royale on the night after her supposed disappearance. You can see the official time stamp that it was taken two nights ago. UZI owns this club and many others."

Caroline looked beautiful in a dark, strapless dress with her hair swept up into a French twist. A man's arms encircled her waist from behind with his fingers splayed, nearly touching her breasts. She was leaning back into him, lips parted. Peter could see large diamond teardrops hanging from her ears. *A gift from UZI to replace his little diamond hearts.*

Golokov handed him more pictures. The man's hands were all over Caroline, but his face remained obscured. All Peter could determine was that he was tall. "This could be anyone," he said, tossing the photo on the commander's desk. "Don't you have a clearer picture? I'd like to know what UZI looks like."

"You seem to have a strong personal interest in this woman," said Golokov. "Is that why you've come?"

"I intend to find Caroline Luke and bring her home to Seattle. I ask you again, commander. Do you have a photograph that shows UZI's face?"

Golokov ignored his question. "Miss Luke is here on an official performance visa hosted by the Pushkin Theater. It is good for one year. We can't make her leave and you can't force her to go if she doesn't want to."

"Let's find her and ask her about that, shall we?"

"There is a contract involved." Golokov waved another folder. "She has legal obligations to the theater and financial obligations to her patron."

"Can I see it?" asked Peter.

"Of course not. Contracts are confidential. I have a copy because it supports her visa status."

"Did she have legal counsel when she signed it?"

"Apparently not. It seems that she didn't feel the need for professional advice. Women are fickle, temperamental creatures. They operate on instinct, not logic. I have never trusted them to use good judgment in business." Golokov sighed. "Now let's get back to the more interesting character in this drama—UZI. He's the one that I'd like to discuss with you—one forensic psychologist to another. I have studied the man for years."

The door opened. The stern-faced young woman entered balancing a tea tray and electric kettle. The cord trailed behind her like a tail. She poured tea for Golokov. Peter accepted a cup, pausing to recover his composure before he said anything regrettable. He took a bite of stale biscuit.

Golokov was probing him like an adversary. His refusal to share photos of UZI was strange. Surely, he had them. Peter didn't know what to think or feel about the commander's insistence that Caroline had left him for a

Russian gangster. Maybe Golokov was right and she was in some love nest with UZI. *They're laughing at me for being a fool.* He even felt some relief at the thought. *She's left me. She's found herself a rich patron. Money is all she cares about now. I can go home.* He shook his head at the hopeless idea. There was no home without her and it was his fault that she was here alone.

"And now, Doctor Stone, I would be grateful for your professional assessment of UZI." Golokov interrupted his reverie.

"I've never met the man," said Peter, switching into professional mode. "From what I've read about him and his poetry, he appears to be a sociopath with a narcissistic obsession for recognition. In my professional experience, sociopaths like him are creative, notoriously self-serving and extremely manipulative. They kill without conscience or remorse. If Caroline is with him, she is in extreme danger."

"You're right, of course. The man is an amoral assassin with a compulsive need to keep us informed about his grisly deeds through poetry. Personally, I find his crimes far more interesting than his poems." Golokov shrugged. "But the Russian people love the damn things. They put them to rap music and play it all day on the radio."

"Why do you think he's so popular?" asked Peter.

"It's simple really," Golokov replied. "UZI resonates with our Russian condition. He wants to show the world how much he feels, but he has been so damaged that he feels nothing. His only way of connecting with another person is through violence. He sees no difference between violence and affection."

Golokov opened another file and extracted a news clipping. "This is just one of a dozen examples of murder for profit, UZI's usual fare. He and his associates have been killing rival gangsters and taking over casinos and brothels around Moscow. Perhaps you noticed the Savoy Club on Tverskaya Street? It's hard to miss when you enter Moscow." Golokov smoothed the clipping in front of Peter. "This was published a few weeks ago."

Three whores died,
Pumping their beating hearts
Into a puddle of red.
Is it my fault
That life is worth so little under the sheets?
UZI

Golokov scowled at the poem. "Parliamentarian Barlov was found dead with two prostitutes at the Savoy. They'd had their throats cut. Barlov was no great loss, so there wasn't much of a fuss. The public didn't care. Just another local pimp who'd bought himself a seat in Parliament. He owned brothels in Berlin, too— many Parliamentarians do. We knew that he was hiring young Russian women to work as nannies in Germany and forcing them to be prostitutes in his clubs there. But the Germans don't care about Russian girls and there's nothing we can do in the European Union. Barlov's brothels were taken over a few days after his death by a company called Moscow Traffic."

Peter recalled standing beside the old colonel the night before—the sudden blaze of neon lights, the throb of rap music, and Pavel's words before he collapsed: "God save us from Moscow Traffic."

"What exactly is Moscow Traffic?" Peter asked.

"It's the most popular night spot in Moscow. It belongs to a criminal cartel called the Kurzaniks. UZI is their leader. That is why we surveil him." Golokov eyed Peter and said, "Miss Luke appears to have found him exciting company. Maybe she is attracted to dangerous men. Are you a dangerous man, Dr. Stone? I have my suspicions."

"I'm a boring psychologist from Seattle. Nothing more."

"I don't believe you. Rugby players are violent men. They are never boring." Golokov leaned closer. "You are a troubled man. Are you also a violent one?"

Peter flinched, annoyed by Golokov's probing. He countered by pulling the folded fax from his pocket and holding it up. "Commander, someone wrote 'KURZAN?' on this. Was it you?"

"I hadn't meant for you to see that." The commander blushed, moving papers on his desk. "It was just my scribbling, trying to put things together in my own mind, looking for links to UZI."

"I've seen Kurzan. It's just an old ruin. Why are these criminals called Kurzaniks and what does it have to do with UZI?"

"After the CHEKA destroyed Kurzan Monastery, they turned it into a prison for boys— Kurzan Prison for the Children of Enemies of the People. The Kurzaniks all grew up there. They became blood brothers, a feral tribe that matured into a fearsome mafia."

"How did a monastery become a prison?"

"During the purges, there were too many leftover orphans and no place to put them. The monasteries were empty. They had high walls with locking gates so they put them in there. It's as simple as that. The prison was closed about ten years ago when the grounds were contaminated by explosive gas from a munitions factory."

"How awful," said Peter recalling the cemetery with the crumbling angel holding the scroll of boys' names.

"Yes, it was. The children's prison system was terrible and Kurzan was the worst." Golokov turned toward the window. "They adopted a program developed by captured Nazi scientists. Their plan was to take the children of dissidents and intellectuals—our best and brightest—and shatter their personalities. They thought they could rebuild them into perfect soldiers, spies, whatever. The State was successful in destroying them psychologically but could never build them up again. Only the strong ones like UZI survived to adulthood."

"UZI grew up at Kurzan?"

"He was there for eleven years. Those boys were transformed from the best of our genetic pool into savages with no loyalties except to one another. There are many such groups in Russia—as many as there were children's political prisons. The Kurzaniks are the worst and UZI is their leader."

"Why do the people tolerate these killers?" Peter shifted in the springless chair. "Why is a dangerous sociopath like UZI still on the streets?"

"It's political. UZI has influenced a generation of Russians through his poems and made it 'cool' to be a gangster. Now everyone is writing songs and stories about the underworld like crime is something to aspire to. Arrests would lead to a public backlash against the police."

"Can't you bring him in and have a friendly chat—or beat him to a pulp, I don't care. Just find out where Miss Luke is."

"Sometimes the power of the Kurzaniks exceeds the power of the police." Golokov spread his hands, palms up in surrender. "We are limited by our legal system—the Kurzaniks are not. Until there is a public outcry, there is little that we can do against him or his gang. Currently, the public adores him."

"You're telling me that the only way I can find Caroline Luke is to track down this assassin who sits at the center of an untouchable criminal cartel called the Kurzaniks, and that you can't help me because the Moscow Militia is too weak?"

"Basically, yes. And if you do find him, he will kill you. I don't recommend trying." Golokov frowned at Peter. Then his voice softened. "Go home, Dr. Stone. Your girlfriend ran off with someone dangerous. Forget her. She's gone. The best advice I can give you is to go back to Seattle. Live your life. Stay away from Russia."

Golokov glanced at his watch. "You must excuse me. I'm overdue for an interview with one of our officers. My secretary will escort you downstairs."

Peter struggled to extricate himself from the springless chair. When he stood up, he towered over Golokov. "I will find UZI with or without your help."

Golokov sighed. "If you are determined to follow such a reckless course, I suggest you start by talking to Tanya Pavlova."

"Tanya? From *Eleven News?*"

"She's the one who made UZI a celebrity. She publishes his poems in her column."

"I'm staying with the Pavlov family." Peter was stunned. "Why didn't she tell me?"

"What have you done to earn her trust? Anything?" Golokov opened the door. "You must understand. Russians are chess players and chess is a game of the soul. There are souls playing on this board who are truly evil. You may be out of your league, Dr. Stone."

Chapter Ten

THE PUZZLE

Moscow, October 6, 1997

Peter retrieved his passport at the front desk of Petrovka 38 and left feeling off-kilter. How could he discern truth from misdirection in this world where everything was askew to begin with? He'd been in Moscow for less than twenty-four hours and been lied to by everyone, except possibly the old soldier who was now drugged and unable to speak. On top of that, two armed mercenaries were following him. Were they really protecting him?

He paused halfway down the front steps and saw the Mercedes waiting down the block. He wasn't ready to face the Chechens. Golokov's interview had awakened self-doubt, and left him uncertain of his own perceptions, particularly about whom to trust. Some of it he recognized as jet lag, the skewing of reality as if half of his molecules remained on the other side of the world. The rest was an unwelcome muddle of emotions he had tried all his life not to feel. Doors in his psyche that were best left closed and locked had cracked open, revealing an unpleasant sliver of light. He needed time alone to think in English.

He ignored the car and walked in the opposite direction toward the Moscow River. In summer, the embankment was a pleasant gathering place for fishermen. Now in winter, the stone bulwark rose above street-level as an oasis of solitude, a frozen refuge in the middle of the teeming city. He crossed under Tverskaya Street and climbed the granite steps to the top of the rampart. A bone-chilling wind off the river burned his cheeks. He didn't care. He sat on the ledge and dangled his feet over the ice-clotted river.

On the far shore, the golden cupolas of Kremlin churches gleamed above the multi-colored domes of St. Basil's Cathedral. The pale, yellow light and cacophony of church bells chiming midday did nothing to ease his disquiet. Instead, he felt even more foreign and out of place. He breathed deeply as if taking in the frozen air might help him understand this strange world. It burned his lungs, causing him to cough and sneeze simultaneously. His eyes watered and his eyelashes froze.

The photograph of UZI's splayed fingers sliding up Caroline's waist as if to touch her breasts had unhinged him. He clapped his hands to warm them and thought of her face in the photograph. Her lips were parted as she leaned into the man who held her from behind—but something was wrong. Caroline wasn't smiling. In fact, she didn't look happy in any of the pictures. What he saw in her expression was closer to pain.

The oversized diamond pendants weren't right either. When Peter gave her dainty diamond hearts for her birthday, she was worried that they were too ostentatious. Now she was wearing gaudy baubles.

"Poor as a mouse," Golokov had said of her. Who's fault was it that she had gone in search of a patron?

He broke off a chunk of ice and hurled it. It bounced and shattered on a larger block of ice drifting downriver. Golokov had played him. The meeting was a setup from the miserable chair to the harsh light that forced him to squint. And what was that nonsense about sports and playing chess? The commander wasn't helping. He was covering for UZI and trying to make Peter abandon Caroline.

Did the policeman lie about everything? Did UZI put him up to it? He must have. Maybe Tanya was telling the truth about the cops at the airport. Maybe she had saved his life. Clearly, he had underestimated her. But if she wasn't outright lying, she was still holding back. And if UZI was the young vulture, who was the old one?

The Mercedes pulled alongside the bulwark and parked on the sidewalk. Ruslan leapt up the stairs. "Never sit on cold stone like that. You'll freeze your nuts," he said, crouching on his haunches next to Peter. "Besides, you're too exposed here in that yellow coat. Petrosyan is worried about snipers."

"That name again. Why does everyone seem to know who Petrosyan is except for me?" Peter remained sitting. "I won't get up until you tell me who he is."

"No problem. Petrosyan is our boss. He pays us to keep you alive. If you get shot or freeze to death, we don't get paid." Ruslan stood and helped Peter to his feet. "Now please, get in the car."

"Is Petrosyan the 'old vulture' that Tanya referred to?" Peter stood slowly, his legs stiffened by the cold.

"I know nothing about birds." Ruslan took his arm and helped him down the steps. "Your Tanya is a journalist. She likes her riddles."

Peter was grateful for the overheated air and warm leather upholstery. He looked at his watch as they sat in traffic on the Ring Road. It was 2:00

a.m. in Seattle. In a few hours, he could call Lex. "Where can I get an international phone card?"

"Central Post Office on Tverskaya."

"Can we get there in this traffic?" Peter looked around at the snarl of automobiles snaking slowly through the center of Moscow. "Maybe I should walk and take the Metro home."

"Enough walking." Ahmed attached a flashing blue light to the roof of the car and flipped on a siren. "One of the many privileges that money buys in Moscow." The Mercedes drove onto the sidewalk, scattering pedestrians.

****

Back at Apple Street, no one answered the door at the Pavlov flat, so Peter used his assortment of keys to unlock the grate and then the door to Caroline's former apartment. He checked the time—still too early to call Lex. He put the kettle on, pulled the files out of his carry-on bag, and sat at the kitchen table. He had barely skimmed through the documents Lex had sent over. It was time for a thorough examination.

On the top of the stack was the death certificate, signed by Dr. Ivan Krimsky at 1:00 a.m. on October 2. It declared that Caroline Luke had died of an acute infectious disease resulting in rapid decomposition of the flesh. Next was a Customs declaration signed by Victor Vasevsky of the Moscow Morgue at Perovo, approving shipment of the sealed coffin to the United States. Attached to the declaration was a Bill of Acceptance and Lading from George Tanner, Citizens' Services Officer at the American Embassy in Moscow. His affidavit declared that he had confirmed the identity of the body and ordered that the coffin remain sealed until burial. Presumably, it was Tanner who punched the hole in her passport. He had also approved the invoice to King County from American Airlines for transporting the coffin.

Peter decided to call Tanner. No one answered the main number of the American Embassy. He tried again. This time, the line was busy. After ten minutes of trying, it was time to call in a favor from a college rugby buddy, Curtis Jones, who worked as a senator's aide in Washington, DC.

Peter dialed Curt's private line. "Curt, I have an urgent problem here in Moscow and I can't get through to the embassy."

Curt laughed. "Tell me about it. Who are you looking for? I'll see if I can drum him up. They do answer when a senator's office calls. We have a back line."

Peter gave the name: "George Tanner in Citizens' Services."

"Hold on. I'll give it a try." Curt was back in a few minutes. "I found someone in the State Department who helped me get through."

"Good work," said Peter.

"Yes and no. They searched the records of everyone who has worked at the embassy in the last five years, but there isn't any listing for George Tanner."

"How can that be?" Peter had counted on talking to an American. Everyone else on the list was Russian.

"All I can tell you is that Tanner isn't on their roster. Maybe you should go to the embassy and ask in person. Their roster might be out of date."

Next, Peter called Hospital 70 and spoke to the head of the medical faculty. "I'd like to speak with Dr. Krimsky about a death certificate he signed for an American on October 2."

"I'm sorry. He's gone away."

"Where did he go?" asked Peter.

"He won a free vacation to the Black Sea, the lucky sod. He won't be back for a month." Peter thanked him and rang off. Phony coffin. No body, plus no embassy witness, plus a disappearing doctor added up to no convincing evidence that Caroline was dead. The dates on Golokov's photographs showing her alive two nights ago might be accurate.

The next papers documented the route of the coffin. It was flown from Moscow to New York and held overnight in a warehouse at JFK. *Why overnight?* He found another invoice to King County for the warehouse fee and was startled by the date. It was billed a week in advance of the coffin's arrival. How could that be?

He needed to talk to Lex, but it was 3:45 a.m. in Seattle. Lex wouldn't be at the office for another fifteen minutes. Peter paused to eat some spicy Borodino black bread and wash it down with tea. Then he dialed his friend.

"Frasier here." Lex sounded wide awake.

"Lex, it's Peter. I'm looking through Caroline's papers and there are some inconsistencies."

"Like what?"

"Like it took three days to transfer the coffin from Moscow to Seattle. Does that seem right to you?"

"Nope, too long."

"Maybe it was some Customs delay? Paperwork?"

"Doesn't happen. Coffins clear first."

"It overnighted in a warehouse at JFK."

"That's a new one—but it's hardly front-page news."

"The strangest thing is that the warehouse fee was invoiced to King County on September 29, a week before the coffin got to JFK."

"Impossible."

"We need to follow this up. The warehouse belongs to a company called Russian Traders. There's no phone number. Can you find out who they are?"

"I'll give it a try. Got an invoice or payment number and a Telex?" Peter read them out. He heard Lex's computer booting up.

"Got it," Lex announced. "Russian Traders is owned by Daniel Karlov—an attorney out of New York. It doesn't give a contact telephone either."

"Karlov, you say?" Peter gasped at the sound of the familiar name. "Thanks Lex, I have his number."

He hung up before Lex could ask questions that he didn't want to answer. He felt sick—the old gut-wrenching sick like when he was a child and heard his parents fighting. He pulled out his wallet and found the card he had carried since he was nine years old. It had arrived in the mail addressed to him shortly after his father died.

The name on the card was Daniel Karlov Esq. Attorney at Law, Trustee of the Petrosyan Fund. It gave an address on Avenue of the Americas, New York City. Peter's monthly statements that he never opened were mailed from that address. On the opposite side was a phone number that he had never dialed. He fingered the card and remembered the horror he felt when his father let go of him saying, "I've given you a great gift… You are a fresh new boy… Never look back." He had clung to those words. Today they sounded like a warning instead of a gift. With enough time left on his phone card for one short call, he dialed Daniel Karlov.

The phone rang. He envisioned an elderly man with a long white beard who sat by the phone year after year, waiting for him to call. "Hello, Peter." The voice that answered was paternal. "How can I be of service?"

"I need to know about my trust fund," Peter blurted, knowing that time was short. "Who is Petrosyan?"

Before Karlov could answer, the line clicked several times. A cheerful woman's voice informed him in Russian that his international phone card had expired and he could buy a new one at the Central Post Office when it opened again at ten a.m..

Peter wrapped himself in the duvet and stood at the window. The black Mercedes was parked in plain view on the street. Cigarette smoke curled from the windows. *Is this what it means to be a fresh, new boy?* He wanted to call Lex back to tell him about the strange meeting with Golokov. It would have to wait until the post office opened. He would purchase several phone cards next time.

Back at the table, he rechecked the envelope and discovered one more piece of paper—a 1991 newspaper clipping from *The Seattle Times*. Peter recognized the photograph that had been taken from the top of the Federal Building in downtown Seattle. Rows of open coffins lined Federal Square. Students sat in the boxes waving American flags. A banner said, "End the Iraq War Now."

"Is there hope for us, my love?" he said aloud, tracing his finger around the angry face of Caroline Luke. "There must be hope."

Chapter Eleven

THE THEFT

New York City, October 6, 1997

The icon sat on Petrosyan's mantle—immutable and inanimate. *A beat-up block of wood, that's all you are. The rest is in my head.* The old man fidgeted in his chair, unable to shake the feeling that a vengeful pagan goddess held him accountable for his grandson's predicament. *She'd be right, wouldn't she?*

The whole mess started just over a year ago with a surprise visit from his older brother Ephraim's grandson, Alexei Kaminsky. Petrosyan had thought his nephew long dead, shot in the purge with Ephraim and the rest of his family. Apparently, he had been spared execution and grew up in Kurzan Prison for Children of Enemies of the People.

Alexei seemed well-spoken. He was tall, blond, and had the Kaminsky good looks. Petrosyan reminisced with him about Ephraim, showing him photographs of their young days in Kolomeno Settlement. After two days, the men parted on friendly terms.

Following a year of silence, Alexei contacted Petrosyan again—this time with the enticing story about finding Russia's long-lost icon, the Virgin of Kurzan. The old man was skeptical at first, but as he listened, Alexei's story began to sound credible. Apparently, Alexei and the other boy prisoners used to go exploring in the tunnels under their prison. The subterranean warrens had been there since the 14th Century and had once extended in a maze from the Kurzan River, which was covered over in the 16th Century, all the way to Pskov. On one such adventure, Alexei discovered a cave beneath the ruins of the Church of the Kurzan Goddess. He crawled inside and saw a light glowing around a hidden panel. He tried to pry it open with his hands but it didn't budge.

He left Kurzan Prison shortly after that at the age of seventeen and the incident was forgotten for years—until a few months ago. An ORT television special featured the Virgin of Kurzan as Russia's most valuable lost treasure. There was a dramatization of the destruction of Kurzan Monastery by the CHEKA in 1928. The heroic monks were tortured and executed one-by-one, but no one revealed the hiding place of the Virgin of Kurzan. It had been missing ever since.

Alexei returned to the ruins of Kurzan with power tools and unearthed it. The icon was sitting on his desk. when he called Petrosyan in New York.

"I've already spoken with your man at Sotheby's," Alexei said. "According to Arthur Wellington, you own a collection of old parchments that document the history of the icon, something called the *Book of Miracles*. That kind of provenance will triple the price. He wants to auction the whole package under your name." After a pause, he added, "This may sound strange but I want to get it out of here, uncle—soon. It's giving me bad dreams."

"Nightmares, you say?" Petrosyan perked up at that bit of news. Was Zemyna working her devilish magic on his nephew? He had an extensive collection of documents recording centuries of visions and nightmares induced by proximity to the Virgin of Kurzan. He demanded that his nephew describe the dreams in detail. At that point, he became convinced that the icon was genuine. "Give it to me and I'll see that you clear twelve million," he exclaimed.

"That will be enough to buy the charter for my new bank. I'm going to call it the International Bank of Kurzan," said Alexei. "I'm taking my business global. What do you need me to do now?"

"Get the damn thing to New York. I'll take care of the rest." Petrosyan hesitated. Smuggling icons wasn't as easy as it once had been. The Russians had gotten touchy. "How will you ship it to America? It is a registered historical treasure."

"Don't worry. I have a plan," Alexei answered, sounding very much like Ephraim. "We need an American to lie in a coffin long enough for some embassy official to take a quick look and declare him dead. Then we substitute the icon for the body, add some ballast, seal the box, and send the coffin with the US passport to one of your warehouses at JFK. You take the icon out and ship the coffin on to the bereaved family in America."

Petrosyan balked. "Murder might work for you in Russia, but not with an American citizen."

"The American won't be dead, just drugged enough to look dead. We have a doctor on payroll who is a specialist in human smuggling. He is very skilled. Our Yankee will wake up twenty-four hours later with a hangover and minus a passport. We need that to accompany the coffin."

"Won't people here get suspicious when they discover the coffin is empty?"

"Who cares? Once you have the icon, we will drop the American at the embassy to get a new passport and go home. What happens beyond that isn't our problem."

Petrosyan thought it over. It seemed like a good plan, unlikely to arouse much interest from law enforcement on either side of the Atlantic. "He won't suffocate?"

"It won't be a real coffin—just one of those porous papier-mâché boxes we use for smuggling people across borders. They look good and hold up well—as long as it doesn't rain."

"Do you have an American in mind?"

Alexei paused. Warning bells clanged in the old man's brain.

"I was thinking of my cousin Peter Stone," Alexei said. "Don't you think it's time our Pyotor earned his inheritance?"

"No!" Petrosyan's voice was forceful. "Not Pyotor. You keep your hands off my grandson." The old man might have lusted after the icon for seventy years and already killed a dozen men to get it, but he would not put his heir at risk. *Think. Think!* Finally, the answer came to him. "Your body doesn't need to be a man. You can use a woman named Caroline Luke," he said. *Why not? She has clearly broken Pyotor's heart.*

"Peter's girl? The one who left him?"

How does he know that? "She's been in New York for the past few weeks auditioning for operas. I understand that she has considerable talent but not much luck. Become her friend. Buy her a starring role in one of the major Russian operas. Opening night at the Pushkin Theater will get her to Moscow. After that, do whatever you need to, but get her into that box—and out alive."

"Of course, uncle, I'll do what you say," Alexei replied and rang off.

What will you do to her? Petrosyan wondered, then put the question out of his mind. *None of my concern.* She walked out on Pyotor. She made him unhappy, so what did he care.

He contacted his New York investigator to check up on Caroline and discovered that she had just purchased a ticket back to Seattle. She would be leaving in a week—going back to his grandson. That would ruin Alexei's chances of getting her to Moscow alone. He called Alexei and urged him to act quickly.

A few weeks later, the coffin arrived in his warehouse accompanied by Caroline's passport and documents. The icon was in it. Everything was just as it should be. Or it had been until Pyotor boarded the Aeroflot Ilyushin and flew to Russia.

Chapter Twelve

MOSCOW MEAT MARKET

Moscow, October 6, 1997

Gogol barked in the hall. The elevator door slammed, waking Peter. He sat up and checked his watch. He had slept face down on the table for two hours. His head ached; his brain felt like oatmeal. He fumbled in his bag for a bottle of aspirin and swallowed three with two glasses of cold boiled water from the refrigerator. He pushed aside the lace curtain in the tiny kitchen and watched Gogol pulling Tanya along the sidewalk. The dog weighed more than she did. Peter needed to talk to her as soon as she returned, but first he could use a wash. Clean clothes and a shave would help clear his mind, too.

He showered quickly. The jet of hot water did wonders for his head, but he wasn't quick enough getting dressed. Tanya must have returned with the dog while he was still in the bathroom. He was pulling on his trousers when he heard the Pavlovs' door close. When he looked in the hall, Tanya had stepped into the elevator. She wore her white fur and high-heeled black boots.

"Tanya, wait," he called, but the lift doors shut. He grabbed his coat and raced downstairs. The nine flights seemed to take a long time. He was certain that he'd lost her—but he hadn't. She was standing at the curb. "Tanya," he shouted. She didn't hear him. A black Chaika pulled up in front of her. When the door opened, women were laughing inside. Tanya got in and the Chaika sped away.

"Shit, shit, shit." Peter swore, oblivious to babushkas scurrying by. He had to follow her, but there were no taxis and not enough time to go back for the Mercedes. He remembered that Russian drivers would pick up anyone if the price were right.

He fumbled in his pocket, found a twenty-dollar bill and waved it at the next car—an old blue Moskvich. It skidded to a halt. Peter handed the twenty to the young man driving and climbed in. "Don't lose that Chaika," he said.

The icy roads slowed traffic to a crawl and the Moskvich had no difficulty maintaining its position behind the other car in the heavy traffic. It was dark when they reached a bend in the Moscow River where one of the gigantic gothic constructions known as Stalin's "wedding cakes" dominated the skyline—the Hotel Ukrainia.

Peter asked the driver to stop at the bottom of a circular drive that curved up to the hotel portico. He climbed the rest of the way on foot. The Chaika was parked in a row of cars. Tanya leaned against it, smoking. Her coat was open to the hem of her miniskirt, exposing slender legs. On the other side of the car, two statuesque women—one in black mink with huge gold hoop earrings and one wrapped in red fox—shared a cigarette. Around the Chaika were Zils, Volgas, and Gazel vans with their motors running.

Men in fur hats and heavy boots haggled over open wooden crates. A tall, leopard-clad woman in stiletto heels brushed against Peter, running her hand across his shoulders. "Hey cowboy," she murmured in a husky voice. "Are your pants full of pleasure yet?"

Older women with bad teeth and too much makeup pressed in close. They jostled one another and shouted, "Not expensive…not expensive." Well-dressed Japanese men with flashlights and magnifying lenses examined gemstones on the hood of a Rolls-Royce. Young men with wide Yakutian faces leaned against a silver Volga. They slid white paper packets through the windows of foreign cars that drove up slowly and sped away.

"Hey, you." An enormous man in a black fur hat, one gold earring, a full-length black leather coat, and laced-up boots stepped in Peter's way. "*Durak*! I am talk with you. You want narco-mans? You speak them," the giant said in broken English, nodding toward the Yakutians. "You want womens, you speak me, Oleg the Cossack. I am boss."

"I'm just leaving." Peter tried to turn away but was blocked by another brute with a forelock and gold earrings. People stared and moved closer. He tried to back up but was surrounded. "I don't want any trouble," he said, holding up his hands.

"This is the capital of trouble and you are in the middle of it," said a voice in soft, clear English. The driver of the blue Moskvich had come up beside him.

"What is this place?" asked Peter.

"This is the Moscow Meat Market. We need to get you out of here." The man addressed Oleg, flicking his hand dismissively: "Excuse us, please, Mr. Cossack. This man is a guest at the hotel. Let us pass." Oleg bowed and stepped back deferentially, as if he knew him. The driver propelled Peter toward the bright foyer.

Peter balked. "But I'm not staying here."

"You'd better be," the driver chuckled. "Unless you want to be worked over by that mob."

"What about Tanya…the young woman over there? Maybe she should come with us?"

"If you want to pay that Cossack pimp for her, then do it."

"She's a prostitute?"

"Of course, she is. I see that you have a lot to learn about Moscow." The driver laughed and tugged at Peter's arm with unwelcome familiarity. Peter looked back at the hostile crowd and chose to follow him to the safety of the hotel.

"Come on, hold up your documents," said the driver. Peter displayed his passport to the armed hotel guard. Other uniformed men watched from the glass vestibule inside. They opened the door to let him in. "I am Alexei Kaminsky, his interpreter," the driver said with a wink. They nodded as if they were in on the joke.

In the lobby, Asian men hovered in the shadows, smoking cigarettes and ogling a group of blond women dressed like schoolgirls, who giggled and flirted. Two Americans in Stetson hats and string ties walked by complaining about the "rising cost of ass in this town."

"I'm guessing that you like to watch the girls without paying," said the driver, looking Peter over. "I know just the place for that."

"I'm not interested in any of this," said Peter. He pulled out his wallet. "I'll pay you forty dollars to drive me back to Apple Street. Or if that is too far out of your way, I'll call a taxi."

"No taxis will come in this traffic. You are stranded. Let's have a drink. I'll get you home when the roads clear."

"How long will that take?"

"Usually an hour, plus or minus." said the driver with a shrug.

He led Peter to the elevators. One opened with Arab men in headdresses and Russian girls in skin-tight leather pants and filmy blouses. One of the women with spiky white hair raised a leather whip and snapped it at Peter. An Arab grabbed her and bit her breast. She slapped him hard with the whip, cutting his lip. She smeared his blood on her nipple. They screamed with laughter while the door to the elevator slid shut.

"Now those girls are expensive." The driver laughed. "There is a real art to drawing blood like that. It is very sexy. The pain is exquisite."

Another elevator opened—empty except for two babushkas with mops and a bucket that smelled like vomit. The driver propelled Peter in.

He pushed the button for the third floor where he led the way through a dimly lit maze of hallways that opened onto a lush winter garden. A pink marble fountain surrounded by voluptuous nude statues of men and women marked the entrance to a restaurant.

Peter followed the driver through a jungle of orchids and bromeliads to a long, marble-topped bar. Bartenders in white aprons polished glasses in front of a floor-to-ceiling mirror. Glass shelves displayed more varieties of liquor than Peter had seen in one place. Beyond the bar, the dining room was wood paneled with ornate gilded ceilings and abundant foliage. Men in suits ate with gusto and laughed loudly, speaking many languages. Women in skimpy shorts and high-heeled boots passed among them offering trays of cigarettes and cigars. Tobacco smoke hung in the air.

The driver spoke to the maître d', then said to Peter: "This is our lucky night. My favorite table is open." A waiter led them to a table in front of a large, round window that overlooked the parking lot. Beyond it, the four-lane roads on either side of the river had fused into unmoving ribbons of red and white lights.

"What did I tell you—traffic. It's the same every night in Moscow. At least it doesn't last too long." The driver handed his coat to the hostess and pointed through the window at Tanya. "There's your girl. Isn't that the one you wanted?" Tanya was arguing with Oleg. The Cossack grabbed her arm. She spat at him. He let her go.

"She looks so small," said Peter. He leaned close to the glass, but she had moved out of his sight, away from Oleg. "That man's a giant."

"Don't worry. Those girls are tough. They do this for a year or two then marry a rich foreigner and get the hell out of this country." The driver pulled off his black knit hat and ran a hand through thick, blond hair. "Care for a drink?" His blue eyes met Peter's. "I could use one."

"I'm buying," said Peter. A hostess in a black sequined gown helped him out of his coat while the waiter delivered a bottle of Krystal Vodka with two shot glasses and plates of bread and pickles. Peter put a twenty dollar bill on the table. "Sorry, no rubles."

"No rubles, no problem." The waiter pocketed the money, broke the seal on the Krystal and filled their glasses.

"We'll do this Russian style. Drink up," said the driver, downing his in one gulp. He closed his eyes and pressed a piece of black bread to his nose, then took a bite of pickle. "Ahhh … That's a very fine pickle. Now you."

Peter drank his shot and pushed the glass away. Getting drunk was not on his agenda and it was easy to lose track with Russian vodka. The driver refilled his glass to the brim and pushed it back to him. "One more won't hurt a big strapping lad like you." They clicked glasses and drank. The driver poured another. "Do you have a name?" he asked.

"My name is Peter Stone, Dr. Peter Stone."

"What a coincidence! My name is Alexei Kaminsky. Kaminsky is Russian for Stone." They shook hands, then Alexei leaned forward, "Maybe we're cousins. Maybe your real name is really Pyotor Kaminsky. What do you think? Do you have Russian relations?"

Peter shrugged, wary of the cat-like narrowing of the other man's eyes. Based on looks, they could easily be related. Both were tall with broad shoulders, high cheekbones, and round faces. Peter had sandy hair that was streaked with blond. Alexei was a little taller, slimmer and a platinum blond. Half of Moscow had the same Slavic looks with a touch of Tatar in the slant of their blue eyes. "I don't know anything about my family," he said. "In America, no one cares."

"Fair enough." Alexei drank another and slammed down his glass. "So, what are you doing such a long way from home?" He lit a Stoli. "Not looking for a good time, I see. You're such a serious fellow." A plate of fresh greens arrived at the table—sprigs of parsley, cilantro, dill, garlic and fennel. Alexei pushed the plate toward Peter. "Never drink on an empty stomach. Have some Siberian garlic."

"I'm here on business." Peter examined the garlic and bit into a pungent clove. "Just for a few days."

"In that case, welcome to Moscow." Alexei poured two more glasses. "Russians love Americans. They are much better tippers than Germans or French."

A white-haired woman in black leather hot-pants and sheer blouse came into the restaurant, whip in hand. Peter recognized her as the one who had cut the lip of the Arab in the elevator. There was no blood on her blouse now. Her unblemished skin and slender figure gave her the look of a naughty child wearing too much makeup and not enough clothing.

She perched on a barstool and ordered a bottle of Perrier. Peter observed her in the bar mirror. Her eyes caught his and she rotated slowly on the stool until she sat facing him. She spread her legs and carefully poured Perrier on her nipples, which grew erect beneath the blouse. She began to suck at the bottle with an exaggerated slowness, drawing it all the way into her mouth.

Peter sat transfixed until Alexei thumped his shoulder and called the maître d' to the table. "Better give this man fifty bucks for the show. That is if you want to walk out of here on your own legs. I told you those girls are expensive." Peter pulled a fifty from his wallet. When he looked up, the woman was gone. He turned back to the window. Tanya was standing alone.

"You really want that little girl from the Meat Market, don't you? Well, here you sit with a wallet full of dollars. All you need to do is pay for her. The women here are for sale."

"She's a successful journalist. I don't understand what she's doing out there."

"They've all got day jobs, but their pitiful wages aren't enough to buy bread. Even your remote-control blow job is probably an accountant or a doctor. You can bet that she's on her way home with a purse full of cash to buy meat for her two kids and vodka for her no-good unemployed husband." Alexei leaned on the table. "Don't look so shocked. Sex is just a business for them. When the economy crashes, women sell what men will buy. This is the new thing in Russia. We call it capitalism." Alexei turned and raised his arm to order another bottle of vodka. He tensed abruptly.

Peter followed his line of sight and was surprised to see the Chechen bodyguards taking seats at either end of the bar. Ahmed had his hand inside his jacket and Ruslan wore a pair of black-framed eyeglasses that Peter had not seen before. If the Chechens could track him to the Hotel Ukrainia, they must have the technology to follow him anywhere.

"Do you know those men?" he asked.

"The Butchers of Grozny?" Alexei spat. "I know them by reputation."

"What do you mean—butchers?"

"Men, women, little children mutilated and shot by mercenaries during the Chechen War, led by that guy Ruslan Amiroev. Stay away from those two. They are killers." Alexei opened the fresh bottle of Krystal when it arrived and poured himself a shot. "Drink up. It's time to go somewhere else."

"No, thanks," said Peter, covering his glass with his hand. "I'll stay here until the traffic clears, then call a taxi."

"That simply won't do," said Alexei, swigging his vodka. "I must insist that you come with me. Now."

"Why?"

"Because of her." Alexei pulled a coil of blond hair from his pocket and shook it. Long golden strands unwound and cascaded to the floor. "She is where you want to be. Am I right?" He leaned into Peter's face and smiled. "You know that I'm right, Pyotor."

Peter grabbed the locks with one hand and Alexei's arm with the other. "You aren't just a random driver. Who the hell are you? Where did you get this?"

Alexei shrugged. "Didn't your American writer Kurt Vonnegut say: 'We are who we pretend to be'?" He grinned and broke Peter's grip. "The hair is from the songbird—who else?"

"Is she all right?" Peter pressed the locks to his nose—China Rain. "Where is she?"

"She is happy and fulfilled. Tonight she becomes an international star." Alexei stood and signaled the hostess to bring their coats. "Come, be my guest. See her triumph for yourself."

Peter hesitated. He was tempted to call Ruslan and Ahmed for help—but what could they do? He still had no idea where Caroline was. The vodka wasn't helping him think. "Is she with UZI?"

"Do you mean that famous poet—the handsome one? Possibly," said Alexei, tossing Peter his coat. "You won't know anything more unless you join me."

Trusting that his bodyguards would follow, Peter stood up and tossed another twenty dollars on the table. "Let's go," he said.

"Did I tell you that I'm a free-market economist?" Alexei laughed as he zipped his coat. "There are thousands of us in this town, but I'm the very best." He stuffed the vodka bottle in his pocket, put on his hat and said: "Now, let's lose the two black-butts."

On his signal, they were surrounded by a flurry of waiters and waitresses who rushed them to the back of the restaurant and into a stairwell. Alexei bolted the door behind them and Peter followed him down the exit stairs to the parking lot. The Chaika waited by the door with the engine running. Oleg the Cossack stood by the car grinning ear-to-ear. He grabbed Peter in a bear hug, kissed him squarely on the lips and pushed him into the backseat next to Alexei.

Tanya stood staring at him, open-mouthed. "Tanya," he called.

She backed away, but Oleg grabbed her arm and pushed her in beside Peter. The Cossack climbed onto the driver's seat. "We go party now!" He turned to leer at Tanya. "You like my girl? She's yours for two hundred American dollars."

"Pay him, or he'll kill you," Tanya hissed in Peter's ear. "Worse, he'll kill me."

"Pay Stepan," said Oleg, tilting his head to the passenger seat.

Peter paid the pimp's wingman, the brute with a forelock and gold earrings. The man grinned and tossed a box of Red October chocolates onto Peter's lap. "For you. A present."

Oleg threw back his head and howled. He ground the gears until the Chaika jerked forward and accelerated out of the parking lot. Oncoming traffic scattered and skidded on the ice. Brakes screeched.

Peter grasped Tanya's shoulder with one hand and held tight to the door strap with the other, afraid that the rattling door might fly open and dump them onto the road. The Russian men smoked and passed the vodka. Tanya lit a cigarette.

Peter whispered in her ear: "Are they taking us to Caroline?"

She shrugged and gazed out the window.

Across the river, a yellow moon hung low over the Kremlin. Peter stared at its reflection in the river and remembered a night in Seattle a few months before when rain pounded the windshield of Caroline's Volkswagen.

The little car sped across the Lake Washington Floating Bridge with Caroline at the wheel and him in the passenger seat, wishing that she would slow down. The anemic heater had given up and they were bundled in ski hats and down parkas. Their breath formed plumes that steamed the windows. He wiped the windshield with his sleeve.

"I can't believe this." She pounded her fist on the steering wheel. "The part was mine. I deserved it. I am fucking Norma!"

"Yes, you are," he said. "No doubt about that."

She had every right to be angry. They'd sat together for hours waiting for her to audition for the starring role in Seattle Opera's production of *Norma*, He shared her growing elation listening to the different sopranos. Not one of them could sing like Caroline. She was Norma, the druid priestess, in every other way as well—statuesque, strong, beautiful. In the end, the role went to a dumpy, middle-aged singer who hadn't auditioned for it. She was known to be the paramour of the opera's biggest donor.

"What's the bloody point? Where is justice? Fairness?" Caroline demanded. "Why do I keep trying when I never get a break?"

"How can you ask? No one can sing 'Casta Diva' like you can."

"Talent isn't enough." She pulled over to the side of the road and braked. "All that work. My whole life devoted to becoming an artist. In the end, no one wants me because I don't have money."

It hurt his heart to see her so unhappy. That was the first time in his life that he considered dipping into the Petrosyan Fund. He didn't know how much was in the account but there must be enough to turn some heads at the Seattle Opera with the prospect of a generous donation. Anyone with eyes and ears could see that Caroline Luke had what it took to be a diva—all she needed was a break on the stage. The fame that she craved could be hers and he had the power to grant it.

But then what? He'd wondered. Did he want her travelling to other countries and surrounding herself with admirers? Not really. To him, she was perfect the way she was—his flustered little bird, always late, rushing around the houseboat searching for misplaced sheet music, tossing up a cloud of hair ribbons and scarves, her costume jewelry rattling from every doorknob. There were pros and cons to consider. Accessing the fund was not to be taken lightly.

He needed time to mull it over. Fortunately, he had plenty of time. It was too late for *Norma*—that role had been cast, and the next set of auditions was weeks away.

He had not considered it again until the fateful night when she cornered him and said: "Can we talk?"

Chapter Thirteen

THE BRIDE MARKET

Moscow, October 6, 1997

Twenty minutes later, the Chaika drove into another crowded parking lot and Oleg backed into an open space. Rap music pulsed and pounded. Rings of neon encircled a building, rising like flames.

"I've seen this place before," said Peter. "This is Moscow Traffic. Your grandfather brought me here last night."

"Swell," said Tanya. "What was the old fool thinking?"

Armed men in fatigues waved their party down a flight of weathered steps into a dank, stone-walled tunnel. At the end of it, Alexei pushed open a set of heavy doors. Glowing neon sky bridges floated overhead in a cloud of tobacco smoke. Men in tuxedos tossed down shots of vodka and snorted cocaine or danced on the flashing bridges with scantily clad young girls. Peter squinted against the strobe lights.

Onstage, a rapper sang and danced to a synthesizer so loud that it rippled the drinks. They were no sooner seated than the rapper did a backflip off the stage and a man in a pink tuxedo strode to the microphone. "Welcome gentlemen! Are you ready to meet the woman of your dreams?" The crowd cheered. Bottles of cognac and boxes of cigars appeared on the tables.

"Sit," said Oleg, directing Peter to a chair near the stage.

"Smile, Pyotor." Alexei sat next to him. "You are my guest. You can ogle all of the girls without spending a kopek."

The house lights dimmed. Spotlights shone on a band that played a jazzy, sexy rendition of "Moscow Nights." A glowing pink catwalk appeared to unroll down the length of the building. Next, the band launched into "New York, New York" and a line of young women stepped onto the catwalk. The first one, a redhead in a tailored blue suit, strutted to the turnabout at the end of the runway, where she struck alluring poses. She paraded back, replaced by a blonde in a white suit with a hip-swinging stride.

"The suits are just to warm up," Alexei confided. "No one really wants to see them with clothes on."

At the end of the first round, a bare-breasted woman dressed as Nefertiti danced around the stage playing the flute for two dancing bears. Waiters refilled drinks, lit cigars, and cut lines of cocaine.

"Where's Caroline? You said she was here." Peter tried to stand. It was difficult to see in the smoky club.

"Sit!" Oleg pushed him back down and karate chopped him hard on both shoulders. "Stay put, or I hurt you," he growled.

The band struck up "Singing in the Rain" and the women walked out again, this time in elegant head-to-toe furs—mink, fox, beaver. They looked regal in high-heeled boots and fur hats.

Programs in several languages were scattered around the tables. Women were listed by name and age with a photo. There was a rating grid and a place to write a bid, starting at $50,000. Peter searched for Caroline's name.

"You won't find her there. The songbird is not for sale," said Alexei, shaking his head. "This is her big night as a singer. Just look around this room. We have producers, directors, agents—the cream of entertainment from all over the world. This parade of silly women is just a warm-up for her debut."

With a round of "Getting to Know You," each woman, now dressed in an evening gown, stepped up to the microphone and stated her name, age and catalogue number before she turned and swept down the runway. The effect was stunning. Some gowns were tight-fitting and low-cut. Some were high necked with low backs and long slit skirts. There were black silks, emerald greens with sparkling sequins, pure whites with appliqués of pearls and lace. One tall, red-haired beauty with eyes so green they glowed in the stage light, wore a Cossack uniform—tight black pants, high boots, and a red jacket with gold braid laced across her breasts.

"They make the costumes," said Oleg. "Families work on them for a year sometimes."

Now the band was silent, the crowd restless. The announcer stepped to the microphone to a drum roll. "Gentlemen, this is the moment we have all been waiting for—when nothing can be hidden, the moment of truth when you see what you are paying for!" He pointed to the band, which started a hip-grinding rendition of "The Stripper." Raucous whoops and whistles exploded in the hall and the women started down the runway—this time wearing only high heels. They looked vulnerable in the pale pink glow. The parade of breasts, pubic hair, and buttocks blurred together in a confusing muddle.

"What is this insanity?" Peter blurted.

"It's actually quite logical. You've seen the Meat Market at the Hotel Ukrainia," said Alexei. "That is the first step where the girls earn enough money to pay their entrance fee for the second step. Some girls have families that put up the money, but most of them have to work for it like your little Tanya. Then once a week, Moscow Traffic closes to the public and sponsors the Bride Market, which is step two. Tonight fifty lucky ladies reveal all on that runway. By the end of the night, they will have rich husbands and go on their way to a new life."

The announcer was back at the microphone. He hushed the audience. "Ladies and gentlemen, while we collect and tally your bids, we have a special treat for you, courtesy of our patron, the owner of Moscow Traffic who is with us tonight." A spotlight shone on Alexei's blond head. "Let's have a round of applause for our host, the world-famous people's poet— UZI!" Alexei stood and raised his arms.

The house erupted with applause shouting, "UZI! UZI! UZI!"

"You! You are UZI!" Peter struggled to stand, but Oleg dug powerful fingers into the nerves beneath his collarbones while Stepan kicked his feet out from under him and held him down in the chair.

Alexei/UZI nodded to the announcer and the lights dimmed. UZI leaned close to Peter's ear. "That's what the songbird screams when I take her to my bed…UZI, UZI."

"Let me go!" It took two more men Oleg's size to hold Peter in his seat. "I'll fucking kill you."

"Watch the show, *durak,*" Oleg growled in his ear.

"Ladies and gentlemen," said the announcer to a drumroll, "It is my great pleasure to present to you the famous American diva—Miss Caroline Luke, fresh from her stunning success at the Pushkin Opera."

A recorded soundtrack played and Peter stopped struggling. He recognized the music. It was the overture to Wagner's, *Götterdämmerung,* one of Caroline's favorites. Several stories up, floodlights illuminated a trapdoor in the center of the ceiling. It opened slowly, reminding him of the cargo doors on the 737 at Sea-Tac Airport when he'd held Baba in his arms.

An elaborate gilded cage lowered through the opening on a chain. Spotlights from every direction focused on its occupant. High-resolution screens showed close-ups of the golden head of Caroline Luke. She was wrapped in strips of fur that barely covered her nakedness. "Caroline!" he shouted. She did not respond. She couldn't hear him.

The announcer bellowed into the microphone, "Miss Luke will sing Brunhilda's aria at the dramatic moment when she throws herself into the flames for love. Then she will burn." The music pulsed through the sound system. Orange, red, and white neon flames flared up the walls of the building. Smoke rose from vents in the floor. The audience was engulfed in neon fire. UZI stood on his chair and pumped his fist shouting: "Burn, burn!"

The audience chanted, "Burn, burn, burn…"

Caroline lifted her face. Peter gasped in horror at what he saw on the screens. She was made up like a doll, with exaggerated lashes and clown tears painted down rouged cheeks. The effect was beautiful, but grotesque.

The overture ended; the music softened. Her voice rose and echoed around the hall. He had never heard such pain in it. It clawed at his heart. *I have to do something, anything.* The crowd was motionless, mesmerized. Peter forced himself to relax and control his breathing. He'd heard Caroline sing the immolation aria a hundred times. He bided his time knowing that the chance would arise for action. Oleg had rendered his arms nearly useless by crushing the nerves, but Peter had other rugby moves. He pumped his leg muscles, warming them up, readying his body for action.

Her voice rose in power, her sorrow echoed off the walls, saturating the hall with reverberating sound. The audience gasped, engulfed in the cocoon of music. When she reached the climactic crescendo, Peter pushed upward with all the strength in his legs. His head smashed into Oleg's nose. He kneed another man in the groin. He charged into their line, arms tucked tightly to his body, head down, spinning to shake them free as they grabbed at him. He used every dirty move he knew to block, kick, and head-butt his way past the thugs

"Caroline! Caroline!" he screamed but she still couldn't hear him. He jumped onto a chair and, using a table as a platform, leapt onto the catwalk. "Caroline…Caroline…It's Peter. I'm here." But he wasn't there. She was above his head in a cage that swung in widening arcs. She couldn't hear him over the surging music and the power of her voice. He had never felt so helpless.

"Caroline…" His head exploded in a burst of white and he fell, curling into a ball. He was kicked from all sides. "Caroline…" He gasped for breath.

He heard a gunshot. Someone screamed. The kicking stopped. Bodies flew. He struggled to sit up. The Chechens were by his side. Ahmed slung him over his shoulder before he blacked out. When he came to outside, he saw flames—real ones. Ruslan shouted, "Those idiots set fire to our car."

Gogol was nearby, barking furiously. Pavel called out, "Get Tanya and Pyotor to Kurzan. Everyone go to the convent before this whole place explodes."

He was bounced over rough ground on Ahmed's shoulder. Acrid orange mist rose from the ground. "Smells like napalm," said Ruslan.

"It is, or something like it from the munitions factory," yelled the old man. "Get down! It's going to blow!"

Ahmed dropped Peter behind a remnant of brick wall and dove on top of him. Peter raised his head high enough to see a wall of flame burst from the ground and engulf the Mercedes. Flames raced through the parking lot, igniting one luxury vehicle after another. The neon that spiraled up the sides of Moscow Traffic burst in a shower of sparks and popping glass.

"Let me go. Caroline is in there." Peter struggled to his feet. "She's still singing!" He lurched toward the building. Ahmed caught him when he fell.

Chapter Fourteen

BEFORE THE FIRE

Moscow Traffic, October 6, 1997

aroline had clung to the gilded bars as two of UZI's Cossacks guided the elaborate cage through the trapdoor in the ceiling. The winching mechanism was old and required constant hammering, oiling and cussing. Caroline closed her eyes, horrified that her life was in the hands of fools. If they broke the cable or the gears failed, she would crash to the floor of Moscow Traffic.

She had checked that the cage was securely connected by ropes in addition to the chain before they locked her in, but it swayed whenever she moved. She kept still and focused on deep breathing to prepare herself for the performance of her life. According to her contract, this concert constituted her final obligation. After that, her debt to UZI would be cancelled. The nightmare would end and she'd be free.

It was all written in the damn contract she had signed without reading it over cocktails with UZI at the Ritz in New York. *What a fool I've been—beguiled by a monster who flattered me when I was down.* She didn't discover until after her debut at the Pushkin Theater what was in it. Apparently, she owed UZI for both of their plane tickets on Aeroflot, his hotel in New York, her room and board in Russia, the dresses and jewels he'd given her in Moscow—the list seemed endless and kept growing. Even his right to keep her under lock and key without access to a phone as long as she owed him money was in the contract.

It did not say that her body was his, but it didn't have to. She was powerless against him. The only way to free herself was to complete the terms of his contract. After tonight's performance, she would walk all the way to Apple Street barefoot in the snow if she had to.

The chain caught in the winch; the cage bounced. Gears ground in a high-pitched squeal. A man swore, striking the chain with a hammer that sent tremors down to the cage making it swing. Caroline held her breath, willing it to be still, concentrating on not falling. UZI had invited agents and impresarios to hear her sing. They were down below somewhere—

important men who would promote her career in opera. They were also men who could elevate the status of Moscow Traffic from cheap cabaret entertainment to high art. She knew how much UZI wanted a reputation as a champion of the arts. She would give that to him. After days in captivity, she would give him anything he asked for, if it meant her freedom.

"Sing like an angel tonight and go home to Seattle tomorrow," he had said. "See if your American lover will take you back now that you've been loved by a real man."

The thought of collapsing into the safety of Peter's arms brought her to tears. She fought them back, unwilling to let UZI see her cry. "Yes, I'll go home."

But how could she explain to Peter what had happened? Maybe he didn't need to know. She was an actress, but was she good at lying? He was a psychologist and would see through her artifice. Would their relationship be destroyed by her pride and foolish decisions? Would lying to him make it worse? Cover-ups were often worse than the original missteps, weren't they?

These thoughts were too complicated. They drained her energy, pulling her emotions into dark places where death was preferable to living another day as UZI's slave. She could not afford to go there, not when tonight held the promise of freedom and she was reaching for it with every fiber in her being. She was struck by another doubt. Would UZI keep his word and let her go? She would have to take that chance.

The cage jerked and lowered again. She calmed her nerves using an old theater trick. She closed her eyes and mentally packed her suitcase, visualizing each step in the mundane task, recalling the colors and textures of the sweaters, scarves and skirts that smelled like her instead of him. She had been locked in a small room under Moscow Traffic for the past three days without a telephone or hot water. She had only her opera costume and the courtier dresses that UZI had bought for her.

To him, that cell was a special place because he had been confined there as a boy when the building was part of a childrens' prison—sometimes for days at a time without light. He had etched his poems on the walls with a fork. He seemed to think that she would like it there. She didn't.

She wore the exotic black gowns and hats when he took her out to his casinos and clubs, fondling her in front of his rich friends like he owned her. And according to his contract, he did own her—until tonight. Now she wanted a hot shower with enough soap to scrub the stink of him off her skin. She would leave everything that he'd given her behind. Her own things, clothes that he had never touched, were either at the theater or still in her flat with the Pavlovs.

She thought of her sweet neighbors on Apple Street. They must be out of their minds with worry. Had they called the police when she didn't return after the concert? Surely the Pavlovs had reported her missing. Would it do any good? UZI seemed to own the police. Baba must be worried, too. Caroline hadn't been able to call her since the day of the opera. Had Baba told Peter about Moscow? She'd promised not to.

Caroline had wanted to tell him herself once she had achieved success and could prove to him that she was worthy of her dreams. What would he do if he found out she was in Russia? Would he come looking for her? What would UZI do to him if he did come? She gasped at the thought and her pulse quickened. She closed her eyes. *Breathe!* Dark thoughts would not help her sing.

She re-centered herself and wrote a mental checklist of steps required to get from Moscow back to the houseboat on Lake Union. She imagined Peter at his desk right now, head down, working on his next article about psychopaths. She'd fly through the window like a squall, blowing his neat papers into chaos and ruffling his hair. He would pretend to be angry, then make love to her—real love, tender and kind without violence. Would it ever be that way between them again? First, she had to get home. The rest would work itself out once she was safe. She had to believe that, or she would go mad.

Back to her checklist: First thing in the morning when the Central Post Office opened, she'd purchase a telephone card and call Baba and Peter to tell them she'd be on the next flight to Seattle. She imagined them waiting for her at Sea-Tac, waving as she cleared customs and came through the glass gates. Peter would give her flowers, Baba would cry. What should she wear on the flight? Her lucky suit, of course—the one that Peter liked best. Where had she left it—that emerald green silk suit that matched her eyes? She had worn it on the day in New York when she met UZI and believed that her dreams had come true.

It was barely two weeks ago that she stood in the lobby of the Ritz Hotel and extended her hand to Alexei Kaminsky, the wealthy Russian who'd agreed to sponsor her debut at the Pushkin Theater. How thrilling to find a patron who appreciated her for her talent. As a bonus, he was tall, handsome like Peter and a famous poet. "I'm very pleased to meet you, Mr. Kaminsky. I have read your poetry."

"Call me UZI, please." UZI lifted her hand to his lips and kissed it. "The pleasure is mine." He raised his blue eyes to hers and arousal flushed through her. She had spent the evening before in the public library reading articles about this man and knew of his reputation as a poet and a gangster. Meeting him in person was thrilling. Peter worked with criminals every day at Harborview, but she'd never met any. What would he think of her now?

"A starring role at the Pushkin is a great honor," she said breathlessly, her cheeks flushed. "I hope you won't be disappointed."

"How could you possibly disappoint? The selection committee reviewed dozens of videotapes. They were unanimous in their decision. You have won our hearts. You will sing Antonida Susanina, the virgin bride and heroine of Russia."

"To be honest," said Caroline, "I've had so many auditions that I don't remember applying to the Pushkin."

By the time she had downed two martinis in the Ritz's tony Contour Bar and signed the contract, she felt like a beautiful woman again. After Peter's hurtful rejection she wasn't sure if she ever would. A few hours later, she and UZI took their first-class seats on the Aeroflot Ilyushin and UZI ordered champagne. *Look at me, Peter! I'm flying to Russia with a handsome stranger who admires me as an artist.* "I don't even have an agent yet." She laughed.

"With talent and beauty like yours, you don't need one," he whispered, leaning close to tuck a loose strand of hair behind her ear as Peter might have done. "I will take care of you."

Dusk in Moscow looked fresh and exciting from the backseat of UZI's chauffeured Zil. On Tverskaya Street, the garish casinos were springing to life with gaudy bursts of neon. They passed jazz clubs where musicians and waiters prepared for another steamy, smoky night. She watched showgirls, impossibly thin in their tight jeans and boots, checking in at stage doors. *How vulnerable they look.* She glanced at the handsome man beside her, reassured to be watched over by a gentleman. Theatergoers were lining up along the Kremlin wall, waiting for the Pushkin Theater to open. According to the marquee, Philipp Kirkorov was singing in concert. *Will they line up like that to hear me sing?*

"Let me put you up at the Metropole." UZI nodded toward a brightly lit hotel on Red Square. "Wouldn't you prefer a suite with a view of St. Basil's to a homestay with the Pavlov family? The Metropole is across the street from the theater."

Caroline nearly said yes, but UZI continued: "We can see much more of one another—alone, without interruptions."

"If you don't mind," she backtracked, her bravado flagging, "I'd rather stay with the Pavlovs. I'd feel more comfortable with a family."

"As you wish. Let me know if you change your mind."

She nearly did change her mind about the flat on Apple Street when UZI escorted her into the dark, fetid lobby and left her in the lift. But Tanya and the Pavlov family made her feel so welcome that she decided to stay. *What does it matter? I'm here to work, nothing else.* She unpacked and decorated her room with scarves, bangles and souvenirs. It was then that she realized that UZI had kept her passport and both copies of the contract they had signed. *Just an oversight. I'll get them back tomorrow.*

She meant to ask him about it, but every day there were rehearsals, fittings, lines to learn and music to study. UZI sometimes came at the end of rehearsals and insisted on buying her dinner. He obviously knew his way around money and wasn't reluctant to spend it on her. He gave her an open-ended account with the boutique of Slava Zaitsev on Prospekt Mira. Slava designed her a strapless, black velvet gown that she wore on the night that UZI presented her with an extravagant pair of diamond earrings. She gasped when she opened the red leather DeBeers jewel case.

"They're beautiful!" she exclaimed. "I've never seen diamonds so big. They must have cost you a fortune."

"No matter," he said. "Those other diamonds you wear are too small for you. A diva must have jewels that match her beauty."

"These were a gift," she fingered Peter's little hearts, reluctant to remove them from her ears.

"From the man who broke your heart? The man who isn't here?"

"How did you know?"

"You're such a sad little princess," he whispered, caressing her cheek with the back of his hand. "It's time to take these off." She let him remove Peter's hearts and felt naked without them. He replaced the hearts with the heavy diamond drops. "You look stunning," he said. "Would you wear them when you sing on opening night? It would make me happy."

"I'll have to ask Ludmilla, the costume designer."

"You do want to make your patron happy, don't you?" He leaned forward and kissed her throat and shoulders. She froze, sensing the menace in him. "Do I need to remind you that you have a debt to me that must be paid?"

"Of course I'll wear them," she said. *What did I sign?*

****

The cage reached the end of its chain and stopped with a clunk. Caroline opened her eyes but saw only klieg lights, wisps of artificial stage-smoke and neon lights that darted and danced across the ceiling to simulate flames. Invisible below her and on the sky bridges lost in the haze, Moscow Traffic must be packed with revelers. She heard them shouting, "UZI, UZI" and then "burn, burn," terrifying chants from an unseen mob.

If only she could roll back time and erase everything that had happened since she had met UZI. But she couldn't. Her only way out of this predicament was forward. That meant playing her part tonight to perfection. *How will my voice sound after all that has happened?* Emotional and physical trauma could either enhance or destroy a voice. She wouldn't know until she sang. She shook her head, letting her jaw go slack to relax her throat. The long, slow overture to *Götterdämmerung* began. The music drowned out the noise from the club. She let it transport her back to the last time that she had been happy.

Opening night at the Pushkin Theater was only a few nights ago but it seemed an ocean away. The omens had been favorable that day—the weather unseasonably fine, a full house at the theater, the boisterous good humor of the cast as seamstresses rolled racks of colorful costumes to dressing rooms where the thirty-five soloists of the Pushkin Theater of Opera and Ballet were assembled for the 59th season opening of the national opera. It was her night to star as Antonida, the brave young Russian bride in her nationally televised premier. The Pushkin Theater was one of the world's top houses—a star-maker. She intended to be brilliant.

There had been a week of rehearsals and in that time, she had grown to love the company of singers and the crew of artists who supported them. They welcomed her as one of the company, becoming the family that she had never known. She joined in their rowdy antics as they dressed for the performance. When it was her turn to sit at the lighted mirror, Anatoly applied sponges of zinc white, pancake makeup and powder to her face — then bright blue kohl, which made her eyes enormous, and a flourish of rouge which heightened her complexion and lips to rosy perfection. When her makeup was complete, he freed her hair of its thick plait and let it fall over her shoulders in golden waves.

Then came skinny Ludmilla, her dresser, forever chain-smoking Stolis but never dropping an ash. She had pincushions strapped to her wrists and a tape measure draped around her neck. She hummed as she slipped a dough colored muslin gown over Caroline's head and helped her step into pantaloons, then looked her over like a painter eying a blank canvas.

Next she wrapped her in the many layers of Antonida's wedding dress. The ensemble was finished by a high-waisted apron of red, yellow, blue and green ribbons with a matching ring of ribbons that circled her neck and flowed down her back.

Caroline slipped on the gaudy diamond earrings, her gift from UZI. Ludmilla scowled at them but no one was going to oppose UZI. She covered them with Antonida's headdress with its accents of silver, pearls and more colorful ribbons. Caroline watched herself transformed from Caroline Luke, American coloratura soprano, to Antonida Susanina, Russian folk heroine. She felt taller, stronger, unafraid.

Anatoly applied a final touch of rouge and winked at her with satisfaction. Ludmilla completed the tucking and pinning of her gown and smiled. After they left, she sat alone in the dressing room to gather force for the performance. "These are my family. Moscow is where I belong," she'd said aloud, meaning every word.

When she stepped onto the stage as proud Antonida, daughter of Ivan Susanin, hero of Russia, there was magic around her in the moonlit forest of Kostroma. Then the Polish army, costumed in white satin capes and furs, set upon her father, and brutally murdered him with spikes. The tenor Baluta as her love Sobinin, the baritone Pravilof as Ivan Susanin, and her Antonida, brought the audience to thunderous applause when the Poles were defeated and she was reunited with her beloved to consummate their wedding vows. Magic billowed forth from the rousing chorus of thirty-five soloists whose voices melded in a finale that thundered between heaven and earth.

The audience loved her. She couldn't count the curtain calls, the children climbing onto the stage to fill her arms with red roses and carnations. She had never felt so alive and adored. *I'm home.* At the cast party, the mayor of Moscow filled her glass with Crimean champagne and led the first of many toasts in honor of Russia's new coloratura soprano— "Carolina Luke, our beautiful American Antonida." She removed her makeup but stayed in costume, posing for photographs and giving interviews to fans and reporters, growing giddy on the champagne.

She raised her glass and announced that she intended to legally reclaim the name of Lukhinova, the name her father had shortened to Luke when he joined the Marines. She was no longer the wandering exile but a Russian Countess, returning to the Old World from the New World as the toast of Moscow. It all made sense to her in the bright lights and tipsy company of her theater family. From the reaction of the audience and media, she knew that offers would come for starring roles in other operas. Finding an agent would be much easier because, as of tonight, Caroline Luke was a star.

She looked for UZI in the crowd. She stood on her toes and searched the room, wanting to thank him for his belief in her. There he was—lurking, half-hidden under the stairs, apart from the happy party. She waved and blew him a kiss. When he summoned her with a nod of his head, she didn't hesitate. Her stardom and the champagne made her invincible. She grabbed an unopened bottle of Kornet Champagne and followed him away from the light.

"I need you to do something for me," he said, sweeping her into his arms like a child and carrying her out into the night. "It's in your contract."

"Damn the contract," she laughed. "Tonight anything can happen."

The Zil waited by the stage door. He placed her into the car and climbed in beside her, closing the door with the soft thump of a well-made automobile. "The river," he said to the chauffeur.

She shivered in her costume. UZI wrapped her in a fur rug and held her. "You were magnificent, little songbird. You made me proud." She sighed and leaned on his shoulder, warmed in the arms of this powerful man who had taken a risk on her behalf. "We are going to a special place. I want to share it with you."

"Is it in my contract?" she laughed.

"No, princess." He put his fingers to her lips to silence her. "It is in my heart." He slid his cold hand under her muslim sheathe and caressed the warm skin of her belly. Caroline gasped, but didn't pull away. She lay back and became weightless as a falling leaf, invisible, a miniscule disturbance in time. She let him undo the ribbons on her apron and kiss her lips. He tasted salty.

As the Zil glided through Moscow, her imagination erased the noisy, tasteless strip clubs, drunks and prostitutes that shouted from the sidewalks. She summoned instead the old Moscow of Baba's stories, that imaginary city, timeless in its beauty. As UZI touched her breast, he became the handsome prince who granted all that her heart desired.

Streetlights illuminated the red brick Kremlin wall topped by battlements and towers. In her mind, the Zil was pursued by sleigh bells from another century and clattering hoofbeats of metal shoes striking sparks on the cobbles. How many lifetimes, she wondered, how many generations of her ancestors rode in troikas down this very road, pulled through the streets by three prancing horses—their bridles jangling with bells, their breath steaming and nostrils flared as they snorted in the cold. Had life been as glorious for those women tucked beneath their furs?

Approaching the bank of the Moscow River, they passed the remnants of the Church of St. Yaroslav the Redeemer. It had no tower now, no bells—Spetsnaz had pulled them down in 1928. In the modern world, all that remained of the great 13th century cathedral was a hole in the ground. The bells she heard were ghosts. The Zil whisked past the ruin and the bells followed, tolling the days of her births and deaths in the country of her soul.

At the bottom of the hill, a ship was moored at the embankment waiting to ferry them downriver to Kurzan. Lanterns burned brightly on the bow as men in fur jackets and hats stamped their boots and smoked to ward off the cold. The dockers were delighted with her fairly-tale costume. They called her a princess from another time. UZI gave them vodka in a basket and one hundred rubles each.

She stepped down into the cabin of the boat that smelled of petrol. The engines chugged as UZI held her close, his head pressed against her chest, and shared with her the tragic story of his childhood. She stroked his hair and listened in respectful silence. He was bestowing a great honor by sharing his secret sorrows and taking her to see the place of his imprisonment. He wanted to show her the treasure he had discovered there.

It was midnight when they docked at the wooden pier at Kolomeno and disembarked along the well-worn path made by the feet of long-dead pilgrims. For six centuries they came to lay their ailing, lame and dying in front of the Virgin of Kurzan and pray for miracles. Now Caroline and UZI were the hopeful pilgrims.

At the top of the bluff, the ruin of the monastery loomed over them like a two-dimensional stage set. Nothing seemed real. On one side, an ugly brick prison tower soared above the snow like a bloody dagger. On the other, steel gates and barbed wire — inventions of this cruel century that had kept UZI a prisoner in his childhood. She clung to his arm. How terrible it must be for him to return to this place of his defilement.

But they were not alone. Oleg stepped out of a Gazel van with a white coated doctor. He walked ahead to unlock a cellar door and lit a flickering torch that sent tongues of burnished gold up earthen walls as they passed in single file through the narrow burrow in the earth. The air grew still and cold. The scent of dirt surrounded her. She shivered in her fur wrap. UZI rubbed her shoulders. She felt his warm breath on her cheek. It reassured her though Oleg's presence was disquieting.

"Look what I found," UZI whispered in her ear. "This will buy me my international bank." The passage widened and the dome of a cave disappeared overhead into darkness. Ahead, an alcove glowed with its own pale light. "There it is—Russia's most famous icon, the Virgin of Kurzan. And you are going to help me take it to New York. That is in your contract."

Caroline stepped forward, until the universe was reduced to herself and the icon—the gentle face of the Mother and the startled, wide eyes of her Child glowed before her.

"Come into me, daughter," whispered a chill wind. "Danger."

She turned to tell UZI that the icon spoke, but she couldn't move. Oleg had his arms across her chest and waist, squeezing her tight. She struggled to breathe. The doctor held up a syringe and squirted clear liquid. There was pain in her neck—a needle plunged in deep, striking bone. She attempted to cry out, "My voice, not my voice."

Oleg released her. She tried to run away but fell, her legs paralyzed and useless. The weakness climbed her body until her face was pressed into the dirt floor. She tasted decay on her tongue as she fought off the swarm of darkness that engulfed her. With her mind's voice, she shouted a prayer, "Mother, Holy Mother, Help me!"

She was barely conscious when they laid her in a coffin, certain that she was dying. UZI placed the icon on her breast, crossing her arms over it. In the last few seconds of light before the lid was shut and the drugs took total hold of her mind, the eyes of the Mother calmed her.

"Come, daughter," said the wind.

She exhaled and there was no more darkness, only the smell of the ocean in a whirlpool of light. She was running across the sands of Shi Shi beach while the wind whipped through her hair. She inhaled salt spray churned by the surf and raised her arms to the giant boulders that hovered offshore.

She turned and watched beautiful Peter pick his way across the tangle of logs where the beach met the forest. The memory warmed in her heart. He looked delicious in denim shorts with his tousled blond hair and muscular arms. He was scrunching up his face like he did when he wanted something. She laughed. *I know what he wants.* She tossed back her hair, confident in the power of her beauty. *I'm here, Peter. Come for me. I'm yours.*

She danced down the beach away from him, splashing into the waves that raced onto the sand in a hissing tumble of pebbles. Each remembered wave swept her further from the humiliation of her paralyzed body. She grew younger with her twelve-year-old arms and legs warmed by the sun.

She galloped on top of Blue Ridge where the wind gusted off Puget Sound and ruffled her grandmother's roses.

"Caroline…get away from that cliff." Baba stood on the porch, arms akimbo. "You're too close to the edge."

"Okay, Baba," she called out. "But how can I fly away if I don't go to the edge?"

"You're not flying anywhere. Now cut some roses for the table." Baba held out the flower basket. "Put on sandals or you'll step on thorns."

"No, I won't," she laughed, dancing through the garden, clipping pink and yellow blossoms. Pine branches rustled overhead. The briny tang of tidelands filled her nostrils. In the distance, the lights of Seattle blinked on in the fading light. Raising her face to the sky, she sang a Russian nursery song to the parents she had never known:

> *"May there always be Mama,*
> *May there always be Papa,*
> *May there always be sunshine,*
> *May there always be me."*

The wind lifted her hair, caressing her face and limbs. "Daughter," it whispered. Love warmed her veins.

****

She woke up in the Zil, shivering and nauseated, with her aching head on UZI's lap. She struggled to sit up. "I thought I was dead. I thought you killed me."

"Of course not, silly princess," UZI said. "You were tired after your big opera. I let you nap for a couple of hours." He stroked her cheek. His touch was repulsive. "I'd never harm you."

"You did harm me. Why did you drug me like that?" she struggled to sit up. "Where is that coffin?"

"I flew it to Seattle," he laughed. "A gift for your grandmother."

"I don't understand. What about the icon? Where are you taking me?"

"I'm taking you home, little bird. To my home."

Her head pounded. She didn't notice that they drove past the exit to Kolomeno until they entered a walled compound with armed guards. "What is this place?"

"This is Konkova, my private kingdom. You are still a princess, but here I am the king." The car rolled to a stop. He opened the door and got out, signaling to a group of men, "Get her ready."

"I'm frightened," she called to him. "Don't leave me!"

Oleg jerked her out of the car. "Oh, he won't. But you'll wish he had."

"Let me go! I'm not going with you." There were two more of them now, pulling her by the arms. It took three men to force her into a dimly lit room and onto Alexei's bed. She kicked, screamed, and bit, until one of them straddled her chest, forcing the air out of her lungs with his knee. The other two pinned down her arms and legs.

The same doctor injected drugs into her neck again. "A smaller dose this time," he said. "I nearly killed you with that last one."

Her vision warped. She was dizzy, nauseated. She felt hands on her body, pulling off her shift and pantaloons, but she was paralyzed, unable to fight. She tried to scream but could not make a sound. They tied her wrists to the bed and spread her ankles, running their hands up her thighs. She was furious but helpless.

They left her alone and she dozed, waking in horror at the flick of a reptilian tongue. UZI was licking her naked belly. "Wake up, princess," he whispered. "I am going to enjoy this."

He dropped his robe and she saw the hissing serpent. It bared its fangs and ripped into the flesh between her legs, tearing her open, raking her insides with its sharp teeth.

She closed her eyes, waiting again for the death that did not come. In her distress, she called out to the Virgin of Kurzan. "Mother, where are you? Help me."

"Come, daughter…" whispered the wind.

Caroline left her ravaged body, filling her lungs with the scent of summer as she was lifted high into a circle of kedr trees where the Virgin of Kurzan swayed. From the safety of the tall Siberian pines, she watched the reptile devour a pale woman, a naked stranger who lay splayed on the bed like a broken toy.

****

Caroline was jolted into the present by the final notes to the overture of Brunhilde's aria. She took a deep breath and loosened her throat. It was time to sing for her life and freedom. She raised her face and became Brunhilde, the lover betrayed, carrying a lighted torch to a mountain where wood was stacked for her funeral pyre.

Accursed charm! Terrible ring!
My hand grasps thee, and gives thee away.

The music swelled. Her voice reverberated off the walls of Moscow Traffic and echoed back to her. She closed her eyes, pleased with the sound. The trauma had enriched her voice. She gave her soul to the words.

Let fire, burning this hand,
cleanse, too, the ring from its curse!
Ye in the flood, wash it away,
and purer preserve your shining gold

If chaos erupted below her, she saw nothing of it. She sang until the music stopped abruptly and the klieg lights extinguished. Only then did she notice the black smoke that roiled through the nightclub and hear the screams of panicked customers fighting their way to the exits. Alarms shrilled, red lights flashed, sirens wailed. Smoke stung her eyes and throat. She held the fur over her mouth and watched the scene below in terror. *I'm going to die here.*

"Where is that fucking bitch?" UZI bellowed overhead.

The cage rose up through the ceiling and Oleg pulled her out. When she stumbled, he carried her under his arm downstairs to the backstage, where thick-necked men in black leather herded half-dressed women into tunnels. UZI stormed toward her. "Look what you've done, you ungrateful whore!" She'd never seen anyone so angry but she stood up to face him.

"I sang Brunhilde. It's the best I've ever done it. I've paid my debt to you and I want my passport back. I'm going home."

"Your debt will never be paid." He grabbed her chin, forcing her head back. "Look what Pyotor did to my club."

"Who? I don't understand."

"Your Peter Stone, my asshole cousin who has fucked up everything." He shook her until she stared into his eyes. "This was your big night. I did it all for you. Now we have producers, directors, the top executives of MosFilm running for their lives. I look like a fool."

"What are you saying?" She tried to push his hands away. "Peter is here?"

"There's no time for this." Oleg pulled UZI's arm. "We've got to get out of here."

UZI threw him off. "This one..." he bellowed, pointing at her. "This one doesn't get out." He swung his fist. It hit her chin and she flew backwards, lifted off the ground by the blow. She crash-landed onto a table with the wind knocked out of her. She felt her jaw swell. There should be pain, she reasoned, but she felt nothing. She was outside of herself, far away in the sacred kedr circle with the Virgin of Kurzan. Did he say that Peter had come for her? *What does he mean: "his cousin, Peter?"*

UZI crouched over her. He stroked her damaged cheek tenderly and whispered:

"Where do you go
When I split your flesh and crack open your universe?"

She moaned and turned her head away, closing her eyes. "Look at me." He grabbed her by the throat, squeezing until her eyes opened wide. He leaned into her face, so close that she felt his breath on her lips. "Your passport is gone. Everyone in Seattle thinks you are dead. I own you." Smoke darkened the air between them. UZI coughed. He heaved her onto his shoulder and stumbled toward the exit.

They were both choking, blinded by the fumes when Oleg appeared. "Hurry!" He guided them down a back stair, through a tunnel to an idling black van. UZI tossed Caroline into the back. She landed on top of a group of frightened young women. "Drug her up, Stepan," he shouted. Stepan plunged a needle into her thigh, then he locked the door and joined UZI and Oleg in front.

"Get us out of here," UZI roared. The van rolled forward a few feet and stopped. "I said move it!"

"I can't. It's a goddamn circus," whined Stepan. "Look at those news crews with all of their crap. There are people everywhere. Fire trucks can't even get in."

"Fuck my mother," said Oleg. "The club's going up like a torch!"

"It is a torch, *durak*. Which one of you jerk-offs lit the fire under the Chechens' car?"

"How were we supposed to know they were parked on top of a gas leak?" said Stepan. "That munitions factory wasn't around when we were kids."

"We can't sell any of these in Russia now." UZI shined his flashlight on the cowering women in back. "Where are the rest of the girls?"

"All fifty of the high-class girls are accounted for. We have eleven here, not counting your singer. The rest are in other vans." Oleg consulted his clipboard. "As to the kids working the floor, we haven't counted them yet. Everyone is on their way to Konkova. We'll do a head-count when we load them on buses."

"We'll have to ship them to the Middle East, maybe Bahrain."

"Not a problem. We can drive them through Turkey. Auctions are coming up in a few days. The Arabs are paying top dollar for real blondes. I saw a dozen on the runway tonight."

UZI turned to the trembling women, "No rich husbands for you, you greedy little twats. You will be on the Slave Road to Istanbul tonight and whores in Saudi Arabia by suppertime tomorrow." He pounded the dash. "Get a move on, you Cossack cluster-fuck."

"What do you expect me to do? Fly?" Stepan shrugged. "Everybody's watching the fire. Look at them. The idiots are standing all over the street."

UZI shined the light on Oleg's clipboard. "Most of those village girls are under fifteen. We can sell them as virgins in Cairo. Let the Bedouins smuggle them the rest of the way into Israel."

"You got it." Oleg made notes.

"Better call the good Commander Piggie while you're at it. He can earn his keep by keeping the feds off our backs."

"Good idea. Golokov can stall the families, too. They won't be happy when their daughters don't show up with millionaires." Oleg added to his list. "We'll need some phony passports if we're sending them abroad tonight."

"Call the Georgians," said Stepan. "We can pick up new documents at the Turkish border. Just send the drivers with extra cash."

"What about your singer back there? You just made a mess out of her face. We can't sell her like that."

"Forget her. She stays with me."

UZI's voice faded from Caroline's awareness as the drugs took effect. She shivered. It was cold—cold…so cold. Annoying hands patted her face, rubbed her arms. "Wake up, blondie…stay with me." It was a woman's voice. Worried young faces pressed in close around her. "We need to get some more clothes on you."

"Go away," Caroline moaned, swatting the hands. *Where am I? Who are these women?*

"Let's cover her or she'll freeze to death." Someone wrapped a fur around her and pulled socks onto her feet.

"Thank you," she tried to say, but could only moan.

"Shit!" UZI pounded the dash. An animated crowd swarmed around the van—gawkers fresh from the Metro. "Drive on the sidewalks if you have to."

"They're jammed up with people, too. Damn cops are everywhere. At least we're starting to move," grumbled Stepan.

"Give it some gas."

Stepan did. They accelerated, bounced through a pothole and stopped again.

In the back, Caroline opened her eyes to see a pretty face bending over her. "Where's my lucky suit?" she asked. "I need to find my lucky green suit."

The woman grasped her hand and smiled. "I'm Detective Pashkina. I'm an undercover police officer. Tell me your name. I will help you, but I need your name. Are you a prisoner?"

"No, never!" slurred Caroline. "I am a free woman. I am Antonida Susanina, the proud virgin bride.... My father is the peasant hero of Russia, Ivan Susanin..." She sang Antonida's wedding lament. Her voice echoed in the van as it sped through Moscow.

A flashlight shined in her face. "Shut up, silly fool," UZI growled. "We're almost at Konkova. Let's see how much of a virgin you are after the rest of the Kurzaniks take a ride on you. Oleg can have you for breakfast."

"Do you mean that?" Oleg sounded surprised.

"Of course not," UZI snapped. "Anyone who touches the songbird is dead meat." He paused. "Here's what you can do. Go find that whore Tanya Pavlova for me. Her time is up."

Chapter Fifteen

ZEMYNA

New York City, October 6, 1997

At ten o'clock in the morning Arthur Wellington was back for the icon. "I know you're in there, Petrosyan." He pounded his fist on the old man's door. "Open up! The auction starts in an hour."

"Go away. I have unfinished business."

"At least let me see her, for Christ sake." Arthur banged harder. "The Saudis are starting the bid at twenty-two million. It'll only go up from there."

The reinforced steel door cracked open an inch. Petrosyan eyed him suspiciously. "Why so high? Are the test results back?"

"I have them right here." Arthur waved an envelope. "It's confirmed. The icon is pre-Christian. The red pigment in the wood sample is denatured hemoglobin with fragments of human DNA. It's very old blood with a Baltic haplotype. I'd say you've got their goddess Zemyna. She's the real deal."

"Give me the reports."

"Not until you open this door and I see the icon."

"Are you alone?"

"Certainly."

Petrosyan stepped back and Arthur pushed his way in. "You look awful, Pet. Been sick?"

"Family troubles," snapped the old man, scanning the computer printouts.

"Now, where is our Queen of Heaven, Mother of God, Virgin of Kurzan and whatever else they've called her in the name of religion?"

"On the mantel," said Petrosyan, nodding to the library doors. "Look but don't touch."

"My Lord in heaven," Arthur exclaimed. "It's really her. How did you find her?" He raised his hand to touch the wood. A blue spark snapped his finger. "Ouch!"

"I warned you. She's in a foul temper."

"Is this the provenance—the famous *Book of Miracles*?" Arthur sucked on his sore finger and opened a maroon leather portfolio with his other hand. "Simply fantastic!" Adjusting his glasses, he read from a yellowed parchment. "According to Saint Ignatius, the Virgin of Kurzan healed Ivan the Terrible's angina and Peter the Great's gout." He scanned the parchments. "It says that it was carried off to Samarkand by the Mongol Horde to heal Tamerlane's crippled foot. Twenty years later, the icon mysteriously returned to Kurzan Monastery. They found it hanging from a kedr tree. Floods, fires, invasions—the Virgin of Kurzan survived and returned home. She's a tough old girl."

"Fine, fine. Now go."

"Do you think there's anything to these miracles? How did she get back to Kurzan from Samarkand—that's Uzbekistan, isn't it? That's all the way from Central Asia."

"Utter nonsense," muttered Petrosyan. "Folk tales. My old granny used to tell these stories to scare my brother and me when we were children." He shooed Arthur out the door. "Come back tomorrow."

"But the auction… What do I tell the Saudis?"

"There'll be twice as many Arabs bidding once the test results leak out. Now scoot along and make sure that happens."

Once Arthur was gone and the door closed behind him, Petrosyan sank into his chair. He was about to pour himself a vodka when the phone rang. It was Daniel Karlov, his trustee. "Someone just called me on Peter's dedicated number," he said. "For the first time, I might add."

The old man sat up. "Was it Pyotor?"

"I believe so. I confirmed that the call came from Moscow. It was very short, only a few seconds before the phone company cut in to say that his phone card had expired. What shall I do if he calls again?"

"Make sure it's Pyotor, then give him whatever he wants. No limits."

"Yes, sir."

"And keep me informed." Petrosyan hung up breathless, his heart wildly skipping beats. He'd waited years for this call. Was the boy finally reaching out to him? *Anything you want, Pyotor—anything at all.*

The next call was from the Chechens and it wasn't good news. They had followed Peter using a GPS tracker attached to his coat. He was having a drink at the Hotel Ukrainia with someone they couldn't identify.

"Show me," said Petrosyan, booting up his computer.

Ruslan fiddled with his video eyeglasses while Ahmed adjusted the transmitter. After some blurry images, Petrosyan saw a busy bar reflected in a mirror. Seated in front of a round window, Pyotor was drinking shots with another man.

"Turn your head a bit," said Petrosyan. "I want to see that man's face." Blurry images followed as Ruslan turned toward the table. Petrosyan gasped. "My God. That can't be!"

"What's wrong?" asked Ruslan. "Who is it?"

"That's Alexei Kaminsky—my damn nephew. Don't let them out of your sight. He's the one who wants Pyotor dead."

"He's seen us," said Ruslan. "They're moving."

Petrosyan watched the jumbled video until Ruslan reached the exit and pounded on the locked door. "They've gone."

"Follow them." The video switched off. Petrosyan could do nothing but wait for more news. He felt helpless, angry and old. He glared at the icon. "This is *your* fault," he growled.

A few hours later, Daniel Karlov called a second time. "I don't want to be an alarmist, but Alexei Kaminsky's nightclub is on fire. I'm watching it on Russian TV—quite spectacular. I hope this hasn't got anything to do with Peter. You might want to look for yourself."

Petrosyan pushed buttons on his console that brought up ORT News in Moscow: "A fire in the notorious nightclub Moscow Traffic has resulted in a massive explosion in the Kolomeno district this evening." The screen behind the anchor showed the sky over Kurzan bright with flames. "We take you live to our reporter on the scene. Dima? Can you hear me?"

"Yes, Vladimir," the reporter shouted over wailing sirens: "Eyewitnesses tell us that there were at least five hundred people inside. The blaze started in the parking lot and rapidly engulfed the building. Most have escaped through the front door, but an unknown number may still be trapped in old tunnels under the ruins of the Kurzan Monastery which is nearby. Rescuers are searching for them now."

The news anchor cut in. "Dima, callers are asking why the fire is still out of control. It's a concrete building and there are three fire brigades on the scene. Can you shed some light on this?"

"Yes, I can. Last winter I reported on a similar incident on Apple Street. Someone dropped a lit match on the sidewalk and a kiosk exploded. It burned for twenty-four hours. Our investigation uncovered that the explosion was caused by flammable gas leaking from an underground munitions factory operated by Spetsnaz since the 1980s. Sources in the Ministry of Defense confirmed that when the ground freezes, the gas can migrate underground as far as two kilometers...."

Petrosyan muted the sound. "Spetsnaz...The Party's Gold. What have I done?"

Chapter Sixteen

THE CONVENT

Kurzan Convent, October 7-8, 1997

Peter awakened face-down, drowning in pain. Even the weight of a sheet across his naked back was intolerable. He turned his head to the sound of rustling paper and his eyes focused on Tanya. She sat next to the bed reading a newspaper and smoking. She wore a long, black nun's habit dusted with ash.

"Tanya?" he croaked through thick, dry lips. His head throbbed with the effort.

"How disappointing," she sniffed. "The arsonist lives."

"Where am I? Why are you dressed like that?"

"This is Kurzan Convent. The disguise was Grandpa's idea because UZI will kill me for helping you—if he finds me."

"What happened? I can't remember."

"Go back to sleep. I'm supposed to watch you until the doctor comes." She turned the page and returned to reading. "That doesn't mean I have to talk to you."

"They beat me up." He closed his eyes, forcing images to form. "I saw Caroline in a cage. She was singing. There was an explosion—a fire? Is she all right?"

"Look for yourself. Here's the early edition of *Eleven News*." Tanya held the front page up to his face. The headline read: *Twelve Men Killed in Nightclub Fire.* "See that? All men. No Caroline."

"Thank God." He grunted and collapsed. "Where is she now."

"UZI must have her with the other women. I don't know where. Shall I read you the article?"

"No. As long as Caroline is okay, the rest doesn't matter."

"It should matter." She snapped open the paper. "Twelve poor souls have been burnt to bacon because of you. Look at the pictures—all those scorched bodies. Moscow Traffic is a smoking pile of rubble. I told you that someone would die."

"I didn't start the fire."

"You started the brawl." She waved it at him. "What were you thinking? Did your stupid antics save Caroline? And what about all those poor girls who didn't get their husbands last night? Don't they matter? They will be sold to Arabs as sex slaves. God only knows what will happen to the little village girls. Are you listening to me? Peoples' lives have been ruined because of you."

Peter tuned her out as he struggled to assemble the fragments in his mind— Caroline's made-up face, the crowd's terrifying chant: "Burn, burn," the cage swinging over his head as he shouted helplessly from the stage, unable to reach her—then her voice rising in crescendo, laden with such pain that it tore at his soul: "My bosom, how it burns…" There were punches, kicks, a gunshot but she kept singing. Ahmed carrying him outside, Pavel shouting, Gogol barking while flames shot skyward—real flames as the cars exploded and Moscow Traffic caught fire. And through it all, the awful sound of Brunhilde's immolation aria—Caroline singing as though nothing was happening.

He tried to sit up but his arms spasmed. "I need to get to the American Embassy," he groaned, collapsing on the bed.

"Don't be daft." Tanya snorted. "It's four in the morning. The embassies are closed."

"Call their emergency number. They must have one. Tell them Caroline's alive and she needs help."

"We don't have a telephone, remember?"

"I hate this damn country," Peter rasped.

"So do I," said Tanya, wiping away tears. "I almost got away. One more week and I'd have my turn at the Bride Market, my chance to marry a rich guy and get out of Russia." She lit a fresh cigarette. "You've ruined everything. I might as well become a nun for real."

"Better than prostitution." He regretted his words.

"Fuck you." She exhaled a plume of smoke.

"Why do you do it?"

"Selling my body pays," said Tanya. "I thought that I could support my family as a journalist but that was naïve. The pay stinks, but I'm a strong woman. I decided that I could tolerate prostitution for a while if there was a rainbow with a treasure like the Bride Market at the end of it. You saw the foreigners flocking to Moscow Traffic to buy beautiful Russian brides. Why shouldn't I be a bride, too? Then I could take my family to Paris or Berlin or New York where the shops have food." She flicked ash onto the floor. "Anything is better than wasting my life starving in Moscow. But now there is nothing left but rubble. My life is over."

"That's not true. I'll help you ..." Peter's back spasmed. He cried out in pain.

"You?" She scoffed. "I said that you're a complication, but you are even worse. You are another vulture, a curse—the wrecker of everything." Tanya scowled at him, then softened. "You look terrible," she said, cautiously lifting his sheet. "My God! You're black and blue. Mother called the Kremlin Hospital hours ago. Where is that Dr. Plotkin? He should be here by now." Tanya rushed out.

Peter didn't want a doctor but Tanya returned with one. The doctor shined a light in his eyes. "So, this is the man who burned down Moscow Traffic. Does this hurt?" Every place he prodded hurt like hell. "A beating like this would have killed a weaker man but you are obviously a sportsman," said the doctor. "You've got renal contusions and some bruised ribs at a minimum. You should be in the hospital."

Peter was aware of other people in the room. An elderly nun with blue eyes peered over Plotkin's shoulder. "Pyotor is family," she said. "We'll take good care of him right here in the convent."

Peter wanted to shout that he didn't have any family and he wasn't going to find Caroline lying face-down in bed, but the doctor gave him an injection. His eyelids drooped before he could command his mouth to speak.

He woke to the sting of an IV in his arm. He tried to pull it out but couldn't do it one-handed. Empty IV bottles were lined up on the bedside table. Someone had threaded a catheter into his bladder. Ruslan and Ahmed were in the room. One sat quietly in an old armchair and the other perched like a bird of prey on the windowsill.

Ruslan nodded to Peter. "Good morning, *tovarish*."

"Good morning, comrades," Peter mumbled as he drifted off.

When he woke again, Katya was seated on the bed. She lifted a wooden spoon of steaming borscht to his lips. He turned his head away despite his growling stomach. He wanted answers more than food. Katya had other ideas. She put down the soup, yanked the duvet onto the floor, and looked him over. "You're just as stubborn as old Pavel." She adjusted the IV and rolled him onto his side to check the catheter. "Dr. Plotkin will take that out and change those dressings *after* you eat some soup." Katya covered him again and gently tucked in the duvet. This time when she offered him the spoon, he accepted. The warm soup made him feel better.

"Will he be okay?" Ahmed asked.

"Don't worry. Pyotor's a Pavlov. He's made of tough stuff," said Pavel from the doorway. *I'm a Pavlov? What did he say?* He tried to ask but couldn't keep his eyes open.

Peter woke again when Gogol licked his face. The dog had sardine breath that could not be ignored. Pavel sat in the armchair holding a cardboard box. He eyed Peter eagerly. "You're awake," he said. "I brought you Caroline's things from the flat. We have her suitcase, too. We didn't give them to you sooner because we didn't know whether you would turn out to be a good man like your father, our Denis, or one of those vile Kaminskys. You could have gone either way. Denis was never quite able make up his mind and look what happened to him." Pavel set the box on the bed.

What did happen to him? Peter wanted to scream but could barely whisper: "How do you know my father?" No one heard him. He pushed up the duvet with his feet to get their attention. The box flipped onto the floor with a tinkle of scattering trinkets.

"I'm so sorry," said Katya, gathering the knickknacks. "It's too soon for this. We are just confusing you. Rest now." She shooed Pavel and Gogol out of the room and shut the door. Peter heard raised voices in the hall.

"We've got to do something," Pavel insisted. "He doesn't know who he is."

"How is that possible?" said Katya. "Can anyone be this ignorant? It must be an act."

"I'm not so sure. Denis might have decided not to tell him about us— and Denis died before he could change his mind."

"But Petrosyan is still alive. Doesn't Pyotor know him?"

"Apparently not," said Pavel. "And what he doesn't know will get him killed…maybe get all of us killed. We've got to tell him the truth."

"Be careful how you go about it. The truth can be a difficult pill to swallow. What if he is unstable like his father? You don't want to push him over the edge." Katya's voice was shrill. "Denis hung himself in his own orchard. Do you want that for his son?"

My father committed suicide? Peter tried to sit up but couldn't.

"And what if he's no better than that horrible UZI?" Katya fretted. "They are cousins. They even look kind of alike."

"Have some faith, woman. Maybe he will be the one that is finally strong enough to stop the madness in this family. But first, Pyotor needs to know who he is, and he needs to know now."

"What makes you think he'll believe us? He seems rather thick."

"He's in denial, that's all. And he's a psychologist." There was a pause until Pavel said, "I have an idea. Where's my mother's old trunk?"

"I saw it in Maria Pavlova's room. At the foot of her bed."

"Help me carry it."

The next time Katya came into his room, she fed Peter sorrel soup thickened with sour cream, which he devoured, his instinct to live overcoming his lassitude.

He woke again when Dr. Plotkin came to remove the IV and catheter.

"What time is it?" asked Peter.

"Nearly three in the morning."

"How long have I been here?"

"Overnight and then some. You've slept most of the last twenty-four hours. I treated you for shock and contusions and gave you IV fluids. You've responded well." The doctor took his pulse and blood pressure. "I don't know why I bother, though." Plotkin stuffed the cuff and stethoscope into his bag. "The Kurzaniks have a big red bullseye painted on your forehead. This may be a waste of good IV solution. It's hard to come by these days." The doctor laughed. "Don't look so serious. That's a joke. I see you are not familiar with Russian humor."

Katya entered with fried eggs and black bread. She set the tray on the bed and let Peter feed himself. "My arms are working," he exclaimed. "No permanent damage?"

"I gave you steroid injections for the bruised nerves," said Plotkin. "It reduced the inflammation, but you mustn't overuse your shoulders. The damage could become permanent. "I'll be back in a few hours." He snapped his bag shut and left.

Peter slept again. In his dream, Caroline leaned close, and whispered, "It's time to get up, sleepyhead. Doctor's orders." He tried to rise, but was paralyzed, helpless. He couldn't breathe. A spotlight shone in his eyes.

"Stop it," he groaned. "Go away." He finally woke up all the way and discovered that it wasn't a spotlight, but a bedside lamp. He was alone in the room and needed to pee.

He sat up slowly, dizzy, hoping that he wouldn't vomit. He looked around and saw his pants and boots by the door but not the rest of his clothes. His stomach did a turn. *My documents! Where are they?* He stood up too fast. His vision blacked. He braced himself against the wall to keep from falling. His passport, visa, and wallet were on top of his pants along with Caroline's passport. He checked his pockets and found the diamond heart earrings. He staggered to the commode, urinated with some difficulty, and felt better.

He pulled on his trousers and looked for a way to turn off the offending light but there was no switch. He reached down to unplug it and noticed that the bedside table, which had been covered with IV bottles, was now stacked with photograph albums. More of them were stacked on top of a well-worn leather trunk that he hadn't seen before. Some of the albums looked old, others were obviously recent.

He wrapped himself in the duvet and picked up one of the older albums, dated 1929–1934. It was filled with photographs of a blond baby boy who grew into a chubby toddler and then a schoolboy.

The next several albums held more pictures of the same child. There were photographs of the boy next to a nun and group photographs of nuns and children of all ages. In the album dated 1945–1950, a teenage boy was in New York City. Peter looked at the handsome blond man who stood with the boy in front of a shop called "Kaminsky's Gallery of Fine Russian Art."

Peter perused the subsequent albums. They contained photographs of the young man taking in the sights of New York and of family gatherings in elegant homes and restaurants. There was a photo of him standing in front of a sign for Columbia University and another with his arm around a girl. The young man grew to middle age, moving through a series of beautiful women and flashy cars. There were parties in Las Vegas with showgirls, one of whom looked familiar—a lot like his mother––though he had never seen photographs of either of his parents when they were young, so he couldn't be sure.

Next, he discovered photographs of a bride and groom feeding each other cake. After that, the progression of black and white pictures evolved to color, with an eight-by-ten portrait of a family assembled in front of a stone fireplace. They clustered, smiling, around the blond man and his much younger wife. She held a baby in a blue jumper. The photograph was loose, so he turned it over. On the back he read, "Pyotor Denisovich Kaminsky – First Christmas, New York 1965—the year that he was born." *Denisovich? Denis's son? Me?*

Peter opened the next album filled with baby pictures, many of them professionally done. There were no more photographs of the parents, only of a serious-looking tow-headed boy who picked flowers, played with kittens, or climbed an apple tree. Memories of Stone Farm flashed through his mind as he turned the pages. *It can't be.* The photographs were of the apple orchard and the yellow ranch house where he lived with his parents. *I'm hallucinating.*

He lowered his head to his knees. He should lie down—leave the albums alone until he felt better. But the next album was labeled "Seattle." In it were pictures of the boy with a woman who looked like Ruby Mae. They sat in the front seat of a yellow Mercury convertible as big as a boat. Peter remembered the car. *Who took the picture?*

With mounting confusion Peter opened the final album in the stack, labeled "Pyotor and Caroline." Blood pounded in his temples. He lifted the cover and started to sweat. He had never seen any of these photographs, but they were all of him with Caroline. There were even photographs taken through the windows of the houseboat. The final pages showed them kissing on the Winslow Ferry.

He staggered to the door—it was locked. He pounded on it, shouting, "What the hell's going on? Open this door! We need to talk … Now!"

Chapter Seventeen

Maria Pavlova

Kurzan Convent, October 8, 1997

The little room was crowded. Pavel sat on the bed next to Peter. An elderly nun sat upright in an armchair with Katya perched on the arm next to her. Tanya, unusually subdued, sat on the floor with her head in the nun's lap. Ruslan and Ahmed stood guard at the window. Gogol panted at their feet.

"This is my sister Maria Pavlova, Mother Superior of Kurzan Convent," said Pavel. "She's the one that I wanted you to meet. She is Denis's mother and your grandmother."

"No family, you said. What a laugh." Tanya smirked. "You are related to half of Kolomeno and everyone knows it but you."

Peter met the gaze of the elderly nun who shushed Tanya. She was tall and slender with elegant fingers. "Is this true?" he asked. "You are Denis's mother? My grandmother?"

"Yes, Pyotor," said Maria Pavlova dabbing her eyes. "Forgive me my weak emotions. I never dreamed that you would come to me. I assure you that these are tears of joy."

"This is what I meant when I said that your story begins at Kurzan," said Pavel. "I am a soldier, a very literal man. I wanted you to meet your grandmother."

"And is this what you meant when you said that I was a Pavlov?" Peter struggled to construct a family tree in his mind. He needed a computer, or at least a pen and a notebook. Nothing would seem real until he could put it on paper.

"Your father, Denis, was my son," said the old woman. "And his father, your grandfather, is Petrosyan Kaminsky."

"Kaminsky? But my name is Stone," said Peter.

"Kaminsky is Stone in Russian. Your father changed it when he left New York and moved to the other side of the country. We think he was trying to hide from his father," said Pavel.

"Who exactly is Petrosyan Kaminsky?"

"The spawn of Satan." Tanya scowled and spat. "That man is the devil."

"That's not helpful, Tanuchka," said Katya.

"Your husband?" Peter asked Maria Pavlova. His fingers grasped the bed frame under the mattress to keep him upright as he fought back against nausea and disbelief.

"No," she said. "Sadly, he was not. We would have been married in normal times but those were not normal times. We had just been through a revolution and a civil war. People who once lived together in peaceful communities were turned against one another. My father forbade my marriage to Petrosyan because he was a Jew. As a result my son, your father, was born out of wedlock in the labor camp at Sverdlovsk. Having you here with us now is a miracle that I have long prayed for, but never thought I'd live to see."

"Now that we have had our family visit, you must go back to America," said Pavel, slapping his knees. "Immediately—before UZI kills you, or us."

"You said that he's my cousin. Is that true?" Peter recalled the pale blue eyes and blond hair so much like his own.

"Your second cousin—yes, I am afraid so," said Pavel. "UZI's grandfather was Petrosyan's older brother, Ephraim."

"I didn't know that I had any cousins."

Tanya snorted. "Don't be stupid. Even I am your cousin."

"Why didn't you just tell me when we met?"

"I tried. You didn't listen."

"You spoke in riddles." Peter rubbed his aching forehead. "This is a nightmare."

Tanya rolled her eyes. "Welcome to Russia."

"Why does UZI want to kill me?" he asked.

"Simple. You are Petrosyan's heir and Petrosyan Kaminsky is a very rich man," said Pavel. "If UZI kills you, he becomes the heir. There are no others living."

"Heir to what exactly?"

"Everything that remains of the Party's Gold—and probably much more, by now," said Maria Pavlova.

"The Party's Gold?" asked Peter. "What is that?"

"The massive wealth that Petrosyan and Ephraim looted from the palaces and churches of Russia and sold in America. It was known by the communists as the Party's Gold," said Pavel. "It bankrolled Joseph Stalin's rise to power and paid for his secret police—Spetsnaz, or Special Tasks."

"The Kaminskys were well rewarded for their evil work," said Katya. "Their share became known in America as the Petrosyan Fund. Your father, Denis, was the heir to the fund and with his death, you became the heir. How can you not know this?"

"I've heard of it but never touched it. Denis called it criminal money," said Peter, remembering his father's final admonition.

"It is blood money. As bloody as it gets," said Katya. "Petrosyan and Ephraim Kaminsky left a trail of gore and tears across Russia. That devil UZI follows in their footsteps."

"Don't think about it now, Pyotor," said Pavel, patting Peter's knee. "Rest, eat. Regain your strength so that you can go home to America."

"How did my father get to America?"

"War was coming. Schoolboys were being conscripted to defend the western front against the Germans. One day when Denis was twelve years old, he left for school and never came back." Pavel frowned, deepening the lines on his weathered cheeks. "We thought we'd lost him to the Red Army. Later, we learned that Petrosyan had Spetsnaz pick him up and put him aboard a ship to New York. There was nothing we could do to get him back. A few weeks later, the border closed. The Germans invaded. We were at war."

The nun patted her brother's arm. "It was for the best," she said. "He would have been given a broomstick instead of a gun and shipped to the front to fight German tanks with the rest of the schoolboys. They were already bombing Kursk and Novgorod. The boy brigades were slaughtered.

"During the war, I was transferred to Omsk in Siberia, to work in a school for orphans. Most of them died of tuberculosis. I thanked God every day that Denis was safe in New York and not with me in Omsk."

"Sadly, we never saw him again," said Pavel. "Once the border closed, we couldn't send letters overseas. The Post Office stopped working for eight years."

"I was sure that Denis must be terribly worried about what we were going through," said the nun. "He was a sensitive boy. I imagined him crying when he listened to the radio about the fierce fighting in Russia, the stories of death and destruction here."

"But you were wrong, weren't you?" said Pavel. "Everything we'd taught him about being generous and kind went right out of his head when he got to Petrosyan's fancy penthouse. He started going to private schools and living life as a big party. As soon as he could drive, Petrosyan bought him a convertible. When he got drunk and smashed that one, Petrosyan bought him another."

"How did you get these photographs? And all this information?" Peter picked up one of the albums and opened it to see his father as a young man living the high life in Las Vegas. He recognized a publicity photograph of Ruby Mae, his mother. She was beautiful—all legs and bosoms in a slinky lowcut gown, a crown of white peacock feathers on her head. She did not look like the kind of woman who would be content to live in Wenatchee, Washington, or raise a son.

"Petrosyan's man, Daniel Karlov, brought us pictures after the war," said Pavel. "By that time, Ephraim Kaminsky and his entire family had been shot and Petrosyan was a wanted man. He could never enter the USSR again. Mr. Karlov represented his business interests in Moscow and made time to see us."

"Why didn't you immigrate to America?"

"Maria Pavlova had been in prison camps for several years. After that, she was forbidden to leave the USSR. Then the Iron Curtain fell and no one could leave. Somehow Mr. Karlov still visited Moscow two or three times a year. He brought the photographs and we were able to follow Denis's life as an American boy. We gave Mr. Karlov our gifts and letters to take back. They must have seemed meager compared to what his father could buy. We even sent gifts for you when you were small."

"We hoped for letters from Denis, but none came. Who could blame him? He had a new and wonderful life," said Maria Pavlova. "I was grateful to Petrosyan for taking him and I forgave Denis for forgetting me."

The windows lightened with the dawn. Peter asked: "I heard Katya say that my father committed suicide. Is that true?"

"Yes," said Pavel. "He sent his mother a letter before he died. The only one she received from him. It came in the mail."

"It's here," Maria searched under her apron. "I saved it."

Before she could pull it out, Ruslan, who had been slouched on the windowsill hissed, "Kill the light—somebody's coming."

Chapter Eighteen

UZI

Kurzan Convent, October 8, 1997

Tanya dove for the plug. The room darkened. The Chechens crouched on either side of the window. "Cops," said Ruslan. "They're in Kolomeno Park."

Tanya peered over his shoulder. "Federal cops? City cops? Rental cops?"

"They look like phony cops, Commander Golokov's boys."

"We've got to get Pyotor out of here," said Ahmed.

"Me too," said Tanya. "But how?"

"The tunnels," said Pavel. "You can hide in the tunnels."

"Don't be stupid," Tanya snapped. "Piggie grew up here, remember? His mother was the warden. He knows the tunnels better than you do."

"Piggie?" asked Peter.

"That's what UZI calls Commander Golokov," said Tanya. "The Kurzaniks all do."

"His mother was head warden of Kurzan Prison." Pavel spat. "Dreadful cow. The commander grew up here with the prison boys. He's known the Kurzaniks all his life."

"That explains a great deal," said Peter.

"I know a safe place," said Maria Pavlova with a start. "The kagans inside the domes of the church. No one will look there."

"Kagans?" Peter didn't recognize the word.

"That'll work," said Pavel.

"Yuri, bring me Papa's winter coat and sweater, the warm ones from the cedar chest." Maria Pavlova was suddenly all bustle and business. Peter glimpsed the steel in her spine. "Get Pyotor dressed—quickly."

Katya helped Peter into the sweater, jacket and cap that had once been his great-grandfather's. His shoulders were still weak. Pain shot into his hands when he leaned down to tie his boots.

When he was dressed for winter, Maria Pavlova took his face in her hands. "God protect you, my precious grandson." She made the sign of the cross and kissed his forehead. "The sisters and I will pray for your safe return to America." She blessed Tanya, hugging her tightly. "Now go with Pavel and hide until I can deal with these policemen."

"Quickly!" The old man hurried them down a dark flight of stairs followed by Ahmed armed with a pistol and a walkie-talkie. Peter kept pace. His head throbbed, and his bruised kidneys ached with each step. Pavel unlocked a heavy wooden door and pushed it open to the courtyard.

A foot of snow had fallen overnight. The frozen air smelled of tar. The ruined hulk of the Church of the Kurzan Goddess loomed overhead casting jagged shadows. Three nights ago, the moon had been merciful to the old church. Now, a harsh dawn stripped away its mystery. There were no signs of life—no old babushkas lighting candles and selling prayers. The five onion domes, one large in the center surrounded by four smaller ones, sagged precariously. The decorative stars that had reflected the moonlight were dull, flat black.

Pavel ushered them into the church where nothing remained but pillars of charred, exposed brick. Some arched high overhead to an open ceiling, but most had crumbled. The roof was nearly gone. A long wooden ladder was propped against scaffolding that supported the five domes. Snowfall dusted the floor, except for a square under the domes.

"What happened to this place?" Peter asked.

"Petrosyan Kaminsky happened." Pavel spat. "He and his brother Ephraim looted and dynamited this and every other monastery in the Golden Ring. This church has been a ruin ever since."

"And the icons? The treasure? Was that what you are calling the Party's Gold?"

"You're inheritance, yes." Pavel shook the ladder. "It's a miracle these domes never fell."

"Where are we hiding?" Peter saw nothing promising in the piles of rubble and open spaces.

"In the center dome," said Pavel, pointing up. "Climb the ladder and crawl inside the kagan. That's a big upside-down clay pot with enough room for both of you."

"You are full of it, Grandpa." Tanya snapped. She wrapped her nun's cape around her like batwings. "That's crazy."

"No, Tanuchka. There are giant cauldrons—kagans—in each dome. That is how these old churches were constructed. It gives the domes their round onion shape and excellent acoustics. The central one is the biggest. It has a new crack in the terracotta that's wide enough to slip through.

Climb up there and we'll hide the ladder. No one will find you. You will be safe. I promise."

Tanya didn't budge. "I'm afraid of heights."

Ahmed's radio crackled to life. He held it to his ear. "They're inside the convent. Get up there, quickly!"

Tanya started up the ladder. "I'm more afraid of UZI," she said. Peter followed, steadying her when she tripped on her cape and nearly knocked him off. At the top, he helped her squeeze through a wide crack in the thick terracotta. Once she was settled inside, he slid into a pot large enough to boil a cow, or two people.

Wooden slats supported their feet. Through gaps between the boards, Peter watched Pavel and Ahmed pull away the ladder leaving them stranded thirty feet in the air. Tanya was right. This was crazy. He should have taken her and made a run for the American Embassy. His family may have been Russian, but he and Caroline were American citizens.

Ahmed looked up. "Don't worry," he said. "We'll be outside watching the doors. No one can get past us."

"And whatever happens, stay quiet," Pavel warned. "Those old pots make big echoes." The church door scraped the ground as he pulled it shut behind him. Peter had no choice but to depend on these Russians no matter how flawed their judgment seemed.

He sagged back against the kagan, resigned to wait. The embassy wouldn't open for hours yet. He would be there as soon as it was. He closed his eyes and listened to the sea. The round clay kettle had the effect of a giant seashell. All he needed was sunshine, seagulls circling overhead, and Caroline running into the ocean, splashing through waves that reflected heaven.

He would take her back to Shi Shi Beach next summer and make love to her on the warm sand, kissing and adoring every inch of her. Later when they snuggled under the sleeping bag, he would lay the riches of the Party's Gold before her—a platter of golden apples and precious gems that glowed in the moonlight. She could choose from among his treasures or take them all. He didn't care.

He forced himself to breathe through the tightness in his chest and his sense of loss, realizing that even if he got out of this alive, nothing would ever be the same. He pressed his face into his sleeve, hating the smell of moth balls, but grateful for his great-grandfather's warm clothes. He would prefer it if they smelled like the old man's sweat—the essence of another being that belonged to him, another part of his story that he could sense but not yet see.

Time passed. He shivered in the still air, watching the vapor from his breath. Tanya was curled by his side, her arms wrapped around her knees. Like all these new-found relations, she seemed to know more about him than he did. In a way, it was a relief to discover that he wasn't an empty slate and that Caroline was right—he'd been a fool to think so. A thin membrane of deception was all that had ever separated him from this densely populated universe of people and events that were rightfully his. He hoped that he'd survive long enough to embrace the teeming life on the other side.

Tanya shivered. There was just enough light to see her frightened eyes. He put his arm around her shoulders and started to ask: "Tell me, Tanya…" he whispered, then regretted it. "Tell me…tell me…Tanya…Tanya…Tanya…" echoed around the inside of the kagans, a medieval sound system getting louder and louder. Soon they were booming, "Tell me, Tanya…tell me, Tanya…" Tanya faced him. She squeezed his chin, glared into his eyes, and put a finger to her lips, signaling him to shut up.

"Tell me, Tanya…Tell me, Tanya," came an eerie but familiar voice from below.

> "Tell me, tell me, Tanya,
> There's a chicken in the banya,
> There's a rooster in the pot;
> Shall I boil him, boil him, boil him
> 'Til he's hot, hot, hot?"

UZI! Peter tensed his muscles, ready to fight—pain forgotten. Tanya gasped and that sound echoed through the domes as well. Looking down, Peter saw a thatch of blond hair. UZI was pacing the floor. *Where did he come from?* It was Peter's turn to shake his head with a finger to his lips. But Tanya no longer met his gaze. Her eyes were fixed in the blank stare of a doomed rabbit in the headlights of a car. Veins pulsed in her neck. A sheen of sweat oiled her cheeks. He pulled her against him.

"How do you like my old neighborhood, Pyotor? Kurzan Prison is my alma mater," said UZI. "And this used to be my playground. You know, where I learned to write poems and kill people." He picked up a stone and tossed it in the air. "The boys and I liked to throw things at those old domes. They make terrible noises." UZI threw the stone. It hit the kagan, echoed, and amplified into a hundred clanging bells. Peter's ears kept ringing after the echo faded. His mind sought an escape. There was none.

"So, you found your way into one of those old pots. Which one, I wonder? There are five. I will only get one shot before your Chechens come rushing to save you. They are standing right outside, guarding the doors. They didn't know that there are many other ways in, and I know Kurzan's secrets better than anyone. I'll always have an escape. But for you, sadly, there's no escape. Now, let's be quiet and have a think about how to do this. One bullet, two people."

The silence was ominous. Surely, UZI could hear Peter's jagged breath and racing heart. The only way out was to jump thirty feet to the ground. He'd break his legs and UZI would shoot him. It might work if he landed on top of UZI. If he could move the footboards and jump through the hole before UZI aimed and fired. He calculated his attack, but UZI moved out of sight.

"Well, well...look what we have over here." Peter heard him toppling a pile of bricks. Debris skittered across the floor. "Here's my name, 'UZI,' on the wall. It says, 'UZI 1978.' And here it is again, 'UZI 1979,' and again carved in the plaster, 'UZI 1980.'

"What were you doing in 1980 while I was starving, scrounging for grubs in the cemetery? I bet that you were eating a greasy cheeseburger in Seattle, am I right? Pickles, mustard, relish, and French fries? Living in a big house with a swimming pool—fancy school, blue blazer, and a necktie? Big old boat of a convertible out front."

He's seen the photos.

"That's right. I've seen your pictures. Petrosyan showed them to me when I called on him in New York. Don't get conceited. I didn't go all that way to talk about you. I went to get my money back—my money. Ephraim's share of the Party's Gold belongs to me—not you!" UZI threw bricks at the wooden struts of scaffolding. The kagans hummed.

"My mother paid the mother warden of Kurzan to take me into this lovely prison when my family was shot. Ephraim gave Petrosyan my share of the fortune to keep for me. It was more than enough to buy my way out of prison and send me to fancy schools like you. Instead, your grandfather took the money and left me to rot. Thought I was dead, he claims, so he gave my money to you. Now he says that it is in a trust and he cannot give it back. Imagine that!"

Finally, something made sense. UZI's hatred had seemed irrational, deranged. But it wasn't. The source of his sociopathy was like many others of his kind—abandonment, betrayal, abuse and greed. That was sad, but it didn't make him any less deadly.

"Well, my dear cousin, here are my school photographs, carved on this wall, UZI 1980, UZI 1981, and on and on. Every year a smiling school portrait of me…no, that was you. I was locked in here when you were driving that Firebird on your way to university, paid for with the blood of my family and eleven years here in hell for me."

Peter wanted to shout: "Take the money. Take it all—I don't care." But that would be suicidal. *He plans to kill me no matter what I do.*

"Enough about you, Pyotor. Let's talk about your cousin Tanya. What lies has she told you? She is not an innocent victim, you know. She sought me out. She put an ad in the personals. It said, 'UZI. You have what I want, and I have what you need.'

"So, I called the girl. Did you know that our Tanya was number one in her class from journalism school? I went to her office at *Eleven News*. She'd been a two-week wonder, promoted straight up to the esteemed Culture Column; she was that good. It should have been enough for any other cub reporter. But our Tanya wasn't satisfied writing about Mrs. Yeltsin's new hairdo. She wanted to be a real journalist. She wanted the big-time. She wanted UZI.

"She offered to work a deal with me. Not so that she would win a prize for journalism. No—she wanted to walk down the runway at Moscow Traffic in the Bride Market and sell her ass to some rich guy. She thought because we were 'family' that we could help one another. She'd publish my poems and I'd move her up the line at the Bride Market."

He was pacing again, moving in and out of Peter's line of sight. "I told her to strip in that little office of hers and she did. I told her to bend over her desk and I fucked her. She was a virgin, so I did her a favor. I got her ready for what was coming next."

Peter held Tanya against his chest, willing her to stay silent, knowing that he was losing her. She rolled her head from side to side, the will to flight slipping from her body. He rubbed her back, wishing that he could tell her that UZI's words meant nothing to him, that she should let them go. He wanted to say how happy he was to discover his new family. How proud he was that she was his cousin. He wanted to scream: *We have time, Tanya. We have the rest of our lives to talk this through, figure this out. You don't need the Bride Market. I'll help you. We'll be a real family.*

UZI was back. "We made a deal, Tanya and me. She would publish my poems and in return, I would let her pay me five grand instead of the usual ten for the Bride Market. Then she could strut down the runway and into the hands of some horny foreigner. Stupid whore. She thought she was such a great poke that she'd gained some power over me—as if she meant something to me."

UZI mocked in a woman's voice: "'That was so good, UZI. I'd like to do it again.' I told her that she would do it again—and again and again and again. I told her flat out that's how she'd earn her money for Moscow Traffic—and she agreed. Imagine her surprise when Oleg arrived and drove her to Hotel Ukrainia. You changed your prissy little mind, didn't you, Tanuchka? Poor Oleg had to throw you down on the hood of the car and poke some sense into you."

Tanya was shrinking, pummeled by shame. Peter lifted her face, signaling with his eyes to stay strong and not let UZI humiliate her. He willed her to banish UZI from her mind. *Fight him, Tanya. He's nothing. You're everything. You're what matters.*

"When Oleg jabs his junk into a little girl like our Tanuchka, she can't walk for a week. One session with him and our girls behave. They know they don't have much time before their looks go and nobody will buy them. Right, Tanya? You've been fucking four, five men a night for two years now and, next week, if my math is correct, you'll be walking down the runway at Moscow Traffic. My congratulations! You'll be going to a rich asshole in America or maybe Paris or Berlin. You'll have furs, cars, caviar, a yacht. You can get your folks out of that shithole flat on Apple Street."

Tears rolled down Tanya's cheeks onto Peter's coat. UZI kept talking—his words a merciless barrage. "You'll have nice clothes, sleep on good sheets. You'll grow to be a fat, happy babushka with lots of grandkids. Moscow Traffic will grant you every woman's dream. But wait…it won't, will it. Moscow Traffic is gone. Pyotor blew it up. He blew up your life, Tanuchka. You aren't anything now. All your good fucking, up in smoke. You're dirt for the dustbin, nothing but a used-up whore."

"I can imagine you up there—Dr. Stone, forensic psychologist, analyzing me. You know what I'm doing. I've picked on the weaker one—little Tanuchka. It's easy to destroy her self-esteem because it's already so low. Simple to rob her of hope because she's never had any, not really. I am letting you watch me work my magic, like I do on all women. They start out all bravado and self-importance. But beneath the paint and powder, they're just whores—even Caroline. I want you to watch how skillfully I suck Tanya's soul from her body. You wonder how I'll do that? Well, there is an ironic twist to this plot. I won't do it. You'll do it for me."

He was pacing again, kicking stones across the floor. "I don't know which dome you're hiding in, but I can see you in my mind holding the terrified Tanya to comfort her, to keep her quiet so that she won't give you away—because as soon as she makes a sound, you are both dead.

"You're feeling noble and wise, protecting a beautiful woman. You think of her as the sacred prostitute who will help you find your lost lover. Did she tell you how she lured Caroline to the Pavlovs' flat for me? That she invited the lonely little American to stay in the safety of a nice Russian family? Did she tell you how much I paid her to do it? How many thousands of rubles she made, spying on Caroline for me? Telling me her every mood?

"But our Tanya, the little over-achiever—she did so much more than that. Your sweet cousin befriended your lover in the way that only a woman can. Caroline poured out the secrets of her heart to Tanya and Tanya told them all to me. What a treacherous viper you are, Tanuchka."

A moan escaped from Tanya's lips. Peter heard the slide and snap of a chambered round. He clamped his hand over Tanya's mouth, holding tight. UZI drew closer. "Those intimate, late-night confidences shared between two women were the bullets I used to take Caroline down. I could have seduced her without Tanya's help, but it was oh so much more satisfying to know every secret place in her soul.

"Now I own Caroline—body and soul. She is never coming back to you, Pyotor. And what is Tanya's reward for all the long, cold nights standing by the Chaika at the Ukrainia Hotel or in Caroline's apartment, whispering lies so she could betray the woman who trusted her? There is none. Moscow Traffic is gone. She cannot escape this place and she can't escape me. She'll die here and so will you because she betrayed you also. How do you think I knew to come here? How did I know that the Chechens took you to Kurzan Convent?"

For an instant, UZI's words made chilling sense. Peter pushed Tanya away from him, holding her by the shoulders. When she raised her eyes to his, he saw raw desperation. She held his gaze, her eyes wild, mouthing the word *no*. She reached for him in a silent plea to hold her again, but he kept her away.

"Do you know how I paid our deceiving whore on the night I entered your woman? She got her packet of rubles, of course, but I gave her a special bonus for all her good work—earrings, diamond earrings shaped like little hearts. I ripped them from Caroline's ears and gave them to Tanya."

UZI's words were a bayonet to Peter's heart. His grip on Tanya's tightened. His doubt was reflected back to him in the desperate pleading of her eyes. A primordial howl of grief and capitulation burst from her throat. It hung for an instant in the frozen air. A shot shattered the kagan and his eardrums. Tanya exhaled a shuddering sigh and collapsed—a bloody rag in his arms. Her head flopped grotesquely, eyes open, a trickle of red from her parted lips.

"Tanya." He shook her limp body. "Tanya, Tanya," he screamed again and again, hearing nothing but the roar of the sea in his head. He rocked her in his arms—willing her alive, unwilling to give her up to Ruslan and Ahmed when they climbed the ladder to carry her down.

Chapter Nineteen

THE AMERICAN AGENT

The American Embassy, October 8, 1997

The Chechens carried and dragged Peter back to the convent—nearly deaf and covered in blood. He was sedated. stripped and examined by Dr. Plotkin, who found no wounds. The blood was Tanya's. Pavel and Maria Pavlova immersed him in a metal tub of hot water and scrubbed him clean, dressing him in his great-grandfather's stiff winter suit. No one spoke a word—or they might have. Peter couldn't tell because sirens were going off in his head.

"We saw this often in the Great War," Pavel mouthed, pointing to his own ears. "It might get better, or not."

"American Embassy," Peter shouted. It was time to invoke the power of the United States Government. "I need the Americans."

He had no idea how to accomplish that without a telephone at the convent, and he knew how difficult it was to get through to the embassy even when he had access to one. The Americans were not going to take him seriously if he showed up unannounced with a black eye, stinking of mothballs in a Soviet era suit and chaperoned by the Butchers of Grozny.

Ruslan slipped through the door and handed him a white business card. It had the U.S. Department of State gold emblem embossed on the top. The card was from Ambassador Richard Baynor. On it was written, "South Gate, 11:30."

"What is this?" Peter shrugged.

"An appointment with Ambassador Baynor at 12:30," Ruslan shouted. "We'll drop you at the South Gate an hour in advance. Your escort will be waiting."

Peter was surprised. "You know the ambassador?"

"Ahmed and I were mujahideen. We worked for the Americans in Afghanistan, then Blackwater in Iraq. Ambassador Baynor was a field agent."

"Agent of what?" asked Peter. Ruslan shrugged and Peter decided that he didn't really care. He needed to pull himself together enough to convince the ambassador that Caroline was alive and that a monstrous crime had been committed against an American.

He was distracted every time someone opened the door across the hall, revealing Katya prostrate and sobbing over Tanya's body. His mind went blank at the sight, his throat tightened and his eyes burned with tears as he relived her horrifying final moments in slow-motion—the gunshot blast and her body flopping lifeless into his arms.

By 11:00 a.m., Peter was seated in the back of the Chechens' new Mercedes as it crawled through Ring Road traffic on the way to the embassy. The sidewalks were thick with commuters, heads lowered against the wind, walking faster than the cars. His hearing had improved but his skull still felt like a diving bell full of bees. The march of pedestrians barely registered as his brain replayed Tanya's death on an endless loop. *So much blood for such a small person.*

By 12:30, Peter was seated on a leather sofa in the ambassador's suite. Ambassador Baynor sat in a matching wing chair. He poured Peter a mug of Lapsang Oolong tea and introduced the other embassy personnel. They included Head of International Narcotics and Law Enforcement, Jack Howard, whose nametag read 'INL,' and Chief of Citizen's Services, red-haired George Tanner. Several young staffers took notes but were not introduced.

"Wait a minute," Peter interrupted. "Did you say Tanner? I called the embassy asking for Mr. Tanner, but they said there was no such person."

"I don't know why." Tanner smiled. "Here I am. I've been here three months."

"What can we do for you, Dr. Stone," asked the ambassador.

Peter launched into an explanation of how he'd been tasked by the King County Executive to find Caroline Luke, an American citizen, who'd been declared dead at the Moscow Morgue by Mr. Tanner. He produced Caroline's passport with a hole punched in it and passed it around. "In fact, I've found Miss Luke. She is very much alive and being held prisoner by Alexei Kaminsky, also known as UZI, leader of the Kurzaniks." He told it all as succinctly as he could, knowing that his time would be short and that he was speaking too loudly.

Tanner scowled. "I cancelled Miss Luke's passport myself after identifying her body. She matched our facial software perfectly," he said, handing the passport back to Peter. "See the hole? That means that she's dead."

"She's not dead. I saw her two nights ago at Moscow Traffic. She was in a cage. They were forcing her to sing. UZI told me that she was his prisoner. I'm here to get your help. She's an American citizen who's being held against her will. She has been trafficked and her life is in danger."

"This sounds like a case for the Moscow Militia—GUVD. Have you contacted them?" said Baynor.

"Of course, I did. They tried to kill me," said Peter in frustration, knowing that it made him sound crazy. He wondered how he must look to them with his bruises and pungent, rumpled suit, shouting over the buzzing in his ears.

Jack Howard from INL interjected, all patronizing smoothness, "The solution is simple. Ask Miss Luke to come to the embassy and prove to us that she's alive and we'll issue her a new passport."

"She's a prisoner in a cage, being held by a monster," Peter shouted. The embassy officials looked everywhere but at him.

There was a knock on the door. "Come in," said Baynor.

The pretty, dark-haired receptionist poked her head in. "Ambassador, the Minister of Foreign Affairs is waiting to see you," she said.

"Thank you, Martina." Baynor slapped the arms of his chair, making it plain that the meeting was over. He stood and extended his hand to Peter, saying, "Keep us updated of any new developments."

"I hope we have been of assistance to you." Howard and Tanner handed him cards with their direct line numbers and moved him skillfully out the door.

He was ready to lash out in frustration when a hand on his arm brought his attention to the receptionist. She held up a folded scrap of paper, "You dropped this." She stuffed it into his pocket and turned him toward the elevator. "Your escort is waiting."

As soon as he was out of the compound and back in the Mercedes, Peter unfolded the note. On it was written, *ZOOPARK THIRTY MINS. MK.* "What the hell is this," he exclaimed. "What's a zoopark and who is MK?"

Ahmed leaned over the seat and took the paper. He showed it to Ruslan. They laughed. "Martina Kay. Now we're getting somewhere."

"Who's Martina Kay?"

"You'll see," Ahmed grinned, showing his gold front tooth.

It took thirty minutes to drive the short distance through traffic to the fanciful entrance of the Moscow Zoo at Barrikadnaya Metro. When the Mercedes glided to the curb, a blond woman in dark glasses and a frumpy green coat got into the backseat with Peter.

"Hello, Martina," said Ruslan.

"Ruslan, Ahmed." She returned the greeting, reaching forward to pull off Ruslan's glasses and look at the wires. "I didn't think you wore glasses. These are cute. Ahmed, what have you got for me? Any fancy gear that you shouldn't be wearing when I'm around?"

Ahmed pulled out his cuff transmitter and passed it to her. "Are we clean now?" she asked. They nodded. "Let's get going, gentlemen. Drive to Dzerzhinsky Square—we've got a meeting at Lubyanka at 14:00."

"Who are you?" Peter demanded. "What's at Lubyanka? What meeting?"

"Lubyanka is the headquarters of the Federal Bureau of Detectives," she said, pulling off the blond wig and shaking her short, dark hair; Peter recognized her as the ambassador's receptionist. "They work the human trafficking cases. They had a sting operation underway at Moscow Traffic involving foreign nationals and Russian women—except that everything went haywire two nights ago when some crazy American with Chechen bodyguards set the place on fire. Wonder who that was? Any ideas?"

"We didn't do that," said Ruslan. "It was that Cossack, Oleg Sherepov. Dumb as a post. The asshole set off explosive gas from that secret factory on Apple Street. We barely got this guy out alive."

"Doesn't matter who lit the fuse," said Martina. "The point is that the police had an undercover detective inside the club. As of right now, federal police are stopping and boarding all the buses crossing from Moscow Oblast into Vladimir Oblast. Hopefully, the women who were taken from Moscow Traffic are on them—including Detective Pashkina."

"Why would they be on buses?" asked Peter.

"After the fire, Kaminsky couldn't sell them at his nightclub, so he's sure to send them on the Slave Road through the Republic of Tatarstan to Turkey. From there, they can be auctioned off and sent all over the world."

"And Caroline?" Peter's voice cracked. "Is she with them?"

"I don't know. That's what I hope to find out at Lubyanka." She pulled out a compact and powdered her nose, using the mirror to look behind them and at the cars on both sides.

"Why did the ambassador blow me off?" asked Peter.

"Don't be silly. I'm here, aren't I? I wouldn't have come without his imprimatur." She took off the dark glasses and squinted at his face. "Is that mess on your face all from Moscow Traffic?"

"UZI tried to kill me this morning. He blew out my eardrums—though it's getting much better, less buzzing."

"We thought from the chatter on the GUVD channels that he *had* killed you. We were surprised when Ruslan contacted us to say you wanted to come to the embassy." She checked her mirror again, "So, who died in the Church of the Kurzan Goddess?"

"Tanya Pavlova, my cousin," said Peter. The words felt untrue coming from his damaged lips. He cringed at the thought of nuns rolling Tanya on her side and washing the blood from the hole in her spine.

"Tanya Pavlova, the journalist? From *Eleven News* Culture Column?"

"Yes," said Peter, choking on the words, "the popular journalist—an amazing woman. I was just getting to know her."

"What a shame," Martina sighed. "Journalism is a dangerous profession." They rode in silence for a few minutes. "So, who are you really—and why are you here?" she asked.

"The 'why am I here' part is easy: I came to find Caroline Luke and take her home to Seattle. The 'who am I?' question gets more confusing by the minute." He looked up and caught Ruslan scowling at him in the mirror. Who should he trust—the receptionist from the American Embassy who was wearing a disguise, or the Butcher of Grozny who had saved his life more than once? He didn't trust anyone except Pavel and in retrospect, and far too late, Tanya.

"I'll ask you again." She smiled. "Who are you?"

"I'll let you know when I've figured that out myself."

"Let me help you. Obviously, you aren't an innocent tourist from Seattle. Americans don't generally get greeted at the airport by Golokov's thugs. UZI had a hit out on you before you even arrived. Next thing we know, you are speeding through town with Chechen mujahideen fighters and a famous journalist. Then you're spotted at the Hotel Ukraine drinking shots with UZI himself, and you take off in a car driven by the Kurzaniks' chief capo and UZI's right-hand man, Oleg Sherepov. A short while later you burn down the Bride Market at Moscow Traffic and ruin a federal undercover investigation."

"That was Sherepov," interjected Ahmed. "Pyotor didn't do that."

"It wouldn't have happened if Dr. Stone hadn't been there, right?"

"Well…technically, no."

She continued her litany, "You spoiled the police sting and a dozen people burned to death. Plus, the fire drove the Kurzaniks into their armed fortress at Konkova where they will be much harder to track. Then we hear that Kaminsky has shot you dead in the ruins of the Church of the

Kurzan Goddess. So, imagine our shock when you show up at the embassy shouting at everyone, and smelling like camphor."

She leaned forward to scrutinize his face. "It took twenty minutes to confirm your identity using our facial recognition computers, what with all the swelling and bruises. It took ten more minutes to find the records of your name change from Pyotor Kaminsky to Peter Stone in the seventies. You and this Alexei Kaminsky are related, I take it? Cousins?"

"Cousin or no cousin, he's a monster. He's taken Caroline Luke and held her against her will. I've come to take her home. She'll need a new passport so we can fly to Seattle and forget all of this."

"What is your relationship to Miss Luke? Are you married?"

"We intend to be. We've been together for six years working our way through university degrees and starting careers." He couldn't meet Martina's gaze. He should have married Caroline years ago.

"I was at the Pushkin Theater on opening night. I heard her sing in *Ivan Susanin*." Martina smiled. "Her voice is spectacular. You must be proud of her great achievement."

"I wasn't there." Peter sighed. "I didn't even know she was in Moscow. She was supposed to be in New York."

"You didn't know about UZI, either, I take it?"

"No, he must have met her in New York and offered her the part in Moscow." Peter rubbed his chest. "Apparently, she wanted to succeed on her own, without my help."

"Or to deceive you with another man. She may have gone to him willingly. That makes this less of a sex trafficking case and more of an affair gone wrong—a very gray area as far as the embassy is concerned."

"I don't care what it is, she's now his prisoner. If she turned to him for financial help, it's my fault not hers. I should have stepped up and been her patron. She doesn't know it, but I have money in a trust fund."

"Oh yes, the Petrosyan Fund," said Martina.

"How do you know about that?" he asked.

"We'll get to that in a minute," she replied.

"I've never touched that damn money. I've made my own way by hard work and that was enough for me." He scowled defensively, then softened his words. "Caroline's needs are different. An opera star has to hire a top agent. She needs clothes, jewelry, travel expenses, voice lessons—all things I could have paid for. Instead, I got my hackles up and the poor girl went off half-cocked looking for a patron in New York City."

"She went alone? Was that wise? Clearly she found more than she bargained for."

"I thought she'd give up and come home—that things would return to normal. Instead, she signed a contract with UZI. I doubt she even read it. She is a creative but impractical person. I always loved that about her."

"Do you have a copy of the contract?"

"No, but Commander Golokov does." Peter recalled the chubby officer waving his files. "He showed it to me but wouldn't let me read it."

"I've seen some of UZI's contracts. They are devious and clever," said Martina. "That is how we can prove entrapment. For now, we will assume that this is a legitimate trafficking case involving an American citizen." Martina put her hand on his arm. "I know you're a highly experienced forensic psychologist, so I'm going to ask you flat-out one of the most difficult questions that arise in any trafficking case."

"Shoot," said Peter, regretting his choice of words.

"Are you sure that you want Caroline back?"

Blood rushed to Peter's face. His cheeks burned. "What kind of question is that?"

"Even if the federal police can save her, she will never be the same physically or psychologically. You will have a long road ahead of you while she recovers––if she recovers. She'll be like a wounded veteran with PTSD except that there are no institutions with services for trafficking survivors. Will you stick by her?"

"I'm a physician and a psychologist. I can help heal her better than anyone else."

"She's been with other men. Can you forgive her for that?"

"There is nothing to forgive. I just want her home. We'll work out the rest when we're safe in Seattle."

"What if she doesn't forgive you?"

"Me?" Peter flushed. "I'm here risking my life, blundering around like an idiot, trying to save her from her own stupidity." He held his head in his hands. "I'm sorry. That sounded terrible."

"Honest anger. It's a first step." Martina smiled. "Chin up, Dr. Stone. More people than you know are trying to help you. Now, what can you tell me about the Petrosyan Fund?"

Peter gazed out the window and recalled his locked desk drawer filled with unopened correspondence from Daniel Karlov. "I don't know anything about it except that my father left it to me."

"You have a trust fund worth hundreds of millions of dollars and you know nothing about it?"

"Millions?" He choked. "No, I didn't want to know. In fact, I worked hard at not knowing. The statements came every month, but I never opened them."

"Who is Petrosyan Kaminsky?" There was an edge to her voice. "What is his relationship to you?"

"Apparently, he's my grandfather. I'm his heir so UZI wants me dead so that he will inherit. What can he possibly have to do with Caroline?"

"I believe that his actions have a direct bearing on what happened to Miss Luke." She searched in her bag and handed him a reproduction of an old Russian icon. "Have you heard of the Virgin of Kurzan?"

"No. What does an icon have to do with anything?" *Bloody Kurzan again.*

"It is among the oldest and most valuable of Russian artifacts. It was hidden by monks on the day that your grandfather and a squad of Chekists looted and burned Kurzan Monastery in the 1920s. They didn't find the icon and it's been missing for seventy years. Two days ago, it was announced for sale at a private auction at Sotheby's in New York. Coincidence? Guess who's selling it."

"Petrosyan Kaminsky?"

"Right! And how did he smuggle a national treasure out of Russia and past U.S. Customs in New York?"

"The empty coffin weighted with sand." Peter sat bolt upright. "It was kept overnight in New York at a warehouse owned by Daniel Karlov..."

"...who fronts for Petrosyan."

"UZI must have drugged Caroline and fooled Tanner into declaring her dead." Peter shook his head. "How could Tanner be fooled? Didn't he check for a pulse?"

"Tanner's an idiot. I'm sure he didn't look too closely. Unfortunately, he won't want to lose face by admitting that she might still be alive. That could present a problem because she needs a U.S. passport in order to go home. After what she's been through, she might not look like her old passport photo any more than you do."

Peter pictured Caroline's open, smiling face. His heart contracted. "I hope that's not true."

"Those are details that we can handle through the ambassador's office," Martina said, "but it will take time. Aha, this is Dzerzhinsky Square. We're here."

"Who do you work for?" he asked Martina.

"For Ambassador Baynor," she replied with a smile. "I'm his reception-ist."

"Who do you really work for?" Peter asked again.

Martina shrugged. Ruslan guffawed and said, "You don't want to know."

Chapter Twenty

THE RUSSIAN FEDERAL
BUREAU OF DETECTIVES

Lubyanka, October 8, 1997

They parked in front of an oversized Soviet-style green façade festooned with concrete garlands, hammers and sickles. Martina looked Peter up and down and pursed her lips in disapproval. "Remember that we're here strictly as observers. This is a Russian federal police action and we have no jurisdiction of any kind. They are letting us sit in on this briefing as a courtesy to the embassy. Our orders are to sit there and be quiet, no matter what. Can you agree?"

"Yes, of course. But what if they need my help?"

"You might have an opportunity to speak to the detectives on the case afterwards, but that's at their discretion."

Peter nodded. "I understand."

Martina winked. "Good. Let's go in."

Once through security, the two Americans were given badges and escorted into a high-tech conference room where they sat on gray metal chairs along the wall. Uniformed officers sat at the conference table including Commander Golokov. Peter watched his eyes narrow when he saw Martina Kay, then widen when he spotted Peter. *Surprise, Piggie. I'm still alive.*

A pair of burly plainclothes detectives entered, followed by a petite woman officer in a neatly fitted uniform. There were dark circles under her large blue eyes. Her tousled blond hair looked like she'd slept on it. Martina nudged him. "That's Detective Natasha Pashkina," she said. "She's the chief of the Federal Task Force on Human Trafficking. She's the one who was undercover at Moscow Traffic. Did you see her at the club?"

"I don't remember anything but Caroline in a cage," he said. "The rest is a blur. Sorry."

Detective Pashkina sat at the head of the table. An older officer next to her cleared his throat to start the meeting. His badge said SKARPOV. "As you know by now, Detectives Pashkina, Markov, and Demidov have been running a sting at Moscow Traffic to catch the Kurzaniks trafficking women out of Moscow. In particular, we sought to observe Alexei Kaminsky, the notorious UZI, in the act of operating a human trafficking ring." There were nods of approval around the table. "We've known for some time that they entrap high-class young women from good families and auction them to foreign men as brides. More commonly, they entice village girls to work at the club and sell them to North Americans or Europeans as sex slaves. Those that they can't immediately sell are trafficked and bused to Turkey where they are auctioned off to the Middle East.

"We knew this was happening to about one hundred and fifty women a week, but we weren't able to act on this information within Moscow jurisdiction until we had proof that women were being sent outside of Moscow Oblast, making it a federal crime. As soon as we obtained that proof, this became a federal case and Detective Pashkina was sent in undercover as one of the brides." There were murmurs of admiration.

Skarpov continued. "You also know about the catastrophic fire at Moscow Traffic. Sadly, five Russians, three Americans, three Frenchmen, and a German were killed—all of them men. The women, including our detective, were removed by the Kurzaniks and taken to their fortified compound at Konkova. From there, they were loaded onto buses and sent via the Nizhny Novgorod Highway toward Vladimir Oblast. As soon as they crossed out of Moscow Oblast, our agents intercepted the buses. I am happy to report that one hundred and fifty women were rescued and five Kurzaniks have been arrested on federal charges of human trafficking. All of the women are safe. As of this moment, they are downstairs giving statements and will soon be on their way back to their families."

Applause broke out. Peter noted that Golokov was not applauding. Neither was Detective Pashkina. She raised her hand to speak. "Colonel Skarpov, I am afraid that isn't quite accurate. There's one woman who's not accounted for."

"How can that be?" Skarpov countered. "We have the program lists of the women for sale that night. All of them have been safely recovered."

"There is one more, a singer. She wasn't for sale. They kept her apart from us. She sang right after the bridal parade and I thought that she was part of the show, a paid entertainer. But when we were evacuated, UZI threw her into the van with me and ten other women. She had been beaten and drugged. I assume UZI did it. He kept swearing at her, shining the light in her eyes. She's a victim and we need to help her. If she wasn't rescued on the buses, she must still be imprisoned at Konkova."

"Do you have any idea who the woman could be?" asked Skarpov, looking through his papers again while Peter squirmed in his seat.

"Wait," Martina hissed, her hand clamped on his forearm to keep him still.

Skarpov continued, "We need some sort of identification before we go busting into Konkova. That's a big step. Maybe she's Kaminsky's girlfriend and they got into a fight. Wouldn't we look stupid?"

Pashkina frowned. "She was a prisoner the same as we were. At least ten other women saw her, including Judge Bartovsky's daughter, who was at the Bride Market. They will testify in court if they have to. But first we need to go rescue her. Based on her condition, we must act quickly. Her life is in danger."

Commander Golokov spoke up. "I think we should be satisfied with the hundred and fifty women that were saved. Detective Pashkina's reputation as a zealot overstepping her bounds is well known. GUVD can't move against the compound at Konkova without so much as a name for your so-called trafficking victim."

"I don't know her name." Pashkina's cheeks flushed with frustration. "She was barely conscious in the back of the van. She was very beautiful before UZI beat her…"

That was more than Peter could bear. He stood and said, "Caroline Luke is her name. She's American." He fumbled in his pocket and pulled out her passport, which he tossed onto the conference table. Martina made a show of pulling him back into his seat.

"Miss Kay," Colonel Skarpov narrowed his eyes, "let me remind you that you are here as a courtesy in gratitude for the cooperation your embassy has offered us on international criminal cases. But I will withdraw that courtesy if your assistant so much as sneezes again."

"Yes, sir," said Martina. "I apologize on behalf of my colleague." She squeezed Peter's hand and whispered, "Good work."

The passport made its way around the table. When it reached Detective Pashkina, she studied the photograph. "Yes, this is her. This is the woman still at Konkova."

"If she's American," Golokov addressed Skarpov, "then this is a case for Interpol. I can see that the GUVD files a request for them to investigate by the end of the week."

Pashkina leaned forward. "The Trafficking Task Force will file the request for an investigation within the hour and, yes, Interpol will investigate. However, we all know that they are far too slow to save Miss Luke.

It's also possible for the American Embassy to file an investigatory request on behalf of an American citizen. That's also too slow to save her," she said through clenched teeth. "If we don't act within the next few hours, that innocent woman will die at the hands of a murderer. Do you want that on your consciences? Or worse, do you want the murder of an American in the international press? Perhaps we should ask our American embassy liaison what their response would be."

"I think we'd better." Skarpov frowned at the Americans. "Miss Kay?"

"Esteemed colleagues." Martina stood to address them. "Ambassador Baynor is always concerned for the well-being of our citizens in your country. This heinous crime against Caroline Luke came directly to his attention this morning. I assure you that he was shocked by it. He is standing by now, waiting for me to report on the response of the Russian Federal Police in preparation for his weekly press briefing. As Miss Luke is a celebrity, an opera star, the press will run with the story in both our countries."

"An opera star, you say?" Skarpov interrupted, holding the passport and pushing his glasses up his nose. "She looks familiar. Isn't she the one who sang on television last week? *Ivan Susanin* at the Pushkin? She went missing, right after. It was in the press until the American Embassy released a report saying that she was dead. GUVD declined to investigate, as I recall."

"Clearly the embassy and GUVD were mistaken," said Pashkina. "Now it's up to the federal police to clear this up before the international press does it for us."

Skarpov looked dubious. "Police action is not required for dead people, even if they're opera stars. If the Americans are satisfied that she's dead, maybe we should be satisfied as well."

Pashkina pushed harder. "Caroline Luke was seen very much alive by Judge Bartovsky's daughter, and the police commissioner's daughter, and the niece of the editor-in-chief of *Eleven News*. They were all captives in the van with me—and Miss Luke. Gentlemen, I may be bound by my oath of office not to speak to the press, but I assure you that those young women have no such restrictions. They will be speaking to the media as soon as they are processed and released from Lubyanka. So, you gentlemen must decide. Do you want to be seen by the international community as heroes, or," her eyes locked on Golokov, "Kurzanik lapdogs paid off by organized crime to let criminals like UZI prey on our daughters? Because that's how it will look in the media."

Detective Pashkina could not have been more than five foot three and one hundred ten pounds, but she carried the room. The men in uniforms around the table bobbed their heads in assent. Peter thought they might break into applause until Golokov, now purple in the face, pounded the table and shouted, "You can't just up and raid a legitimate place of business like Konkova without following the letter of the law. You don't have a warrant."

Pashkina drew herself up to her full height and crossed her arms. "Judge Bartovsky is with his daughter downstairs and will be signing our warrant within the hour."

"In that case," said Colonel Skarpov, "we mobilize immediately. Call OMON."

Chapter Twenty-one

THE BRIBE

Lubyanka, October 8, 1997

The meeting ended. Officers gathered their notes, snapped shut briefcases and left in small groups discussing football scores.

"Shouldn't they be planning a rescue?" Peter asked Martina. "Don't they care?"

"Not their department," she replied. "It's up to the detectives now."

"Whatever's happening, I intend to be part of it."

"Of course." She patted his arm. "Wait here."

Martina moved to the head of the table where Detective Pashkina greeted her warmly. Peter leaned forward in his seat, trying to listen. He didn't see Golokov until the commander straddled a chair and pulled it around to face him.

"I wouldn't put my faith in that little twat," he said.

"What?" Peter was startled.

"The dishy little blond." Golokov smirked, nodding toward Detective Pashkina. "I fucked her in Germany, you know."

"Sure, you did," said Peter, repulsed by the moon-faced little man.

"It's quite true. The Berliner Polizei had a grant a few years back to teach Russian police how to stop sex trafficking from Russia. After class, they would take us out for a few beers, and we'd go bang as many Russian whores as we could buy on our per diem. That little cunt was working in a brothel off Alexanderplatz. Now she's screwed her way onto the federal police force."

"I don't know who you're talking about."

"Yes, you do. She's standing right there with your friend Martina Kay—Detective Natasha Pashkina, the bony blond who's about to stir up a shitload of trouble."

"Isn't she the chief of the Federal Task Force on Human Trafficking?"

"She is. But let me tell you, nobody from GUVD wanted her in the bureau. She is just very good at getting what she wants. Five minutes alone with Colonel Skarpov and she had his pants down and her hand around his gearshift, if you know what I mean. She probably did the whole department for that job."

"Good for her." Peter turned away, willing Golokov to shut up so that he could hear Martina.

Golokov edged closer. "I warned Skarpov that she's a whore bent on revenge, but his dick was in charge. He even made the mistake of trotting her out at a live press conference. She looked like cream and sugar with those big blue eyes—but when she got to the microphone she went off on her own script. She confessed everything on national television. Weepy-eyed Russian grannies were glued to TV sets from Kaliningrad to Vladivostok."

"Why? What did she confess?" asked Peter.

"That she'd been a fifteen-year-old kid on school holiday when she and her friends were trafficked in Moscow and sold to a German brothel."

"How could that happen?"

"You saw the girls partying at Moscow Traffic, didn't you? Not the fancy ones from the uppity families on the runway, the other ones." Golokov grinned. "The peasants."

Peter recalled young women dancing on the sky-bridges. "They looked like children."

"They are primitives." Golokov grunted, earning his porcine nickname of Piggie. "Bumpkins from villages who've crapped in outhouses all their lives. Suddenly, they are in the big city and some handsome guy invites them to Moscow Traffic for a party. They drink, dance, and snort coke until they drop. Nobody tells them they'll wake up as whores in Berlin."

"That's terrible, but what does it have to do with me?"

"Not everything is about you, Dr. Stone. This is about her." Golokov nodded toward Pashkina. "She bellyached to the Russian public on live TV about how German pimps forced her to stand in a window dressed like a schoolgirl and made her fuck ten men a night. By the end of the broadcast, she was a national hero. She had the whole country bawling, ready to declare war on Germany. Now she's cleaning up Casino Row on Tverskaya, getting that ass Skarpov to close the topless clubs and causing serious trouble for the Kurzaniks. UZI wants her nailed to a cross."

Peter's veneer of patience evaporated. "I get it. You are UZI's inside man," he snapped. "Why should I waste one more minute listening to you after you tried to have me killed? Go away and let us do the job you couldn't or wouldn't."

"Don't pretend to be so high and mighty," Golokov sneered, "or I'll arrest you for murder."

"I haven't killed anyone."

"I've got twelve charred bodies in the morgue that say otherwise. And there is the matter of a shooting at Kurzan that left a journalist dead this morning. You were involved in both incidents. Is that a coincidence?"

Peter's jaw tightened. The burn victims were an abstraction that he'd set aside to deal with later. But Tanya had died in his arms. He'd washed her blood from his hands. "UZI shot Tanya. His men set fire to the club. Do your job. Go arrest them."

Golokov held up his hands. "Pardon me, Mr. Cowboy. I forgot that you're an American. You think you have rights. You don't know how it works in Russia, do you? Here, you're guilty if I say so and you stay guilty until you can prove that you're innocent. You can't do that very well in a Russian prison. That's where you'll rot, getting your neck tattooed by your horny lover-boy while you wait years for a court hearing. No exercise machines, no libraries—just thick-necked goons with big dicks, too much testosterone, and, did I mention, AIDS?"

"That's enough, Commander. What do you want?"

"Your attention."

"You have it. Why are you telling me this?"

"Without my help, you and Detective Supergirl have no chance of rescuing Caroline Luke. The Kurzanik compound at Konkova is a fortress, most of it underground. I know how to get inside without triggering the compression mines at the entrance. I know because I installed them myself. And I know where UZI's private quarters are. That's where your girlfriend will be."

"You would go against UZI?"

"For the right price. Remember, I'm offering you the only chance you have to save the songbird." Golokov leaned close, "Decide quickly. I'm taking a big risk even talking to you. I need to know what's in it for me, and I need to know it now."

Peter didn't hesitate. "I'll give you fifty thousand dollars if you draw us a map with a big red X on the spot where Caroline is.

Golokov grinned. "So, what UZI told me is true. You are a rich bastard. Make it a hundred thousand, and I'll take you to her myself."

"It's a deal." Peter didn't hesitate. He stood up. "Let's go."

"No, you don't. The money must be in my account before we leave Lubyanka. No ripping me off once I do the job."

"Done," said Peter. "Get me an international phone line and we're in business." He looked up to see Martina nodding in approval.

"Let's get Dr. Stone to a telephone," said Detective Pashkina.

Chapter Twenty-two

THE LETTERS

New York, October 8, 1997

Petrosyan strained to hear Ruslan shouting on the satellite phone over the traffic noise on Dzerzhinsky Square. "He's inside the Lubyanka building with federal detectives."

"Have they arrested him?"

"I doubt it. He's with the American embassy liaison, Martina Kay."

"Don't you have a bug on him?" Petrosyan did his best to stave off panic.

"We do, but everything inside Lubyanka is jammed," said Ruslan. "We can't hear him."

"What's that racket? It sounds like tanks."

"Spetsnaz is mobilizing an OMON unit. Looks like they're going to raid Konkova."

"Konkova?"

"The Kurzaniks' Moscow stronghold—an old munitions factory with bomb shelters and bunkers. I've heard that's where they keep their bank with the gold and cash they intend to launder once they get an international banking charter."

"Is Pyotor going with them?" Petrosyan's right hand started to shake uncontrollably. His fingers weren't working properly.

"I don't know. He's still inside."

"Call me when you're back in contact." He dropped the phone in its cradle. Lights flashed around his eyes. His vision skewed. If only it would stop snowing in his penthouse. Hooded apparitions surrounded his chair—monks that he and Ephraim had killed. He heard the orthodox chanting. The air smelled of charred timber. Beyond a wooden sign for Stone Farm, tree trunks materialized. *The apple orchard.* Wind gusted. A creaking rope drew his eyes to a corpse that swung from a branch.

"Denis," he groaned. "My dear, dear son. I loved you from the first moment I saw you."

****

Denis had been a wide-eyed, skinny twelve-year-old when he walked down the gangplank of the *Queen Mary* to shake hands with his father. The boy was excited by everything that Petrosyan showed him in New York. He was a bright student and learned English quickly. Still, the adjustment from Russian to American life was difficult, especially when he heard the news reports of atrocities on the eastern front. Conditions in the USSR were appalling and getting worse. Denis missed his mother and worried about her constantly. He pined for the Pavlovs, fearing for their safety. The Soviet Post Office and Telegraph had shut down. Petrosyan tried but was unable to discover where Maria Pavlova, had been sent— only that she was somewhere in Siberia.

In a way, Germany's invasion of Russia came as a double blessing for Petrosyan. Not only was he able to purchase art from Russian museums for huge bargains, but the closure of the Soviet borders gave him a chance to separate Denis completely from his Moscow relations.

After the war, he kept up the deception by intercepting Maria's letters to her son, and his to her. Denis eventually seemed to accept the reality that he would never see his Russian family again. He grew up to be the rich, handsome playboy that Petrosyan had always wanted to be himself. Denis was charming and witty. Petrosyan encouraged him to lavish money on beautiful women. The last thing he expected was that he would marry Ruby Mae, the Peacock of the Bellagio, just because she was pregnant. That was bad enough—but even worse, Denis found the intercepted letters that Petrosyan kept hidden in the basement.

"There are five more boxes just like this," Denis said, dropping a banker's box at Petrosyan's feet.

"What were you doing in the cellar?"

"Looking for my immigration papers. I need them for the marriage license. I found these instead." Denis lifted a handful of letters with boyish script on the envelopes. "You never sent them, did you? My poor mother must have thought that I forgot her. And what about the Pavlovs? You've been lying to me all this time. How can I live with this? How can I live with you?"

****

The ghosts faded when the phone rang again. Petrosyan managed to press the speaker button.

"Hello…hello?"

It was Daniel Karlov. "Pyotor called again—from Lubyanka. I thought I should clear this with you."

"What does he want? Is he in trouble? Is he hurt? Why is he at Lubyanka?"

"He asked for a hundred thousand to be wired into the account of a Commander Alexander Golokov. It's the first time that he has requested money from the Petrosyan Fund. What should I do?"

"Wire it! Is that all he wants?"

"For now, apparently."

"Whatever he asks for, give it to him … as long as you're sure it's Pyotor."

"I have him on the other line. You can listen in." Karlov punched the conference-call button. "Peter? Are you still there?"

"Yes. Will you send the wire now? It's urgent." Petrosyan's heart warmed to the sound of his grandson's voice.

"It's been approved. The wire was sent," said Karlov. "Are you sure that's everything you need? Can I make a hotel reservation or order a car for you?"

"No, thank you. I'll be busy for the next several hours." Peter paused, then said: "On second thought, can you arrange for a private jet to get Caroline and me out of Russia?"

"I'll have one standing by at Vnukovo Airport. I can also open an account for you at Citibank in Moscow. It is a simple matter to set up a line of credit. You can withdraw whatever cash you need."

"Let's do that."

"Will one million be enough? Two million?"

A pause. "One million will be fine."

"Where are you staying? I'll have the credit card delivered today."

"I'll let you know when I know." Peter hung up.

"What should I do?" Karlov asked Petrosyan.

"Get that account set up," the old man rasped. "And have my Lear standing by at LaGuardia. I'll pick up Pyotor myself."

"Shall I meet you in Russia? I'm at the London office. I can get there before you do."

"Let me think about it." Petrosyan hung up. Half an hour later the phone rang again.

Ruslan said, "Pyotor's standing in front of Lubyanka. He's wearing Spetsnaz gear. There are six OMON transports on Dzerzhinsky Square. I can't count how many troopers. Pyotor's getting into the second car with the detectives. The police escort just arrived. They're moving south fast. Gotta go…." Ruslan hung up.

Petrosyan stared at the Virgin of Kurzan on his mantlepiece. The spotlighted faces had more color and detail than before. The eyes were sharper, the pupils flared in pinpricks of fire.

"You are out of time, penitent…" said the wind.

Something spun in Petrosyan's chest like a rusty gear that had snapped and broken free. He gasped for air, nauseated and sweating—unable to catch his breath. He speed-dialed Karlov. "Come at once. I need you in Moscow," he rasped. "Bring the documents—all of them." He gave Karlov further instructions, then hung up.

The eyes of the icon bored into his skull.

"Take me home, penitent…" said the wind.

Chapter Twenty-three

THE DETECTIVES

Lubyanka, October 9, 1997

Peter shivered in the cold men's locker room of Lubyanka. He was in his skivvies with detectives Markov and Demidov as the three of them changed into heavily padded blue and gray camouflage jumpsuits issued by Spetsnaz. He was careful to zip Caroline's diamond heart earrings in his pocket before discarding the old suit. When they were dressed, Demidov tossed him a black bullet-proof vest that said OMON across the chest and back in white letters. "Put this on."

"What does OMON mean?" Peter asked.

"Omonovsty is the militarized branch of the federal police," said Markov.

"That means they get all the fancy gear from Spetsnaz," said Demidov.

"Is Martina Kay coming with us?" Peter asked.

"Not allowed," said Markov. "She's a foreign diplomat. You're coming instead— as our psychology consultant."

The detectives strapped on handguns, then belts with extra clips and flashlights. "Do I get a gun?" asked Peter.

"Have you ever been in combat?" Markov asked.

"No."

"Have you been trained to use a handgun? An automatic weapon?"

"No to either."

"In that case, I'm not giving you one. You are safer without it and so are we," said Markov, handing him a black OMON helmet. "And here is your flashlight. Don't lose it."

"Stay behind us. We'll tell you when we need you," said Demidov.

Detective Pashkina was waiting by the exit wearing the same insulated fatigues and OMON vest. She looked at Peter with a skeptical expression that reminded him of Martina. "Are you sure you're up to this? You look pretty banged up."

"I play rugby," said Peter. "What's a few bruises."

"But your face…Can you see all right?"

"Faces always look worse than they are." Peter shrugged. "I'm fine—really."

"Let's go," said Markov, pushing open the door. Below them Dzerzhinsky Square was a hive of activity. Blue and white OMON transport vehicles loaded with armed men were organizing into a convoy. Traffic police were on site to redirect angry drivers.

"We're waiting for the GUVD escort," said Pashkina. "Then we go to Konkova."

"How far is it?"

"About an hour to the south," said Demidov. "There's our car."

"Get in," Pashkina said to Peter. "You'll ride with us."

Demidov climbed in front with the driver. Peter sat in back between Markov and Pashkina.

"No gun?" she asked. Peter shook his head.

"He can't shoot," said Markov.

"Stay close to us. Don't go off on your own." Pashkina loaded a clip and slid it into her Tokarev TT33 semiautomatic pistol. "Where is Golokov?"

"One car back," said Markov. "And we've got Dr. Stone's bodyguards tagging along at the end of the convoy." Peter looked back but saw only OMON vehicles.

"Here's the escort," Demidov shouted over approaching sirens and the roar of engines revving up. "Let's roll."

The convoy took off at speed. This time the Ring Road traffic parted for them and they flew past the zoo and the American Embassy, moving south on Leninsky Prospekt. The bouncing vehicle didn't bother the detectives as it jerked them from side to side, but Peter felt the motion in every bruised facet of his body.

"Are you all right?" Pashkina shook his arm. "You look gray."

"I'm fine," he said.

"I need you focused and strong. We don't know what we're going to find at Konkova. Miss Luke may be in bad shape."

"If she's still alive," said Markov. "She may not be."

The sudden thought of Caroline flopping limp like Tanya was a punch to his gut. Peter grunted and fought off the urge to vomit.

"We always take a psychologist on our rescues. Martina tells me that you're a good one." Pashkina was all business. "But if you aren't up to the job, we can call someone else."

"I am a good one and Caroline knows me," Peter agreed. "I've just been through a lot the past few days."

"And you're about to go through a lot more," said Markov.

"I'll be okay." They rode in silence for several blocks—then Peter asked, "Why didn't you stop those gangsters at Moscow Traffic? You could have rescued the girls and Caroline."

"That was the plan." Pashkina frowned. "But someone messed up our operation and burned the place down. By the time I met Caroline, I was in the back of UZI's van in nothing but my coat and underpants. All I had was a GPS tracker in my hairclip and total faith in Detectives Markov and Demidov."

"I saw Caroline in that cage and couldn't think of anything else but saving her."

"So, you went full-on *cowboy*." Markov snorted. "Not much of a strategy but that was some commendable head-butting."

"My arms were useless, thanks to that bloody Cossack pimp, Oleg," said Peter. "I'm sorry about your operation. I never meant to interfere."

"On the bright side, we now have a bigger and better operation than before," said Pashkina. "We've got OMON with us and you bribed Golokov to get us into the compound. The rest is up to us."

"What's the story with you and UZI?" Markov asked Peter.

"He's my cousin. This is all about an inheritance."

"Your what? Explain that a little better, please?" Pashkina rubbed her forehead. "I've been undercover for two nights. I have a bloody awful headache, and nobody's told me anything."

"My grandfather is Petrosyan Kaminsky. UZI's grandfather was Ephraim Kaminsky, Petrosyan's brother in crime, apparently."

"So this is all about the Communist Party's Gold?" Her eyes opened wide. "That Petrosyan and Ephraim Kaminsky?"

Peter nodded. "I'm afraid so."

Markov whistled softly. "That must be some inheritance."

"With me dead, UZI becomes the heir and gets the lot."

"Where does Caroline Luke come into this?" asked Pashkina. "Or Tanya Pavlova?"

"Martina Kay thinks that UZI and my grandfather used both women in a scheme to smuggle a famous icon to New York in a coffin."

"Which icon?" asked Markov. "I thought they were all in private collections."

"It's called the Virgin of Kurzan."

Markov whistled again. "The lost treasure of Russia. I saw that TV documentary."

"I saw it, too," Pashkina said. "That icon must be worth millions."

"It isn't worth one hair from Caroline's head—or Tanya's," said Peter. They rode in silence for several blocks, then he asked: "Martina said that Caroline will never be the same after this. What do you think?"

"When I saw her in the van, she was drugged but defiant. She's brave, strong and she's fighting. But rape is a terrible violation of body and spirit. No one recovers completely. Some of us refuse to surrender, but that's not the same thing."

"How do you know all of this, detective?"

"Didn't Commander Golokov tell you? He likes to tell everyone how he met me in a brothel in Berlin. I was trapped there for six months. He liked my type—lots of men did."

"He did tell me, but I didn't believe him. How could you go from being a victim of trafficking to becoming a federal police officer and head of the task force?"

"The usual way. I graduated top of my class at law school and outperformed most of the men. I can fire a Kalashnikov and take down a suspect as good as these guys. When the federal police formed the Trafficking Task Force, I did what it took to get the top job."

"How did you escape from Berlin?" Peter asked.

"An angel saved me." She smiled. "I was locked in a tiny attic. The pimps had been tipped off and left town. The German cops showed up and did their usual sloppy search. I was banging on the door, but they never came upstairs. They were getting into their cars to leave when Sergeant Dieter saw me at the attic window. He broke the lock and pulled me out. 'No one should ever be left behind,' he said, and that has become our task force motto. We're living up to it today for Caroline."

They rode in silence for a while before Peter asked, "What about Commander Golokov? He took my money, but can we trust him?"

"Of course not," she snorted. "My detectives have been sitting on him all day, making sure he didn't tip off UZI about the bus rescues or this operation. That's why he was at Lubyanka. Between the federal detectives and the mob of angry parents waiting for their daughters, Golokov couldn't do anything but pretend to be helpful."

"We've got his balls in a vice," said Markov.

"That's why I thought he might be open to a bribe, if it was big enough," said Pashkina. "He'll want to take his money and run. Hooking him up with you was Martina's idea. No offense, but you don't look like a rich guy."

"I'll take that as a compliment," Peter sighed, hoping that they would get there soon. The speed, the sirens, and an endless loop of Tanya's pleading face in the split second that his faith in her had flagged were draining his confidence. It worried him that he had let UZI manipulate him and Tanya had died because of it. He should have known better. His reaction to Caroline would have to be different, better.

"There's the roadblock." Markov pointed. "We're almost at Konkova."

Pashkina patted Peter's hand. "Stay focused. Stay strong…for Caroline."

A Spetsnaz officer approached the car. "Wait here, detectives. We're blowing the gate."

Chapter Twenty-four

THE GODDESS

Konkova, October 8, 1997

In the depths of the old underground bunker at Konkova, UZI sat cross-legged in his dressing gown and read aloud to Caroline:

> *"Where are your sacred molecules?*
> *I have pushed every part of me*
> *Into every bit of you,*
> *But cannot douse your fire…"*

Caroline was handcuffed to his bed. She lay on her back and flexed her numb fingers, afraid to make a sound. Her hair spread over her shoulders was greasy with sweat. She hated the way she reeked of him, how his scent was on her skin, in her hair, up inside her.

"Time to go," said Oleg leaning in from the doorway. "OMON is nearly here. They've set up roadblocks on every highway."

"Looks like our fun little party is over." UZI dropped his robe and stood naked facing Caroline. "All good things come to an end, right, my little songbird?"

She wanted to turn away but stared instead. Through her tears he became Peter with his smooth skin, broad muscular shoulders and narrow waist. She had betrayed the man she loved by trusting this monster. She wanted to spit at him, but her mouth was too dry.

UZI was busy with his trousers and sweater. "Are we ready to go?"

"The Sikorsky's loaded," said Oleg. "The hard drives are pulled and crated. Everyone's in position."

"What about the bank vault?"

"The barge has docked. The forklifts are moving the bank aboard now."

"Good." UZI found his coat and knit watch cap. He searched under the bed for socks. "Who's coming with the feds? Detective Pashkina is bringing guests, I assume."

"They have Piggie with them," said Oleg. "Do you think he's been turned?"

"Who cares? He's a dead man either way. Speaking of dead men, what about Pyotor?"

"It looks like he's with the detectives, too. We'll know soon enough."

"Is the new videotape in the system?"

"Of course," said Oleg.

"Tell Viktor to warm up the chopper." UZI buckled his boots. "I'm done here."

Oleg spoke into his transmitter. The radio squawked an answer. Caroline heard the Sikorsky rotors rev up with an accelerating whine.

"What are we going to do with her?" Oleg nodded at Caroline. "We can't sell her—not with her face looking like that." An explosion rocked the compound. Plaster dust fell onto Caroline's eyes and into her mouth. She coughed and spat out sand. "OMON's blown the outer gate," said Oleg. "It's time to move."

UZI bent over the bed and kissed Caroline's forehead. She turned away in disgust. He grabbed her chin and forced her to face him. She winced. "I can't understand it," he said. "No matter how much I hurt you, I can't possess your soul. How does it slide away from me? Where do you go?"

"Give it up, brother," said Oleg. "Just cut her throat and let's go." He pulled a lever. A trapdoor snapped open in the floor revealing stairs.

"No... Drug her up, then cut the power. Let her freeze to death. It won't take long. I want Pyotor to see her die." UZI pulled on his hat and hurried downstairs.

Oleg plunged a needle into Caroline's thigh. She closed her eyes, grateful for the rush of drugs. Her breathing slowed.

When she opened her eyes, the room was dark and silent. She was transported back to the Pushkin Theater on opening night of *Ivan Susanin*. The orchestra tuned their instruments while the stragglers in the audience were seated. Backstage was hot, crowded, teeming with excitement.

The conductor tapped his baton. The house quieted. The orchestra burst into the overture to *Ivan Susanin*. Caroline gargled warm saltwater and limbered her throat. Magic sparked when she stepped onstage and sang of love, honor, and devotion, while the Polish army set upon her father and pierced him with pikes.

So much love. The audience loved her and she loved them back. She couldn't count the curtain calls. Children scampered onto the stage to fill her arms with red carnations. She was a creature of light and beauty— soaking up the praise, vibrant, and alive.

"You are safe with me, daughter..." whispered the wind.

Chapter Twenty-five

KONKOVA

Konkova, October 8, 1997

OMON took up positions around the perimeter of the Konkova complex. Spetsnaz had blown the outer gate into bits of smoking, twisted metal. Now they approached the inner door to the Kurzanik's compound.

"Stay low and follow me," said Pashkina. She and Peter crouched behind Markov and Demidov. Golokov led the way.

Suddenly the grounds were awash in light, wind, and noise. "What the hell is that?" shouted Peter, shielding his eyes. Whirling snow and ice stung their faces and the percussive thwump…thwump…thwump… of a helicopter pounded their ears.

"We're too late," said Golokov. "That's their Sikorsky. They're leaving."

"Who tipped them off?" Markov shouted over the whine of the rotors.

"Who knows?" said Golokov. "They've got people inside OMON just like GUVD. It's a rich man's world, detectives."

The dual-rotor helicopter hovered above their heads.

"We should shoot the damn thing down," shouted Demidov.

"With what?" Markov shouted back. "I didn't bring my rocket launcher. Did you?" The chopper banked east and disappeared.

"Do you think Caroline is on board?" Peter asked.

"Only one way to find out," said Pashkina. "We're going in."

OMON troopers unpacked boxes of C4, preparing to blow open the steel entry door. Golokov pushed through them. "Get out of my way, you Spetsnaz idiots. You're going to get us all killed." He flipped open the cover of a hidden keypad, punched in a code and waited. After a series of metallic clicks, the door slid open. "Those claymores would have turned us into ketchup. It's safe to go in now."

He stepped inside, followed by Peter and the detectives. Demidov gave orders to the troopers, who moved down corridors to sweep the darkened building and secure the perimeter.

"The power's off," said Markov, trying the light controls. "How do we turn it back on?"

"There are backup generators, but they're down in the basement. We'll have to make do with flashlights for now." Golokov switched his on.

They were rounding a corner when a video monitor lit up in front of them. Monitors flickered to life down the length of a long hall. Cheerful music from the 1930s blasted. A young woman riding a bicycle sang in English, "I love to whistle because it makes me merry, makes me feel so merry…"

"What the fuck is that?" shouted Pashkina.

"Deanna Durbin, the American movie star." Golokov smiled. The others stared at him. "At Kurzan Prison we had three Deanna Durbin movies. Mother Warden would play one every Saturday night. I can recite them all by heart. I'm sure UZI and the Kurzaniks can also." Golokov whistled with the cheerful little girls on the grainy film.

"Shut it off!" Pashkina demanded.

"Can't," said Golokov. "These screens are controlled from UZI's room. He has cameras in there too. When he's sticking it to someone, he likes others to watch."

As if on cue, the music faded. UZI moved in front of the camera. "Did you like the entertainment, Pyotor? How about you, Piggie? Bring back fond memories of Kurzan?"

Golokov's bravado dissolved. He was wide-eyed with horror.

"I'm going to make this easy for you, Pyotor, because there isn't much life left in your girl. There she is." The camera swung toward a bed. There was nothing visible in the pile of bedclothes except two slender arms and a cascade of hair. "She's a little tired. She had all of the boys last night—couldn't get enough of them. One after the other and she was still crying out for more. We had to call in Oleg and the Cossacks. They satisfied her. She's been quiet ever since." A slow moan rose from the tangled sheets. "She's alive, but barely. You better hurry. I'll be watching. I want to see her face the moment that you kill her—because you will. Just like you killed Tanya."

Pashkina grabbed Peter's arm. "Don't you dare let him into your head. He's a psychopathic asshole. Get moving." She pushed him along.

A few meters further on, another screen sprang to life. UZI's face filled it. "Poor little Tanya. She watched you believe my lies, Pyotor. Why did you believe me and not her? I'm the scoundrel and she has…or had…a heart of gold. Now, thanks to you, she has no heart at all."

"Keep moving," Pashkina shouted. "Don't listen."

They rounded a corner to yet another full screen of UZI's face. "Is it because I'm a man and she's a woman? Or was it because I made her into a whore and that meant that she was less than human in your eyes?"

The next monitor sprang to life. "Your Caroline is as much a whore as Tanya. She's been had by every man in this place…twenty-two, last count. She screamed with pleasure…wanting more, more, more. So, who will you believe when you look in her eyes? The answer is simple. You'll believe me because I'm UZI. I've bet the rest of the boys that one look from you will mortally wound her and she will die." He swung the camera to show several men waving wads of cash. "They don't believe me, but then again, they don't know you like I do. We are so much alike, you and I—more like brothers than cousins."

"He's your cousin?" Golokov looked surprised. "I knew it. I saw the resemblance."

"Keep moving," Pashkina shouted, "Don't listen to that subhuman piece of shit! Blondie's here, and she's alive. Nothing else matters. Commander, take us to that room."

Golokov led them down a series of hallways. Peter moved next to Pashkina. "I was with her…with Tanya. UZI started telling me how she betrayed Caroline. For just a second, I believed him. Tanya knew it. She gave up a terrible sound and he shot her. I feel like it's my fault."

Pashkina looked ready to slap him. "Who fired the shot?"

"UZI."

"He's the killer—not you. He's fucking with your head. I thought you worked with psychos like this?"

"All the time, but it's not personal. It is with UZI."

"When Caroline looks into your eyes, she needs to see love. That and only that. No shock, no horror, no fear—just love. Do you understand? Can you do that?"

"Do you think that UZI's telling the truth? That they've all had her?"

"Does it matter? If you can't accept that possibility and still love her, then stay back and let me handle this."

"This is it," said Golokov. "UZI's room." Pashkina elbowed her way past him and followed Markov and Demidov into a darkened room.

"She's like ice," exclaimed Markov, rubbing Caroline's hand. "Get the medics…now!"

Demidov tried the transmitter. "The radio's dead."

"They've scrambled your signals," said Golokov. "Just like at Lubyanka."

"Peter?" A weak voice rose from sheets. "Peter, is that you?"

Peter pushed past Pashkina and dove to his knees by the bed. He wanted to gather Caroline in his arms. But what he saw repulsed him. He nearly gagged. The only feature that could identify her was her hair. Her face was swollen purple. Her lips were cracked and bloody. Her eyes were rheumy, her breath putrid. The stink of semen was all over her.

"She's hypothermic," said Markov. "We have to get her out of these handcuffs and into the ambulance."

"Our keys don't work on these. We'll have to cut through," said Demidov.

"Well, start cutting," said Pashkina. "We can't wait for the medics. She'll die of shock."

"Caroline, it's Peter," he whispered, working up the courage to touch her. He brushed strands of oily hair off her face. She opened her eyes and turned to him. Her face brightened.

"Is it really you?" She smiled, searching Peter's eyes, but her face fell at what she saw there. She turned away from him. "I want to die. Let me die."

Natasha covered Caroline with the blankets that were scattered on the floor. "Blondie, do you remember me? I'm Detective Pashkina. I've brought the federal police. I told you we were going to rescue you. You're safe now." But it was no good. "She's giving up," shouted Pashkina. "Hurry!"

The video screen in UZI's room came on to the sound of men's laughter. "UZI said he'd do it," said Oleg, "He said Pyotor would polish her off and he did."

Then it was UZI's face onscreen. "Good work, Pyotor Kaminsky. Two dead whores in one day. I'll have to write a poem, set it to music."

"There's a camera in this room," Demidov shined his flashlight over the walls.

"Forget the camera," shouted Pashkina. "Get the cuffs off. Get her out of here now."

"Oh, I forgot to mention, the cuffs are titanium. You can't cut them," UZI howled with laughter. "Damn you, Pyotor. You just can't help killing every woman you touch. I guess you're a Kaminsky after all."

"Shut the fuck up," Pashkina screamed. She swung a metal chair and smashed the screen into splinters of glass. Then she turned on Golokov. "There's only one agency that has titanium cuffs: GUVD. These cuffs came from Petrovka 38. That means you have a key."

Golokov reached in his pocket and pulled out a set of keys. He dangled them in the air and backed toward the door, brandishing his Baikal pistol.

"Another hundred thousand dollars. Wire that to my bank and you can have the keys."

Pashkina approached him menacingly, "Give them to me, you pompous ass."

"Or what, Detective Twat? What's a pipsqueak like you going to do to me? I know what a runt you are under that uniform."

"This isn't helping," shouted Peter. "I'll pay you whatever you want. Just give her the keys."

Golokov eyed him, "First, you go out to the truck and use their satellite phone to wire the money. Then we'll talk."

"We don't have time," shouted Pashkina, but Peter was already out the door. "Bring the medics," she shouted after him.

"We're losing her," Markov said. "She's not responding."

"You pig." Pashkina held the chair in front of her like a lion tamer, her face twisted with rage.

"That was Mother Warden's chair," smirked the commander. "And over there is her desk. She sat in it for years, meting out punishment to the bad boys in prison. Now UZI sits in that chair. You think it will stop a bullet, you stupid cow?"

"I don't care, you psychopath." She raised the chair. Golokov pointed the gun at her head. She rushed him, and he fired point-blank. The shot went wild when Peter struck him from behind with his flashlight. Pashkina grabbed the keys and tossed them to Markov, who opened the cuffs. Peter wrapped Caroline in blankets and lifted her in his arms.

"I'm so, so sorry." He kissed her bruised cheek. "I love you. I'm taking you home."

"No...I'm ruined. I'm filthy. I want to die," she groaned. "Leave me here."

"Not a chance," he whispered.

"What about Golokov?" Markov pointed to the inert commander.

"Leave him," said Pashkina. "We'll send the medics to get him."

They moved back the way they'd come. The music had stopped, and the monitors were dark. "Wait a minute," Peter said, signaling to the others to stop. "That last video feed, the live one. Something was missing. It was too quiet."

"What do you mean?" Markov asked.

"He's right," said Pashkina. "There wasn't any background noise. If they were on the Sikorsky, they'd need headsets and mics. I didn't hear a chopper on the video, did you?"

"Oh shit! They're still here," said Demidov. "We've got no radios, no sat-phones, and they could be anywhere in this building…or the tunnels."

"How many did you see on the screen?" she asked.

"Six or seven. UZI, Oleg Sherepov and his Cossack thugs," said Markov.

"OMON has the place surrounded, but the Kurzaniks love their tunnels."

"Maybe we should go back and get Golokov. We might need him," said Peter.

"Let's just get out of here," said Pashkina. "Keep going."

The screens leapt to life again, filled with the green face and cackling laughter of the Wicked Witch from *Wizard of Oz* against a backdrop of flying monkeys. Then UZI's face came on. "How clever you are, Detective Twat. Looks like it's going to be your pussy that entertains the boys tonight. I always wanted to give you a ride."

"Where in the hell are they?" Markov glanced around.

"Who cares? Keep moving," said Pashkina. "The door is straight ahead."

Peter followed Markov and Demidov. Pashkina brought up the rear. The two detectives stepped into the vestibule. The door slid shut behind them with a clang. They were isolated and trapped.

"Don't move," Pashkina shouted. "The claymores might re-arm." A series of metallic clicks affirmed her statement.

"Go get Golokov," she shouted at Peter. "We need the codes to get out of here. I'll stay with blondie."

Pashkina sat on the floor and Peter laid Caroline on her lap. From his pocket, he withdrew the diamond earrings. He held the little hearts out to Pashkina. "Please, detective. Can you put these in her ears? For good luck."

She nodded. He started to go, but Pashkina said, "Wait!" She pulled out her Tokarev TT33 pistol and slid it to him. "Careful. There's no safety."

He picked up the gun between thumb and forefinger. "What do I do with this?"

"Point it and shoot."

Chapter Twenty-six

THE INTERNATIONAL BANK OF KURZAN

Konkova, October 8, 1997

Peter ran back toward UZI's room. Suddenly the hallway echoed with porcine squeals.

"Here, Piggie, Piggie. Nice little Piggie." Peter pressed his back against the wall, gun raised. "Where's that big, pink pork-butt?" Men laughed.

"Get away from me, you Cossack bastards!" Golokov shrilled in terror.

"Don't hide your tight little piggy hiney. Pants him, Vanya."

"Get your filthy hands off of me!"

"Or what, Piggie? You're gonna tell Mother Warden on us? The old sow can't save her precious piglet this time, can she?"

"UZI said to fuck you on her desk. We'll video the whole thing and send it to her."

"And to ORT-TV. This is sensational stuff. I can see the headlines, 'Kurzaniks rape GUVD commander—see it on the eleven o'clock news.' We'll get cash for that. But wait, wouldn't we get more money for a snuff film? What do you think? Fuck him, then kill him? Sell it to *48 Seconds*?"

"Yeah—polish him off with the crowbar up his ass. That'll make great TV."

"No, no! You bastards," screamed Golokov. "Not on Mother Warden's desk."

"Tie him down. I'm getting a hard-on."

Peter startled at the sound of a struggle and hard slaps on flesh. He looked at the gun in his hand.

"Poke him good, Vanya. I've been wanting to do this since we were kids."

Golokov screamed. Vanya yelled, "Oh yeah, Piggie. That feels good… That's the way to squeal."

"Curse you to hell," Golokov shrieked.

Peter crouched and peered into the room. Golokov was stretched face down and pant-less across the desk. His hands and feet were pulled taut and tied to the legs on either side. A thick-necked Kurzanik was pumping hard, his back to Peter. Another poked Golokov in the gut with a crowbar. "Come on, Piggie. Squeal." Golokov let out a piercing scream.

"There's our Piggie. There's our fat little porker."

Point and shoot. Peter leapt into the room and shot the humper in the back of the head. Blood sprayed over Golokov and into the face of the other Kurzanik. The man threw the crowbar aside and raised his gun. Peter shot him through the neck. He fell, gurgling blood.

"Fuck, fuck, fuck." Peter tried not to vomit. With trembling fingers, he untied the ropes that held Golokov. "Come on, Commander," he shouted, but the commander lay still. "Pull up your pants and get moving. We need you to open the door."

Golokov didn't move. "Shoot me," he whimpered. "I'm finished."

"Well, I'm not," Peter shouted, yanking the smaller man to his feet. "We're getting out of here and if you don't pull yourself together, I'll shoot your fingers off." He looked at the half-naked man and pointed the gun at his genitals. "No, I'll start by shooting off your balls."

"Okay, okay," Golokov stood and zipped his trousers. "Let's not overreact." Peter almost laughed at this absurdity, but pressed on.

"The detectives are trapped in the vestibule with the doors closed. The claymores are armed. We need to open the door without blowing ourselves up."

"I only know the code to the exterior doors."

"Then we'll have to get out of here through the tunnels and double back from the outside. Can we do that?"

"What's in it for me?"

"I'll forget what I saw here...and look, there's the video camera." Peter grabbed the recorder from the wall. He slammed it to the floor and stamped on it. "Now, move!"

Golokov pulled a lever and UZI's trapdoor opened. "Follow me." He snapped on his flashlight and started down the stairs. The air grew colder as they descended. Eventually Golokov stopped, "Holy God—this is it."

"The way out?"

"No, the way in." Golokov stopped and raised his flashlight, shining it around the inside of a cave.

Peter made out rows of shelves, stacked with equipment and boxes. "What is this place?" he demanded. "Why are we here?"

"We are inside UZI's heart—the International Bank of Kurzan. Everything he cares about is here." Golokov stared transfixed at a long row of shelves stacked with gold bars.

"Commander, we've got to get out and save the others." Peter's frustration rose. A wooden crate containing AK-47s was open. Peter picked up a gun. "Can we use these?"

"They won't work," said Golokov. "No bolts or firing pins." He ran his hands along a shelf and picked up a shrink-wrapped packet of $100 bills. "Behold one of the world's great criminal treasures. When UZI buys his bank charter, all of this will be washed clean and disappear into computers where it will be multiplied a hundred-fold. It's called re-hypothecation and it's happening all over this country... all over the world."

Peter's flashlight flickered and went out. "Damn," he exclaimed, throwing it aside. "I broke it on your head." He hurried to catch up to Golokov who wandered the stacks shining their only light on UZI's treasure.

"I don't think you understand the significance of all this," said the commander examining a pyramid of silver bars. "Once they have their bank charter, the Kurzaniks will be free to operate their enterprises in every country of the world. Their crimes will become undetectable."

"Let's get out of here," said Peter. "We can come back for this later."

"I just wanted to see this place once in my life. Look over there." He pointed his light at a long stretch of wall covered with writing. "UZI's stinking poems." Lights bobbed towards them. Men's voices echoed. "They're coming. Hurry." He sprinted through the room with Peter close behind. They ducked into a storeroom and closed the door before the Kurzaniks entered.

"Turn off the goddamned light," hissed Peter, tripping over a box of AK-47 firing pins. He had just enough time to see that the small, square room was stacked floor to ceiling with boxes of C-4 plastic explosives.

Chapter Twenty-seven

THE FUSE

Konkova, October 8, 1997

Inside the secure room, Golokov rummaged through boxes of firing pins, bullets, and bolts while Peter held the light. "Piggie, do this. Piggie, do that. UZI's made my life hell since I was three years old." He pulled out something that looked like a Frisbee and examined it in the light. "Here we are. This is perfect."

"What's that?" asked Peter.

"A mine casing. Hold that light steady for God's sake."

"Won't they see it under the door?"

"This is a sealed chamber."

"What do you mean?"

"It's a shock-proof box built for storing explosives. If the C4 ignites, the lack of oxygen contains the chemical reaction and the whole place won't go up. There are no cracks, no leaks, the walls are a meter thick, and that door is solid steel. Titanium bolts seal it at the top and the bottom and there's very little air. Now, shine that light here so I can assemble this."

"Why don't we just stay in here until they leave?"

"Because we'll suffocate in about ten minutes. Now hold the light steady, so I don't blow us up first."

"What are you doing?"

"I'm building a mine. I've got everything except a fuse mechanism. I'll have to strike the firing pin myself. Do you see a hammer or something heavy like that?"

Peter shined the flashlight around the room. Nothing.

Golokov pointed. "That flashlight should be heavy enough. I'll use that."

Peter sat on a crate of ammunition and steadied the light against his knee. Heavy machinery scraped the floor in the next room. "Sounds like a forklift," he said.

"They'll be loading the International Bank of Kurzan onto a barge. One of the tunnels runs down to the river. That's why UZI stayed behind. After they've loaded everything else, they'll come for the explosives." Golokov unwrapped a brick of C4. "I've got to work fast."

Peter watched Golokov's hands flying with practiced skill. "Where did you learn to handle that stuff?"

"Afghanistan," said Golokov. "Best four years of my life. Building land-mines in Kandahar was like a vacation after Kurzan." He opened two more bricks, deftly molding them into crescents and packing them tightly into the round casing.

"Tanya Pavlova told me that you grew up at Kurzan Prison."

"Mother was head warden. I was nothing more than an inconvenience that popped out of her womb during a wheat harvest. She stuck me under her apron and kept on threshing. She was made a hero of Soviet mother-hood for that and appointed Mother Warden at Kurzan. She raised me as a model proletariat. That meant spending my days with the boy prisoners. They hated me."

He turned his attention to removing the springs from firing pins. "I had food— they did not. At night, I'd sit in Mother's kitchen, eating dump-lings and watching the hungry boys through the window. The skinnier they got, the more I ate. UZI threatened to eat me if I didn't do what he wanted. He would have, too, if it weren't for Mother Warden. She was the only person that UZI feared. Any shit from him and Mother Warden locked him in the basement in the dark for weeks, sometimes. It was a break for me." Golokov paused to look around. "Pass me that bolt. Make it two bolts, then dig some bullets out of that box you are sitting on. Six cartridges should do it."

"What was it like—the boys' prison?"

Golokov fitted firing pins into the bolts. "What do you think? Hun-dreds of starving boys confined together for years, sleeping six to a bed and spewing tuberculosis over one another. Most of them died."

Golokov took the cartridges from Peter and pushed them into the C4. "Night after night, the KGB lined up dissidents outside the walls and shot them. Their daughters were driven off to God knows where and their sons were herded into Kurzan."

"And UZI came out on top?"

"He always preferred to be on top…me and the other boys just bent over with our pants down. Any boy who didn't submit was killed. After a while, even Mother Warden wouldn't enter the grounds without an armed guard. Yet she left her little Piggie to the mercy of the brutes every day." Golokov stood up. "Voila! A thing of beauty." The mine that balanced on his splayed fingers looked like a pie with a nail sticking out the top. "Give me the flashlight. What you're going to do now is unbolt this door, let me through, then bolt it again very quickly. You only have a few seconds. ..."

"But you'll be killed."

"I'm a dead man anyway. At least I'm going to take out as many of those Kurzanik bastards as I can. I just hope UZI's standing on the other side." Golokov unlatched the door.

"What about me?"

"I'll send you a postcard from Hell." Golokov sprinted out the door.

"Commander, you forgot the codes! Give me the codes!"

Peter had scarcely re-bolted the door when an explosion lifted the secure room and knocked him down. The roar that followed rolled on and on, shaking the room and burying Peter in a pile of cardboard boxes.

Chapter Twenty-eight

THE ESCAPE

Konkova, October 8, 1997

The floor of Konkova heaved. Caroline heard shouting through the echoing thunder. *Good,* she thought, drifting away from the noise in a drug-induced haze. *This will be over soon.*

She tried to return to the forest where she could shelter with the Virgin of Kurzan, but the leaves along her path were hostile, withered and sickly, fading from green to yellow. The trees had an electric edge that buzzed and burned. She tried to crawl beneath a comforting blanket of leaves, but they turned into beetles with sharp little feet. They ran up her arms and legs. She thrashed, trying to brush them off, but they kept coming. They swarmed over her, pricking her skin. She coughed, losing her dream. The beetles were eating it and she wanted it back. *I'm leaving now. I'm going home.*

She spread her wings to fly above Seattle, high up where the beetles couldn't go. Lake Union was easy to spot, a dark circle surrounded by city lights. A well-lit houseboat floated in the middle. Inside, a blond man bent over a desk. *There's darling Peter with his papers stacked on his desk.* She drifted down, reaching out to touch his hair. "I'm home, Peter, my love," she said.

It wasn't Peter, but a cartoon spider with yellow fangs and rotating eyes that captured her in its hypnotic stare. "I don't want you back," the creature hissed, growing huge, bursting through the roof of the houseboat. "You are dirty. Go away!"

"Forgive me," Caroline cried, buffeted by a powerful updraft that pushed her away. "I've been a fool."

The lake became a sickly pink and waves churned the waters brown. Sparks flew into the air, snapping at her with sharp teeth.

"Baba," she cried. "Take me to Baba's." The skyline shimmered and buzzed. *Beetles! They're everywhere!* Blue-black insects covered the house on Blue Ridge, beating the air with millions of wings, grinding the building and trees to dust with powerful jaws and pushing them over the cliff and into Puget Sound. She saw Baba's face in the window, screaming as she was swept away by the sea. "Make this go away," Caroline sobbed, but no one noticed. "I need more drugs. I need another shot."

The detectives were screaming at one another. The door to the vestibule slid open with metallic clunks and the screech of steel. The cold air smelled like burning butter. A giant black beetle with OMON stamped on its shiny round head scooped her into its arms and ran away with her. She shrieked and kicked. More shouting and another explosion knocked them to the ground. Now she was surrounded by giant beetles. They lifted her onto a rolling platter.

"Don't eat me," she screamed as they strapped her down.

"She's too cold," shouted a chef in a white coat. "We've got to warm her up. Get her into the oven. Start an IV."

"Don't eat me," she begged, straining against straps that bound her arms and legs. A siren wailed. Her strength ebbed. "Help me," she whimpered and lost consciousness.

****

She woke with a start. The insects had gone, but everything was askew. Her mouth was dry, her tongue swollen, her eyes barely focused. She was in a moving ambulance with an IV in her arm. An oxygen mask covered her nose and mouth. She recognized Detective Pashkina, who was talking to a dark-haired woman that she hadn't seen before. She moaned but they didn't see her.

"I thought we were goners," said Pashkina. "How did you get the door open?"

"Ruslan Amiroev, Peter's bodyguard, called me," the other woman responded. "I used to work with him in Iraq. He told me to grab our keypad decoder and get to Konkova. I flew over in the ambassador's little Bell helicopter. I'm sure GUVD is screaming at Ambassador Baynor right now. I violated more than a few Moscow laws by flying it over the city."

"Thank God you did. Another second and we'd have been killed."

Through the oxygen mask, Caroline croaked, "I'm alive."

The stranger smiled at her, leaning close. She said in English, "My name is Martina Kay. I'm from the American Embassy. I'm here to help you."

"I need a shot."

"Can you give her something?" Martina asked the white-coated medic.

"Not until I know what she's already got on board. She's got needle marks on her extremities and her neck. We could give her the wrong thing and kill her."

"Peter...where's Peter?" Caroline groaned. "What have you done to him?"

Martina rubbed Caroline's hand. "We don't know where Dr. Stone is yet. Don't worry. We'll find him."

Sobs shook her. "Peter...Peter doesn't want me anymore."

"Poor girl," said Martina, watching Caroline drift away. She turned to Pashkina, "Why wasn't he with you?"

"He went back to get Golokov. The commander knew the key codes. I hope he wasn't caught in that explosion. I saw those two Chechens run into the building with respirators on once we were outside. Do they know what they're doing?"

"Absolutely," said Martina. "They'll find him, one way or another."

"Oh God, I want to die..." moaned Caroline.

"What's wrong with her? Physically, that is." Martina asked the medic.

"She's dehydrated. She's in shock. She's coming down off some powerful hypnotic. She's been sexually assaulted. She's been beaten, she's been starved, and she's hypothermic. We need to get her to a hospital." He adjusted the IV.

"Did you bring her new passport?" Pashkina asked Martina. "You know Russian law. We'll need that to admit her to any hospital."

"I don't have it yet," she replied. "And she needs it to get back to the U.S. I just spent the last two hours arguing with Citizens' Services at the embassy. George Tanner insists on talking to her before he issues a new passport."

"What do we do?" Pashkina asked.

"I've taken care of that. The ambulance is taking us to the embassy. Tanner agreed to come out and look for himself. We're on Novinsky Bulvar now, so it won't be long. I'll call Tanner now."

Caroline dozed until a light shone in her face and a man with red hair shouted, "No way. This is not Caroline Luke. Luke was beautiful. This woman's a wreck. Is she even American?"

"Ask her," Martina urged.

"What's your name, ma'am? Are you an American citizen?"

The light burned Caroline's eyes. She squinted. Her head buzzed. The world spun. *I'm so dizzy.* Then she heard the overture to *Ivan Susanin* and it was opening night. She stepped onto the stage. Klieg lights glared. The audience applauded. Children piled red carnations into her arms.

"Who are you, ma'am?" Tanner repeated in English.

"I am Antonida Susanina...the virgin bride," she replied in Russian. "Let me sing for you..."

"This is a fucking waste of time, Martina. I don't know what you're trying to pull. Caroline Luke is dead."

Chapter Twenty-nine

WHITE CRANES ARE FLYING

Kurzan Convent, October 9, 1997

Bong… bong… bong… bong… Caroline woke slowly to the sound of the Kurzan bell tolling for Tanya's funeral. In her drugged mind, each slow stroke shook a spray of pine needles from the sky and stuck them into her skin. She moaned: "What's happening? What is that terrible sound?"

"It's our bell," said the sister sitting by her bed. "It's beckoning the souls of the dead to fly to heaven as white cranes."

"I want to fly away. I can't stay here anymore." Caroline's body ached. Every joint felt stretched to breaking when she tried to move. "It hurts too much."

"I must go tell Dr. Plotkin that she's coming around," said the sister. "Will you stay with her, detective?"

"Yes, of course." Someone rubbed Caroline's hand vigorously and patted her cheeks. Caroline opened her eyes and Detective Pashkina's smiling face came into focus. "Hello, blondie. You're going to be all right."

"Where am I?"

"You're in Kurzan Convent," said the detective. A man with a stethoscope entered the room and stood next to her. "This is Dr. Plotkin. He's been taking good care of you."

"I need to check your vital signs." He stepped up and shined a light in Caroline's eyes. "You're lucky to be alive, Miss Luke. We nearly lost you to that drug. I could only guess on a proper antidote. If I'd been wrong, it might have killed you. I guessed right. You were loaded with a local specialty called 'wild squirrel,' perhaps because it makes people nuts. Do you remember anything from last night?"

"I remember Peter." Caroline looked around. "Where is he?"

"Oh yes, Dr. Peter Stone. I treated him after he burned down Moscow Traffic. He'd gone there looking for you, as I recall. Open your mouth… say aaah." He looked down her throat. "He was lucky to be alive, too. You Americans must be made of tough stuff. The Kurzaniks gave him a serious beating, but he's a rugby player. He's used to rough stuff."

"Where is he? Where's Peter?" She tried to raise her arms, but her wrists were tied to the bed. She panicked and fought against the restraints.

"Shhhh…Stop that!" commanded Plotkin. "Those are to protect you. You keep pulling out the IV. I'll remove it as soon as your mind clears, and you eat something." She lay still, but her heart raced. Plotkin slid a cold stethoscope under her clean linen gown and pressed it between her breasts. "Breathe in and out, slowly, deeply."

Caroline followed directions. She could see Detective Pashkina in the hall talking to the American.

"Who is that woman with the dark hair?" she asked.

"That is Martina Kay, assistant to the American ambassador. She has been trying to get you a new passport…something about you being officially dead." The bell quieted; the bonging ceased.

"Thank you," she whispered, meaning the bell.

"Thank your benefactor," said Plotkin. "He's paying me a bundle for your care."

Tears filled her eyes. "Peter paid you?"

"No. Some American millionaire named Petrosyan Kaminsky."

"Who?" She struggled to make sense of it but couldn't. If he was related to Alexei Kaminsky, then she wasn't safe at all. A tall Middle-Asian man joined the two women. Martina introduced him to Pashkina as Peter's bodyguard, Ruslan Amiroev. *Bodyguard? For Peter?* She strained to hear what they were saying.

"We went as far in as we could," said Ruslan. "Most of the upper floor had collapsed. We found two dead men in UZI's room—both shot at close range. They were Kurzanik Cossacks, part of UZI's inner circle."

"I gave Dr. Stone my Tokarev. Maybe he used it." said Pashkina.

"We found a trap door in there, but it was filled with rubble." Ruslan shook his head. "We found what was left of Commander Golokov, but no sign of Dr. Stone."

"We were lucky to get anyone out alive," said Martina. "And this begs the question: Why did the Kurzaniks blow up Moscow Traffic and Konkova? They've destroyed their own enterprises."

"Moscow Traffic was a mistake. I was undercover in the van with UZI. He was furious. I thought he was going to kill Oleg Sherepov. Konkova was something else. I presume that they set off an explosion in the tunnels once they had us trapped and expected the claymore mines in the entry to finish us off. In any case, they are most certainly going to regroup at their other compound in Tver."

Another man joined the group. He carried two black duffle bags and tossed one to Ruslan. "Time to go," he said.

"You can't leave now, lieutenants," said Martina. "At the very least, that poor Luke woman needs protection until we can get her on a flight to Seattle."

"Did you forget, Miss Kay? Working for the CIA cost us our commissions in the Red Army. Now we work for whoever pays us. Petrosyan Kaminsky missed our last payment. Ahmed and I have other offers."

Ahmed said, "What about your colleagues at the Federal Bureau of Detectives, or your friends at OMON? Can't they help you?"

"They're busy cleaning up after Konkova. Besides, they only agreed to help with the rescue. Thank heaven none of them were hurt. I'm no longer officially on this case either. I talked Lieutenant Skarpov into sending out a press release indicating that an American woman had perished at Konkova. That will buy us some time, but it's not going to fool the Kurzaniks for long."

"Won't the American Embassy help?" asked Ruslan. "Pyotor and blondie are citizens."

"Not while Caroline Luke is officially listed as dead," said Martina. "We need you at least until that's sorted out and she can leave Russia."

"Our instructions were to protect Dr. Stone. The old man never said anything about the Luke woman."

"Can't you call him and ask?" said Pashkina.

"We've tried. Petrosyan isn't answering his phone."

"Is that your only way to contact him? No telex, email, fax number?"

"Just the phone."

"We can send someone to his address in New York, but we'd have to put that request through the NYPD. It could take hours," said Martina. "There must be some other way."

"Wait a minute," said Pashkina. "What number did Dr. Stone call from Lubyanka? We should have a record." She didn't wait for an answer. She punched a button on her sat-phone. They watched her walk out of earshot, issuing instructions.

A nun entered Caroline's room with a tray. "Aha, breakfast," said Plotkin, startling Caroline. "Here's the good Sister Makarova with food for our patient. That cabbage soup smells delicious."

Caroline turned her head to the wall. "Take it away."

"Nonsense. You must eat something. Sister will feed you while I get my breakfast. It's been a long night." He walked away.

The little nun lifted a wooden spoon to her lips, but Caroline ignored the food. She concentrated on the conversation in the hallway—trying to understand who they were talking about. "Where's Peter?" she called out, but no one seemed to hear.

Pashkina rejoined the group. "Ruslan, is this the same number you have for Petrosyan Kaminsky?"

"No, it's different. What's this number?"

"Dr. Stone called it to have $100,000 wired into Golokov's account."

"It must be the Petrosyan Fund," said Martina. "They'll know how to reach the old man. Give me the sat-phone and I'll call." She started to punch in the number. "Wait…What should I say about Stone?"

"What do you mean?" asked Pashkina.

"If I tell the truth about how bad this looks for him, the old man might stop paying. Miss Luke needs money for medical help. He owes it to her."

"She's Stone's girlfriend. Petrosyan should help her," said Pashkina.

"I'm not so sure," said Martina. "It looks to me like Petrosyan is the one who handed her over to UZI."

"That's monstrous. He's guilty of human trafficking on top of stealing antiquities," said Pashkina.

"What did he steal?" asked Plotkin.

"An old icon, the Virgin of Kurzan," said Martina. The doctor whistled.

Caroline smiled, recalling the glowing eyes and gentle wind that had comforted her. *Holy Mother… I remember you.*

Martina spoke again. "Petrosyan Kaminsky is as responsible for what happened to that poor woman as UZI. I intend to see that he is prosecuted in an American court. But first, we need his money and to get that, we've to keep Stone in play whether he is alive or not."

After a pause, the other Asian man said, "There is a way that he might have escaped. I saw a barge…"

Martina frowned. "What barge?"

"I was standing on the bluff when the first explosion blasted out of the cliff. There was a barge docked close to the compound."

"It's a busy river. There are dozens of barges," said Pashkina.

"This one had no lights even though forklifts were working on deck. Maybe that's how UZI and the Cossacks travelled to Tver if they weren't on the Sikorsky," said Ahmed. "If Petrosyan wants this job done properly, we should follow the barge upriver. He'll pay for that if there's a chance that Pyotor's on it."

Martina punched in the number.

"Where's Peter?" Caroline called out. "Is he all right?"

Plotkin walked back in. He scowled at the full bowl of soup and pumped up the blood pressure cuff.

"Where is Peter? Tell me now!" she demanded.

Plotkin checked her pulse. "It sounds like your friends are still looking for Dr. Stone."

"My friends? I don't know these people."

"They've risked their lives to rescue you. I'd call them friends."

"I don't know you, either," she snapped. "You're all strangers. I hate strangers. Everything hurts." She shivered. "I need a shot."

"Not until I get your lab results back. Eat your soup while I go see if they are ready."

The sister pulled her chair to Caroline's bedside and offered the wooden spoon again. "Here, Miss Luke. Please eat something. You'll feel better." Caroline took a sip, straining to hear Martina.

"Hello? Hello? This is Martina Kay from the American Embassy in Moscow. I would like to speak with Petrosyan Kaminsky....I got this number from Dr. Peter Stone....Yes, Mr. Karlov, we did try Petrosyan Kaminsky's personal number. He isn't answering....I've been assisting Dr. Stone in the rescue of his fiancée Caroline Luke....Yes, that's correct, sir. Federal detectives rescued her from the Kurzaniks' enclave in Konkova with the help of OMON....Yes, sir. She's safe for now at Kurzan Convent. She is receiving medical treatment....She is expected to recover, but she needs ongoing medical care....Thank you, sir, but we can't fly her back to the States yet, even in a private jet. There's a problem with her passport. We can't even take her to a Russian hospital because the American embassy has declared her dead. We've hired a private doctor and need to pay him....Yes sir. Thank you, sir."

Martina gave a thumbs up. "Dr. Stone appears to be pursuing Alexei Kaminsky with the assistance of Commander Golokov of GUVD...Yes, on his own...I'd like to send Ruslan Amiroev and Ahmed Kadyrov to follow him...No, sir. They won't go until they are paid...No, they haven't been able to reach Petrosyan either...They are both here with me."

She handed the sat-phone to Ruslan. "Hello? Yes, sir, this is Ruslan Amiroev. Inshallah, I am well, thank you. What Miss Kay told you is correct...No, sir. We tried all night to phone Petrosyan. It's urgent that we follow Pyotor, but we haven't been paid since day before yesterday...We followed him to Konkova. He went into the building with the detectives, but we lost track of him during the explosions. We suspect that he escaped through a tunnel and is traveling by barge on the Moscow River to Tver....He is following the Kurzaniks....Yes, sir. It is extremely dangerous and we have a blizzard closing the roads. We'll leave right away in our UAZ all-terrain vehicle, sir.… You can reach us on the sat-phone. Do you have that number?…Yes sir, that's correct." He handed the phone back to Pashkina.

"Petrosyan Kaminsky is on his way to Moscow," said Ruslan. "That's why we can't reach him." He and Ahmed picked up their duffels.

"Where are you going now?" Pashkina asked.

"To Tver. Mr. Karlov said to follow Pyotor and he's the one who's paying. Miss Luke will be well guarded while we're away."

Dr. Plotkin returned waving a sheet of paper. "Well, Miss Luke, your electrolytes have improved, so I'll give you a mild sedative. Then Sister Makarova will bring you a fresh bowl of soup. I expect you to eat all of it this time and then I will remove the IV."

He held up a glass vial, pulled liquid into a syringe, and inserted the needle into her IV tubing. Warmth flowed into her. She closed her eyes and became a white crane flying. *Peter, I'm coming.*

The bell pealed again—a call for the living to come honor the dead. She soared through an open window. Leafless birch trees threw stark silhouettes on the snow. Smoke rose from chimneys. In the distance, she saw the barge that carried Peter. It sailed north toward Tver, following a curve in the river. "I'm coming…wait for me," she cried out. The wind gusted and blew against her. She couldn't fly fast enough to keep up. The barge sailed out of sight. "Peter," she screamed. "Peter…wait!"

"Miss, miss," the sister stroked her arm. "Stop struggling. You'll pull out your IV. Doctor will be upset."

"Make it stop. That bell is driving me mad." Caroline tried to cover her ears, but her wrists were tied. "Get these ropes off of me," she wailed. "Untie me, now!"

"I can't do that, miss. We have to wait for the doctor."

"Untie me!" Caroline screamed. "My head is going to burst."

"I can't untie you and I can't stop the bell. It's ringing for the funeral."

"I knew it. Whose funeral?" Caroline's breath caught. She recoiled. "Who died?" Her stomach twisted. "Who…is…dead? Is it Peter?"

"I can't tell you." The girl's eyes were wide with fear. She backed away, knocking the soup to the floor.

"A man or a woman?"

"I can't tell you."

"An American? Did Dr. Stone die?" She was suddenly strong, fierce in her rage, struggling against the restraints that bound her limbs. "Untie me!"

"I can't," the nun sobbed, running from the room.

Caroline thrashed, arching her back and rolling from side to side. One hand came free. She undid the other restraints and pulled out the IV. The world spun when she stood up. She lurched into the hall, crashing into walls.

Where is everyone? She had been surrounded by strangers, but now she was alone. *They must be at the funeral.* She had to find them and tell them that they couldn't bury Peter. He wasn't dead. He was on the barge. She had seen him.

Barefoot, she padded toward the stairs. An open door diverted her attention. She stepped inside. Lit candles surrounded a bed. Tanya lay there in a long white dress, her hair a black halo on the pillow. Her hands were crossed on her breast.

"Tanuchka! I'm so glad to see you." Caroline stood by the bed and stroked her hair. "Your earrings! You forgot to put them on." Caroline pulled the diamond hearts from her ears and put them into Tanya's. She pressed her hand to Tanya's cheek. "You're freezing! I'll get my blanket." She ran to her room and pulled the duvet from the bed, covering Tanya with it. "That's better." She climbed under the coverlet and wrapped her arms around her friend. "I'll warm you up. I'll sing to you. I'll sing Antonida …."

****

The flickering candles became the klieg lights at the Pushkin on the night of dress rehearsal. The beaming director hurried toward her with arms outstretched. "Beautiful, my dear Carolina, just beautiful! You sing like a heartbroken angel." Facing the rest of the cast, he clapped his hands and boomed, "It's midnight, my darlings. Go home and get a good night's sleep. We open tomorrow."

The stage emptied. The director drove her home. "Have some soup, a hot bath and a good rest." He kissed her on each cheek and left her at the door.

Restless, she paced the apartment. Who could sleep with a world debut the following day? *I need to talk to someone.* She tried to call Baba but her international phone card had expired. She heard a key in the Pavlov's lock and rushed to the door. "Tanya! Come in for a minute. I have peppermint tea and apple cake."

"No, not tonight, blondie." Tanya kept her face in shadow.

"Tanuchka, good heavens! What happened? You've torn your clothes. Where's your hat?" Caroline draped an arm across Tanya's shoulders and pulled her inside. "Come in, dear. Sit at the table and tell me what happened?" She poured tea and sliced the apple torte that Mrs. Radina had baked.

Tanya did not touch her tea or cake. Her makeup was smeared. Twigs and leaves were tangled in her hair. "I can't do this," she murmured. "I can't live like this and I won't lie to you anymore. Go home to America before it's too late. Go home before you end up like me."

"Tanya, what do you mean? Is it your work at *Eleven News*?"

"Open your eyes, blondie. I'm a prostitute. That's what I do at night. I go to the Hotel Ukrainia and sell my body because I need the money for the Bride Market."

Caroline sat back, stunned. "But you're a journalist. You're famous."

"It's not enough. I need more money if I'm going to marry a wealthy foreigner and get out of Russia. I've paid four thousand dollars, but I need a thousand more. Then I'll be auctioned off to a rich man at Moscow Traffic. I don't care who he is as long as he has money." She dropped her face on her arm and sobbed. "That john nearly killed me tonight."

Caroline's heart ached for her friend. "If I had money, I'd give it to you, but I'm broke until the performance. Wait! Wait a moment." She pulled the diamond hearts from her ears and pressed them into Tanya's hand. "Take these. Sell them. I'm sure they're worth at least one thousand dollars."

"But Peter gave them to you."

"Please sell them. I don't want them." She opened a polished leather jewelry case. "UZI gave me these. He wants me to wear them tomorrow night."

"Oh no, Caroline." Tanya's eyes widened in horror. "Don't take anything from that terrible man. Get out of this country tonight before something happens to you."

"I can't leave now. I'm opening at the Pushkin tomorrow night. The opera will be on television."

"Caroline, you're too naïve for Moscow. UZI is going to hurt you. You must leave Russia—immediately. Trust me. Your life is in danger…."

"Tanuchka!" Katya stood in the doorway and scowled at her daughter. "Come home this minute! I've drawn you a hot bath."

Tanya rose wearily and kissed Caroline's cheek. "Good luck with the opening, little songbird. Please, please, be careful."

Katya put her arm around Tanya's shoulders and led her out of the apartment. Caroline locked the door, pleased that she was able to help her friend.

Sleepy at last, she turned out the light.

Chapter Thirty

THE BARGE

Moscow River, October 8, 1997

The secure room had lurched sideways and stopped shaking. Peter lay on his back, eyes wide open, but he saw nothing. *Am I dead?* He pushed away the boxes and tried to stand. Disoriented in the dark, he fell hard on his elbow. *I hurt too much to be dead.* When he tried to stand again, he realized that the room was askew—jarred loose and tilted by the blast of Golokov's mine. He felt along the walls, praying that he would find the door before he ran out of air. He was lightheaded by the time he found the handle and raised the bolt.

The door opened a crack. Something heavy blocked it from the outside. He pressed his face to it and sucked in smoky air. The oxygen revived him. He realized that the chamber outside was as dark as the room. *Maybe I can force this door open.* He wedged a heavy box against it to keep the air flowing and felt along the walls for some sort of tool. He tripped on an open crate. The contents spilt onto the floor. He slipped on loose firing pins, lost his balance and slid to his hands and knees.

He picked up a handful of the smooth metal pins, remembering Golokov's hands flitting around the mine casing like birds. He threw them down in frustration. He tried to stand but fell against the cardboard boxes. He ripped one open and ran his fingers over plastic-wrapped bars of clay. *The C4.* He tried the door again; it wouldn't budge. *I'm trapped.*

Exhausted, he sat on a box, startled when white light streamed through the crack, accompanied by the grinding of heavy machinery. The forklift was back.

"Stepan," someone shouted. "Pick up the whole damn thing and let's get out of here." The secure room vibrated to the screech of metal scraping through the rubble until the secure room lifted free. A sudden jerk forward slammed the door and sent Peter tumbling with the boxes again. The room bounced and lurched. With a final bump, the forklift rolled onto even ground. Pulling himself up, Peter released the bolt and threw his weight against the door. It swung open easily and he nearly plummeted headfirst under moving treads. The forklift was one of several in the process of boarding an unlit barge.

He pulled the door closed, then propped it open a crack—just enough to observe shadowy figures moving on deck. He heard Oleg shout to the forklift driver. "Did you get everything?"

"This load of C4 is the last of the explosives."

They cast off lines and the barge churned upriver. Men stood smoking on the stern. Beyond them, lumberyards lined the riverbank with brightly lit gigantic claws that slid back and forth on overhead tracks, shifting logs from one pile to another. The air smelled of sawdust, diesel, and cigarettes.

Stepan leapt down and secured the treads of the forklift with chains. He lit a cigarette and stood next to Oleg. "Who'd have thought that Piggie had it in him?"

"Did you see him do it?"

"I saw him with a goddamned mine in his hand. One look and I knew he was serious. Lucky for me this baby can hustle, or I'd be dead, too."

"How many did he take with him?"

"He shot Vanya and Misha upstairs. The blast killed four others. We're down six brothers. Where's UZI?"

"On the radio talking to the boys at Tver. We'll be docking in about an hour. Come on. Let's crack open that bottle of Rasputin and remember our lost comrades."

"That crappy vodka rots your bowels, makes you shit green." Stepan slapped Oleg on the back and the two men moved away. "Got pickles?"

Peter crouched behind the door, wondering what to do. He'd been running on adrenaline for hours. Sweat soaked through his clothes. He needed to calm down and think logically. He opened the door enough to chill his flushed face, but the icy wind made his eyes water. His wet hair froze. *It must be below zero.* If he didn't keep moving, he would freeze to death. He looked at the shoreline, trying to gauge how close they might be to Tver.

People walked their dogs under streetlamps along the embankment. Behind them rose blocks of generic apartment buildings that could be anywhere in Russia. *Think.* His greatest threat at that moment was hypothermia. He crawled to the back of the room, pulled cardboard boxes around him for warmth and considered his options. *I'm alive, I have a gun, and they don't know I'm here.* But when he thought about the factors aligned against his survival, he started to sweat despite the cold. Then he yawned. *I'm so sleepy.* He closed his eyes and dozed.

"It's freezing," laughed Caroline, slipping naked under his clothes. He enfolded her in his arms, warming his hands on her belly and thighs. "Yikes! You're an ice cube! This was a dumb idea. Couldn't you hide in a storeroom with heat?"

"I'll warm you up." He rolled on top of her, their bare skin belly to belly.

"That's so much better." She sighed. "Let's sleep a while."

Thunder shook the room, bouncing Peter around with the boxes again. He was startled by men's voices. "Those idiots triggered the claymores.... They blew up Konkova."

"On the bright side, they blew themselves up with it." Peter recognized the voice—UZI! "Those OMON sons of bitches are as dead as Piggie...."

Men laughed and cheered. Peter staggered to his feet and peered through the crack. The Kurzaniks were drinking and throwing vodka bottles on the deck. Glass shattered.

UZI stood a few yards away, his arms raised in victory. "Good-bye, Detective Twat and your rent-boy cops. Farewell Peter Stone and your blond cunt. May you roast in Hell, Piggie."

Rage heated every inch of Peter. He slid his hand around the steel grip of the Tokarev pistol and charged through the door.

Chapter Thirty-one

THE PARTISANS

Little Rodinko, October 9, 1997

> *"May there always be Mama,*
> *May there always be Papa,*
> *May there always be sunshine,*
> *May there always be me."*

Little boy Peter ran down rows of apple trees that stretched to the horizon, singing the Russian nursery song.

"Young Peter, where are you?" Denis, his father, called. "I have your favorite treat—blinis with honey."

Peter laughed and kept running. Leaves rustled. Branches, heavy with red fruit, groaned in the summer wind. He became a tiger, slinking unseen through the orchard—a predator choosing the moment to pounce on his prey. He leapt out with a roar and wrapped his arms around his father's legs.

Denis scooped him up, tossing him high until he fell into his father's embrace with shrieks of laughter. "You frightened me, Mr. Tiger," said Denis. "Come sit in the shade." They sat on a blanket, eating sweet, sticky *blini* pancakes from paper plates and licking their fingers. "You're getting so big and strong, son—like a real tiger."

Emboldened, Peter asked the forbidden question. "Where do you come from, Papa?"

The slap knocked him off the blanket. He scrambled to his feet, pressing a hand to his smarting cheek. His lips quivered. He struggled not to cry. Denis raised his arm to strike again. His voice trembled. "There are things that you must never ask. There are things that you should not know." Denis pointed to the house. "Go to bed and never speak of this again."

The dream faded. Peter awoke in a bed that wasn't his own, in an unfamiliar room that smelled like hot plaster. His body ached. A little girl with blond curls sat on the floor, coloring a picture. She sang:

"May there always be blue sky;
May there always be white clouds;
May there always be Mama;
May there always be me."

"Where am I?" Peter asked.

"Little Rodinko," the child said, without looking up.

"How did I get here?"

She jumped to her feet shouting, "Grandpa Igor, Grandpa Igor. The bad man woke up."

Bad man? Peter was lying shirtless on a cot. He was in a log cabin, a dacha. Most of the space was taken up by a Russian stove that radiated heat. His clothes were draped over it, except that they weren't his clothes. He'd been wearing a Spetsnaz jumpsuit and bulletproof vest with OMON printed on them when... *When what?* He couldn't remember. He tried to move, but his ribs caught painfully. When he tried to touch the sore places, he discovered that his hands were tied together. He saw three dense purple bruises on his bare chest. *How did this happen?* He closed his eyes until an old man poked him in the flank with a shotgun.

"Spetsnaz scum," the man snarled through bad teeth. "Wait till the comrade partisans see what I fished out of the river."

"How did I get here?" Peter groaned, struggling to remember.

"I'm asking the questions, smartass," the man snapped. "And the big question is: What's a lump of Spetsnaz shit doing in my river?"

"I'm not Spetsnaz. I'm American."

The old man cocked the gun. "Worse! Foreign Spetsnaz scum. Shut up or I'll blow your head off."

"Grandpa Igor, look!" The girl tugged on the old man's arm and pointed to the tiny window. Peter could see hunched figures moving through heavy snowfall. "Uncle Murat and Uncle Petya are here. Uncle Kolya, too. Will Auntie Anna be coming?"

"Yes, Lena, my dove. All the partisans are coming. We've waited a long time for this. Ask your mama to make tea and piroshky." The girl didn't move, so he called out, "Rita! Come get Lena and make us some tea!"

Three old men with shotguns crowded into the room. Peter noticed that Pashkina's Tokarev semiautomatic pistol had been disassembled and the parts displayed on a white cloth. The men seemed more interested in the gun than in Peter.

"What do you think of that little beauty, Murat?" Igor chuckled.

"Incredible," said the taller man. "These TT33s were built specially for Lubyanka. You can't even buy one on the black market. Good work, comrade."

"I keep telling you boys," smiled Igor. "Midnight's the time for eel fishing. That's when you catch the big ones. Look what else I netted." He tossed them the bulletproof vest. "We could have used a few of these during the war."

"OMON," said Murat, running his fingers over the white lettering. "That's what they call Spetsnaz in Moscow these days." He nodded toward Peter. "What're we going to do with him?"

"Hang him, of course," said Grandpa Igor.

"What? Hang me?" Peter struggled to sit up, but Igor pushed him back with the gun.

Murat was skeptical. "He's pretty young. I doubt he had anything to do with the Great Patriotic War."

"Then his father did, or his grandfather. Evil's in his blood. I can smell it on him." Grandpa Igor turned to Peter. "I'm asking you again, you goddamn scum of the earth. What's your name and rank?"

"I'm Dr. Peter Stone. I'm not Spetsnaz. I'm an American psychologist. I don't have a rank."

"You sound like a hoity-toity Muscovite to me," sneered another man.

"I learned to speak Russian in school—in America and at Moscow State University." Peter studied the weathered faces. They were ruggedly handsome men, even if they had barely a dozen teeth between them. They lit cigarettes and glared at him.

"What were you doing on a barge that belongs to that spawn of Satan, Alexei Kaminsky?" demanded Igor.

"He was on the Kurzaniks' boat?" asked Murat, surprised.

"Yep. Shooting right at UZI. He wasn't four meters away, but he missed every shot. Kaminsky didn't miss. He plugged our boy here three times and knocked him over the side. I thought he was dead. I fished him out for the Tokarev pistol."

"But he's alive," Murat said. "How can that be if Kaminsky shot him?"

"The vest saved him. Look at those slugs. They're stuck right in it. You can see where he's got bruised ribs, but he's alive enough for executing."

Peter remembered stepping out of the secure room, but the memory evaporated. When he pushed for answers, his memory rewound all the way back to childhood again. "I don't shoot people," he said, but images of the two men he'd shot in UZI's room—one with his skull blown open and the other grasping his throat and gurgling blood— materialized.

Recalling the stench of blood and gunpowder made him want to vomit. He coughed. "I'm not a killer."

"You're a liar," Igor shouted, jabbing him until he cried out in pain. "I saw you empty a clip at Kaminsky. The question is: How could you miss with a gun like that Tokarev?"

"I'd never fired any gun before last night. Yes, I tried to kill Kaminsky. Why do you want to hang me for that if he's the spawn of Satan? What have I done to you?"

"Explain it to him, Petya," said Igor, beckoning to a shorter man with a goatee. "You're the professor."

Petya cleared his throat. "It's not complicated, comrade. We are partisans and you're Spetsnaz. You killed our comrades, so we will kill you."

Peter blinked. "Partisans? What are partisans?"

Igor pointed the shotgun at Peter's head. "We're the death of you, that's what we are. We've had enough of your mind games, you Special Tasks psy-ops fuck!"

"Wait a minute," Peter struggled to remember what Pavel had told him. "Partisans… the heroes of Russian resistance, the freedom fighters of the Great Patriotic War."

"Right," said Murat. "We're the ones who saved Russia from the bloody Germans. We were too tough for those Kraut bastards. We could live rough and blow them to pieces every place we found them. Five hundred thousand of us brave souls there were."

Petya continued, "Whoever could lift a weapon took to the woods and fought for the motherland."

Igor smiled, "Best days of our lives, eh? Remember when we buried ourselves in snow outside the munition depot at Tula? Five days without food, but we blew those bloody Nazis to pieces. It's a miracle we didn't freeze our balls off—just lost some fingers and toes."

"We've had our share of miracles," said Murat.

"But did we get medals? No sir," said Petya. "After the war, Comrade Stalin set Spetsnaz on us. They hauled our heroes from their beds for hanging. Young lads, like us, were sent to labor camps. I was sent to Yakutia for ten years to work in the diamond mines."

The room fell silent except for the snap of wood in the stove. The men smoked. Peter watched them and strove to comprehend his predicament. "Why do you call UZI the spawn of Satan?"

"The Party's Gold, of course," said Petya, his eyes widening. "Didn't they teach you anything in America? It funded the secret police, the

Spetsnaz, while the Kaminskys made a fortune looting Russia and killing good patriots like us."

Peter shivered. *The Petrosyan Fund.* He recalled his father's words: "It's dirty blood money. I won't ever touch it again." When he looked up, the men were staring. "He's sweating like a goddamn Nazi collaborator," said Murat.

"He's playing us for fools," said Petya.

Igor leaned close. "So, you do know about the Party's Gold. What aren't you telling us?"

Deceit oozed from Peter's pores. *What can I say? My life has been nothing but lies.* To survive, he had to refocus their momentum away from himself and his secrets. "Don't partisans abide by the Geneva Convention? Russia is a signatory. I am an American citizen and that makes me your prisoner of war. I have rights."

"Okay, son, if you're American, show us your passport," said Igor. "I didn't find any documents on you. Believe me, I looked."

Peter paused. He had left his passport in his great-grandfather's suit at Lubyanka, Spetsnaz headquarters. He could hardly admit to that. "I left it at Kurzan Convent," he lied.

"Kurzan?" The men guffawed. "That convent in Moscow with the crazy nuns?"

"Yes. My grandmother is the Mother Superior."

"I thought you said you're American?"

"I have Russian family."

"Who's your grandfather, then? What's your Russian family name?"

Peter had said too much. "I don't know. Pavlov, I think."

"There you go pulling my shlong again," growled Igor. "Let's see if I've got all these lies straight. You came to Russia to shoot a gangster, but you can't shoot a gun. Your grandmother is a Russian nun who doesn't know who knocked her up. You're wearing the uniform of the secret police and carrying a special issue TT33 but claim to be an American psychologist. Do I have it right so far? Oh, and you're not carrying a passport?"

"Spetsnaz agents never carry documents," said Petya. "Who do you think you're fooling?"

"It's time for a hanging," said Kolya.

A young woman entered the room. She used hot mitts to carry a hissing brass samovar. Little Lena followed with a platter of piroshky.

"No, Uncle Kolya," she said. "It's time for tea."

Chapter Thirty-two

IGOR'S MIRACLE

Little Rodinko, October 9, 1997

Rita pulled a stool to Peter's cot while the old partisans drank their tea. She spoke to him in English: "This is all your fault. Yesterday they were just sweet old uncles and grandpas. Now they're fighting the Great Patriotic War again. I've never seen them like this."

"What did I do?"

"For one thing, you're lying to them. It's making them crazy. And if you think this is bad, wait until my aunt, Anna Lemirova, arrives." She shook her head. "She's a fanatic. I expect she's behind all this hanging business. I want to help you, but you've got to help yourself, and so far, you're doing a poor job of it."

"I really am Dr. Peter Stone from Seattle. I'm the chief psychology resident of the King County Psychiatric Unit at Harborview Hospital. You can call the Moscow Militia at GUVD, or Detective Pashkina at the Federal Bureau of Detectives. Better yet, call Martina Kay at the American Embassy. They know me. They'll come for me. I give you my word that these old men won't be in any trouble."

"I would gladly call, but there are no telephones in Little Rodinko," said Rita. "I'd have to get to the post office in Tver. In this blizzard, that would mean driving the tractor and it's too slow. They'd hang you before I got to the main road. Besides, if the police come, these old fools might decide to die in a hail of bullets." She looked askance at him. "Are you really a psychologist?"

"I am a physician and a forensic psychologist."

"That might be the only thing you have going for you."

"What do you mean?"

"Use your skills to try to understand these old soldiers. They might look senile to you, but don't underestimate them. And for God's sake, stop lying." She opened the drawer of a breakfront and pulled out a faded photograph. She held it up for Peter to see. "Here's Grandpa Igor and his comrades in 1942. There were twenty-five of them. By 1946, there were only five left—this lot and Anna Lemirova." Peter looked at handsome young men and women posed in a snowy wood. They were bundled in heavy coats and wore fur hats with earflaps. They looked like students on an outing, except that they carried rifles.

Rita pointed to a smiling youth with a head of blond curls, his arm around a stern-faced beauty. "That's my uncle, Yuri Lemirov, and his wife, Anna. He was their leader, a brilliant tactician. After the war, Spetsnaz hanged him in front of his house. Auntie Anna has never gotten over it."

"You and Lena have the same hair."

"This is Little Rodinko. Ten families have lived in this village for a thousand years."

"Rita! Stop fraternizing with the enemy," shouted Kolya. "Step away from the prisoner."

She replaced the picture and turned to the men. "I've been speaking with him in English, He is definitely American. We should turn him over to the police."

"Why? So that he and his OMON death squad can come back and execute us?"

"He's not a Spetsnaz agent. He's an American psychologist. Let the police sort this out before it gets any worse, please."

"Shut up, stupid girl," Igor raged. "How dare you speak to us like that. I let you go off to Boston University and you came back pregnant and spouting claptrap." He slammed his fist on the table. "Get back to the kitchen where you belong."

"I suggest you start telling the truth," she told Peter in English. "Now."

Murat tapped his watch. "First it's time for the news. Do the honors, Igor."

Igor plugged in an ancient box-style radio and fiddled with the squealing dials until they honed-in on the call sign of *ECHO Radio Moscow.* The weatherman opened with an emergency bulletin: "Weather stations from Karelia to Kaliningrad are reporting blizzard conditions with high winds and record snowfall in central and northwest Russia. Citizens are advised to stay home. The Transportation Ministry is working to clear major highways, but most rural roads remain impassable due to fallen trees...." Peter ignored the broadcast until the news reader came on: "Now the headline news from Moscow. Just two nights after the disastrous fire at the nightclub Moscow Traffic, the Kurzanik brotherhood suffered further losses during a federal raid on their commercial compound at Konkova. Eyewitnesses told *ECHO Radio* that two explosions flattened most of the structures there. Apparently, the first blast came from a tunnel beneath the compound. It was followed by an explosion on the main floor. An unknown number of Kurzaniks were killed along with decorated GUVD commander Alexander Golokov. It is also reported by the Federal Bureau of Detectives that one American woman was killed…"

"Noooo…" Peter groaned, recalling the barge and the rumble of thunder.

The signal deteriorated. Igor slapped the radio a few times and the news reader returned, but Peter was lost in grief. Caroline had felt so light in his arms. She'd been injured and weak, but she was alive. Did the claymores explode before they got her out? Was she trapped in the second explosion—the one he'd thought was thunder? He couldn't just lie there and think about it. Numb to the pain of his injured ribs, he struggled to sit up. Blizzard or no blizzard, he'd run all the way back to Moscow on foot, if he had to. "Nooo…nooo," he groaned again, trying to free his hands. "Let me go, you old fools."

The barrel of the shotgun jammed painfully against his ear. "Shut up! Somebody's coming," Igor hissed.

The partisans moved away from the window, melting into shadows until the little girl shouted, "It's Auntie Anna. Auntie Anna's here."

Igor's face brightened, and he lowered the gun. "Okay, Spetsnaz. Now you're in for it. You think we're tough, wait until you meet the Witch of Tver. Sit up and be respectful." He opened the door and a tall, lean woman swept in, trailing the scent of wet wool. She wore a long, black coat and heavy boots. A white braid hung to her waist. She carried a rifle slung over her shoulder.

She regarded Peter icily. "Is this the best you can do, boys?" She swaggered to the cot where Peter had finally managed to sit up. "Twenty dead partisans and you net me one puny Spetsnaz? Yuri was worth a hundred of this lousy excuse for human shit."

"He claims that he's an American psychologist and not Spetsnaz at all," said Rita. "I believe him."

"Then how do you explain these?" Igor handed Anna the vest and pointed to the Tokarev. "Lies. He's telling us nothing but lies."

"These were built special for Lubyanka." Anna inspected the pistol pieces. "Enough bullshit. Let's get on with the hanging."

"What's wrong with you," Rita yelled. "This is crazy," She wrung her hands in frustration. "Listen to yourselves. The Great Patriotic War has been over for fifty years. You are talking about murder. Turn this man over to the police or the American Embassy."

Anna slapped her hard across the cheek. "Stupid girl! He was wearing in a Spetsnaz uniform and that makes him the enemy. This is the kind of war that never ends."

"Auntie Anna, Grandpa Igor, Uncle Murat," cried Rita. "The war is over. You cannot kill this man."

Kolya grabbed Rita by the hair and shook her. "What's he to you, silly little bitch. What do you know about this man? Are you fucking him?" He looked to Anna, "I think this tart's starting to sound like a collaborator. We shoot collaborators."

"Stop it," shouted Igor, pushing Kolya away. "Rita, take Lena to the kitchen. Stay there until we are done. I mean it." Igor pushed them out of sight.

"What should we do now?" Kolya asked Anna.

"Dress the American in these." She tossed an old leather suitcase onto the cot next to Peter. "They're the clothes that Yuri died in."

Peter didn't move. "Put them on!" Kolya shouted.

Peter lifted his hands. "You will have to untie me."

"Do it," said Anna. "But if he makes a move, shoot him."

It was a slow, painful effort for Peter to pull on woolen coveralls and maneuver his arms into a stiff, brown sweater. At least he was getting dressed in warm clothes. There were heavy trousers, socks and boots in the case. Fortunately, the boots fit. He tied the laces and sat on the cot observing his captors.

The fight had gone out of Murat and Petya. They sat hunched on a corner bench and smoked. Igor stared out the window, looking more sad than angry. Anna clapped her hands energetically, "Come, comrades. Why such sad faces? Igor, let's look at our photos of the old days and re-member what we fought for. Where are the pictures?"

Igor brightened. He opened the drawer and pulled out stacks of old photographs, tossing them onto the table by the Tokarev. Many showed hanged bodies. Peter glanced at them, thinking of his father's death. Did Denis look like that— his neck stretched, his face swollen and discolored?

"Look at this one," said Kolya. "Isn't this the day we shot Masha Mash-inkova for sleeping with a Kraut? That's her body in the snow. Hard to tell with all that blood, but I'm pretty sure that's her."

"So much death," Igor sighed. "Far too many young lives wasted."

Anna held up a picture of a boy and girl holding hands. "Look at my Yuri—how handsome my husband was. He should have lived. We should have a farm with livestock and a garden. We should have children and grandchildren…" Her words trailed off when an engine rattled noisily to life, shaking dishes and silverware. The air was saturated with diesel fumes.

"What's that?" Kolya jumped up and cocked his shotgun.

"Someone's stealing the tractor!" Igor shouted. "Get to the shed." He tried to open a door at the rear of the cabin, but it was blocked. "It's blocked from the outside. Where's Rita? Where's Lena?"

Petya pointed out the window. "They're in the tractor." Something crashed against the front door. "They've pushed over the woodpile."

Murat put his shoulder to the door. "It won't open. We're trapped."

Petya shouted, "The window, comrades. Open the window."

"It's been nailed shut for years," said Igor. "And the panes are too small to climb through."

"We'll have to cut it open," said Kolya. "Where's your saw?"

"It's in the shed—with the ax."

Anna Lemirova shoved the men aside. "You idiots! Get out of my way." She lifted her rifle and smashed the glass panes with the butt. "Rita's a goddamn collaborator! She's worse than the prisoner." She took aim.

"Anna…Don't shoot!" Igor screamed. Peter lunged across the room and body blocked Anna. The shot missed Rita, but it hit the engine. The crippled tractor lurched out of control, spewing black smoke. It veered into the woods, bumping through underbrush and bouncing off tree trunks. Then it stopped, tilted onto its side and lay burning in a shallow culvert.

"Look!" Igor screamed. "Little Lena's lying in the snow. She's not moving! I've got to save her."

"Rita's not moving either," said Petya. "She's got blood on her head."

Anna struggled to her feet with murder in her eyes. She lunged for her rifle again, but Peter caught her, pinning her arms. She thrashed and elbowed Peter's ribs. He winced but he kept his grip on her. She tried to bite him. "Let me go, you bastard! I'll finish those traitors off. This time I won't miss."

"We have to open this door. My girls are going to die." Igor threw himself against it, but in vain. Kolya and Murat joined him, but it still wouldn't budge.

"Shoot the collaborator! Shoot the Spetsnaz scum," Anna howled. "You're all traitors."

Petya shook his head. "We need a miracle." He turned to Igor. "Where's Granny's icon—the one that saved your ass at Novgorod?"

"Haven't seen it in years." Igor yanked open drawers, throwing papers and photographs on the floor. He opened an old chest and tossed out clothes. "Here it is, the Virgin of Kurzan."

"Put it in the northwest corner. Hurry!" said Petya.

Igor propped the icon on top of the breakfront and knelt, crossing himself. It was mounted on a block of wood with a bullet lodged between the faces of the Mother and Child.

Anna struggled in his arms. "Put that abomination away," she screamed. "You're an atheist. There is no God! The church is a lie. That icon is a fake." She kicked and spat.

"Pray harder," Petya called from his post near the window. "The girls are running out of time."

The old man steepled his hands and pleaded. "Holy Mother, you took this bullet and saved my life at Novgorod. I've never asked you for anything more. I don't ask for myself now. But those are good girls out there dying…those are my generous, kind girls. They're freezing to death before their time because I've been a terrible foolish old man. I can't help them, so it's up to you—you and your precious Baby Jesus. I beg of you, save them. Please don't let them die…I'll do anything…"

Tap…tap…tap…

"My God," screamed Igor, raising his arms. "It's a sign from God! He's sent an angel."

"No, Igor. Look," Petya exclaimed, wiping condensation from the glass. "There's a man tapping on the window."

Peter stared in disbelief. "Ruslan!" he exclaimed. His grip on Anna loosened.

"Mujahideen!" she screamed, breaking free and grabbing her rifle.

Chapter Thirty-three

THE PENTHOUSE

New York, October 9, 1997

"**O**pen up, you bastard! I've got a warrant." Arthur Wellington pounded on Petrosyan's door. "That icon goes to auction at noon, you hear me?"

"Do we break it down?" asked the police sergeant.

"It's solid steel. You'll need a blow torch. This whole place is a fortress." Arthur continued to pound. "Open up or we're coming in!" He turned to the policemen, "Don't just stand there. Get your equipment. I've got an auction in two hours." They retreated to the elevator, leaving him alone in the hallway.

Arthur kicked peevishly at the door. Finally, he tried the doorknob. He was surprised when it turned and the door swung open. He stepped into the dark vestibule and felt for the light switch, flicking it a few times with no result.

"Petrosyan? Where the hell are you? It's freezing in here." He felt his way forward, pausing at the doors to the library. *Should I wait for the police?* He pushed them open and stepped in. "Petrosyan? Are you all right?"

Scorched air chilled his lungs. His breath froze in a vaporous haze. The Gothic ceiling was charred. Soot smeared the walls and glass crunched under his steps. The red leather portfolio with the icon's provenance was open. The *Book of Miracles* was gone. The rest of the ancient parchments were scattered around the floor.

"No!" He hurried to pick them up. Some were wet, the ink smeared. "If they're ruined, I'll sue you!" An upturned bankers' box had spilled out letters. He picked one up and recognized Denis's childish hand. He tossed them away, turning his attention to the upholstered chair facing the fireplace. Petrosyan had commanded the Kaminsky Empire from that seat for forty years. He was slouched there, wrapped in a blanket.

Arthur approached cautiously. His pulse pounded in his temples. "Are you okay, Pet?" He touched the old man's shoulder—no response. He pushed harder and Petrosyan slid to the floor. Arthur shrieked. He ran halfway across the room before he realized that there was no man, only a crumpled duvet.

"The icon," he exclaimed, staring up at the empty mantelpiece. The Virgin of Kurzan was not there.

Chapter Thirty-four

BABA

Kurzan Convent, October 9, 1997

Bong... bong... bong... bong...

"Make it stop," Caroline groaned. The mournful tolling of the Kurzan bell was magnified by the drugs still in her system. It echoed inside her skull and reverberated in her brain. She covered her ears, burying her face in the comforting scent of Baba.

A hand touched Caroline's cheek with soft, warm fingers. "I can't do anything about it, my sweet. The bell tower is above our heads." The voice sounded like Baba. *Another hallucination?* "Open your eyes, darling. I've come to take you home."

"Home," said Caroline, squeezing her eyes shut tighter. "I don't remember the way." She clenched her fists, pushing through the fog of memory until she stood in Baba's garden. Storm clouds blackened the sky over Puget Sound. Yellow running lights marked the shipping lanes even at midday. A gale whipped the pines and churned the sea. The air was thick with rose petals.

The red door to Baba's house opened and her grandmother stepped onto the porch calling: "Come home to me, precious. The world is a dangerous place."

"I'm trying." Caroline shouted above the rising storm. She opened her arms and took a step, but a fierce wind whipped her back toward the cliff. "Help me!" She leaned into the gale and fought her way toward Baba's embrace. The skirt of her nightgown billowed. It caught the wind, snapping like a spinnaker. She was sucked into the tempest and tossed far out to sea. "I'm drowning," she screamed.

"No, my darling. You are safe at Kurzan Convent. You've had a bad reaction to the shot the doctor gave you, that's all. It will wear off soon." Fingers stroked Caroline's cheek like Baba had done when she was a child. "Will you open your eyes and look at me?"

Caroline shook her head. "Don't make me believe you are here when you're not. I can't bear it."

"But I am here, precious. Detective Pashkina brought me from the airport a few minutes ago. She told me everything that has happened."

Caroline kept her eyes closed but reached up, searching until she touched Baba's face. "I feel your breath on my hand. You are so warm." She remembered touching Tanya and grew frantic, clutching at the bedclothes. "Tanya was cold, Baba. I wrapped her in my duvet and held her against my body like we learned in Mountaineers. I told her that she was right about UZI. He is a terrible man, a monster. I promised to take her to America. I put the diamond hearts in her ears, the ones that Peter gave me. She opened her eyes and smiled. She was about to speak when that awful bell started.

"God is calling for my soul," she sobbed. Strong arms gathered her in an embrace and rocked her like a child. "I saw Tanya turn into a white bird and fly out the window. Hundreds of cranes were flying. I couldn't find her. I couldn't save her."

"Darling, look at me."

Caroline opened her eyes wide. "It really is you." She ran her hands down Baba's arms, then hugged her tightly. "Oh Baba, I've been a fool…" The words caught in her throat.

"This is all my fault. I trusted an evil man. I signed his contract without reading it. I let him touch me. I've betrayed Peter with a monster."

"You are not the first, my darling." Baba sighed. "And you won't be the last."

Detective Pashkina appeared in the doorway. "I have good news. The Chechens have Peter. They are driving him to Moscow."

"Is he all right?"

"He seems to be," Pashkina replied. "He called on my sat-phone from the Tver Highway. I was bringing it to you when the connection failed. Maybe he will call again."

Caroline turned away. "I can't talk to him."

"But why not?" Baba stroked her hair. "He risked his life to save you. He loves you."

"He hates me." Caroline rocked on the bed. "I saw it in his eyes."

"I was with him at Konkova," said Pashkina. "What UZI did to you made him so angry that he chased the Kurzaniks all the way to Tver. He did that for love. He even shot at UZI."

Caroline gasped. "Peter killed UZI?"

"I don't know if he did or not. He'll be here in about twenty minutes and we can get the whole story."

"That is wonderful news, my golden one." Baba hugged Caroline. "Aren't you happy that Peter is coming? You will be together soon."

194

"He can't see me like this." Caroline relived the moment when Peter had knelt beside her and the look in his eyes stripped her of hope. Until that moment, she had been fighting for freedom and her life, defending her soul from UZI's onslaughts. Peter's eyes told her that she had lost the battle. "I'm dirty, a freak. Just look at my face." She drew up her knees and rocked back and forth.. "I deserve to die."

"Those bruises will fade in a day or two." Baba tried to hold her but Caroline pushed her away. "You will be your beautiful self, just like before."

"I will never be any good to anyone again." She was rocking faster, racked with sobs. The toxic storm in her blood was winning the war for her mind. "I should be dead. Even the embassy says so."

"You don't look dead to me." Baba stroked her hair. "You will get your new passport and the three of us will fly back to Seattle—you, me and Peter. Everything will be all right."

Bong… bong… bong… bong… .

"That cursed bell. It's coming for me," Caroline screamed, her eyes wild, her pulse racing. She could no longer fight the madness. "It is time to die." She broke free of Baba's embrace and ran for the window, clawing at the latch, struggling to open it.

The window flew open. Caroline climbed up onto the sill. Pashkina pulled her down and restrained her, pinning her arms from behind. "Let me go!" Caroline fought to break free. She was inches taller, but the detective held tight and wrestled her onto the bed.

Caroline thrashed and screamed through her delirium. She was back in Konkova, face down on UZI's bed. "Get off me, you devils. UZI, stop them…Don't let them hurt me…Save me! Save me!" The Kurzaniks swarmed over her, holding down her arms and legs. She fought back but they overpowered her. "Let me go!"

"Hold her still," said Plotkin, hurrying into the room. "I'll sedate her with something different."

Caroline saw the hypodermic needle and fought harder. "Stay away from me, you murderous quack!" A needle pricked her neck. A flush of drugs swept through her body in a soothing tide. The bell stopped. Her panic deflated, she rolled onto her back and whispered, "Thank you."

"What did you give her, doctor?" Baba asked.

"Demerol," said Plotkin. "It's stronger than I'd like, but the sedative from this morning made her hyperactive—it happens sometimes. We found her in bed with Tanya trying to revive the corpse."

"Oh, my poor child," Baba murmured, her hand on Caroline's arm. "What have they done to you?"

"The good news is that she'll recover completely once we get the drugs out of her system—physically, at least."

"But what about her mental state?"

"Not my department." Plotkin looked at his watch. "It's time for hospital rounds. I will be back in a few hours to check on Dr. Stone when he gets here. Lord knows what damage he's inflicted on himself in the last twenty-four hours."

My mental state? Caroline wondered. She floated in the arms of the Virgin of Kurzan. Together they hovered high above a woman with a swollen, purple face. *Is that me?* Her multitude of cuts and purple bruises had been painted yellow with iodine. *Such unbecoming colors.* A blond braid coiled over the woman's shoulder and nestled between her breasts. It hissed at her. "The snake!" She gasped, batting at her chest. "It's trying to bite me."

"Hush, my golden one," Baba whispered. "It is only your beautiful hair."

"Cut it off!" She struggled to sit up, but the room spun.

"Poor blondie," said Dr. Plotkin from the doorway. "I saw her at the Pushkin Theater on opening night. What a beautiful Antonida she was. Such a voice. This is a fairytale gone wrong, eh?"

"All fairytales go wrong," said Baba.

Caroline let out a long sigh. She floated back against the pillow and surrendered to sleep.

Chapter Thirty-five

THE RETURN OF PETER STONE

Tver Highway, October 9, 1997

The snow was three feet deep on the Tver Highway. They barely seemed to be moving. Peter used his sleeve to wipe the windshield of the Chechens' UAZ off-road vehicle. It did nothing to improve visibility under the onslaught of falling snow. He swiped at it again until his pique got the better of him and he snapped at Ruslan: "Can't you drive this damn tank any faster?"

"There's a blizzard," said Ruslan. "Do you see any other vehicles on the road?"

"I don't see anything at all." Peter sat wedged between the Chechens in the overheated cab. He was exhausted to the point of the jitters and had not eaten in twenty-four hours. Ahmed had filled him in on what happened at Konkova. Now he was laser-focused on reaching Caroline at Kurzan. He squirmed in his seat, afraid that if he stopped fidgeting he might fall asleep and never wake up. His stomach growled loudly.

"I know how you feel," said Ahmed. "We haven't had any food either. Even sheep dung shawarma would taste good about now."

"Don't worry Pyotor. You can sleep." Ruslan said. "Caroline is safe at the refectory. We have armed men around the building and Dr. Plotkin is looking after her. He said she would recover."

"The Petrosyan Fund paid for everything," said Ahmed.

Peter frowned. "You contacted the fund?"

"We tried to contact Petrosyan in the usual way, but he didn't answer his phone. Detective Pashkina traced the number that you called from Lubyanka and we reached Mr. Karlov who is well known to us. He helped us finance our business in Grozny."

"You contacted him without my permission?"

"You would be dead if he hadn't paid us to go after you," said Ahmed. "Those partisans were ready to hang you."

"How did you find me—in Little Rodinko, of all places?"

"We drove through all of the villages along the river looking for the barge. Most of those roads aren't paved and it was tough going in the snowstorm, even for our UAZ," said Ahmed. "We were approaching Tver when the blizzard let up long enough for us to see the burning tractor. Igor's cabin was fifty meters further."

"When we got there, a little girl was unconscious in the snow," said Ahmed. "Her mother was trapped in the tractor. We pried her out with a crowbar. She revived the child and stayed with her in the warm UAZ while we checked out the cabin."

"The old coots were stuck inside," said Ruslan. "I didn't know you were in there until I looked through the window."

"That's when that witch, Anna Lemirova, tried to shoot us," said Ahmed. "Thanks to Allah and your excellent tackle, she missed."

"Yes, thank God." Peter checked the dashboard clock and fiddled with the dials of the radio, to no avail. "We left Tver five hours ago."

"In weather like this, slow and steady wins the race," said Ahmed. "It would be a shame to kill you on the Tver Highway after so much work to rescue you."

"These UAZs aren't fast but they are the best military transports the USSR made," Ruslan added with pride. "Equally good on sand and snow. We used them in Afghanistan, Iraq, Chechnya...."

"Where are we now?" Peter asked.

"Outskirts of Moscow," said Ruslan. "About two hours from Kurzan. Ahmed is correct—slow and steady gets us there alive."

"Can you try the sat-phone? We might be close enough to get a call through," said Peter. "Caroline doesn't even know that I'm alive. I thought she was dead, until you told me. The radio said an American woman had been killed at Konkova."

"The news story was a fake to fool the Kurzaniks." Ruslan switched on the phone. "No signal."

"Keep trying."

"I will. You should get some sleep. I can wake you when I get through to Kurzan."

Peter fought to stay awake, as if he could make the UAZ move faster by sheer will. But the snow falling against the windshield proved hypnotic. The sticks and rags that passed for wipers clicked rhythmically—back and forth, back and forth until he dozed.

Bong...bong...bong...bong.... Peter opened his eyes, startled by the sound. The blizzard had cleared. Sunlight glistened on the pristine white city.

Snowplows were venturing onto the roads. In the distance the blue domes of the Church of the Kurzan Goddess rose above the trees. "What's that noise?"

"The Kurzan bell. It must be tolling for Tanya's funeral," said Ahmed. "We're getting close."

"I've got Detective Pashkina on the sat-phone," said Ruslan. He passed it to Peter.

"Hello, detective. Can I speak to Caroline?"

"She's upstairs with her grandmother."

"Baba's there?"

"Martina arranged it with your friend Lex Frasier. They decided that if Caroline couldn't go home right away, they would bring Baba to Russia. Frankly, we didn't know if you were still alive. The odds were not in your favor. Where are you now?"

"Close enough to hear the bell. Fifteen to twenty more minutes in this tank, according to Ruslan. Please, let me talk to her."

Peter waited and listened as the static on the line crescendoed. "I will try... not herself..." The connection failed.

He swore and gave the phone back to Ruslan.

"We're almost there," said Ahmed. "Fifteen minutes on the road or five if we cut through Kolomeno Park."

"No contest," said Peter. "Through the park."

"Hang on!" The UAZ bounced off-road, across the sidewalk and through the forest, dodging between trees. After a few minutes, they reached a clearing behind the Wooden House Museum. They drove onto the service road, which had been cleared, going off-road again when they reached a wide field. They crossed it, leaving two lines of tank treads in the pristine snow and stopped at the south gate. Peter jumped out, ran across the courtyard, and banged on the door. A young sister opened it and stared open-mouthed as he rushed past her with Ruslan and Ahmed close behind.

"Where's Caroline," he demanded.

"She's upstairs. But you can't go up there yet."

He nearly collided with Detective Pashkina on the stairs. She spread her arms and blocked his way. "Slow down, Dr. Stone. We've finally got Caroline settled. Dr. Plotkin gave her an injection and she is sleeping, which is what she needs most. Baba is sitting with her."

"I need to see her—just to know that she's all right."

"Follow me." She led him up the stairs to the room where Caroline slept. Baba was curled on the bed beside her, also asleep.

Sister Makarova put her fingers to her lips, then covered the women with a duvet. "Let the ladies rest," she whispered, shooing them out and the door.

"My poor Caroline." Peter descended the stairs. The relief of seeing her safe in Baba's arms crashed his adrenaline high. He sat down exhausted on the bottom step. "Her face—all those bruises."

Pashkina sat next to him. "Her injuries will heal, and she'll be beautiful again—different maybe, but still a beauty. What did you tell me? Faces always look worse than they are."

"I know," he said. "I need to take my own advice. Her bruises will fade but the psychological trauma? That's what worries me most. How deep does it go? Will those wounds ever heal?"

"I told you, she won't ever be the same. You must accept that."

"You recovered, didn't you?" he asked. "You've made a great success of your life. Commander Golokov even called you 'Supergirl.'"

"I'm flattered." Pashkina smiled. "He also called me a zealot and a twat. It's true. I became a vigilante. Law enforcement was my way of coping with the crimes committed against me. The federal police became my life—my only life."

"I can't imagine Caroline joining the FBI." Peter smiled.

"She will overcompensate in other ways. For me, busting bad actors was a way of proving my worthiness," said Pashkina. "For Caroline, it could be singing and stardom—a fierce ambition to be the best. She was a huge success at the Pushkin Opera. UZI stole her triumph for himself. Will she give up? Or will she fight back?"

"My money is on her as a fighter," said Peter. "When can I take her home?"

"Martina is at the embassy working on her passport. She will need it to fly back to America. Until that is done, there's nothing you can do but wait." She put her hand on Peter's arm. "Speaking of trauma and psychological damage, what about you? Everything has changed for you, too. Take this time to assess your own damages. You aren't the same people that you were, either of you."

"You're a better psychologist than me," said Peter. "I used to think that I knew what I was doing."

"Don't be too hard on yourself. I've thought a great deal about trafficking victims over the past few years."

"Tanya called me the 'wrecker of everything,' and I'm afraid she might be right." Peter rubbed his hands through his hair until it stood up. "Tanya was a good, brave girl. I owe her a debt that I can never repay. She saved my life and I failed her by letting UZI mess with my head. I let him do it again with Caroline."

"He is very good at it," said Pashkina. "I'll give him that. He is the master of the half-truth."

"Where is Tanya now?"

"Upstairs. Maria Pavlova and the sisters are preparing her body for the funeral. That's why the bell has been ringing. Most of Kolomeno will be making their way to the Church of the Kurzan Goddess for the viewing."

"She died in that church—in my arms." He looked away, trying not to see Tanya's half-closed eyes, or her blood on his hands.

"By the way, where's my Tokarev?" Pashkina patted her empty holster. "I hope you didn't lose it."

"Certainly not," said Ahmed. He handed her a paper bag full of gun parts. "It's all in there. The old partisans took it apart, but they couldn't get it back together again. They send their apologies."

"Partisans? What partisans?" Pashkina stared into the bag. "What the hell…"

Footsteps sounded on the stairs above them. The funeral procession had begun. The detective pulled Peter out of the way. Chanting priests descended the stairs in a line followed by the grim-faced mother superior, Maria Pavlova. She blinked in acknowledgement of her grandson as she passed by him. She was followed by two lines of weeping nuns, each with a flickering candle. Pallbearers carried the open coffin.

When they reached the bottom step, Peter glimpsed Tanya lying like a porcelain doll on a bed of red satin. *This isn't right.* Where was the feisty woman who had confronted him at the airport and risked her life to save his? Or the fair-skinned beauty smoking in the parking lot of the Hotel Ukrainia and holding her own against Oleg the Cossack?

"This isn't finished, Tanya," he whispered with murder in his heart. "I promise you."

Chapter Thirty-six

THE ATTORNEY

Kurzan Convent, October 9, 1997

The funeral procession passed through the refectory and into the courtyard. Peter tried to follow but Ruslan held him back. "You are exhausted. Sit down and have some dinner first." He pointed to the long refectory table set with heaping platters of pastry. "The piroshkies are onion, egg and cabbage. My favorite."

"I am famished," said Peter, "but I won't miss the funeral."

"Russian funerals go on for a very long time. The viewing can take hours. The actual service won't start until everyone in Kolomeno has paid their respects," said Ahmed. "You have time for piroshky."

"And here comes soup," said Ruslan. The sister placed a cauldron of steaming borscht on the table and served up bowls with a wooden ladle. A brass samovar hissed on the sideboard.

Peter finished two bowls of soup and six piroshky. He was starting on his third bowl when Pashkina returned with the assembled Tokarev. She set the empty magazine next to his plate. "You fired eight rounds. Who did you shoot? Was it UZI?"

"I tried," he said, staring at his blood-red soup. "I shot two men in UZI's room. They were about to kill Commander Golokov."

"So, what did happen to the commander?" asked Ahmed. "OMON found pieces of his uniform mixed in with body parts from several people. We went through the whole mess looking for pieces of you."

Peter pushed the soup away, his appetite gone. "He built a landmine and blew himself up. He took some of the Kurzaniks with him."

Ahmed looked skeptical. "He'd never be that careless. Golokov was a legend in Kandahar. He could make a bomb out of anything."

"He did it on purpose. He intended to kill UZI as well as himself." Peter remembered Golokov's final words. "He said, 'I'll send you a postcard from Hell,' and kaboom! That was it."

"Why weren't you injured?" asked Pashkina.

"I was locked inside a portable secure room filled with C4. After the explosion, the Kurzaniks loaded it onto their barge with me inside. That's how I got to Little Rodinko."

"Is UZI dead?" asked Pashkina. "Did Golokov kill him?"

Peter shook his head. "UZI's alive, no thanks to Golokov, or to me. I don't remember any of this, but the partisan who pulled me out of the river claims he saw me on the barge deck firing at UZI. I missed."

Pashkina raised her eyebrows. "With six rounds?"

"Apparently." Peter shrugged. "Then UZI plugged me three times in the bulletproof vest. I was knocked overboard next to the partisan's boat and woke up with the old man's shotgun in my face. There are still some holes in my memory, but that is pretty much it.."

"The partisans wanted to hang him because of the Spetsnaz gear he was wearing," said Ruslan.

"How did you get out of that one?" Pashkina snapped her re-loaded magazine into the Tokarev. She pointed it out the window and sighted down the barrel.

Peter recounted what had taken place at Igor's cabin. "Eventually, the old partisans came to their senses and took care of Rita and the girl. They were fine once they settled down. Uncle Kolya thinks he can fix the tractor."

"Even that crazy Anna Lemirova put down her rifle and made tea," said Ahmed. "Now the old coots want to canonize Pyotor. They figure that our arrival was a divine miracle."

"It seemed that way to me," said Peter.

Pashkina holstered the gun and ladled borscht into a bowl. She noticed his untouched soup. "Aren't you eating? You need your strength."

"That's what I told him." Ruslan thumped Peter's back. "You're a lousy shot, but a good body blocker, so bulk up." He slid the borscht toward Peter. "Eat."

He pushed it away. "It looks like brains."

Ahmed laughed. "You better get used to seeing body parts in your soup."

"Why do you say that?"

"You're a Kaminsky. Blood and brains are your fate," said Ruslan. "I recommend you learn to shoot, so that they aren't your brains next time."

Peter shook his head. "Caroline and I are going back to Seattle. I'll never touch another gun."

"I've just spoken with Martina," said Pashkina. "The embassy still insists that Caroline is dead. She still can't go anywhere without a passport, I'm afraid."

"Why didn't you take her to the embassy? Show them she's alive."

"We did that—directly from Konkova."

"Did that Tanner guy speak with her?"

"He did but Caroline was so drugged that she refused to answer him in English. They couldn't use facial recognition because her face is distorted. They fingerprinted her, but it didn't help because she isn't in any database. If Martina can't straighten this out, Caroline will have to show up in person once she's detoxed enough to make sense."

Bong… bong… bong… bong… .

"I'm going to the service." Peter stood. "I owe it to Tanya."

"We'll take the tunnel," said Ruslan. "Ahmed and I discovered a maze of tunnels under the church after UZI got by us and into the church. One of them comes out right here, under the refectory stairs." Ruslan tossed him the Kevlar vest with three dents in it. "Put this back on."

Peter held it at arm's length. "Do you really think the Kurzaniks will return?"

"Maybe." Ruslan shrugged. "Why take a chance?"

"What about Caroline?" Peter buttoned the heavy leather jacket that Anna Lemirova had given him over the vest.

"We have guards at all the entrances and on the roof," said Ahmed. "I'll stay here at the base of the stairs. Caroline will be secure."

"Go on, Dr. Stone." Pashkina squeezed his arm. "I'm sure that Caroline will feel differently about seeing you after a good rest and some dinner. Tanya's death was a terrible shock to her on top of everything else."

Ruslan's sat-phone squawked three times. He moved quickly to the window. "That's the lookout's signal." He peered through the curtain. "Someone is out there."

Pashkina unholstered the Tokarev. "It can't be law enforcement. My team is still at Konkova. More mourners maybe?"

"No…they'd be on the path to the church. There is a man coming through the courtyard pulling boxes on wheels…Wait! I know him!" Ruslan opened the refectory door. "Come in, Mr. Karlov. Welcome."

An elderly man in a camel-hair coat pulled a trolley stacked with bankers' boxes over the threshold. "Hello, Lieutenants. How's your halal meat business in Grozny doing?"

"Very well, sir. Inshallah." Ruslan shook his hand. "We have a second butcher shop in Nazan now. You won't regret your investment."

"Let me help you with your boxes." Ahmed rolled the heavy trolley to the table.

When he spotted Peter, the older man extended his hand. "And you are Dr. Peter Stone, born Pyotor Denisovich Kaminsky. I'm Daniel Karlov, your attorney."

"I'm pleased to finally meet you, sir." Peter stepped forward and shook hands with the man who looked like he'd always imagined him to look—dignified, with thick white hair, except that his beard was stylishly trimmed. "Why have you come?"

"Your grandfather told me to meet him at Kurzan. He flew from LaGuardia in the Learjet. I flew commercial from Gatwick. I'm a bit ahead of him but there's plenty we can accomplish before he arrives. You and I have years of lost time to cover, so we'd best get started.

Karlov shrugged off his coat and handed it to Ruslan. "Your grandfather is dying, I'm sorry to say. It is my job to maintain continuity in the management of his global affairs while everything is transferred to you as his heir. Any sign of weakness in the Kaminsky empire and there will be chaos. People will be hurt. We haven't a moment to waste." He rubbed his hands and looked at Peter expectantly: "Are you ready?" He sat at the table and opened the first box. Sister Makarova served him tea and a plate of piroshky.

Peter nodded and took a seat across from Karlov. His mind was far away in time, drifting down a long, paneled hallway where an old man stood in front of a fireplace. He had been four years old the last time that he'd seen his grandfather. Now, in Kurzan where this story began nearly a century ago, he had completed a circle and arrived at the moment of reckoning that he'd hoped would never come. He had ignored the Petrosyan Fund and locked away the unopened bank statements, doing his best to forget them. But the man in the castle in New York City had not forgotten him—the photo albums made that clear—and the burden that had destroyed his father was about to become his. The guilty knowledge that had driven Denis to hang himself was there in Mr. Karlov's boxes.

As he watched Karlov stacking thick files on the table, he longed for the bland certainty of his office in Harborview's locked ward with its austere, gray furnishings and bank of video monitors that pried into the lives of the insane without his having to touch them. He sensed that, that kind of certainty was lost to him forever.

A sister came downstairs to report that Baba and Caroline were sleeping peacefully. Another sister brought out a fresh apple tart to the table and served it to them.

Barely audible over the sound of the Kurzan bell that tolled again, Peter heard the *thwump...thwump...thwump* of a helicopter.

Chapter Thirty-seven

Long-ago Love

Kolomeno Park, October 9, 1997

Petrosyan Kaminsky made his way down the metal steps of his silver Learjet and onto the tarmac of Vnukovo Airport. A liveried chauffeur held open the door of an idling black Volga. "Welcome to Moscow, sir. We had a blizzard this morning, but it's turned into a lovely afternoon."

Petrosyan leaned on his stick and squinted into the sunshine. He was in no mood for a chatty chauffeur. He grunted and shuffled silently toward the car. The driver reached for his aluminum case. "Let me put that in the trunk for you."

"Hands off." Petrosyan grabbed it away. "This stays with me." He held it to his chest and eased onto the backseat.

"Do you have any more luggage, sir?"

"No," he said. "I'm not staying."

The Volga exited to a rural avenue lined by leafless poplar trees, their bare branches dusted white. Petrosyan observed the distant gray blocks of Soviet apartment buildings. Their stark ugliness reminded him why he never returned to Moscow. "I need a drink," he said. "I ordered Krystal Premier."

"It's in the bar, sir. Just pull down the back of the seat."

Petrosyan broke the seal on a fresh bottle and stared through the window. People bundled in black coats and fur hats scurried toward a covered bus stop. Beyond their dark silhouettes, white fields sparkled under a cloudless sky. The Volga slowed. "What's the problem?" Petrosyan prodded the driver with his finger. "Can't you drive faster?"

"I'm sorry, sir. We're stuck behind a snowplow. They're clearing the roads."

"Well, pass the damn thing. I haven't got all day."

"Yes, sir." The Volga passed on the right, skidding along the icy shoulder. Thirty minutes later, the driver announced that they'd entered Kolomeno Region. "That round building on your left is the Atomic Research

Center and the long brick building on your right is the Nuclear Cyclotron. We're turning onto Andropovsky Boulevard. We're almost there."

Petrosyan scowled at the traffic— ramshackle buses and trams packed with sour-faced commuters. "There used to be apple orchards from here to the Moscow River," he said, recalling the day that he and Ephraim had left Kurzan. They'd driven their Zil through a tunnel of fire. He recalled flames from the burning orchards arching over the roof of their car, blistering the paint. Petrosyan blinked and the flames vanished.

"Long before my time, sir. You might find some apple trees at the Wooden House Museum in the park. That's where Kolomeno Settlement used to be."

"And Kurzan Monastery? What's it like now?"

"An eyesore, sir— a disgrace, nothing but ruins. Nuns are trying to restore it as a holy place, but how? It was a prison for children. The land is cursed."

"I heard there was a night club nearby— Moscow Traffic?"

"In an old KGB warehouse next to the cemetery. It burned down a few nights ago. We could see the flames from our flat five kilometers away."

"People died?"

"Cooked alive down in the old tunnels. It was terrible." The car turned through a wrought-iron gate and stopped. "This is it, sir—Kolomeno Park. It looks like they've cleared and sanded the footpath. There must be a funeral today." He opened Petrosyan's door. "Are you sure you want to get out? I could drive you to the convent."

"I'm getting out right here." Petrosyan handed the driver his case to hold while he worked his way out of the car, ignoring the man's proffered hand. "I won't be needing you again," he said. "Just leave my case on the ground."

He waited until the car drove off before picking up the case. It seemed heavier than before. "What are you up to now, Zemyna?" he grumbled. In answer, the case handle flared with heat. Petrosyan dropped it on the frozen ground. It sprang open revealing the Virgin of Kurzan wrapped in leather. "How dare you play games!"

He leaned on his knees and snatched the icon from its protective covering, dropping his walking stick in the process. Black spots swam in front of his eyes when he bent down to retrieve it. When he stood back up, he realized that it wasn't his cane in his hand, but an old crosier used to carry icons in processionals. He'd kept it for years in his umbrella stand. *I must have grabbed it instead of my walking stick.* The icon radiated heat again, burning his fingers. "Okay, okay. I know what you want." He mounted it on the crosier.

The assemblage was surprisingly light but raising it above his head required two hands. *How am I supposed to walk without a stick?* He tested his footing on the gritty walkway. A gust of wind nudged him onto the foot path and after several tentative steps, he felt lighter. The pain in his spine eased and his knees no longer ached. *I'm getting younger.*

He entered Kolomeno Forest through the ancient Gates of Muscovy amongst the second growth of snow-rimed birch, larch, and poplars. With the broad strides of youth, he followed the familiar path of his childhood. Above him soared ancient white Siberian pines. The kedrs were the only trees that had survived the orchard fire of 1928. *Granny always said that kedrs don't burn.* He reached a clearing where a carved sign said: "Welcome to the Kolomeno Wooden House Museum—Absolutely No Smoking."

Petrosyan looked down on an idyllic village of two-story log buildings. The architecture was perfect. The doors were freshly painted in bright colors. The window glass was spotless with geraniums on every windowsill. The layout of the houses and barns was exactly how he remembered. He could name the families who had lived in each of those homes for generations.

"Something's not right," he muttered, staring at the pristine homes. Where were the smoking stoves, rotting fences and moss-covered walls? He sniffed the air—no stench of outhouses, or fermenting slop buckets. And there should be apple trees everywhere. He blinked with the realization that he was looking at a modern reconstruction—nothing more than a museum.

"Come penitent…" The icon lifted him off the ground, transporting him through time.

"You can't do this to me," he shouted, flailing his legs.

The snow melted on the ground beneath him. Pale green leaves unfurled. Wildflowers sprouted from the earth. The air grew thick with pollen and petals. He recognized the scent of apple blossoms. Cattle lowed in attached barns. Pigs and geese patrolled the yards. A white stone church with a golden dome gleamed at the near end of the single street. At the opposite end stood the wooden synagogue with its bright green shutters. "This is the past. It can't hurt me," he said, but his heart pounded wildly. *The past is the past,* he repeated in his mind like a mantra. *It can't hurt me.*

The citizens of the settlement strolled along the street in their summer clothes. He floated unseen among them, a ghost from another era. A dog barked. Children kicked a ball, raising a cloud of dust. He smelled the familiar aromas of burning peat, compost and freshly baked bread.

A young man in a European-cut gray suit and Italian shoes swaggered past with a bouquet of wildflowers. "That's me," he said. "It's 1928. I was twenty-two years old. I'd been working as an agent for Joe Stalin for three years." He approached the only brick house in Kolomeno. "That's the home of the mayor, Artyum Pavlov. And there's my beautiful Maria Pavlova, his daughter."

A long-legged beauty with a mane of golden curls swung out toward him, her hand on the rail of the front porch. Her hair was a flaming corona, backlit by the sun that revealed every detail of her body through her thin muslin shift.

She lowered her eyes and raised them again coyly. "Good morning, Petrosyan."

"You're very beautiful, Masha."

"I'm sixteen years old today."

"I've brought you flowers." He held them out to her delight. "Now that you've become a woman, I guess I can't call you Masha anymore."

"Yes, you can always call me Masha, Pet. In America, I will change my name to Marsha."

An upstairs window flew open. Mrs. Pavlova's head poked out. "Maria Pavlova—get into the house this minute. You can't go outside in your nightgown. You're a young lady now."

"You're so lovely," Petrosyan whispered, "I'll wait for you by the forest at dusk. I have something important to show you. Will you come to me?"

"Of course I will."

Mrs. Pavlova spotted Petrosyan, "Get away from my daughter, you filthy Jew." Maria slipped into the house and closed the door. From the window, she blew him a kiss.

The old man looked up at the icon. "By then, I was a rich man. I could buy and sell every soul in Kolomeno. I was the perfect match for Maria Pavlova. We were going to marry on the ship to America and make our home in New York but those Pavlovs thought I was dirt on their shoes." He floated along the central road toward the synagogue. Its shutters were thrown back, the windows open. A baby cried. He heard the cantor intoning prayers for a bris and his mother's cheerful voice chatting with other women in the kitchen. They were boiling soup bones. The air smelled of marrow.

The crosier warmed in his hands. It lifted him over the synagogue and forward in time. Below him, Mayor Artyum Pavlov's automobile raised a streamer of dust before stopping at his home. At the far end of the meadow, a young man sat smoking in a copse of trees. "I waited there until she came. I had our tickets to America."

Maria Pavlova emerged from the house with her arm raised against the low-hanging sun. Her skin was milky white, and light glowed through her hair. She wore a pale-yellow shift that was too short for her. When she leaned over a fence to scratch the nose of a pony, her skirt rode up, revealing smooth, white calves and knees. She began to dance—careless, detached, drawing closer to the edge of the meadow. When she saw him, her lips curled in a smile. Her cheeks flushed. "Hello, Pet."

He stood up, brushing the forest from his clothes. "Come here, Masha." He held out his hand. She approached him shyly and took it. He lifted her chin with his other hand and kissed her.

"Do you love me then?" she asked, raising her arms to encircle his neck.

"Of course. There is no one else for me."

"When will you take me away with you?"

"Tonight." He held out two tickets for the passenger ship Frisia. "This is what I wanted to show you. We take the train to Hamburg and sail for New York in the morning."

"How wonderful," she beamed.

He kissed her cheeks, the nape of her neck, her collar bone. She opened her mouth to his. "This is how much I love you." He slid his hands up her shift, caressing the curve of her spine. He bent her backwards over his right arm, sliding his left hand to her breast.

"Oooh," she shivered, easing back until she rested on the soft bed of leaves that he had prepared for her. She raised her arms above her head and closed her eyes in surrender. He pulled off her panties, separated her knees and pushed into her gently. She winced when he groaned his release.

He rolled onto his back. She cuddled against him, curled in the fold of his arm. "Did I hurt you?" He asked stroking her cheek. "It always hurts the first time."

"No, Pet. You could never hurt me." Her earnest wide eyes melted his heart. "Are we man and wife now?"

"Yes, in spirit, my love," he said. "We will be married in law before we reach New York." Their lips met. He entered her again. This time she moved with him, matching his passion with her pleasure. He took his time and they climaxed as one.

"In America, you must call me Marsha." She laughed and tickled his nose with a long stem of wheat grass. "We can learn English on the boat."

Across the meadow, a door slammed. Masha's father stormed from the house, cocking his shotgun. "Maria Pavlova, where are you? What are you doing?" he shouted.

Maria leapt to her feet. "I have to go."

"No, don't go to him." Petrosyan tried to stop her. "Come with me. Now. We'll leave this minute."

"I need to pack my things."

"I will buy you all new clothes. You will have the latest fashions from Paris, the best shoes, hats, jewelry—whatever you desire. But you must come with me now. I don't trust your father."

"Don't be silly. Mama and Papa will be happy for us." She pulled her hand away and sprinted out of the woods calling, "I'm here, father."

Her father caught her by the arm and squinted at the blood between her legs. "Who did this to you?" he demanded, shaking her, "I'll kill him." He spotted Petrosyan and sighted down the barrel of his gun. "I'll shoot you, you goddamn kike."

"No, Papa," Maria screamed, pushing up his arm. The shot went high, raising a flock of pigeons. "We're getting married and going to America. I love him."

"You love that Jew? How long has this been going on?" Pavlov turned on her. "You've dishonored your family!"

Her eyes were wide with terror. "It's not like that. Petrosyan loves me and I've always loved him. I've known him all my life. We will be married on the boat. I have my ticket."

"Stupid fool!" Pavlov slapped her, knocking her to the ground. He reloaded, scanning the woods. She jumped to her feet, fighting him for the gun.

Mrs. Pavlova came running. "Oh my God," she wailed, shaking her daughter. "What have you done?"

"I am Petrosyan's wife, or as good as." Maria pulled up her skirt. "Do you see? I'm going with him to New York."

Mrs. Pavlova gasped in horror. "Where are your panties? There's blood on your legs." She turned to her husband. "Our family is ruined."

"This is your fault," Artyum screamed at his wife. "I told you to discipline your daughter."

They dragged Maria to the horse trough, stripped her, and pushed her under the cold water. Mrs. Pavlova was all business now. "Get the scissors."

While the mayor sharpened the scissors on a whetstone, she scrubbed Maria with a stiff brush, ignoring her cries of pain. Then she hacked off her crown of hair. It flew in golden wisps around the meadow. "Thank God, no one else saw anything."

"Dress her in black. We're going to the bishop," Artyum announced.

Chapter Thirty-eight

THE PETROSYAN FUND

Kurzan Convent, October 9, 1997

"Sign here, here and here," said Karlov indicating colored tabs.

Peter signed, then pushed aside the stack of papers. "I'm late for a funeral,"

"Your cousin, Tanya Pavlova—yes, very sad," said Karlov. "I must extend my condolences to the Pavlovs before I go. Now don't worry, Russian funerals go on for hours. You won't be late. The sooner we finish, the sooner you can go pay your respects." Karlov pushed the documents back to Peter. "This is for the Petrosyan Fund, making you the sole trustee as well as the beneficiary. Sign at each tab and initial each page."

"I've had the Petrosyan Fund all of my life. What's different now?"

"Your grandfather wants to protect you after his death, which will be very soon."

Peter signed. "Done." He set down the pen and rose to go. "We'll do the rest of this later."

"Oh, no." Karlov pulled another stack of papers from the box. "We've barely begun. These boxes contain the documents for each of the accounts that must be turned over to you as specified in Petrosyan's will—preferably notarized and filed before he is dead."

Peter looked at the stack of boxes. "How many accounts are there?"

"Two thousand, seven hundred, and sixty-seven enterprises, involving one hundred banks around the globe." Karlov opened another folder and pushed it towards him.

Peter picked up the pen but was overwhelmed by a premonition that this was precisely what his father had warned him against. He tossed the pen away. "I just want everything to go back to normal."

"You've only had a normal life because of Petrosyan's protection. He has kept you safe under a glass bubble, so to speak."

Peter recalled the albums stacked by his bed upstairs. "You mean the creepy photographs? The private detectives?"

"Surveillance was necessary for your safety," said Karlov. "If Petrosyan had not been informed that you were on that Aeroflot flight and hired the Chechen lieutenants, UZI would have picked you off as soon as you set foot in Russia. You would be a corpse by now. They'd be burying you, not poor Tanya."

"Petrosyan had Caroline kidnapped? How did that protect me?"

"I make no excuses for your grandfather's morality," said Karlov. "If I made judgments on wealthy people like Petrosyan Kaminsky, I wouldn't have many clients. I was relieved to hear that Caroline is safe and under Dr. Plotkin's able care."

"We are leaving for home as soon as the embassy gives her a new passport."

"That's fine." Karlov looked at his watch. "Petrosyan should have landed by now. We can all fly to New York on the Learjet."

"I'm taking Caroline back to Seattle."

"You need to understand," Karlov frowned. "There's no possibility of you returning to Seattle."

"What are you talking about?" A knot tightened in the pit of his stomach—the same galling sensation that he'd felt when forced to leave his father. He had devoted his life to never feeling that way again. "We're going home to our houseboat."

"That's not going to happen." Karlov pushed another folder to Peter and pointed. "Sign here … and here. Finish with these and then I will explain."

Peter swept the stack of papers onto the floor. "You have no right to tell me that I can't go home. I'm a free man."

"Yes, I know the story," Karlov said softly. "Denis told me how he'd set you free, that he'd made you a *tabula rasa*—a boy with no past."

"I promised him not to touch the Petrosyan Fund. Until a few days ago, I kept that promise. So, do not expect me to sign away my life. I won't do it."

"Your father was a sweet but hopelessly impractical person."

"This damn fund killed him." Peter leaned forward on the table and glared at Karlov. "It sucked the life out of him—drove him mad. He hung himself because of it, didn't he?"

"A terrible tragedy." Karlov shook his head. "I'm sorry to say it, but Denis was too soft for his birthright. He could take the money—the man loved to spend it—but not the responsibility. He thought he could change his name and run away. It didn't work for him and it won't work for you."

Peter's anger waned at the memory of the high stone wall around their ranch house. It was the only wall of its kind in Wenatchee. Denis had installed a solid steel gate that he kept bolted. Peter stood and moved to the window. Across the courtyard, candles flickered in the Church of the Kurzan Goddess. "I don't even know where my father is buried."

"There is far too much that you don't know. Now, sit down and hear me out while you sign," said Karlov. "I'm on your side."

"Old Pavel said that what I don't know could get us all killed." Peter sat. "Is that true?"

"Yes, it is. Just look at poor Tanya. What you have experienced these past few days is nothing compared to the danger you will face when Petrosyan is dead. You are the heir to a criminal empire that employs thousands of people—from politicians and CIA agents to hitmen. Right now, they are afraid of Petrosyan and that has kept you safe. But will they fear you when he's dead?"

"I'm not a criminal. I can't even aim a pistol."

"But you are the heir. No king asks to be born a prince. Yet, princes are born, and you are the Kaminsky prince because you are Petrosyan's heir. The question is: What kind of king you will be? This is the privilege and the burden of your inheritance." Karlov stared over the rims of his glasses. "I hope that you've heard of the Party's Gold by now?"

"Yes, sadly." Peter nodded, visualizing the torrent of Russian blood that had flowed into his grandfather's coffers. "I don't want blood money," he said. "I'll give it back."

"That's what Denis said. But it isn't that simple. All fortunes are blood money, one way or another." Karlov smiled. "Over time, they take on a life of their own."

"I need more time to think about this," he said, rubbing his temples.

"There is no time." Karlov was emphatic. "You are in extreme danger until you sign these documents and so is Caroline. If you won't do this for yourself, think of that poor girl upstairs. An orderly transition must be made. Then you and she can go do what you want—with bodyguards, of course. Sell it all off and go save the world together if that's what you desire—just do it sensibly. Make a plan and stick to it."

"What if I refuse to sign? Why should I care what happens to the Party's Gold or the Petrosyan Fund?"

"If you refuse your birthright, the Kaminsky criminal empire will go to UZI, the next in line. UZI and the Kurzaniks will charter their international bank and ascend to great power. They will become an untouchable global force. Is that what you want?" He held out the pen. "Now, let's get busy. If we show one moment of weakness after Petrosyan's death, violence will erupt. Dozens may be killed in the power struggle."

Peter took the pen and started to sign. A week ago, he would not have understood the threat in those words. Five days in Moscow had changed all that. "I'm just one man. How can I stand up to criminals like the Kurzaniks?"

"Petrosyan did it by controlling the purse strings. I'll wager that you can, too. You're certainly stubborn enough." Karlov chuckled.

"Why didn't my grandfather just pick up the phone and call me. He could have stopped this madness from ever happening."

"Losing Denis was a terrible shock and he never got over it. Petrosyan was afraid that you might react the same way, so he always gave you the choice—to know or not to know. The opportunity was there for you. You had my card. You received the monthly statements. All you had to do was call and ask. You never did. All that accomplished, I'm afraid, was to postpone the inevitable. Now sign on the pages I've marked."

"What is this stack for?"

"The penthouse at Petrosyan Towers. It's a transported and restored 17th century castle overlooking Central Park. You'll find that it's quite lovely and very secure. You and Caroline can live there safely. Please sign and initial."

The castle in New York City—the memory of a time before Stone Farm. "I'll sell it and go back to my houseboat." Peter signed and pushed the folder back.

"You cannot go back to Seattle—at least not right away and never to a houseboat. You'll have to accept the reality of bodyguards and high-security facilities for the rest of your life."

"I'm not going to live in some castle. I'll sell it."

Karlov sighed. "You can't sell. Petrosyan Towers is in a trust. When you have children, they become heirs and will share the use of the property on your death, but they can't sell it either. If there are no heirs, the property will become the Petrosyan Library. You're not authorized to sell any of the furnishings or books. Nor can you sell any of the numerous works of art." Karlov pushed the file back to Peter. "Now get started on the next batch. We've got a long journey ahead while you get educated and take the reins of power. I'll help you find your way through Petrosyan's records. I'll introduce you to his team of attorneys and accountants. It may take months to visit the sites and meet the management, which you must do if you are to make informed decisions. Then I'm retiring."

"I'll sell everything and put the money into a foundation for peace or the environment."

"You can do that, but it'll take years. Much of the money is in real estate in places like Abu Dhabi and Kinshasa. Large chunks are in specialty trading platforms, which are not considered legal by most governments. Money is legally invested in gold, nickel, and cadmium mines, but they front for human trafficking rings and hide the profits from prostitution. The trafficking rings in turn transport heroin from Tajikistan and Waziristan to the United Arab Emirates. If you disassemble that process too quickly, your life will be worthless. That's not to say that you can't cash it all out, just slowly and not in my lifetime."

"What am I expected to do in the meantime?"

"Marry Caroline, move into the castle and start producing heirs. I've arranged for the Chechens to fly to New York with us to manage security in the penthouse until you get permanent staff and relocate to another secure home, if that's what you want. How you manage your empire after I complete your orientation will no longer be any concern of mine."

Peter set to work signing, barely glancing at the pile of documents that seemed endless. Ahmed and Ruslan kept watch at the windows. They were joined by two other Chechens that Peter hadn't seen before. He listened to their report, aware that his life now depended on these strange, war-seasoned men.

"What's our status?" asked Ahmed.

"There's activity along the park perimeter, sir," said the taller one.

"More mourners?" asked Ruslan.

"They just keep coming. The Pavlovs must be related to everyone in Kolomeno."

"And that's not all," said the second man. "A Sikorsky flew by about twenty minutes ago. It circled twice. We lost sight of it by the river."

"Could the Kurzaniks be coming back?" Ruslan asked, opening a pack of cigarettes. They each took one and lit up. "What are our tactical advantages?"

"We've dug defensible positions on the inner perimeter. The monastery walls are excellent cover."

"Disadvantages?"

"The riverbank drop-off is too steep. We can't see the river. We have limited visibility through the forest. That will become more of a problem after sundown. Also, the Kurzaniks know their way around the old tunnels and we don't."

"Sign here," said Karlov tapping a document and drawing Peter's attention. "Initial here, here and here."

The scout continued. "There's also some kind of procession coming through Kolomeno Park."

"Do they have weapons?" asked Ruslan.

"I don't believe so. It looks religious and there is news media following it—TV trucks and the like. It's about half a kilometer out near the Wooden House Museum and moving slowly, but it's definitely headed this way."

"Divert them if they get too close."

"Yes, sir."

"Where are the rest of the men posted?"

"We've got two on the roof, four guarding the walls."

"Good work, comrade." The men saluted and left.

"Congratulations," said Karlov clapping Peter on the shoulder. "This is the last one."

Peter flipped through the pages. "This is the contract for the Chechen lieutenants, isn't it?" He signed with a flourish. "That means that I'm now their boss." He stood and said to Ruslan: "We are going to the funeral."

"Yes boss," said the Chechin with a grin. Peter picked up a flashlight and followed him to the tunnel door beneath the stairs.

Chapter Thirty-nine

THE CABBAGE CAR

Kurzan Convent, October 9, 1997

Caroline woke up with a clear head and a voracious appetite. "Peter... where's Peter?" She sat up in bed.

"He has gone to the church to pay his respects to Tanya," said Baba.

"Is he all right? He wasn't hurt?"

"A few bruises but he's fine. He looked in on us while we were sleeping," said Baba. "He'll be back soon. You have time for some dinner and a wash-up."

"I'm starving. What's that wonderful smell?"

Sister Makarova entered with a steaming platter of piroshkies. A samovar hissed on the windowsill. "There is borscht in the tureen and sweet tea in the pot. If you don't mind, I'd like to go to the funeral as well," said the sister. "Ahmed is on guard downstairs, there are Chechins on the roof and Dr. Plotkin will be back soon."

"Go ahead, sister. We will be fine," said Baba. "We'll eat and clean ourselves up before Peter returns."

Caroline and Baba sat side-by-side on the bed and shared the platter of piroshkies followed by bowls of soup and cups of sugary tea.

"I've brought you something from home," said Bubba. "I thought these pictures might cheer you up."

"It's your chocolate box. How wonderful." Caroline pried the lid from the old tin box that had "Elysium Chocolate" imprinted in Cyrillic and a snowy winter scene of a troika pursued by wolves. She and Baba had spent hours exploring the old family photographs and inventing stories to go with them.

Caroline held up a faded photograph of the stone lions that had once flanked an elaborate iron gate. The snarling beast on the right displayed the crest of the Lukhinov family, the one on the left, the ancient shield of Rus. She smiled. "Do you remember how we'd sit under the quilt when the power went out and look at these with a flashlight?"

"Seattle in November. Happens every year." Baba laughed. "I kept us stocked up on batteries."

Caroline's smile faded. She stared out the window. "I want to go home. When can I go home?"

"Soon, darling," said Baba. "You must keep up your spirits. The embassy is working on your passport and Peter has arranged a private jet for us. Now rest and enjoy our keepsakes."

"This is you, Baba—when you were ten," said Caroline, forcing a smile and wiping her eyes. She lifted a tinted photograph of a blond girl in a cotton frock standing in front of the Lukhinov lions with an armful of daisies. Caroline ran her finger over the child's face, recalling the oft-told story of how her grandmother had escaped from the Bolsheviks by stowing away in the cabbage car of General Kornilov's death train. "This must be just before the Revolution."

"Look at this one. This was taken in happier times." Baba held up a picture of her mother, the Countess Lukhinova, standing at the top of the stone staircase at the entrance to the palace. She wore a dark sailor dress and a broad-brimmed hat with ostrich feathers. Surrounding her were children in white sailor suits and caps. Behind them, nannies and tutors were stiffly posed. Further down the steps, merchants and civil servants postured importantly. "This is the day my father presented the deed for a new school to the magistrate. Wasn't he handsome?"

"Yes, he was," said Caroline. Count Lukhinov looked gallant with his wavy white hair and handlebar moustache. Caroline pointed to a blurry figure at the edge of the photo. A little girl with a long braid had been captured in mid-jump, leaping from the edge of the fountain. "Do you remember this story?" said Caroline. "It was always my favorite. Tell it to me now."

"That's Caroline," Baba said, pointing to the photograph. "The wind blew your hat away. 'Run after it, precious,' I would say. Then I'd tell you how the playful wind carried that hat high above the trees and into the Lukhinov Palace rose garden. The flowers, blooming pink, yellow, white, and red weren't in the photograph, but roses were part of every story."

Caroline closed her eyes and ran through the labyrinth of rosebushes while the naughty hat danced ahead out of reach. She scampered through the stables where four white stallions whinnied and stomped. She came to the wrought-iron aviary with peacocks, parrots, and cockatiels. The hat skimmed through a green meadow where her pony Snowflake grazed and pawed the earth.

"Thank you for bringing our treasure box." She hugged Baba, forgetting how much she hurt. "These are my oldest, dearest friends."

"Yes, they are," said Baba. "Don't ever forget that." Baba picked up more photographs to spread on the bed. "I thought you'd need some happiness."

"I love seeing the Lukhinov Palace—the parties, the picnics, the balls. Your life was like a dream." A glint of light caught her eye. *The mirror inside the lid.* She hadn't seen any mirrors in Kurzan. Even the lavatory walls were bare. She lifted the mirror to her face, but Baba snatched it away.

Caroline recoiled. "Why'd you do that?" She looked down at the cuts and bruises on her arms. They had gone from purple to green and yellow. "How bad is my face?"

"It's nothing that time won't heal."

"Why can't I look in the mirror?"

"You can, when you're better." Baba took Caroline's hands in hers. "Right now, I need to tell you something important—something that I never wanted to say to anyone except that it will help you get through these difficult times." She took a deep breath. "I haven't been honest with you about the past, about our family."

Caroline held her breath. She had never seen Baba so somber. The Kurzan bell had gone silent, the room cold and still.

"All your life I've treated you like a child," Baba continued. "I made up a fairytale past to make you happy."

"I've always loved your stories. You made our lives magical." Caroline tried to smile but her jaw ached. "Remember the stormy nights when I was afraid of lightning? You told me funny stories about Thor and Vulcan and the gods of thunder who were no bigger than my thumb. They had little squeaky voices. We laughed and laughed. I wasn't frightened anymore."

"Of course, I do. But now I'm not sure it was the right thing to say. If I had told you the truth about how dangerous life really is, you might have been more cautious, less trusting, less of a dreamer. My fairy tales didn't prepare you for the evil in human hearts."

"Are you telling me that the Lukhinov lions weren't real?" Caroline stared at their picture. "This isn't our family in the photographs?"

"Oh, the lions were real. Lukhinov Palace is ... or was ... a real place. But I was just a girl when that world was swept away. Right after my tenth birthday, the lions disappeared. A few days later my father was arrested."

"Arrested? You said he went to Switzerland with your mother and they lived in a mountain chalet." Caroline held up a portrait of the count as a young man with his arm around his bride. "They died in a freak spring avalanche—on a picnic in the alps."

"I lied. The Bolsheviks shot him."

"What about the four white horses? You said they went to Austria and became Lipizzaner Stallions. And the peacocks?"

"We ate the peacocks. I don't know what happened to the horses. It was a terrible summer in 1918. Moscow was burning. Everyone was starving. Mobs set fire to anything that they couldn't eat. They were looting palaces and shooting aristocrats. They hung our neighbors." Baba was trembling, biting her lip.

"You don't need to do this." Caroline shook her head. "It's too hard for you."

But Baba was determined, her eyes fixed on the untempered truth of another time. "My brothers were in Siberia fighting in the White Army when word came to Moscow that the Tsar and his family had been murdered. The next day, Father was arrested. My mother and sisters and I were left alone in the palace. Our only hope of survival was to escape to relatives in Germany." She wiped her eyes. "We sewed Mother's jewels into peasant smocks and snuck aboard the night train to Berlin."

"You said that you stowed away by yourself in a cabbage car."

"That's true—but later. I started the journey with my mother and three sisters. There were no passenger trains anymore. People were packed into boxcars like cattle. The toilet was a stinking pile of straw." She shuddered. "We were huddled on a wooden pallet trying to keep warm. I woke up in the middle of the night when the train stopped. I heard a commotion outside and leaned out the sliding door to see what was happening. The train jerked forward, and I fell out. I was too small to get back in."

"Stop, darling Baba! You're making yourself ill." Caroline grabbed her grandmother's cold hands, frightened by her pallor. "You can tell me this once we're home."

"I want you to know how I fought for my life even when I thought there was nothing to live for. The truth of my struggle will make you stronger. It will help you survive like I did."

Baba pressed on. "A bright light blinded me. It was another locomotive, moving slowly toward us on a parallel track. This one flew the blood-red Bolshevik flag. Men were walking alongside it with guns. They pulled people from our train, forced them to strip and then shot them. They were approaching our car with my mother and sisters sleeping inside.

"I took a step back and fell down the embankment. That's all I remember until I woke up. It was morning with thick fog. When the fog lifted, the trains were gone. I could see bodies along the tracks, but I was afraid to climb up and look for my family." Baba looked away. "I wandered all day through the endless corn. I didn't see General Kornilov's train until I tripped on the tracks and stood in front of it.

"It was stopped. Soldiers sat in a pasture eating apples. They were skinny peasant boys with red stars sewn on their caps. I stood there, waiting for them to shoot me. After a while, a boy tossed me an apple. I took a bite. Then he pushed me to the ground and lifted my skirt. He forced something up inside me. I screamed and tried to push him away. But the others held my arms and legs. They covered my mouth. I couldn't breathe."

"Poor, dear Baba," Caroline kissed her grandmother's hands. "How awful."

"When he was done, the other boys did the same. I thought I would die but afterward, I ate their apples. Then they locked me in the cabbage car. Every time the train stopped, I'd hear the gunshots and screaming. Afterward, the boys would take me out. They'd make me drink beer and lift my skirts. When I fought, they beat me."

"I woke up one morning in a hospital in Berlin. They said it was a miracle that I was alive. I lay in a strange bed with strangers caring for me—just like you did here at Kurzan. After a month, my Aunt Sofiya, my mother's sister, found me. She took me to her apartment and informed me that everyone else in my immediate family was dead. Lukhinov Palace had been looted and burned, my brothers hanged. I'd lost everyone.

"I grew up in the Russian émigré community of Berlin. I married my distant cousin, Nikolai Lukhinov, and we had a son, Mikhail—your father. It was silently agreed among the surviving family that we would never talk about the past. It was a wound that hurt too much. We wanted to build a new life and live in peace.

"It wasn't to be. Russians who had just begun to build a new life for themselves in Germany were again taken from their homes and put into labor camps or shot, this time by Nazis under a secret agreement with Stalin. He was obsessed with stamping out White Russians.

"We were lucky. Your grandfather was offered a visiting professorship at the University of Washington and he brought us to Seattle. We bought the little house on Blue Ridge and the brown Studebaker. After the war, Nikolai returned to Germany as an advisor to the State Department. He knew that the work was dangerous but it offered us U.S. citizenship. He died in East Berlin. The State Department brought home his body and said they were sorry. I have lived on their widows pension.

"Your father changed his name to Mike Luke when he entered the University of Washington. As soon as he graduated, he was recruited by the

Marines. His Russian language skills were invaluable in Southeast Asia. Mike disappeared into the jungles of Vietnam and his body never came home. He didn't know about his daughter.

"You came to me as a surprise—a tiny gift from heaven with your pink cheeks and downy golden hair. You saved my life at the moment I had despaired of living another day. Keeping you safe and happy is all that has mattered to me ever since. But in the end, I failed you because I could do neither."

Baba looked into Caroline's eyes, her fingers touching the photographs scattered on the duvet. "Auntie Sofiya gave me the Elysium Chocolate box with these photographs while I was hospitalized in Berlin. They became my reason for living. Every time I looked at the pictures, my family cried out to me: 'Don't let us fade away. Keep us alive. Make our story beautiful.' So, I lied to you and for that I am deeply sorry. I thought that I could protect you by raising you in a world that has only happy endings. I forgot that there is no such thing.

"And when you brought Peter to my house, I saw him as the charming prince who would always protect you. Again, I forgot that no man is perfect." Baba touched Caroline's cheek. "We were happy together, weren't we? In our little house above the sea?"

"Of course, we were." Caroline wrapped the old woman in her arms and rocked her. "Let's rest a while—just the two of us under the duvet, like the old days."

"I am very tired," Baba said with a yawn. "It must be jet lag. I'll just close my eyes…" Soon she was snoring.

Caroline thought of the weather-beaten old cottage that was doomed to slide into Puget Sound and the Studebaker rusting on blocks in the garage. They'd never had a car that worked. She went to school with girls who had mothers and fathers and nice houses around Woodland Park. She was ashamed to have her friends over to play and grew adept at pretending not to care. The only time she was popular at school was when she sang, so she sang… and sang. She spent hours in Baba's garden playing a game called "when I'm famous," singing and dancing for their tabby cat Koshka, who lurked among the flowers.

There weren't any photographs of her mysterious mother in Baba's tin box. When Caroline had asked about her as a child, Baba brushed her off. If she insisted, whining and cajoling, Baba would take out the old sepia of the Lukhinov Estate and point to the little girl in mid-jump at the edge of the fountain: "There you are, little one. Hurry—chase the hat! The wind is blowing it away. Don't you hear the peacocks? They're saying that your mother's in the rose garden. Hurry or you'll miss her."

"Mama! Mama!" Caroline ran outside into Baba's garden. She searched under the shrubs and through the flowerbeds. "Where are you, Mama? Where did you go?"

"You're too late," Baba would say from the stoop. "She sailed to Vietnam with a basket of roses for your father. Look, you can see her ship's running lights crossing Puget Sound." Caroline would fall into Baba's arms and cry tears of frustration. She was always too slow to catch her. "Your mother and father are together now eating chop suey."

"Why won't she wait for me?"

"Next time." Baba stroked her hair. "You'll just have to be quicker."

"When I'm famous," Caroline would say with certainty, "Mama won't run away from me when I'm famous."

"That's a lovely dream," said Baba. "Dreams come true."

Lies, lies, lies! Her mother lived in Eugene, Oregon. Her name was Carla Orlova. Caroline had found the name on her birth certificate that she'd obtained from Swedish Hospital for her passport. It hadn't been difficult since the adoption by Baba was never formalized and the records weren't sealed. Carla was a graduate of the University of Washington where she must have met Mike Luke. Later, she married R. Rutz, MD. They had three sons. There was no further mention of her illegitimate daughter.

The next time Peter stayed on-call overnight at Harborview, Caroline loaded a basket with sandwiches and a thermos of coffee. She drove all night, traveling south on I-5 to Eugene. By daybreak, she was parked outside the Rutz home. There were lights on inside and movement—a family starting their day. Should she knock on the door? What would she say? "Hi. I'm your daughter." What if her mother slammed the door in her face? Could she bear it?

She decided to wait and watch for any sign that the plump woman in a rumpled lumberjack shirt, jeans and white trainers was really connected to her. She followed Carla through her routine of carpooling, shopping, housework and shepherding sons to soccer practice. By the time the noisy family returned to their tract house, the ache in Caroline's throat had spread to her chest. This woman had no place in her busy day for a grownup daughter. *I'll come back when I'm famous. She will care about me when I'm an opera star.*

She barely remembered driving back to Seattle except that it rained.

225

Chapter Forty

THE DUNGEON

A young sister pushed open the door to Caroline's room with her elbow. She carried a fresh pot of tea and a plate of apple tart warm from the oven. Caroline helped herself to a slice. She thought of waking Baba but the old woman slept peacefully.

"Where is Peter?" she asked, taking a bite of the pastry. "Has he come back from the church? Why hasn't he been to see me?"

"You refused to see him," said the sister. "You were very insistent."

"I don't remember. I've been drugged out of my senses." From the girl's wide-eyed expression Caroline knew that it was true. "Poor Peter. I must go to him."

"He's still at the funeral with Ruslan."

Tanya's funeral. "The church is just across the courtyard, isn't it?"

"Yes, ma'am," said the sister. "You can see the candles from the window. Pyotor and Ruslan took the tunnel under the stairs."

Caroline climbed out of bed. "Will you please sit with my grandmother? Give her tea and that delicious tart when she wakes up." She kissed her grandmother's cheek and tucked her snuggly under the duvet. "I'll be back with Peter."

"Yes ma'am," said the sister, pulling up a chair and taking Baba's hand.

Caroline crossed the hall to the room where Tanya's body had lain. Tanya's white fox fur coat and hat were hanging behind the door. She put them on over her linen night dress and looked for shoes. There weren't any. She padded barefoot down the stairs. *There must be shoes by the front door.*

Ahmed stood between her and the door to the courtyard. He was looking through the window with binoculars and talking on his sat-phone. She ducked into the shadows under the stairwell to avoid him. She'd have to wait until he moved away. She shifted from side to side on the stone floor, her toes aching with cold.

She stubbed her toe on something hard—a boot. She felt around the dark floor and found a row of heavy leather boots caked with dried mud.

She found a pair that should fit and discovered that they were stuffed with thick wool socks. She pulled them on.

She tried to stand. Her sleeve snagged on something—a metal hinge. While she worked the fur loose with her fingers, she recalled Sister Makarova mentioning a tunnel from the refectory to the church. Was this the door under the stairs? Could she get to the funeral this way without Ahmed seeing her go? She leaned out from the shadows and grabbed one of the flashlights. She switched it on and saw a latch. She raised it and crept down uneven stone steps. When she reached the earthen floor, her flashlight flickered. *Low batteries?* Should she go back and take another one, or hasten to the church? *How far can it be? Fifty yards maybe?* She shook the light until the beam was steady and hurried into the tunnel.

After several yards, the passage divided. *Which way?* She paused long enough to feel the cold climbing her bare legs. The fox fur over a nightgown was barely enough to keep her warm. Aside from her rapid breathing, the silence was absolute. She chose the larger tunnel, but there were side branches with footprints everywhere.

She paused at the next bifurcation and once again, chose the larger branch. The cold kept her moving. She shivered and longed for the crackling fire at Baba's house, recalling the night she first brought Peter there. She was only nineteen, wearing the first of her lucky green suits.

"That green matches your eyes," said Peter as they walked through the garden.

The afternoon sun was not kind to the old cottage with its faded blue shutters, and the red door with a childish sun that she had painted in grade school. It looked rundown and shabby. She would have to distract him until sunset. Everything looked better in the dark.

"I'm going to show you my secret place." She took his hand and led him into the garage where the rusty Studebaker had stood on blocks since before she was born. "Follow me!" She slipped off her green pumps and scampered up a wooden ladder. He followed her and they sat side-by-side on an old Smokey the Bear blanket that had always been there. "Look at the sea lanes." She handed him binoculars and pointed through a round window. "Those lights on Puget Sound are ships coming and going from Seattle. I'm going to go where they go. I'm going to sing in the great opera houses around the world."

"Why don't you swim out there and stow away?" he teased, enfolding her in the warmth of his arms, his cheek brushing hers. "Or I have a better idea. Let's buy a boat of our own—a houseboat. We can live on Lake Union." The sweet taste of his lips and tongue filled her mouth.

Later, Baba welcomed him into her parlor that smelled like cinnamon. "Come in. Come in." The house was clean and cozy with a vigorous fire. On the mantel sat a portrait of Caroline's father in his Marine uniform. "That's Mike, my son," said Baba. "Sit down, I'll make tea." Peter sat in a straight-backed rocking chair. Koshka the tabby cat jumped on his lap.

"You have a lovely home," he exclaimed. stroking Koshka who purred and kneaded his thigh.

"We are very happy here," said Baba. "This is our private world."

Across the expanse of Puget Sound cargo ships plied the shipping lanes in route to the Strait of Juan de Fuca and the Pacific Ocean beyond. But inside Baba's cottage time stood still.

How did everything go so terribly wrong? The Saturday of her blow-up with Peter had started like any other rainy Saturday. They had shopped for groceries at the upscale Thriftway Market on Queen Anne Hill. They cruised the aisles sipping lattés from Peet's Coffee and debating the merits of melons versus pears for chevre salad. They unloaded their parcels at the dock and rolled them to the houseboat in a metal cart. Peter steered it over the uneven planks. Caroline ran alongside, trying to keep the rain off the groceries with a plastic tarp that threatened to blow into Lake Union with each gust.

Once inside, Peter built a fire in the woodstove. The little houseboat warmed nicely. Caroline sang to radio KEWB and unpacked the soggy paper bags. Then she chopped pears and made chevre salad topped with a drizzle of balsamic vinaigrette. While the salad chilled in the fridge, Peter seasoned a red fillet of king salmon that they'd purchased fresh off a fishing boat at Interbay. With the fish in the oven, Peter opened a bottle of 1982 Bordeaux and poured them each a generous glass. They drank, and he kissed her. His lips tasted of red wine. Heat rose in her belly when he pressed his hardness against her. She leaned back and relaxed, feeling loved.

The wind howled. Water slapped beneath the floorboards. He kissed her again, pulling her against his body. The salmon popped and spattered in the broiler. She straightened and peered through the window. "There's a squall coming," she said.

Peter reached over her head for a copper saucepan. "In that case, I'll make hot chocolate with peppermint schnapps."

That should have been enough for my entire life. Why did I have to push for more? She knew the answer. There was a driver in her soul, a promise that she had made to herself long ago when she first understood what it meant to be an orphan.

They will love me when I'm famous.

****

The tunnel branched in every direction. Caroline spun around, lost. She should have been paying attention. Had she gone past the church? She must have. A cold draft blew through the tunnel, raising a familiar scent of decay. She froze in place, seized by the feeling that she had been here before. Had she veered off course and wandered all the way to the caves beneath Moscow Traffic?

Her flashlight flickered. She shook it—it blinked and died. Now there was only darkness. She felt her way along the walls for several steps. Another gust of cold air meant that a door had opened to the outside. Pinpoints of light bounced in the distance. *Flashlights.* They came toward her. *Peter's come for me. Everything will be all right.* She heard voices and froze again.

"Give me a Stoli." A flashlight shone on Oleg's face. A match flared. The glow of burning tobacco illuminated UZI's features. If either of the two men raised his torch, Tanya's white coat would glow like a beacon.

She flattened her back against the earthen wall, fearful that they could hear her pounding heart. The two men had just come through the same door they'd used on the night that UZI brought her to see the icon. The cell she had been locked in for three days must be close by. She dug her fingernails into the dirt wall and bit her lip.

"Tell Viktor to have the Sikorsky ready in twenty minutes," said UZI. "Now go. I need to be by myself."

"Why don't we just leave together right now?" asked Oleg. "The funeral will go on all night. You won't get another shot at Pyotor until it's over—too many people."

"I have more important work to do." UZI drew on his cigarette. "This is where I do my best writing. I always have."

"You spent too much of your childhood down here in solitary confinement." Oleg snorted. "Mother Warden's favorite punishment scrambled your brains."

"She did me a favor," said UZI. "Weeks alone in the dark made a poet out of me."

"Why can't you write your damn poems in Tver? Why can't you write on paper, or use a word processor like other people? Who writes on walls with nails?"

"I write with a fork. A good, solid Soviet fork," said UZI. "How else could I write in the dark? And what do you know about art, you stupid Cossack. Get out of here. I need to think."

"Okay, okay," said Oleg. "You have twenty minutes. Then the chopper's leaving, with or without you."

The door opened with another rush of cold. When it closed, she heard UZI reciting:

> One shot, two shots, three shots, four,
> Five shots, six shots—close the door.
> Seven shots, eight shots, nine shots, ten.
> Mama's not coming back again....

His flashlight moved toward her. Her knees buckled. She slid to the ground. She held her breath until she saw stars.

Chapter Forty-one

THE FUNERAL

Kurzan, October 9, 1997

Ruslan stood next to Peter at the back of the Church of the Kurzan Goddess. Black-clad mourners shuffled past them smelling of sweat and moth balls. They packed into the church with pale faces contorted in grief.

"Wait here," said Ruslan. He turned away, covering one ear, to answer his vibrating sat-phone.

Peter leaned against the rough brick and thought about the documents he'd signed. He had a fortune at his disposal. Maybe that wasn't all bad. If Caroline wanted a house in the Hamptons, he could snap his fingers and buy it for her. It would be big and airy, spotlessly clean, with windows facing the sea. If she wanted diamonds, he would cover her in diamonds. He could build her an opera house anywhere she wanted to sing. In a few hours, they'd be back in America—Seattle or New York, it didn't matter as long she was by his side. They could forget about UZI and everything that had happened in Russia. They would marry and start a family.

Peter hadn't been in the church since the morning Tanya died. It had been cleaned and decorated with pine boughs and flowers for the funeral. Candlelight revealed the shattered bones of the glorious church it once had been. Tiers of flickering tapers illuminated reproductions of icons taped to bare brick in each ruined niche. The hoard of villagers gave scale to the massive structure. They brushed against exposed arches and pillars, some of them reinforced with scaffolding or metal jacks, others merely propped up with rubble.

His hand brushed against a smooth patch of wall plaster. He examined it with his flashlight and found names crudely carved in it—Kolya... Vova...Valodya, dozens of names. In his imagination, the boys from Kurzan Prison materialized, ragged starvelings scratching on the wall. A little blond boy appeared, scraping frantically—UZI 1979, UZI 1980, UZI 1981. "Will you remember me?" he asked. Peter looked away. *How could*

I forget? The veil between past and present had been breached; the ghosts of Kurzan were set free.

The rich basso of an Orthodox priest rose and fell, intoning the litany for the dead. A choir of women's voices responded. The air was thick with incense and melting candle wax. The crowd swelled and surged toward a ring of tall candles. He was tall enough to see Tanya's coffin laid in the center beneath the dome where she died. He made out the jagged edge of the shattered kagan and recalled the deafening gunshot. "Tanya, Tanya," he'd screamed through the ocean roaring in his ears. He'd shaken her, staring into lifeless eyes until Ruslan climbed the ladder and said, "She's dead. You have to let her go."

Now Ruslan was back. "The old man's Learjet is parked at Vnukovo Airport. Petrosyan must be on his way here."

"When will he arrive?" Peter asked.

"No one knows. They're trying to find him." He detached a leather case from his belt and handed it to Peter. "Here's my sat-phone. Press one to get me, two for Ahmed, and three for Detective Pashkina in case we get separated."

"What will you use?"

"I'll get my spare from the UAZ."

"You're leaving me here alone?"

"You're hardly alone. There are at least a hundred people here with our Chechens on guard outside." Ruslan looked Peter up and down. He took off his black watch cap and pulled it over Peter's blond head. "That's better—less conspicuous." He put his arm across Peter's shoulders and eased him into the throng. "Go mix with the mourners. You'll be invisible."

"Where will you be?"

"I'm going to strategize with the detective about getting some federal help. If the Sikorsky's come back, so have the Kurzaniks. We need OMON."

Peter wanted to be anywhere except among the grieving Russians. "I'll go with you."

"You're safest here." Ruslan saluted and disappeared into the crowd.

Peter was pushed forward by an influx of new arrivals. They pressed in on him from every side, their gaunt faces framed by ragged caps and headscarves—an anonymous human sea of sorrow.

Before he realized it, he'd been pushed through the ring of candles and stood gazing down at Tanya. She looked perfect—as if she would open her eyes, light a cigarette, and call him an asshole. They'd have a good laugh. He'd give her enough money to buy her freedom and bring the whole Pavlov family to America. *Whatever you need, Tanya, I'll buy it for you—just come back.*

Something glittered under Tanya's hair. He leaned close and spotted the little diamond heart earrings that only Caroline could have put there. She had given the earrings to Tanya in life, and again in death. "I'm so sorry that I doubted you," he whispered. Every certainty he'd held about his judgment turned to sand. He stood unmoving, his feet rooted to the ground, afraid of sinking. The annoyed mourners had no choice but to push their way around him.

Old Pavel appeared at his side and took his arm. "Come join us, Pyotor." Yuri and Katya beckoned from the head of the coffin. He took his place with the Pavlov family. Katya squeezed his hand. .

Peter recognized the neighbors from Apple Street who approached on the other side. He nodded to Mrs. Pandova. She stood with Mrs. Karasova, who was sobbing into a handkerchief. The women from the parking lot of the Hotel Ukrainia were next. They laid flowers before the coffin. With faces scrubbed and red from crying, they looked like schoolgirls.

The priest droned on and sprinkled Tanya with holy water. Another priest swung incense, thickening the air with sweet, musky smoke. The sky darkened through the open ceiling. More candles were lit as dusk deepened until flickering light radiated from every niche and corner of the ruins. The choir drifted off key. Mourners murmured prayers for Tanya and for generations of loved ones who had left the world and moved on through the Church of the Kurzan Goddess.

If there had been a hundred people when Ruslan left, there were two hundred now. They could no longer move forward, although they kept trying. They knocked against the scaffolding that held up the domes. A board clattered to the floor, followed by the rumble of falling brick. Peter looked for a way out before what was left of the church collapsed but he was boxed in. No one else seemed concerned. The crowd had melded into a single organism that swayed to the hypnotic liturgy leaving Peter with no choice but to sway with them. He envied these people their grief that flowed over him, but not yet through him.

With no hope of escape, he finally closed his eyes in surrender. A dark swarm rimmed the edges of his inner sight, spreading like ink through water. Peter took a shuddering breath and let years of grief pierce his heart, slicing it deep. He gasped at the searing pain, jerking up his head, desperate to escape this place and these feelings. But the suffocating crowd was lost in prayer, each person consumed by private sorrows. No one noticed his distress or cared that the walls of his identity were crumbling, leaving his soul exposed and vulnerable.

The crowd shifted, allowing him to squeeze his way toward one of the niches where the brightest light flared. A dozen rows of candles illuminated an empty brick wall. The other alcoves held reproductions of the icons that had once been displayed there. He watched colors shift and swim on the brick until an image materialized. It looked familiar. *Grandpa Igor's icon—the Virgin of Kurzan.* Wasn't this the same icon that Petrosyan and UZI had kidnapped Caroline for?

"Where are you now?" he asked aloud.

"Come penitent…" A warm wind brushed his cheek like living breath. "Come into my temple." Peter blinked. He was alone in an empty church.

"Where are the mourners…?" His words echoed back to him through the perfect acoustics of a high, vaulted ceiling and well placed kagans. He stood motionless, enthralled by an elaborate iconostasis that rose to the ceiling under the domes. A host of saints looked down on him, encircling the mournful face of Jesus. Gilded mosaics of angels covered the arching columns to either side. At the high point of the middle dome, the very place where Tanya died, a white dove spread its wings. *The holy spirit.*

Tall candelabras illuminated wall frescoes painted in deep blues, reds, and golds. The polished floor was a mosaic of Siberian stones in all the colors of the ephod—pink marble, green malachite, purple charoite. The surface reflected the beams of sunlight that slanted through stained-glass windows. *Is this how it was before Petrosyan? Is all of this the Party's Gold?*

Gold tiles inlaid with floral mosaics decorated the niche where the Virgin of Kurzan was now displayed in its perfect beauty. A blaze of candles illuminated the delicate faces of Mother and Child surrounded by haloes of gleaming gold leaf. Precious stones set in the silver mantle reflected the light.

"Come…penitent…" The wind sucked him upward with such force that his ears popped. He hovered above the ruins of Kurzan. In the distance, beyond traffic-clogged boulevards, he saw the skyscrapers of modern Moscow. Below him, a procession moved slowly through Kolomeno Park. It followed behind an old man who floated several feet above the ground. He held aloft an icon. The glow of it lit the forest. Behind him trailed a ragtag host of the living and the dead.

"Who is that old man?" Peter asked.

"Petrosyan Kaminsky…a penitent."

"Who are those people with him?"

"Pilgrims...Muscovites, ghosts, and memories of pilgrims...."

The procession swelled as spirits emerged as wisps of light from branches, tree trunks, and fallen logs. Forgotten legions rose from the snow. Tatar horsemen galloped on piebald ponies. Pagan Balts wrapped in bear skins walked beside Cheboksary horsemen, Polish officers, Latvian soldiers, and Russian boys crossed themselves and marched in the uniforms of a thousand years of holy wars.

"My people love me..." said the wind.

Peter floated over the broken concrete angel that he had seen on his walk with Pavel. *The children's cemetery.* Little boys in rags huddled under her broken wings. A child ran toward him, followed by another. Soon, a crowd of boys scampered across the snow, shouting out their names. "I'm Seryosha—remember me." "I'm Stepan—remember me." "I'm Genya... remember me...remember me."

"What can I do for those boys?"

"Remember them," hissed the wind.

The vision faded. The church was once again a ruin. Around Peter, the crowd prayed and shuffled in constant movement. He rubbed his chest. His heart hurt. It had grown too large for his ribs. He could barely breathe from the pounding of it. A lifetime of grief shook free from his soul. He collapsed to his knees gasping for breath.

"Give him room...he needs air," shouted Pavel, pushing the crowd away.

Maria Pavlova knelt by his side. She wrapped her arms around him. Above her head, Peter saw stars carpeting the sky, winking through the open roof. "Are you all right, my dear child?"

Every fiber in his body shrieked with pain. His head throbbed, and his ears rang. He had been swept beyond the limits of his human capabilities and returned alive. He had survived the unwelcome invasion of powerful emotions, traversed the veil and finally discerned the core of steel in his own spine. He took his grandmother's hand and pressed it to his cheek, reveling in its warm strength. "Yes," he said. "I'm better than I've ever been."

Ahmed burst through the tunnel door. "Has anyone seen the blondie?" he gasped breathlessly. "She's gone."

Chapter Forty-two

ANOTHER VERST TO GO

Kolomeno Park, October 9, 1997

Moscow was abuzz. Word spread like lightning across the airwaves that there was a miracle in Kolomeno. Russia's lost icon, the Virgin of Kurzan, had returned.

Muscovites put on their coats and hurried to the park. They arrived on buses, trams and in automobiles to see for themselves and join the procession of the faithful. Every functioning bell in Moscow started to ring. They joined the basso of the Kurzan bell to spread cacophony over the city. The Kolomeno Park parking lot was jammed with believers, gawkers and TV news trucks that aimed their spotlights at the old man with the icon.

Petrosyan squinted, irritated by the growing crowd of living souls in heavy boots and fur hats that carried bobbing flashlights and candles. They were nearly as annoying as the dead whose murky world he was about to enter—those spiritual emanations that popped and glowed in the forest.

"We're almost there and I'm not dead yet," Petrosyan said to the icon. "Why don't you just bring me Pyotor and let's call it a deal."

"Patience, penitent. ..."

"I'm not your damn penitent. Put me down, now! I'm cold." He tugged at the crosier. It quivered and warmed in his hands.

"Remember..." A warm gust lifted him high over the old growth of Kolomeno Forest and into a memory of late summer. "Not 1928 again," Petrosyan complained. Apple trees bowed under the weight of ripening fruit. Waves of barley swept toward the river. Orchards and fields stretched from the forest across the river and up the other side. Gold stars on the bright blue domes of the Church of the Kurzan Goddess gleamed above the high white walls of Kurzan Monastery.

Below them, young Maria Pavlova crossed the courtyard and climbed the steps of the church. She wore a black wool dress with sleeves that hung past her hands. She clutched the skirt, which trailed on the ground. Her head was bowed, her shaved scalp barely covered by a black scarf. *My poor Masha. What have they done to you?*

Petrosyan heard her father, the mayor, shouting at the Bishop of Kurzan and glimpsed them arguing through an open window. Mayor Pavlov leaned over the bishop's desk, striking it with his fist. "My daughter is ruined. Our family is ruined. What Christian man will want her after this defilement? Damn that Kaminsky. Does he think I'd ever let my daughter marry a Jew?"

The bishop tented his fingers and replied in a deep voice, "Calm yourself, Comrade. The district magistrate will be here on Tuesday. He'll mete out justice where it's due."

"Justice? We won't get justice. Those Kaminsky brothers work for that devil Stalin. They'll pay off the magistrate... or shoot him."

"Comrade Mayor, we must have faith in our legal system. It's here to protect us," the bishop countered. "As to the girl, I gave her forty lashes with the birch switch. Isn't that enough? Why not let her marry Petrosyan and emigrate to America? So many young people are leaving these days. Who can blame them?"

"I forbid it," screamed the mayor. "No Jew will defile my daughter and go unpunished."

"In that case, Maria Pavlova will take the veil and become a novitiate as you've requested. Her husband will be the Church. The bastard child will be born in a labor camp. Its fate is in the hands of God and the CHEKA. In the case of Petrosyan Kaminsky, we will wait for the magistrate. What else can we do?"

"We can enact our own justice, that's what we can do."

"Stop that talk," begged Mrs. Pavlova. "You're the mayor of Kolomeno Settlement. You of all people should respect the law."

"Your wife is right," said the bishop. "Russia is a civilized nation. We have a government with laws that protect us. Maria and Petrosyan have committed no crimes except to love one another. I beg you, Mayor, let them go to America. Let them build their lives together in a new land."

Mayor Pavlov struck the desk again, startling the bishop. "Wake up, you fool! This government is looting monasteries from Irkutsk to Perm and selling the spoils. Their Party's Gold funds the very same CHE-KA that's going to kill you and dynamite this monastery. Petrosyan and Ephraim Kaminsky are their agents. Believe me, they'll come for Kurzan before the year is finished."

"I don't think we need to worry," said the bishop. "I have assurances from the Metropolit of Moscow that Kurzan Monastery is quite safe. Our 538th annual Procession of the Faithful is next week. They've denied us official permission again, but we don't anticipate any problems. Rabbi Epperstein told me that they were denied permission for the Feast of Av, but they'll be gathering at the synagogue tonight as usual."

"Will the Kaminskys be there?"

"I saw Dr. Kaminsky go into the synagogue about an hour ago," said Mrs. Pavlova. "Mrs. Kaminsky is probably baking with the other ladies. Most of our Jewish citizens will be there. Why do you ask? You're not getting any crazy ideas into your head."

"Monsters like Petrosyan Kaminsky have declared war on us. Not only are they robbing us of our daughters, they are destroying our churches *and* synagogues. They are beyond justice as long as they funnel loot into Stalin's black accounts to bankroll the Communist Party. What do they call it? The Party's Gold? You'll see. We'll all be under the heel of the CHEKA soon. Until then, I'm taking whatever justice I can get."

The mayor stormed out, slamming the door. Mrs. Pavlova hurried after him, shouting, "Artyum, wait! You're talking nonsense. Don't you dare do something foolish!"

****

"Come into my temple, penitent...." The icon lifted Petrosyan across the courtyard, up the steps and into the Church of the Kurzan Goddess.

"No," he muttered. "I'm a Jew. I'm not allowed." Candles reflected on the polished mantles of icons packed into every niche. Gemstones gleamed in the light of oil lamps. Intricate mosaics covered the walls with saints, and gilded arches rose to the top of the dome where the white dove soared. "We dynamited this to dust," he grunted nervously. "This is the past...it can't hurt me."

A gust pushed him into a brightly lit niche and toward the Virgin of Kurzan. He blinked and was inside the icon, looking out at the white oval of Maria Pavlova's tearstained face. She lit a candle and placed it among dozens of others. Her blue eyes brimmed with tears.

"Oh, Holy Mother, forgive me! I will devote myself to your Church for the rest of my days, but please, please don't let Papa kill Petrosyan. It was my fault that he sinned. I'm a wretched girl. I tempted him. I thought that Papa would let us marry and go to New York. I thought Mama would understand how much I love him. I have loved him since we were children."

"Masha, my love," old Petrosyan called out across the decades of lost time but she couldn't hear. The wind blustered and swirled, blowing him out of the icon and through the carved wooden doors of the church. They closed behind him with a bang.

He floated down the street of Kolomeno Settlement at dusk. The quality of light had changed, flattening buildings and leaching them of color. Night fell too quickly. The crosier burned in his hands. He sniffed the air—smoke! The synagogue was ablaze. Every window in town reflected flames. Someone screamed, "Help us! We can't get out!" *Mama! Papa!*

Villagers ran with pails of water, but the old wooden temple collapsed before they threw the first bucket. Smoke roiled from the ruins. Petrosyan glided through the gathering crowd, hearing their whispers: "The mayor threw a torch into the synagogue." "He wanted to kill Petrosyan, but he wasn't there...." "Everyone got out except his parents." "What will we do without Dr. Kaminsky?" "Mrs. Kaminsky was always so kind. How could they have such awful sons?"

Petrosyan kicked and shrieked. "Stop this! It's not my fault that Artyum Pavlov torched the synagogue." Petrosyan's words froze in a plume of breath. The crowd of villagers dissolved into the past.

****

He became an old man again. A young bearded monk walked beside him in the snow. "Welcome home, Petrosyan," said the Bishop of Kurzan in his deep basso.

"This can't be you. You look the same as the day I killed you."

The bishop stared up at the icon, crossing himself. "I've told the brothers that the Virgin of Kurzan is coming. They will join us soon."

"The monks? We killed them years ago. I shot you myself. You are all long dead. Kurzan is dead—it's finished. We burned it. There are no more bells."

Bong... bong... bong... bong....

"I know that awful sound," Petrosyan gasped in recognition. "That's the bloody Kurzan bell!"

"Of course, it is," said the bishop.

"That's not possible. We dynamited the bell tower. That bell made a hole a meter deep when it hit the ground. I ordered the Chekists to cut out the tongue and send it to Siberia."

"Yes, I remember," said the bishop. "Then everything burned."

The forest erupted in a sheet of flames that burned around them. Heat singed Petrosyan's skin. He kicked and struggled, but the hot wind carried him forward. "This is the past. It cannot hurt me." he screamed. "Let me free!"

"No, penitent..." hissed the fire. "You have another verst to go."

Chapter Forty-three

THE GIFT

Kurzan, Underground, October 9, 1997

UZI was so close that Caroline smelled his sweat. Her instincts screamed—*run!* But where? She couldn't go back. She'd never find her way to the convent without a flashlight. Moving forward delivered her to UZI. If she stayed where she was, he would see her the moment he raised his flashlight. She crouched against the wall, willing herself to dissolve into the earth. She hugged her knees, pressing her face into the fur.

A minute passed—nothing. Then a few feet away, keys rattled in a lock. A bolt scraped. A door swung open with the screech of rusty hinges. She knew the sound. He was in the room that had been her prison for three days. The light in the tunnel dimmed. UZI must have carried his flashlight into the room and left the door open. She heard him scraping at the walls. *This is my chance!*

Caroline took a deep breath and stood up. The way out of the tunnel, the way that Oleg had taken, was past that open door. She edged along the wall to the chamber. UZI muttered inside.

> *"Tanya, Tanya,*
> *Tainted rose…"*

The sound of his voice sapped her strength. Her courage flagged. What would Baba think of her now, splayed against the wall, paralyzed with fear? She thought of the brave ten-year-old girl clinging to life in a cabbage car. Baba had gone through hell with no one to help. She'd borne her secret scars into a new life in Seattle. She had only come forward and shared them because she thought it would help her granddaughter. What did Baba always say? "You only lose if you give up—so, never, ever give up."

Vignettes of Moscow Traffic, the cage, flames of neon and stage-smoke erupted in a hot adrenaline rush—a visual tangle of being dragged out of the Zil by the arms and hair…men stripping off her clothes…tying her to the bed…spreading her legs…running their hands over her body…UZI violating her.

She clenched her jaw. Her cheeks burned. Rage drove out fear. *I need a weapon.* She felt the ground and picked up a heavy brick. Her heightened senses screamed *kill him* as she crept to the door. She peered into the room.

UZI was on his knees with his back to her—searching the wall with his flashlight. He found something. "Here you are," he said, reading aloud:

> *"A shadow struggles in the light—*
> *Papa fills my doorway like a cornered bear!*
> *Hands grasp him from behind—*
> *Blood on the door frame!*
> *I blink,*
> *But he has vanished.*
> *'...until I'm home again,'*
> *He calls."*

Caroline shrank back. She too had a father immortalized in a frame, a picture frame—the official Marine Corps portrait of Mike Luke on Baba's mantelpiece. He had died a hero's death in the fairytale land of Vietnam where he ate mangos and papayas with her mother. *My life is a fabric of lies.*

She studied the steel door. The keys were still in the lock. All she had to do was to close it and lock him inside. But there was a problem—it opened away from her into the room. She would need to step inside and grab the handle. He would see her but there was no other way. *Am I fast enough? Strong enough?* She took a breath and stepped through the doorway.

He startled, leaping to his feet. His torch blinded her. "You're alive!" She threw the brick, striking him in the neck. He staggered back. She jumped into the cell, grabbed the handle, and pulled with all her strength. The door slammed. She slid home the bolt and turned the key.

She didn't realize that UZI had caught hold of her coat until she tried to back away. The fur was wedged so tightly in the door that she could barely move. She tried to squirm out of it, but the heavy coat held her captive in a stiff cocoon. The only way to free herself would be to tear the coat apart, or re-open the door.

She heard UZI breathing on the other side, mere inches from her face. "Is that my beloved songbird?" he cooed. "The radio said you died at Konkova. Thanks to God, it isn't true."

"Fuck you!" She pushed against the door until her arms and knees gave out, but the coat held her upright.

"I understand why you are angry. Open the door and I'll make it up to you."

"No!" She pressed her burning forehead against the cold metal while she caught her breath. A week ago, she had been a glamorous woman. Admiring eyes had ogled her as she dined and danced with this elegant man, this monster.

"Don't you like your earrings?" cooed UZI. "I was assured by DeBeers that they were the best diamonds that money could buy. I have them here in my pocket. I'll have a necklace made to match—if you'll let me out."

"Never!" She sensed his hands pressed against hers through the door. She jerked hers away. "I hope you die in there."

"Silly darling, you're a prisoner same as me. Only one of us will be saved. Who will it be? Who will come first—my Oleg or your Pyotor?"

Oleg! If he found her trapped like this, he'd snap her neck.

"We've become two halves of the same person," UZI went on. "If we work together, we can both go free."

"I am no part of you." She searched the seams of the coat. One sleeve was torn at the shoulder. She yanked at the threads, making the hole big enough for her fingers. What good did that do? Maybe she could loosen the stitching between the sleeve and collar. She might be able to slide out that way.

"We are creative people. We can write ourselves a happy ending if you'll open this door."

"Shut up!" she screamed, then berated herself. He fed on human emotions. To survive, she needed to take control of herself. *Breathe. I know how to breathe.* Years of vocal training had honed her skills at breath control. She could even inhale while singing a perfect note.

"Don't be angry at me, princess," UZI cajoled. "I am an imperfect man. I realize now that the Pushkin Theater wasn't good enough for you. Next time, you will star at the Marinsky or the Bolshoi. Will that make you happy?"

The gentle lilt of his speech fogged her mind. He was so close, only inches away. *Stop listening.* She struggled to dampen her rising terror but lost control. "I-I hate you," she sputtered.

"But why, my darling? I'm your patron. I invested money in you and made you a star. After your triumph in *Ivan Susanin*, I was the one you came to."

"You raped me!"

"You invited me. Don't you remember our kiss in the back of the Zil? Or how you let me open your shift and caress your breasts?"

In a burst of rage, Caroline ripped the coat's lining from collar to hem, but the fur remained flawlessly stitched. "Peter will kill you when he comes. He is ten times the man that you are."

"You greatly underestimate him. He's much more than that." UZI laughed. "My cousin Pyotor's fortune is a hundred times mine."

"Why do you say that Peter is your cousin?"

"He didn't tell you? Shame on Pyotor."

"How are you related?"

"Your Peter was born Pyotor Kaminsky. Our grandfathers were brothers."

"You're lying."

"You've never heard of Petrosyan Kaminsky, Pyotor's grandfather? Ask him where the Petrosyan Fund comes from."

"What are you talking about? What fund?"

"The Party's Gold. I'm talking about the stolen wealth of Russia. Look around you at the ruins of Kurzan. Look at the sad state of this looted country. Haven't you seen the mass graves and the poverty?"

"What does that have to do with Peter?"

"Ask him where the riches of Russia have gone?" UZI said it so softly that Caroline had to lean against the door to hear him. "Ask him how many Russians died—one million, ten million, fifty million—so that he could live life as an ignorant fool—a blank slate."

"You're lying," she gasped.

"Poor songbird. I'm the only person telling you the truth." UZI sounded sad. "You've paid a tragic price for loving him, haven't you? How did he repay you for your years of loyalty? Why wasn't he your patron? He could have picked up his checkbook and funded your career. He could have made a telephone call and bought you the starring role in any opera house in the world. Why didn't he? It would have been kopeks to him. Your love has been wasted, little songbird."

"I won't listen to you. I don't believe you."

"Ask him then. He'll tell you that he's one of the richest men in America."

"Peter risked his life to rescue me from Konkova...from you!"

"Completely unnecessary—foolish, really. One phone call from his grandfather and I would have set you free," said UZI. "He didn't call, so you were mine. It was just business."

"You are a liar," she gasped. "He brought OMON to save me."

"That may be true. But tell me, what did you see when you looked into his eyes? Remember—I was watching."

Caroline searched her memory. The rescue was a drug-soaked kaleidoscope of screams, explosions and giant OMON bubble heads that threw her into an oven. Nothing was clear except the moment her eyes met Peter's. What she had seen there was not love.

"It was disgust, wasn't it," said UZI. "He'll never forgive you for what you've done with me. You are damaged goods to him now that I've had you. He will think of me inside you every time he looks at your face."

His words cut deep. "I still don't believe you," she exclaimed. Yet she did. She was unable to shut out the revulsion in Peter's eyes.

"Even if Pyotor kills me, it scarcely matters," said UZI. "I should have been executed with the rest of my family twenty years ago. My mother bribed the Mother Warden to hide me in this prison so that she could die in my place. Spetsnaz didn't care whose bodies they tossed into the lime pit as long as there were enough of them."

"That's very sad, but I'm not letting you out."

"I only ask that you let me read you one last poem. It's one of my best. I wrote it on the wall down here after a month in solitary confinement. Let me bare my soul to you while I'm still breathing. Please, will you listen?"

Her back ached. Her fingers were numb with cold and bloodied from scratching at the door. She longed to lie down and relieve her trembling knees. "Do I have a choice?"

"No," he said. "None of us do." He began:

"I drift near
The edge of another lifetime,
Heralded by the smell
Of woodsmoke and thunder—
'UZI—come home!'
A woman's voice!
I must be vigilant
Lest I weaken and call out 'Mama!'
For then I'll run through tall grass
Toward the wood stove.
When the first drops of rain
Kick up red earth.
I'll see her in the kitchen—tall and strong
A white apron tied around her skirt.
I'll run into her arms,
Frightened by the lightning.
She will dry my face, towel my hair—

She has smeared flour on my face.
'Cookie boy,' she teases, kissing me.
She is soft and warm.
She smells of butter."

UZI's mother had loved him and given her life to save his. Her own mother had discarded her like unwanted trash. Whose was the sadder story? "What was she like—your mother?" she asked.

"She had long hair like yours. She liked to twist it on top of her head or braid it like you do. She was a sculptress—famous for huge stone monuments of mythical women. You can see them in parks all over Russia. When she left me with Mother Warden she promised it would only be for a little while, but her eyes couldn't hide her sadness. I knew that she was lying."

"She was a brave woman," said Caroline.

"You can see her soul in the sculptures. Her spirit lives on in her art."

"And where is my soul? My power?" Caroline wondered aloud, not meaning to.

"It's in your beauty," said UZI. "Men will kill to acquire a woman of such beauty."

Acquire my beauty? The irony of anyone possessing her scarred, battered body suddenly struck her as funny. She laughed. a little burst of giggles at first, that grew into peals of near hysteria. She laughed until she cried. "That's very funny," she gasped. "Coming from you. You destroyed my face so that you could own my beauty? How absurd. You are as much of a fool as the rest of us."

"I'm begging you," said UZI. "Let me be the one to possess you. You will recover and have everything a woman's heart could desire—a mansion in Moscow, furs, jewels, a Mercedes. I will protect you from all harm."

Caroline started laughing again until her sides ached. "You protect me from harm? That's simply too much," she said, wiping away tears. The tension had gone from her body. Her breathing was steady. Her hands no longer trembled. The wild pounding of her heart had slowed to a strong, regular rhythm. She drew in a breath—a deep singer's breath— with her diaphragm. It kindled a fire in her belly. The heat rose like warm honey to her throat. "My voice is my power."

"Sing for me, then," he said. "It would make me happy."

"I will sing, but not for you." Her speech was clear, her voice controlled. She stood as straight as the restrictive coat would allow and sang her favorite aria,.

"Queen of Heaven, Maiden mild
O, listen to this maiden's prayer!
For thou can hear amid the wild;
'Tis thou, 'tis thou can save amidst despair…"

The earthen walls dissolved. Caroline stood in the circle of kedrs. Puffs of pollen filled the air with summer snow. Peacocks fanned their tails. White horses grazed nearby. The aches were gone from her limbs. Strength returned to her body, flowing from her core to her fingertips. She was no longer cold and disfigured, but young, beautiful and unafraid.

Her hands were on the bolt and key. "I do not fear you," she said calmly. "Do you swear on the soul of your mother that you will never touch me again?"

"I swear it on the soul of my mother."

"No more talk of 'possession.' I am not property. Not yours—not anyone's."

"I swear it on the soul of my father and all the saints in heaven."

"And that you will keep the promises you've made to me? All of them?"

"I swear it. Your next performance will be anywhere that you desire. You will be swaddled in diamonds. I'll be a good patron to you and demand nothing in return."

"I want to sing Norma at LaScala. Promise me Milan."

"I promise."

She pulled back the bolt. UZI was free.

Chapter Forty-four

LADY OF THE LAKE

Church of the Kurzan Goddess, October 9, 1997

"She didn't go outside," said Ahmed, bending at the waist to catch his breath. "The door under the stairs was open. I ran all the way here through the tunnels—no sign of her. She must be lost underground."

"We've got to find her," said Peter, "before the Kurzaniks do."

"An OMON team will be here in a few minutes," said Ruslan. "They can help search."

Peter shook his head. "We can't wait that long." He started toward the tunnel.

"Stop, Pyotor," said Maria Pavlova. "That's an underground maze that goes for miles. There are caves and deep rivers. You don't know your way. We'll lose you too."

Pavel switched on his flashlight. "I'll lead," he said. He entered the tunnel, followed by Ahmed, Ruslan, and Peter. At the first split in the passage, the old man stopped. "This goes to the refectory. I'm not sure about this other branch, or this one. Footprints are everywhere."

The three men conferred. Peter paced, turning off his flashlight to save the batteries. Darkness closed around him. He listened to the odd echoes muted by soft earthen walls. Something brushed past him in the dark with the sound of rustling feathers.

He flipped on his torch to see the fan of a peacock's tail. *This is insane. I'm seeing Caroline's fairy tale.* He blinked—the bird was still there. It shook its feathers and strutted into a side-passage too low for Peter to stand upright. Before he could call the others the high, clear tones of Caroline's voice echoed from deep in the earth. She was singing Ellen's Song from *Lady of the Lake.* He knew it well. She'd sung it to him in Baba's garden, her voice raised to the wind, her hair a halo against the setting sun.

He crouched low and followed the peacock.

"What is that?" asked Ahmed.

"Schubert," Pavel exclaimed. "Caroline is singing *Lady of the Lake.*"

"Where is it coming from? It's impossible to tell." Ruslan turned, shining his light down each passage. "And where is Pyotor?"

"Pyotor! Pyotor!" they shouted.

Peter couldn't hear them. Their voices were lost in Schubert's ethereal song of love and disaster. Peter struggled to keep pace with the peacock. When the passage became too low for him, even in a crouch, he dropped to his hands and knees and crawled. The tunnel narrowed further until he could barely wriggle through. *I'm mad. I'll get stuck.*

He tried to back up, but his heavy jacket bunched and held him tight. It was forward or nowhere. *I'm going to die chasing a hallucination.* At a curve in the passage, his shoulders wedged. The walls of limestone bound him. He could go neither forward nor backward, so he rested panting, eyes closed, while the familiar words of Sir Walter Scott washed over him. Caroline sang:

"Queen of Heaven, undefiled,
The flinty couch we now must share
Shall seem with down of eider piled,
If thy protection hover there."

Using his toes, he inched his body ahead. His arms were pinned to his side, but he made progress until the tunnel widened enough for him to crawl on knees and elbows. Peter followed a glimmer of light and emerged into a niche in the wall. The singing had stopped. He froze at the sound of another voice.

"That was either very kind or terribly foolish," said UZI.

"It was neither," Caroline replied coldly. "You can't harm me anymore. None of you can. I am beyond your pain."

"I don't want to hurt you, princess. I want to love you. I owe you my life. I want you to be with me."

Peter peered around the corner to see Caroline in Tanya's white fur. She stood with her back to UZI, who leaned close to her, his hands extended but not touching her. Peter moved into a crouch, prepared to attack. He hesitated. The monster could grab Caroline by the neck and crush it with his thumbs. He cringed as UZI said, "All I ask is that you let me love you. Pyotor isn't good enough for you, my love. Take my heart as a gift. I will give you everything he has denied you."

Peter felt his blood rise. UZI was poisoning her with lies. Or worse, he had told her the truth. How could she listen to that monster? The forensic psychologist in his brain warned, "She has Stockholm Syndrome. She's mistaking her pain for love." If Peter attacked UZI, she might even defend him.

"These are yours. You left them behind." UZI whispered. The torch-light danced in colorful prisms as he dangled a pair of diamond earrings, the oversized bangles Peter had seen in Golokov's surveillance photos. "Will you make me happy by putting them on again?"

Caroline inserted the gaudy teardrops in her ears.

"What more can I give you to show my devotion? What more does your heart desire?"

"I want to be beautiful again." Her words tore at Peter's heart. He should be the one promising her the world. "Then I want La Scala."

"You shall have it, my dark queen, my druid priestess. You shall sing at La Scala."

"I'm going to kill you," Peter howled, launching himself at UZI.

"Peter!" Caroline startled, as if waking from a trance.

"Get away from her," Peter screamed. He had almost reached her when a blast of wind pushed him tumbling back in a cyclone of light, ice, and debris. The door had blown open.

Thwump… thwump… thwump… thwump…. Downwash from the Sikorsky pinned Peter to the ground. Oleg stood at the top of the stairs backlit by lights from the helicopter.

"Peter! He has a gun!" shouted Caroline. Peter ducked. A shot rico-cheted and echoed through the limestone caverns.

"UZI—get in the chopper. We're leaving," Oleg yelled. "Pashkina's back with OMON."

UZI started up the stone steps, pulling Caroline by the arm. They were halfway to the top when Peter overcame the force of the wind and lunged again. He wrapped Caroline in his arms and jerked her away. They rolled down the stairs. Caroline landed on top, knocking the wind out of him.

UZI wrestled with Oleg in the doorway. "I'm not leaving without her."

"I'll shoot that damn bitch before I let you bring her. She's ruining you." Oleg fired and missed again.

The door slammed while Peter lay gasping alone in darkness. He had lost his flashlight and sat-phone. "Caroline…where are you?" he called. "Come back" When he finally found the door and pushed it open, he couldn't find her. "Caroline…Where are you?" His voice was drowned by the helicopter rotors and the bells that tolled from every direction. He'd never heard so many. Through the cacophony, the throaty basso of the Kurzan bell continued its slow, steady bong.

He watched the Sikorsky bank steeply over the Moscow River and fly north. *Is she on it?*

Frantic, he scrambled to the top of a wall that supported the prison gate. "Caroline…" The skyline of Moscow City glittered above the forest along the rim of horizon. A jetliner flew between him and the moon, casting a shadow. Below him spread the ruins of Kurzan. He saw the refectory lights beyond the church. Would Caroline go back to Baba at the convent, or maybe into the church? He scanned for her in the direction of Kolomeno Forest but saw only a snowy field stretching to the trees.

He leapt from the wall and ran to the church. The mourners had gone. Only a few babushkas remained, sweeping the floors. "Have you seen the blond woman in a white coat?" He panted. They shook their heads. "Where did everyone go? Where's the coffin?"

"The cemetery." They pointed to a line of lights snaking uphill to a rise where moonlight shone on the cement angel. *They're burying Tanya.* He rushed toward the funeral procession, following the lingering trail of incense and trodden snow. He was part way up the hill when he caught sight of her.

She wasn't with the funeral—she was crossing the field that had once been an orchard following the tank tracks laid down by the UAZ that morning. Her white fur coat blended with the snow and made her difficult to see. She was moving toward the snow-dusted pines and leafless birches of Kolomeno Forest. She was running away from him.

"Caroline…wait!" he shouted, knowing she couldn't hear. How could he catch her? He remembered the footpath he'd taken with Pavel that traversed the park. It was a shorter route to the forest. He pushed through the slow-moving mourners, drawing their ire, and past the priests intoning prayers and the pallbearers bent under the weight of Tanya's coffin. At the head of the procession, Yuri and Katya supported his grandmother.

He detoured through a copse of trees alongside the path, so they wouldn't see him. When he reached the top of the rise, he was stunned to see the lights of a second procession led by a glowing icon. It approached Kurzan from the direction of Andropovsky Boulevard and extended all the way through the park from the Gates of Muscovy. The Kolomeno parking lot was jammed with cars and brightly lit news trucks. A bus disgorged passengers who hurried through the Gates of Muscovy. Another horde emerged from the Kolomeno Metro. If Caroline disappeared into that mob, he'd never catch up to her.

He raced downhill to the woods and stopped where the footpath disappeared into trees. There were no tracks from Caroline's direction. Had he missed her? Should he search the field? Should he go back and wait with Baba?

Tendrils of light threaded toward him through the trees, taking the shapes of horsemen, soldiers, and children. Chanting monks from another age matched their slow, sad litany to the melancholy heartbeat of the Kurzan bell. He froze in place, trying not to be distracted by the approach of spirits. At the head of the procession, an old man hovered above the ground—half spirit himself.

"Petrosyan Kaminsky," he whispered, afraid to say the name aloud.

Chapter Forty-five

BOLT FOR FREEDOM

Kolomeno, October 9, 1997

UZI yanked Caroline off of Peter. "You're coming with me," he shouted over the wail of the rotors. She kicked and thrashed but was off balance, disoriented by the sudden tumble in Peter's arms. UZI overpowered her, dragging her through the cellar door.

"Liar!" She screamed, trying to push him away. "You're all liars!"

"Welcome to the Kaminsky family."

He slung her over his shoulder and ran across the snow. He had nearly pulled her into the Sirkorsky when Oleg's bulk blocked the door.

"I won't let you do this, brother," he said. "Not for any woman." He pulled UZI inside and pushed Caroline out with his boot.

She came to her senses face-down in a snowbank. When she lifted her head to breathe, slivers of ice swirled around her with a high-pitched whine. She curled into a ball, hands over her face, pinned to the ground by the blue-lit downwash of the Sirkorsky. It hovered above her for several seconds, then banked steeply and flew away. When it was gone, she flopped onto her back taking in deep gasping breaths and became aware of other sounds. The Kurzan bell was tolling, answered by the bells of Moscow. When she sat up, she saw a long line of candles climbing the hill to the cemetery. *Tanya's funeral.*

She needed to get out of the snowbank—but what then? Should she go back to Baba at the refectory and wait for Peter? She shivered at the idea without knowing why. Her alternative was the Kolomeno Metro station in the opposite direction. It wasn't far. Twenty minutes across a snowy field and onto the Metro train. She would be safe at the Pushkin Theater.

She had clean, dry clothes in her dressing room, shoes that fit, and her professional makeup case. She could shower, blow dry her hair, and do something to hide the damage to her face. She would feel safer in her own clothes—able to meet Peter as herself, not some pitiable victim of sexual violence that he might despise.

She recalled the disgust in his eyes, and felt the sting of it. His look had struck a blow to her soul. Did she believe what UZI had said about Peter and his family? Yes, at least enough to know that Peter had lied to her and probably to himself for all the time she had known him. His stubborn belief that his life was a blank slate had deluded him and injured them both.

"Caroline...Where are you?" She heard Peter at the cellar door a few yards away. He couldn't see her. The white fur coat and hat made her invisible in the snow. Her eyes welled with tears. Her chest burned with love for him. Why didn't she call out instead of covering her mouth and bawling like a fool? Her wounds were too raw, her face bruised and her soul exposed. *I can't risk his eyes again, not without my dignity.*

"Caroline...?" He ran off toward the church calling her name.

She struggled to her feet and headed toward the Metro. She crossed the moonlit field by stepping in the tracks left by the UAZ's treads that morning. She gulped cold air as she stumbled and ran, dizzy from the blow to her head, taking in gasping breaths and shedding snot and tears that froze on her cheeks. Snow packed into her clumsy boots. Her feet and hands were numb with cold.

One hundred yards further and she would be safe on an overheated Metro train into Moscow. Her face burned; her legs ached. She had to stop, bend over and gasp for air. Would she make it the last few yards?

Another jetliner flew overhead, casting its shadow. *Everyone is going home but me.*

She heard the wind at her ear. "Yes, penitent. I am going home..."

Suddenly, she was not alone. The pathways and forest from the street to the monastery were trodden by the ghosts of pilgrims of all ages and seasons in the clothing of the past five hundred years. They walked toward her, around her and through her. They were widows, soldiers, lepers, lords and beggars, children walking, or carried, on their way to the see the Virgin of Kurzan. Her pain eased and she could breathe. She straightened her back, determined to give it her all.

"My people love me..." said the wind.

The Metro station was fifty yards further if she cut through the trees. She saw Peter standing at the edge of the field looking away from her. A strange procession of Muscovites, living and dead, approached him at the crossroads in an untidy mob. It was led by an old man carrying the glowing icon, the Virgin of Kurzan. In its light, she saw that Peter had a black eye. a thickened lip and bloody nose. His hands were scraped and bleeding. His shoulders drooped in exhaustion. *Poor Peter, what did they do you?*

"Should I go to him?" she asked aloud. "Can I help him?"

"Save yourself, penitent..." whispered the wind.

Head down, fur collar high around her face, she continued to Kolomeno Station and the safety of the train.

Chapter Forty-six

THE CROSSROADS

Kolomeno Park, October 9, 1997

Spirits swarmed around Peter. They whispered and chattered, giving off the scent of gun powder. He and his grandfather were no more than a meter apart, but the distance was as wide as the Atlantic Ocean.

"Pyotor," the old man extended his trembling hand, but Peter couldn't move. "The last time I saw you was your birthday. You were four years old."

"It was a long time ago."

"I wrote you letters. I left them with Karlov. Why didn't you ask questions? Nothing was secret."

"My father died because of you and your filthy money."

"My darling Denis." Petrosyan shrank a little. "What did he say to turn you against me?"

"He said that your blood money was killing him. He wouldn't take it. It was driving him mad."

"Yet he spent it freely—even after he went into hiding. Did ignoring where it came from make it less evil?"

"My father promised that I'd be a clean slate with no past. That was his dying gift."

"Sadly, that wasn't his gift to give," said Petrosyan with a sigh. "Is Karlov here yet? Have you signed the documents? The penthouse? The Petrosyan Fund? The bank accounts?"

"All of those…and I don't want any of them."

"What you do in the future is up to you," said Petrosyan with a wave of his hand. "This is as far as I go. I have a few matters to complete, starting with this." He tilted the crosier toward Peter. "Take this icon and give it to Maria Pavlova. She will know what to do with it."

Peter lifted the Virgin of Kurzan from its carrier. He barely recognized the smudged face and dull eyes. Even Grandpa Igor's old reproduction with a bullet wedged in the wood looked better. "You kidnapped Caroline for this?" He glared at his grandfather, torn between rage and heartbreak.

"It was just business," said Petrosyan. "This icon and I go way back. It's the last of the Russian treasures and the crown of my career."

"What about my father? What was he to you? Just business?"

"He meant the world to me. I tried to give him everything—but couldn't save him when it mattered most. The loss of Denis is my greatest regret." Petrosyan shrank a little more. "I'll tell you what I told your father: There's no escaping your connection with me. You are my blood, my heir."

"What about UZI? He's your blood too. You left him to rot in Kurzan Prison."

"Spetsnaz said they'd shot him with the rest of his family. How was I to know any different?"

"He said that I have his money. Is that true?"

"It's in the Petrosyan Fund—in your name, yes."

"So, if he kills me, he gets back what's his—and mine?" Peter's mounting anger was mirrored in the crackling angst of the spirit circle. Excited spirits released a shower of blue sparks. The old man morphed into a younger one who looked like Denis. Peter blinked, and he was old again. "That's what this is all about—money and this hideous icon?"

"Be careful what you say," Petrosyan rasped. "She's got a temper." The warning came too late. A swirling vortex opened.

"Bring the other penitent..." howled the wind until all that remained of Kolomeno Forest was the circle of ancient kedrs, the burnt stumps of trees and the ashen smell of ghosts.

"UZI! UZI! UZI!" sparked the spirits of dozens of children—little boys dressed in rags. "He remembers.... He knows our names..."

UZI stepped into the circle. Seeing Petrosyan, he smiled. "Hello, uncle. I was waiting for you." Seeing Peter, he pointed a Glock at his head and snapped off the safety. "Him, I can do without."

"Stop!" Petrosyan bellowed with startling force. "If you harm Pyotor, you'll get nothing. Do you understand? Zero."

"I beg to disagree," said UZI. "I've seen the trust papers. With Pyotor dead, I am the heir and the Petrosyan Fund is mine. It's irrevocable. You can't change it. With both of you dead, I get all of Kaminsky's."

"Don't be naive," Petrosyan scoffed. "Nothing is irrevocable. I changed it before I came. All it took was money—the clean kind that comes from a registered bank, the kind you'll never have unless you put away that gun."

"You're lying."

"It cost me a two-million-dollar campaign contribution to bribe a federal official. She changed the trust a few hours ago. If you harm Pyotor, or me, you will get nothing—*nothing*! And Chechen mercenaries will be generously funded as long as it takes to make you disappear."

"This is crazy." Peter looked from one man to the other. "Caroline is getting away from me, and all you two can do is argue about money?"

"Why do you hate me so much, uncle?" UZI ignored Peter. "I'm your flesh and blood. My grandfather was your brother. My father tried to do something good with his inheritance. He spoke out against the Communists and was rewarded with a firing squad. You could have stopped that. You could have brought him to America, too. Was he any less tragic than Denis? But Pyotor..." UZI waved the Glock in Peter's direction, his face a mask of pain. "...Pyotor you always loved. Me you condemned to prison. Why?"

"I was told that you were dead."

"Why didn't you check? Wasn't it suspicious that my mother disappeared?"

"Your mother hated the Kaminsky family. She encouraged your father to write 'Death of My Soul.' It was far too spiritual for the Communist Union of Writers and she knew it. The decision to wipe out all the Kaminskys—you included—was on her."

"I don't believe you. She sacrificed her own life to save me."

"Who knows what women will do? She knew the danger of those ghastly statues she sculpted."

UZI's lips curled into a sneer. "And you weren't sorry about all that, eh? Just more money for you."

"Of course, I was sorry—but Ephraim's poor choices were beyond my control. I told him to come to New York while it was still possible, but he refused. After he died, I had a right to his money. Now put down the gun."

"Let me get this straight. If you both live, I get nothing, and if I kill you, I get nothing." UZI raised his Glock. "I've got nothing to lose."

"You'll lose twelve million dollars for starters. That's your cut from the icon. I'm buying it from you here and now—consider it a cash payoff." Petrosyan held up an envelope. "This will buy the charter for your bank with eleven million left over in capital. Tomorrow you can be sitting in the CEO suite of the new International Bank of Kurzan. If you touch Pyotor or me, it all goes away, and you can spend the rest of your short life as the sewer rat you are now."

"Only twelve million?" UZI scoffed, sighting down the gun at Petrosyan. "The Virgin of Kurzan's worth twenty million at least. Where is it? I'll sell it myself!"

Peter held out the icon. "Here. Take it." But neither Petrosyan, nor UZI seemed to hear him.

"Ha." Petrosyan snorted. "You'd be lucky to find a buyer who'd pay you twenty bucks. No one's going to entrust millions to a thug like you."

UZI recoiled. "I'm not a thug. I'm a poet!"

"Tomorrow you can be a banker. You can launder all the dirty money you have stashed away God knows where and build yourself a skyscraper in New York City. No more living in tunnels and hiding from the police."

"Would someone just take this damn icon?" Peter shouted through the spiritual tempest. "I don't want it. I don't want your houses or your money or your banks."

UZI turned his gaze to Peter. "It's always about what you want, Pyotor," he hissed. "Toss it over."

"Pyotor…don't do it…" Petrosyan gasped.

Peter tried to throw the icon to UZI, but he couldn't release it. An electric pulse shot from his hands thru the top of his head with a pop.

"You're making her very angry," Petrosyan warned.

The wind rose and howled, the icon hummed in Peter's hands, shaking him until his teeth rattled. "Redeem yourself, penitent…." Colors around the circle grew vivid, shadows flattened, and ghosts shimmered.

"I don't deserve this," Peter screamed. "Let me go."

The Kurzan bell and the clamoring bells of Moscow broke the spell. The kedr circle blended back into the dense new growth of Kolomeno Forest. Black-clad mourners led by Maria Pavlova had arrived at the crossroads and converged with the followers of the Virgin of Kurzan. She stopped in front of Petrosyan. Peter watched her transform into a beautiful little girl with a crown of golden curls, then to a pale young woman with shorn head and swollen belly of pregnancy, and a mother with a blond boy who ran toward Petrosyan…shouting "Papa, papa!"

"Denis…" Petrosyan reached for him, but the child vanished.

"Petrosyan," she exclaimed, approaching the old man.

"It's been a long time, Masha." Petrosyan tried to straighten his spine and make himself taller. "I'm afraid I'm not much to look at these days." His breath came in gasps, but his eyes held their intensity. "Forgive me, my love."

"I forgave you long ago," she said. "You gave me Denis—and now Pyotor."

Petrosyan signaled to Peter. "Give her the icon, boy."

Peter placed the icon in his grandmother's hands. She kissed it, held it aloft to the tearful, murmuring crowd, then clutched it to her chest. Both groups fell onto their knees and crossed themselves.

"Enough, you bastard!" UZI screamed in Petrosyan's face. "Give me my bank or I'll blow Saint Pyotor's head off and his brains will be the last thing you see in your cursed life."

Petrosyan held out the envelope. "Don't forget," he said. "I'll be in my grave, but if you touch Pyotor, the International Bank of Kurzan goes away and so do you!"

UZI took it and raised the Glock. "It's a deal, uncle. But if I can't kill him, I'll kill her." He fired two rounds at Maria Pavlova. The impact lifted her off her feet and threw her to the ground. She lay motionless on the cobbles. A keening wail rose from the crowd.

Peter dropped to his knees. He touched her face, her hands. They were covered with blood. "Get Doctor Plotkin," he shouted.

Pavel knelt beside him. He touched her face tenderly. His eyes bored into Peter as he growled the order: "Kill him!"

Peter took off at a run.

Chapter Forty-seven

THE RIVER

Kolomeno Park, October 9, 1997

Peter caught up with UZI in the cemetery and tackled him, slamming him to the ground. UZI wrenched himself free. He punched Peter's face with the butt of his gun—stunning him, filling his head with stars. When Peter could focus his eyes again, he saw UZI silhouetted at the top of the embankment. He was running for the Sikorsky that hovered over the river, shining its spotlight on the two men. Peter staggered after him. "You won't get away," he screamed. Fueled by rage, he bounded through the snow. He tackled UZI at the top of the icy slope, propelling them both over the ridgetop toward the river in a tangle of arms and legs.

When they slid to a stop, Peter was on his back. His head and shoulders hung over the fast-moving Moscow River. UZI straddled him, holding down his arms with his knees. The Sikorsky hovered overhead, pinioning them with its downdraft.

"Pyotor," Ruslan shouted from the top of the ridge. "We're coming." Oleg swung out the door of the chopper, firing an AK 47 at the Chechen positions, forcing them back from the edge.

UZI grabbed Peter's collar and jammed the barrel of the Glock under his chin. "I can't kill you but I'll blow off your ear if you don't settle down."

"You goddamn monster!" Peter spat. "What did that old lady ever do to you?"

UZI jammed the Glock harder into Peter's neck until he gagged. "She fucked your grandfather and whelped that underbred whiner Denis— who lived just long enough to whelp you."

Peter spat in UZI's face. UZI slapped him with the gun, splitting his lip. Peter slipped further over the edge, held only by UZI's knees. "I'm a better man than you," he sputtered, his mouth filling with blood. "You're nothing but a killer."

"And you're not? Do you remember Kostya Korsky or Vanya Barakov?"

"Who?"

"Your kills, you bastard." UZI hit him again. Peter felt his nose break. He spat more blood. UZI leaned close and snarled in his ear. "They were my blood brothers. I've loved them since we were boys."

Peter clutched at the slick embankment. "They were raping Golokov. They were going to kill him."

"And who paid the commander one hundred thousand dollars to turn against his brothers? We were a happy family until you came along. Now they're dead, Tanya's dead, Piggie's dead. The four brothers that Piggie blew up with him are dead." UZI punched him below the ribs. He couldn't breathe. "And what were you thinking when you sent Caroline to Moscow alone without two kopeks in her pocket?"

"You set that up." Peter gasped, coughing up blood. "You raped her. You tortured her. You put her in a cage!"

"I was her patron and that was the price she paid. She'd be a star by now if you hadn't blown up Moscow Traffic. And poor Tanya would be a bride."

Gunfire punctuated the roar of the rotors. The chopper swept over their heads, keeping OMON and the Chechens pinned on the bluff. UZI's blue eyes were locked on Peter's. "Do you even give a thought to the innocent men who died in the fire? There were so many that I can't remember all the names—Pablo Blanco, Herman Gestler, John Bibbens, Clive Smith.…What's the matter? Too many dead Indians on your conscience, cowboy?" UZI leaned so close that his lips touched Peter's ear. Peter clenched his muscles, biding his time. "I have a proposal for you. Why don't we switch places? You come live my life. You take the leadership of the Kurzaniks and I'll take over Kaminsky's. You can live in a bunker in Tver with Oleg Sherepov. I'll go live in Petrosyan Towers and fuck Caroline every night."

With a roar, Peter arched his back, throwing UZI off balance. He grabbed the sleeve of UZI's coat and swung him to the ground. The Sikorsky descended on top of them— the light was blinding. Oleg pointed a pistol at his head. *This is it.* He closed his eyes, ready to die. But the wind gusted, lifting the chopper. Pop-pop-pop! Nothing. Peter fought for traction on the icy slope, but with UZI no longer holding him, he kept sliding headfirst down the steep bank.

He caught a tree branch with one hand, swung around it, and hung there. There was no footing and his feet dragged in the water. The river tugged at his heavy boots. He looked up to see UZI standing over him. "Well now, how could it be my fault if you're so stupid that you fell in the river and drowned?" He raised his boot and stomped on Peter's hand. Pain shot down his arm. His fingers were slipping.

A gunshot rang out. UZI's left eye exploded. Peter was sprayed with blood. UZI staggered and pitched headfirst over him and into the river. Peter caught his jacket sleeve and held on.

"Help me!" screamed Peter, his grip slipping. A hand grasped his wrist just as he lost hold of UZI. Ruslan pulled him to safety on the riverbank. Peter sprawled in the snow, gasping and shivering. The Sikorsky moved away, spotlighting the water. A crowd gathered around Peter. They helped him to his feet, wrapping him in their coats. He saw OMON snipers on top of the bluff, weapons raised. They fired at the chopper.

Thwump… thwump… thwump… thwump… The high-intensity light from the Sikorsky turned their faces blue. They ducked under the down-wash. It thundered overhead and was gone.

Chapter Forty-eight

THE HEIR

Kurzan Convent, October 9, 1997

"You again?" Doctor Plotkin scowled when he saw Peter limping toward him, his arm over Ruslan's shoulders. "I should leave the medical institute and start a private hospital at Kurzan just for your family." Peter winced when the doctor shined a light on his face and probed his nose. "Is this all your blood?"

"Some of it—mostly it's Alexei Kaminsky's."

"Another relative? Will he be in for treatment?"

"He's dead."

"I'm sorry," said Plotkin.

"Don't be. He killed my grandmother."

"Maria Pavlova? You are mistaken. She's fine."

Peter flushed. "I saw him shoot her twice—in the chest."

"Ah…" Plotkin raised a finger. "Do you remember the story of the icon that saved that old partisan's life at the Battle of Novgorod?"

"Grandpa Igor and the Virgin of Kurzan?"

"It saved Maria Pavlova tonight."

"Impossible. I saw her blood."

"She knocked her head on the cobbles—lots of blood, but not much damage. When I revived her, she was still clasping the icon over her heart. It had two bullets in it."

"I don't understand…" Ruslan caught Peter when his knees buckled and helped him onto the bed, where he lay, waiting for the ceiling to stop spinning. He wiped his eyes and grimaced when his fingers grazed his swollen nose. "Can I see her?"

"Not looking like that. Let's wash that blood off, shall we? You've got a broken nose at the very least." Plotkin threaded a probe into Peter's nostril. "Not too bad," he said.

"Where is she?"

"She's with Mr. Karlov. They are sitting with your grandfather's body."

"He's dead?" Peter's vision of his future as Petrosyan's heir contracted to a pinhole of light that threatened to burn him. "What happened?"

"He collapsed while I was helping your grandmother. I found him crumpled on the ground like a pile of old clothes," said Plotkin. "I'm sorry. I thought you knew."

"I need to talk to my grandmother."

"I'll fetch her, but first let Sister Makarova clean up your face. Maria Pavlova is a tough old lady, but she'll have heart failure if she sees you like this." The little nun sat beside him with a basin of cold water. She dabbed the blood from his face and hands with a cloth. Plotkin pushed on Peter's bruised liver, making him grunt. "This was quite a punch up."

"What about Caroline? Where is she?"

"No sign of her here." Plotkin looked surprised. "Have you lost her again?"

"I don't understand. She has to be here." He tried to sit up, but it only made his head throb—too much even to protest. He lay back and moaned. He'd been certain that she would return to the refectory. Where else could she go?

"Pyotor...is that you?" his grandmother called from the doorway. "Are you all right?"

Peter's heart warmed to see her. She had a white bandage around her head, but her eyes were bright. She came to his bedside, took his hand and kissed it. "You're hurt!"

"Just a few new cuts and bruises." He tried to smile. "I saw UZI shoot you. I thought you were dead."

"I was saved by our Holy Mother." Maria Pavlova crossed herself and kissed her crucifix.

"Where is the icon now?" Peter asked.

"Aha," said Dr. Plotkin. "That's quite a story. When I took it from Maria Pavlova, it gave me an electric shock, so I dropped it. It never touched the ground—I swear. Now it's in the Church of the Kurzan Goddess, and no one knows how it got there. The Metropolit came from Saint Savior's to conduct an all-night service. It's still going on. My wife and mother are there now. Just look outside." He indicated the window with his thumb. "Pilgrims are lined up from here to Andropovsky Boulevard. I wouldn't be surprised if most of Russia is on its way here. The TV stations have been running the story all night. They call it the miracle of the Virgin of Kurzan." Plotkin looked at Peter and tapped his watch. "You'd better go pay your respects to your grandfather. The embassy's coming for his body soon."

"Where is he? Take me to him."

Ruslan helped Peter across the hall to the room where Tanya had lain. Burning candles ringed the open coffin of Petrosyan Kaminsky. They sputtered on the windowsill and dresser; the room smelled of tallow. Daniel Karlov sat on a bench, wearing a yarmulke.

Peter stood over the coffin and studied his grandfather. Death had smoothed the skin of his face. He saw traces of Denis in the high cheek bones. The hands crossed on his chest were sinewy, but elegant. He touched the pale forehead. It was cold and smooth. "What kind of a man were you?"

"A very successful man in the context of his time," said Karlov. "A survivor."

"Why destroy Kurzan Monastery like he did? What could inspire such savagery?"

"I didn't know him in those early days. My father once told me that Petrosyan was a man compelled by rage. I never saw it myself."

"I don't understand him, or my father."

"This death marks the end of their eras," said Karlov, "and the beginning of yours. I have boxes full of letters he wrote to you over the years. I suggest you read them. Then let's see if you can do a better job with your life than he did with his."

Peter sank onto the bench beside Karlov and held his head in his hands. "I can't do this alone."

"You're not alone." Karlov clasped his arm. "You have a staff of thousands..." He began to list the names of law firms, accounting firms, mercenary armies, public relations firms and media networks—but Peter didn't need a cast of thousands. He needed one woman.

They were interrupted by a knock at the door. George Tanner bustled importantly into the room. "I've brought the Customs clearances to fly Mr. Kaminsky's remains to New York. We just need Dr. Stone's signature here... and here to release the body." He pointed and handed Peter a pen.

Peter signed. "What about Caroline Luke's passport? We'd like to fly home as soon as we find her."

"You didn't know?" Tanner looked surprised. "She was waiting at the embassy when it opened this morning. I felt so bad about the mix-up that I took her photograph and made her a temporary passport in Citizens Services at no charge. She said she was on her way back here."

"She hasn't arrived." Peter frowned. "But where else can she be? She hasn't got any money with her."

"Well…" Tanner fidgeted. "I hope I haven't done the wrong thing."

"What do you mean?"

"Citibank delivered your new credit card to Citizens Services yesterday. Miss Luke said she would bring it to you. She insisted that you needed it right away."

"Credit card?"

"I had Citibank send it care of the embassy," said Karlov.

Peter recalled the million-dollar credit line. "Why didn't she just ask me for money? I'd have given it to her." *With strings attached—terms and conditions.*

Tanner squirmed. "Well, she did sign for it."

Karlov looked at Peter. "Say the word and I'll have it cancelled, or at least lower the limit."

Peter grappled with the implications. He could block the card and keep her from leaving Russia. But then she might be arrested if she tried to use it and taken to a Moscow jail where they would humiliate her further. Nothing was worth that. He had another idea.

"She can have the card. Call Citibank and tell them she's authorized to use it," He said.

Tanner looked relieved. "I'll file your documents and send a hearse to transport Mr. Kaminsky's body to Vnukovo Airport. You should be cleared to leave within twenty-four hours."

Tanner left. Peter turned to Karlov. "I want to be informed every time she uses that card. When she buys a ticket, I want to know where she's going. Do we still have Petrosyan's private detectives on staff?"

"We do."

"Tell them to follow her wherever she lands. I want to know where she stays and who she sees." Reacting to the surprise on Karlov's face, Peter added, "I can't keep her from leaving, but I can watch over her."

"Should they just follow her, or do you want phone taps, photos…"

"I want her under 24-hour surveillance." The word *surveillance* caught in his throat. Peter thought of the stack of photo albums that had chronicled his life under the unseen but all-seeing eye of his grandfather. "It's for her protection."

"Your grandfather said the same thing about you." Karlov stood. "I should go with Mr. Tanner. There are arrangements to make," he said, closing the door behind him.

Chapter Forty-nine

THE CASTLE IN NEW YORK CITY

Kurzan, October 10, 1997

A lone with the old man's remains, Peter recalled the last time he had seen his grandfather. He remembered clinging to his father's neck in the private elevator to Petrosyan's castle while Denis bounced him and sang in his ear:

> *"May there always be Mama,*
> *May there always be Papa,*
> *May there always be sunshine,*
> *May there always be me."*

"Stop with that stupid Russian song!" His mother, Ruby Mae, licked her fingers and ran them through Peter's hair. "And if you keep jiggling the kid, he'll throw up again. That's his last clean outfit."

"Every Russian boy learns this song." Denis kissed Peter's cheek. He ogled his wife. "Did I tell you how sexy you look in that fur coat?"

"Shut up," she laughed. "Let's get this birthday party over with."

"Be nice to the old man and maybe he'll have some presents for you, too." Denis bounced Peter up and down. "You're such a big boy now— four years old. Are you ready for your party?"

The elevator pinged and opened to the foyer of the castle. A butler waited to take their coats. Peter ran ahead of his parents down the long, paneled hallway and into the great room where Petrosyan stood by his fireplace, holding a brightly wrapped present. Peter grabbed it and pulled off the blue ribbon.

"It's from Abercrombie and Fitch." Petrosyan hugged Denis and kissed Ruby Mae's cheek. "They assured me it's the four-year-olds' favorite."

Peter ripped away the stiff white paper. In the box was a stuffed tiger almost as big as he was. "Wow!" he squealed, shaking the toy and dragging it around the room. "It's Tigger!"

"The boy loves tigers," said Denis, fading into the background with the rest of the adults. Peter gobbled his ice cream and cake and ripped open presents. His mother helped him with a package wrapped in brown paper and string that she cut with scissors. Peter pulled out a hand-knit sweater from Russia. Denis made him put it on. "It's from my poor, dear mother," he said.

Peter wore the sweater, even though it smelled funny and itched, because seeing his father's sadness made his stomach hurt. When the grownups were lost again in their cocktails and cigarettes, Peter ran to the conservatory with Tigger. They played "jungle safari" between the palm trees in the winter garden. They stalked elephants and giraffes until his mother came to get him.

"Go say goodnight to Grandpa." She helped him into his coat and sent him off down the long dim hallway dragging Tigger. The door to the great room was open and Peter heard the strains of his grandfather's favorite music.

"Shhh!" he said to Tigger. They crept in on tiptoe, diving unseen under his grandfather's Queen Anne chair. The old man stoked a roaring fire. Peter was about to growl and pounce on Grandpa's feet when he heard tinkling ice cubes from the next chair.

"I'm sick." His father's voice sounded terribly sad. "It's my nerves."

"We'll find an easier job for you then," said Petrosyan.

"I'm seeing a psychiatrist. He calls it 'survivor's guilt.'"

"Is that necessary?" Petrosyan poked the fire, scattering sparks. "Those head doctors ask a lot of personal questions."

"I can't help it. Nothing's been the same since I read Mother's letters. Why did you stop sending mine? It must have broken her heart to think that I'd forgotten her."

"I was trying to protect you," said Petrosyan. "Who knows what could have happened during the war. You needed to forget about Russia and adjust to life in America."

"I'm so ashamed," Denis said. "She must have thought that I cared more for your money than I did for her. I can't live with that."

"I was the one who hid the letters. Why should you be ashamed?"

"Because I did forget her! I was selfish—I liked the money. When I saw that awful little sweater on Peter it reminded me of how much the Pavlovs gave me, even when they had nothing. How can I live with this guilt?"

"You're forty-six years old, for God's sake. Can't you leave the past behind? There's nothing you can do for the Pavlovs. They are poor in Russia. You're a rich man in America. Enjoy it!"

"We are our pasts. That's what Uncle Pavel always says."

"Bah, Pavel. If you'd stayed in Moscow and managed to live through the war, you'd hate those sanctimonious Pavlovs."

"I offered to send money but they refused to take 'blood money'. Mother is still in Siberia working in that orphanage. It is much too hard on her but she refuses to leave."

"Maria Pavlova is just as thick-headed as the rest of them." There was admiration in his voice. "I'll wire money to the Governor of Omsk. He owes me a favor. He'll make sure that she gets transferred back to Moscow before winter. That is what wealth can do for you. Remember that and be glad you have it." The men were silent. Peter listened to his own breathing, concentrating hard on not moving. Petrosyan asked, "So, how do you like your new Chrysler? It's a honey, eh?"

"I don't want the car. In fact, I'm not going to accept any more money from you. I'm going to work to support my family on my own."

"How? You don't have any skills. You're a trust fund kid," Petrosyan laughed. "And you're married to a woman who expects that big paycheck. How will she manage without nannies and maids? She spends money like water."

"She'll get used to having less."

"Don't be stupid! She'll be gone as soon as the money runs out."

"No, you're wrong about her. She'll understand that we can't live on money that came from looting churches."

"Those churches were toppled by their own greed when the Russian people rose up and stupidly traded one form of oppression for another. Ephraim and I just skimmed some cream off the top in the process. Just be glad that you're in America—and you're rich. You can educate your son. You can give him the life he deserves."

"I wish I'd never had that child," whispered Denis, igniting a fire that roared in Peter's ears and burned in his belly.

"... My nerves can't take it. I look at him and see the curse on our family. I don't want him to grow up with this terrible burden. Sometimes I think we'd both be better off dead." Peter's world went off-kilter. His pounding heart drowned out his father's words.

"Damn it!" Petrosyan threw down the poker. It clattered on the flagstones. "You're such a weakling! How can you be my son?"

Denis was mumbling, incoherent. Petrosyan was hurting him. Peter had to make it stop. He leapt from under the chair and attacked his grandfather, beating at his legs with Tigger. "Don't yell at my daddy!" he screamed.

The old man hoisted Peter into the air, holding him at arms' length. Peter kept swinging. Tigger flew out of his hands and landed on the hearth. "Look at your fine scrappy son!" Petrosyan laughed. "He has more guts than you do. He'll be able to handle what life dishes onto his plate."

Peter screamed and kicked with rage. Denis tried to stand, knocking over his drink. The glass shattered.

Ruby Mae came running. "Put the boy down, you bastard."

Petrosyan set Peter on his feet but held him by the top of his head. "Did you know that your husband is planning to turn off the golden spigot? Are you ready to live on a poor man's wages?"

"What are you talking about?" She faced Denis. "What's he saying?"

"It's my nerves," Denis croaked. "I can't take this blood money anymore. I'll get a job. I'll support you."

Petrosyan laughed. "The only job you'll get will be in a gas station and that's if I own it."

"I know how to farm," Denis said. "Uncle Pavel taught me to grow apple trees. Ruby Mae and I will raise our son in poverty and humility."

The look on his mother's face drove a spear through Peter's heart. "I've had enough of this bullshit!" she snarled. "Get your coat, we're leaving!"

"That's right, my dear," said Denis. "This dirty money is killing me." He yanked Peter's hand and dragged him toward the door. "I'm buying a farm."

"Tigger!" Peter screamed, pointing to his toy.

Ruby Mae scooped it up. "Keep your goddamn present," she snarled at Petrosyan, throwing Tigger into the flames.

Chapter Fifty

THE OLD SOLDIER

Kurzan, October 10, 1997

T he door opened. Dr. Plotkin leaned in. "I'd like to start your IV now. You will feel much better after fluids and pain meds." Peter tried to stand but faltered. The walls closed in. He needed to breathe, but his nose was swollen shut. His liver hurt.

"Take him to his room," said Plotkin to Ruslan who helped Peter limp to his bed and fall back onto the pillow. The doctor inserted an intravenous needle in his arm and opened the line. "I'm giving you fluids, antibiotics, and a sedative. Now start counting backwards from one hundred, please."

"Ninety-nine…ninety-eight…ninety-seven…" Peter slurred the numbers and tumbled into a minefield of memories.

"This is my grandpa Pavel Pavlov," said Tanya, lighting a cigarette. "He's been deaf since the Battle of Stalingrad."

Pavel leaned close. "I know who you are, who you really are."

"Maybe your name is Kaminsky," said UZI, his eye bursting. "Pyotor Kaminsky."

"Peter, where are you?" screamed Caroline from a suspended cage. "I'm on fire."

"We're all on fire," shrieked the twelve charred businessmen. "You're burning us alive."

"And this is a pie," said Golokov, holding the landmine on his splayed fingers. "I'll send you a postcard from Hell." The room upended, tumbling him through boxes of C4 and into the stifling darkness of the safe room—where he slept.

****

"Much better," he heard Dr. Plotkin say, shining a penlight into his eyes as he struggled awake. Detective Pashkina was slumped in a chair at his bedside. She looked exhausted.

"How long have I slept?" he asked.

"Ten hours at least," she said. "We searched the river all night but no body was found. Are you certain that UZI's dead?"

"I saw the bullet come through his head and out of his eye. He's dead," said Peter.

"Unfortunately, we can't say that for certain until we have him in the morgue."

"That helicopter was over the river. Maybe the Kurzaniks recovered the body."

"We'll keep looking." Pashkina ran her fingers through her rumpled hair. "Markov and Demidov spent the night going through ORT TV's videos. There's something I'd like you to look at."

"Not now," Peter groaned. "I can barely see straight. Have someone else look."

"You're the one who needs to see this." She handed Peter a grainy 8 x 10 photo. "It's been enhanced by our technicians. It's the best we're going to get."

"Who's that?" Peter pointed to the lone figure aiming a pistol.

"That's our shooter," said Pashkina. "Can you give us his name?"

Peter looked more closely. The image was blurred, but there was no mistaking the medals on Pavel's jacket. Peter's heart warmed with pride. *Good on you, old soldier.* He handed it back to her, shaking his head. "I've never seen him before."

"I didn't think so," she said, ripping up the picture. "Neither have I."

Karlov poked his head into the room. "Citibank called. Miss Luke just purchased a ticket at Sheremetyevo Airport. She's flying to Frankfurt."

Chapter Fifty-one

THE DEPARTURE

Sheremetyevo Airport, October 12, 1997

Fresh snowfall slowed the flow of traffic through Moscow and on the highway to Sheremyetovo Airport. Ruslan propelled the Mercedes at speed through impossibly narrow spaces, on shoulders and between lanes. The blue light flashed on the roof.

Peter leaned forward in the back seat, willing the car to go faster. Racing through Moscow on an icy road with armed Chechens smoking in the front seat barely registered as dangerous anymore. He stared through the window, ignoring pedestrians who huddled against the wind and casino lights that flashed and cajoled. Ruslan hit the horn and narrowly missed a blue milk truck.

Ahmed rode shotgun, his ear pressed to the sat-phone. He turned to Peter. "Sheremetyevo is reporting flight delays. Lufthansa's on hold. Blondie hasn't gone through Passport Control yet."

"Thank God!" Peter fell back and closed his eyes, allowing himself to breathe. The challenge of finding her in the crowded airport was something he would worry about once they arrived.

"What can I say to make this right?" he'd asked Pashkina before she bundled him into the car.

"You're the psychologist," she said. "You'll figure it out. Now get your ass to the airport."

Peter rested his head on the soft leather and surrendered to overheated air. His mind drifted to simpler times and he remembered laughter. The Blue Moon Tavern was packed with rugby players. The house lights dimmed. The crowd hooted and clapped. Lex elbowed him: "Here she comes. You're in for a treat tonight." The spotlight shone on a long-legged beauty in spike heels swinging her straight blond hair as she strode to the microphone.

"Hi guys." She waved and smiled, showing perfect white teeth. "How are all you ruggers out there?"

"Ca-rol-ine…Ca-rol-ine…" they chanted.

"You boys havin' a good time?" A piano played a few chords. She adjusted the microphone. "I heard that somebody won the intercollegiate championships today. Am I right?" Lex stood and waved the trophy—the team went wild with whistles and applause. "So, what am I singin' for you fellas?"

Someone shouted, "'She-Lyin' Woman.'"

"That thousand-dollar hooker song." Caroline laughed. "Okay, boys…" She nodded to the trio. "You asked for it." The drum tapped. A flute trilled. Caroline snapped her fingers and tossed her mane of hair. "…She-lyin' woman dressed in red…make a man lose his head…"

The audience clapped to the beat, chanting the chorus, "She's lyin'… She's lyin'…"

Caroline shimmied. "…Wiggle, wiggle…purr like a cat…wink at a man and he wink back…" Peter couldn't stop staring. Her minidress barely reached her thighs. "…empty his pockets and wreck his days…make him love her, then she fly away.…" She flipped back her hair. The audience wolf-howled and whistled.

After her set, she strode to their table. The two men stood. Lex thumped Peter on the back. "I'd like you to meet my friend, Caroline Luke." She extended her hand and smiled at him. Their fingers sparked when they touched and heat flushed through his body. From then on, no one else existed but her. When the bar closed, Peter drove her home to her grandmother's house on Blue Ridge.

The wind skimmed the embankment and tall pines swayed above their heads. He breathed the salt air and took in her scent as they walked hand-in-hand into Baba's moonlit garden.

"Your roses are magnificent," he said. "What's your secret?"

"Roses love the wind." She plucked blossoms, tossing petals until he caught her in his arms. "I'm going to be an opera star," she said. "I'm very serious about that."

"Of course, you are." He kissed her and filled her mouth with his tongue.

****

Tires squealed. The Mercedes fishtailed on the hairpin turn from Tverskaya Street to Red Square. Peter barely noticed the car horns or angry pedestrians when the Mercedes jumped the curb and raced along the sidewalk. At this pace, they might just make it to Sheremetyevo in time. The car accelerated into a tunnel.

The roar of traffic and flashing lights made Peter groggy. He struggled to focus his thoughts on what might be his last chance to keep her. Twice, he'd blown it. What could he say now? The car zigzagged, careening toward a future he dreaded, one in which she left him. He dozed and floated above their empty houseboat, watching it spin in the whirlpool of Lake Union before it was sucked to the bottom, abandoned and forgotten.

The car skidded to a halt at the exit to Sheremetyevo. Traffic was at a standstill. "We can't get any closer," said Ruslan. "There's an overturned bus."

Peter could see the clogged drive that curved up to International Departures. Traffic was backed up for a quarter mile. "I'll leg it."

A roar shook the ground. An Ilyushin gained altitude overhead. "The runways are re-opening. You'd better hurry," said Ahmed.

Peter dodged around taxis and minivans that disgorged passengers and luggage onto the highway. He ran with aching ribs between stalled cars and around travelers struggling with children. He ran faster, climbing the curved drive, shoving through the crowds that blocked the glass airport doors with their belongings. In the lobby, hordes of people milled about, hauling suitcases or sitting on piles of bags and boxes.

The air was a haze of cigarette smoke. Tour leaders waved signs, blocking his view. Peter pushed through the press of fur coats and hats. The Customs gate had re-opened and passengers were arranging themselves into unruly queues for Passport Control. He balanced on the bottom rung of the gate and searched the crowd. Nothing.

A mechanical reader-board whirred and clicked overhead, providing information on departures, arrivals, and delays. It updated Caroline's Lufthansa flight from "delayed" to "check-in." He climbed up a staircase and scanned the crush. Under the reader-board, he caught a flash of green. Caroline's lucky suit? Peter leapt the railing and bounded through the crowds to reach her.

She was wearing the elegant suit with matching green pumps. Her face was flawless porcelain, her hair swept into a stylish chignon. She carried her make-up case, a new passport and ticket. The white fox fur had been cleaned. It was draped over her arm. She looked as if she had rolled back time and nothing had happened. "Caroline!" He ran toward her. "I was so worried. Where were you?"

"I went to the theater." She frowned. "Where else would I go?"

The theater—to her friends and colleagues. He should have known. "I have good news for you." He smiled to hide his panic. Her cool demeanor unnerved him. "UZI's dead," he blurted.

Caroline blanched. Her eyes rolled in their sockets. Peter caught her when her knees buckled. He eased her onto the now-empty row of seats and held her close. The neon light revealed bruises under the thick layers of professional make-up. She was in his arms but worlds away.

She sat up slowly, avoiding his gaze. "Did you kill him?"

"I wanted to, but no." *This is it, your last chance.* "He's gone, that's the important thing. We can go back to America and forget this ever happened. We'll move to New York and live in a castle. I'll buy you an opera house if that's what you want."

"I have to go now." She smoothed her skirt. "I have an audition." She opened her make-up case and used a rat-tailed comb to tuck errant gold strands back into her chignon. She brushed powder on her cheeks, then added mascara.

"Don't go, Caroline. I have no life without you."

Tears smeared her mascara. "I love you more than my life, Peter, but I don't know who you are." She looked away. "I'm confused about everything. The only thing I am sure of is that I'm a singer. On that stage, in front of those lights, I'm not afraid of anything." Her lips trembled. "Admit it. Even you fell in love with that sexy woman on the stage at the Blue Moon."

"Every man in the Blue Moon was in love with you." He searched the air between them for the electric charge of their old connection. He didn't find it. "I was the lucky guy who took you home."

"That's all in the past. That story belongs to another girl—a silly, vain impressionable girl, a foolish creature who caused harm to everyone around her. From now on I am a serious artist." She opened her compact and dabbed at her makeup.

When she met his gaze, she was smiling. "You should be happy for me. There were a dozen cables waiting at the theater. I've been offered leading roles at opera houses around the world. I'm a star, Peter. That is all I want right now. I can't handle anything more."

He took her hand and searched the eyes of this strange, cold woman for the funny, lively girl who had done the shimmy at the Blue Moon and decorated his life with music and costume jewelry. She pulled it away, gathered her belongings and stood. "Your love hurts too much," she said. "I can't bear the pain of it."

He realized that he should say something more, at least congratulate her and wish her well, but there was not enough air in his lungs. The reader-board clicked overhead. Crowd noise intruded on all sides. "My flight's boarding. I have to go." She held out the Citibank credit card. "This is yours."

"It's for you. I put it in your name. Use it and I'll pay the bills."

"I don't need a patron anymore." She dropped the card on the floor and stepped to the front of the queue. "I'm a star."

She showed her first-class ticket and disappeared through the gate.

Chapter Fifty-two

LA SCALA

Milan, August 1998

The Kaminsky Lear flew to New York, then to Seattle with Baba, but Peter wasn't on it. Despite Karlov's urging that he assume the reins of power from the safety of Petrosyan Towers, Peter remained in Moscow. Karlov had even suggested bringing the Pavlovs to New York to live in the castle, but Pavel and Maria Pavlova refused. They had work to do at Kurzan and so did Peter. He moved into the refectory, feeling safest there with his Chechen guards. A state-of-the-art satellite video teleconferencing system was installed.

Karlov sent bankers boxes daily from New York and Peter worked his way through them. He was starting to make sense of his inheritance. The boxes were soon stacked to the ceiling of the refectory and covered with his color-coded notes.

Peter was grateful for the mental busywork. It was all he had the energy for. His physical injuries took time to heal. The bones were knitting, the bruises faded, but there was no relief for the wound in him where Caroline had been. The Kaminsky investigators were waiting at Frankfurt Flughaven when she stepped off the Lufthansa flight, but she'd given them the slip and vanished.

Except for tea with his grandmother and dinner with the Pavlovs, Peter lived as a recluse, plagued by memories that erupted unpredictably. He recognized his waking nightmares as post-traumatic stress syndrome—PTSD. There was no relief for him in sleep. Even with the sedatives that Dr. Plotkin prescribed he'd no sooner close his eyes than the room would explode, sending him tumbling through the stifling darkness. One nightmare slideshow would end, and another begin in unresolved chaos. He'd run for help down the dark halls of Konkova and into the midst of Golokov's assault. He would take aim and feel Pashkina's gun fire. Heads exploded, spraying him with broken glass and brains. "Hang him," shouted Anna Lemirova. "Stop lying," said Rita in English. "You're making the partisans crazy." The rugby team at the Blue Moon burst into a chorus of "she's lyin'... she's lyin'..." Denis swung by his neck from an apple tree. The orchard burst into flames.

Peter tossed and groaned, pursued by terrors until dawn when he'd hear the ocean and feel Caroline slide into his sleeping bag. She would spoon into him, her soft breasts warm against his back. "Shi Shi is where heaven meets earth." She rubbed against his thigh, making him hard, then stroked him until he cried out in release. He'd wake to an empty bed and search the sweaty sheets for the woman who wasn't there.

UZI's accusations ran constantly through his mind no matter how he tried to shut them out. He looked up the names of the men who died in Moscow Traffic. They were mainly businessmen or diplomats out for a night on the town. Were they innocent? Why did they have to die? Was it really his fault? Did it matter whose fault it was? The events were tragic.

Finally, he confessed his nightmares to his grandmother. "I don't think I can take this anymore," he complained.

She made a sour face at him. "If we Russians gave up in a blubbering heap every time life got a little hard, there wouldn't be any of us left—including you."

"What's all this about?" asked Pavel, coming in with Gogol. The old dog wagged his tail.

"Our Pyotor thinks he is the only soul who has known troubles," she chuckled.

Pavel poured tea and sat next to Peter. "That Englishman Shakespeare said it well and that's why we Russians admire him." He paused to blow on his steaming mug. "The world is a stage. We are merely players. We are not important, you and me. We're here for a while—then thrown away and others come. Our troubles are as insignificant as we are."

Pavel's words gave Peter an odd sort of comfort. At the very least, he'd finally been accepted as a fellow victim of life's turbulence.

"You've been cooped up in here studying and brooding far too long," said Maria Pavlova. "You're a young man. You need more than moldy old boxes from New York and fossils like us. When do you see Dr. Plotkin for your next check-up?"

"A few days. Until then, I'm working on some ideas to send to Mr. Karlov."

"That's good," said Pavel. "You have your whole life ahead of you. Have you decided what to do with the Party's Gold?"

"I'm not sure yet. Any suggestions?"

"Why not start with something simple?" Pavel's face crinkled into a grin. "Plant some apple trees—that's what we Pavlovs always do. Dirty your hands with God's good earth. I'll teach you how, same as I taught your father."

"Of course," said Peter, perking up. "When do we start?"

"When the ground thaws—another few weeks at most," said Maria Pavlova.

"First, we will plant flowers," said Pavel, "hectares of wildflowers."

"And put a proper stone on Tanya's grave," Peter said. "I've been sketching some designs. I thought she might like an angel."

"That whole cemetery needs repair," said Pavel. "Those poor kids cannot rest in unconsecrated graves. We need to fix that."

As soon as the earth warmed on the surface and pale birch buds greened the trees, they sewed flower seeds that sprouted and burst into bloom on the first hot day. Peter stood at the refectory window drinking his morning coffee and admiring the carpet of calendula. A sea of bobbing orange heads rippled·with the wind, attended by bees and butterflies. It was then that the idea of the Denis Stone Foundation took hold. Soon his mind spun with visions of what the foundation might look like and what it could do. He would accomplish what his father had wished to with the money but was unable.

He called for his car and watched the Mercedes pull into the courtyard, then grabbed his jacket and headed outside. "I need maps," he said. "Big maps—wall sized." They drove him to the Knigy Bookstore on Novy Arbat. Peter bought dozens of maps. He covered the refectory walls with them, ready for Karlov's next teleconference.

"I see you've been busy," said Karlov, eyeing the maps from New York. "What's that behind you? Tajikistan?"

Peter nodded. "I've been plotting the extent of the Kaminsky businesses and determining ways that the Stone Foundation could help local populations. Did you read the outlines I sent?"

"Of course," said Karlov. "You've accomplished more in the past few months than I thought I'd see in my lifetime. I'm glad to see that you are serious."

"It's a start," said Peter.

****

Throughout the summer, Peter rebuilt his strength working with a growing community of volunteers who toppled the watchtower and hauled away the gates of Kurzan Prison. Finally, they dragged the last hunks of rusted scrap metal and barbed wire from the churchyard.

Peter hoed and planted a vegetable garden—his hands slathered with the Russian soil that had been a forest, a farmer's field, a cemetery, a churchyard, and a children's prison. His clothes and hair smelled like compost.

On one unseasonably cold day when the winds blew from Siberia, Peter took shelter in the Church of the Kurzan Goddess. It was cool and dark inside, lit by oil lamps and candles. The roof had been repaired, the domes restored and the clay kagans replaced with new ones. Mosaics covered the reconstructed pillars. Saints rose to the central dome where the dove of peace spread her wings. The only resemblance to the ruin of a few months before was the back wall. Patches of plaster where the boys had engraved their names were preserved under glass—even the ones that said UZI. *We will remember you.*

The floor was still being restored with inlaid malachite, lapis, and charoite to recreate the original. Rows of votive candles and tapers flickered in every niche where icons had been returned from collectors around the world. None burned as brightly as those before the Virgin of Kurzan. The icon had been repaired by experts from the Hermitage and repainted with authentic reds and blues, accented with fresh gold leaf. The missing silver mantle had been discovered in a private collection and donated back to the church. It was cleaned and polished until it gleamed, and reset with uncut gemstones that caught the changing light. Looking closely, he could identify two bullets lodged in the halo. Their copper had been polished until they shone like jewels.

After the brief squall, the colors of the courtyard intensified, and a rainbow arced in the east. Sunlight sparkled on the green lawns and flower beds that bloomed with sweet William, and snapdragons. Sister Makarova shepherded a flock of goats back to the field. Along the newly rebuilt, whitewashed walls, nuns raked the grass free of storm-blown leaves and petals.

Peter climbed the hill to Kurzan Cemetery where the crumbling angel had been replaced by a marble one mounted on a black granite pedestal. He had hired a researcher to scour the Spetsnaz archives and identify the children and parents buried there. Their names were now properly engraved on the polished stone. They included four Kaminskys—UZI's parents, grandparents.

Botanists from Moscow State University had successfully reversed the effects of lime and saponification from the decomposing bodies that had poisoned the soil. A turf of lawn had been rolled over the new topsoil. The grass grew thick and green.

281

Tanya's marble headstone had an angel draping it's wings around her name: Tatyana Yurievna Pavlova, Journalist. He sat on the marble bench at the foot of her grave until the Kurzan bell rang for six o'clock service. It was answered by the bells of Moscow.

****

Peter was hard at work with his maps and papers one morning when Daniel Karlov walked into the refectory.

"I didn't know you were coming," said Peter, looking up in surprise. "Is something wrong?"

"I've found Caroline," said Karlov.

"How? Where?"

"Your hunch was correct. We surveilled the grandmother. She flew to London a week ago."

Peter was disappointed but not surprised to learn that Baba had been lying to him. "Where is she?"

"She's singing at Covent Garden. I was in London, so I went to hear her."

"Is she all right?"

"More than all right." Karlov opened his briefcase and pulled out a newspaper. "I'll read you her review in the *Guardian*. 'Dramatic coloratura soprano Caroline Luke is a stunning but tragic beauty who shines in the title role of Helene in Verdi's *Jerusalem*. Miss Luke sings with the maturity of a seasoned diva. Her musicality is perfection. Every phrase opens a new window into the complexity of a woman's heart. She sings with passion and control seldom heard in the voice of someone so young.'"

Karlov passed him several newspapers. "I've marked the reviews," he said. "They are quite something."

Peter opened the *Moscow Times* and read aloud, "'From the Pushkin Theater in Moscow to her opening at Covent Garden, soprano Caroline Luke is a star.'" His heart ached with pride and loss. He picked up the *World Opera Weekly* and read, "'Caroline Luke is a breathtaking presence on stage with a voice that resonates the pain of the ages, perhaps related to her mysterious abduction in Moscow and dramatic rescue by Russian federal police last year. The resulting trauma to her face required months of plastic surgery.'"

At the end of the article was the sentence: "'The world of opera eagerly awaits her debut in the title role of Bellini's *Norma* at Teatro alla Scala in one week's time.'" Peter checked the date. "That's tomorrow night." He stood up. "Book us a flight to Milan and tickets to La Scala."

"Done," said Karlov, holding up three Alitalia Air tickets. "One for you, one for your bodyguard and one for me. I want to hear her again. The tickets are waiting at the hotel."

The flight departed Domodedovo Airport at midnight. Peter settled by the window in his first-class seat with Karlov next to him and Ruslan across the aisle. He watched the lights of Moscow recede and recalled Caroline at the wheel of her Volkswagen beetle racing across Lake Washington, pounding her fist in frustration. "I am fucking Norma," she'd wailed. How different their lives would be if he'd paid the patronage and she'd sung the role in Seattle.

"Tanya was right," he said aloud. "I am the asshole boyfriend."

Karlov grunted; Ruslan snored.

The poster for Teatro alla Scala's opening of *Norma* was the first thing that Peter saw on deplaning at Malpensa Airport in Milan. Caroline's face was four feet high, framed by a mass of red curls and crowned with a tiara of golden leaves. Her intense green eyes were darkened with kohl and accented with dramatic green and gold shadows. The irregular line of her nose and slight thickening of her cheek added to her exotic look. Caroline was in every way the high priestess Norma. La Scala proclaimed it to the world.

Karlov raised his eyebrows. "Are her eyes really that green?"

"Yes," said Peter, recalling Caroline at Sheremetyevo Airport in her green silk suit.

They followed a uniformed driver holding a sign for "Karlov" to a limousine that had Caroline's face on its side. "Are you here for the opera opening? Everyone's talking about that sexy soprano. Maybe you need tickets?"

"We have them," said Karlov. "Take us to the Hotel Principe de Savoia and pick us up again at six-thirty for the theater."

Their suite had three bedrooms. Peter threw his bag on a bed and opened the envelope propped on his pillow. Their fifth-row center tickets were inside.

"I'm taking a nap." Karlov yawned in the next room. "I suggest you both do the same."

Ruslan looked in on Peter. "Wake me if you plan to go somewhere."

Peter was too restless to sleep. He had decisions to make. When the other men were snoring, he slipped out of the hotel and strolled across the Piazza Della Repubblica. He found a table at an outdoor café and ordered a double espresso, hoping to clear the fog of the red-eye flight with caffeine. Caroline had three performances in Milan, barely enough time to put her under tight surveillance. He hoped it wouldn't be necessary, but if she refused to see him, he could still find out where she lived, where she sang, and whom she slept with.

Was he protecting her? Or was he stalking her? Looking around, he felt like she was stalking him. The square was surrounded by posters of Caroline's face plastered on fences and buildings, the sides of buses, the tops of taxis. Her green eyes followed him everywhere.

By the time he was seated in La Scala listening to the orchestra tune their instruments, Peter still hadn't decided how to approach her. Karlov suggested that they send flowers, but Peter wasn't sure that he wanted Caroline to know that he was in Milan. "It might jinx her performance," he said. It would also alert her to the likelihood that she was being followed. He derided himself for thinking like his grandfather.

He was lost in his broodings when Karlov handed him a program. "You'd better look at this," he said. In red letters across the bottom it read: "Teatro alla Scala gives special thanks to the International Bank of Kurzan for its generous contribution to this production."

"UZI!" Peter jumped to his feet and scanned the audience for any sign of a one-eyed man. In the dim light, they seemed to lurk in every shadow. The lights dimmed to darkness— the house quieted. Peter sank into his chair, haunted by his memory of UZI's eye exploding. *I saw him die.*

The audience burst into applause when the conductor stepped up to the podium. He tapped his baton. The orchestra raised their instruments. The curtain rose on the monoliths of Stonehenge at sunrise. The orchestra played the familiar overture to "Casta Diva." This was Norma's song, the druid priestess's plea for peace after she'd fallen in love with the Roman officer sent to defeat her people. She had slept with the enemy. Whom should she defend—her people or her lover?

A chorus of priestesses gathered among the stones and the spotlight shone on a lone figure descending a staircase—Caroline.

Peter was gripped by a despair so dark that he could find no psychologist's logic to rationalize away his sadness. It was his soul that ached.

"She is magnificent," whispered Karlov. "What a presence." Her wig of waist-length red curls highlighted the whiteness of her bare arms and throat. A clinging gold gown accentuated every perfect curve. She had never looked more beautiful. Peter had never loved her so much. She sang…

"Pure Goddess, whose silver covers
These sacred ancient plants,
we turn to your lovely face
unclouded and without veil...

Peter watched the Stonehenge props on stage recede into the Pacific Ocean. In his mind, the standing stones morphed into the twisted, mist-draped boulders off the coast at Shi Beach A briny gust of wind ruffled Peter's hair. He smelled the sea. His bare toes dug into wet sand. Shrieking gulls circled, buffeted by the wind.

Caroline stood before him, her feet in the swirling water. The sun shone on her translucent skin. The wind tossed her halo of golden hair. Her sorrowful eyes rose to meet his. Their intensity pierced his heart.

She was no longer the laughing, playful spirit that had taken him into herself in joyous frenzy. She had matured into a being far beyond his reach—a goddess born of unimaginable pain.

Peter left at intermission. On the flight back to Moscow, he instructed Karlov to cancel all surveillance on Caroline Luke.

"Why the change of heart?" Karlov asked.

"She doesn't need me anymore," replied Peter.

Chapter Fifty-three

RETURN TO MOSCOW

Kurzan, June 22, 1999

T he seatbelt sign pinged. The Transaero Tupolev-214 banked sharply eastward, then began its approach to Domodedovo Airport in southern Moscow. Caroline raised her seatback and watched through the window as the flight descended over flat Russian countryside—a patchwork of small farms and factories interspersed with dachas of all shapes and sizes. Her pulse quickened. She couldn't see them, but the remains of Konkova were down there along the Moscow River somewhere. *Have I come back to Russia too soon?*

Not that she'd had a choice, or time to consider the wisdom of accepting a last-minute engagement with the Bolshoi Theater. The Maltese diva who had been signed for the lead in *Norma* broke her leg and Caroline's agent had done her job by booking Caroline as the star's replacement. Within twenty-four hours, she was on the Transaero flight from Madrid to Moscow. Fortunately, Baba had been touring with her. Caroline would not have made the journey back to Russia without her grandmother—contract or no contract.

Caroline marveled at how her life had been transformed since leaving Moscow almost two years ago. It had taken months of cosmetic procedures to restore her beauty. It would take years of therapy to overcome her nightmares. She had relived and rationalized each trauma on the psychiatrist's couch. That had helped considerably but not completely. It was the pain in her soul, the combination of guilt, anger and grief, that dogged her—haunting her dreams "You are holding onto your emotional pain," her therapist told her accusingly. "You must let it go or you'll never have meaningful human relationships. You can't suppress your feelings forever."

She had an excuse; she was busy. Her new-found fame had changed everything. Since her triumph in Milan, she had been in constant demand for starring roles. Her agent, Maddie Bear, negotiated contracts and managed her career. She saw to it that they traveled first-class, accommodations were at five-star hotels and the suites stocked with fresh fruit, flowers, and a baby grand piano. Caroline traveled with an entourage that included Maddie, a hair and make-up artist, athletic trainer/voice coach, and security. She should be safe in Moscow this time—surrounded by her own staff.

During the working days, she was an efficient machine—a professional actress who could portray any emotion without feeling it. And as long as she worked her body to the brink of exhaustion, she could override the despair that punished her in her sleep. If she let go of her emotional pain, she argued, what genuine feelings would she have left? At least the pain was familiar and gave a vulnerability to her voice that the public seemed to like.

"Does Peter know that you are coming to Moscow?" asked Baba from the next seat.

"I doubt it. I was a last-minute substitution. It won't be in the newspapers until tomorrow."

"I still don't understand why he stayed at Kurzan." Baba buckled her seatbelt. "I thought he'd be back at Harborview straight away."

"So did I—but Peter is full of surprises." Caroline sighed. "I realize now that I barely knew him."

"He barely knew himself," said Baba. "All this business about the Party's Gold and the Petrosyan Fund must be overwhelming. Inheriting a business like Kaminsky's could take some getting used to."

"Both of our lives have been turned upside-down," said Caroline. "I doubt that we are the same people anymore."

"That's all the more reason to see him while you are in Moscow. You two have so much good history together. Maybe you will still find a happy ending—even if it's only as friends."

"You and your fairy tales."

"But my darling, just look at yourself." Baba appeared surprised. "You are living a fairy tale. This is your dream, isn't it? You are famous with beautiful clothes and real jewelry. The paparazzi follow you everywhere."

"I'm not complaining."

"Nor am I. It's just that you don't laugh anymore and I want you to be happy," said Baba. "When you smile, it's for the cameras or your fans waiting for an autograph. They adore you."

"They are dazzled by the stories that Maddie feeds to the media. She invites the fans and tips off the photographers. I smile and say my lines. It's called public relations."

"Maddie's doing a good job then." Baba held up the latest *People Magazine.* "You are on the cover. I've heard that artists sell their souls to be on the cover. Did you do that when I wasn't looking—sell your soul?"

"Don't tease me, Baba. I've been to that hell." Caroline shivered at the memory of UZI and Moscow Traffic. "It may be in rough shape, but I kept my soul."

"Forgive me, my dear," said Baba. "That was a bad joke. I miss my laughing girl. I want you to find joy and romance." Baba raised her eyebrows. "You're still waiting for Peter, aren't you?"

"Peter has moved on. He has no interest in me."

"How do you know that?"

"Believe me. I know." Caroline had seen Peter arrive and take his seat at La Scala. She'd been watching the audience from her dressing room CCTV and was elated that he'd come—even more so when a huge bouquet of red roses was delivered to her door. She eagerly tore open the card. It was from the International Bank of Kurzan—from UZI, or what was left of him. She let it fall to the floor and checked the other cards on a myriad of bouquets. None of them were from Peter. Maybe his hadn't arrived yet or was waiting at the stage door.

Her dresser and makeup artists crowded into the room. She was powdered, painted, and sewn into the skin-tight, gold *lamé gown.* Norma's heavy red wig was fitted and fluffed. The orchestra played the overture to "Casta Diva" and she took her place at the top of the temple steps.

The curtain rose. Beyond the stage lights, she saw the audience as a sea of black that transformed, in her mind, to the moonlit ocean at Shi Shi Beach. Norma's aria was a prayer for peace among her people. Caroline descended the steps slowly, her voice raised in joy, her heart filled with the happiness she had known with Peter. He was only a few meters away. She stood before him—beautiful and famous, stronger than she had ever been. *Look at me, darling Peter. I have kept my promise. I have made it to the top of the world.*

She reached out expecting him to bound onto the stage and take her in his arms. Instead, the song ended with tumultuous applause. People were on their feet shouting, "Bravo, bravo" and throwing flowers until they carpeted the stage.

At intermission, she hurried to her dressing room and turned on the CCTV in time to see him walking away. *Why, Peter?* His desertion was a dagger in her breast. She couldn't breathe. She grasped at her costume, demanding that they cut it off of her. She drank cold water, and dabbed at the tears that threatened to ruin her make-up.

His leaving should have broken her, but instead her pain gelled into anger. *He won't ruin this for me. Nothing will.* Something split inside and a piece of her entered a new dimension where the pain in her heart wasn't hers anymore. It belonged to Norma.

For the second act, she poured the shock of his desertion into Norma's voice and sang of love, loss, and atonement with a passion beyond anything she had sung before. It exhausted her but did not hurt her. It would never hurt her again. She set a new standard with her art and the critics declared her triumphant. From then on, Caroline Luke became the most sought-after diva for the role of Norma.

She signed with top agent Maddie Bear and the offers kept coming from opera companies. With the money that Maddie negotiated for her, she had no need for patrons. There were recording and television deals as well. She moved to New York and filled her days with music. There were scores to study, librettos in multiple languages to memorize, media interviews, photo-shoots and glamorous new clothes to wear. Baba, meanwhile, closed up her condemned cottage in Seattle. She packed Koshka into his cat carrier, flew to New York and moved into Caroline's spacious Upper East Side apartment that had once been the top floor of an Edwardian house.

Caroline heard from UZI only once after Milan. Maddie received an invitation for her to attend the gala opening of the New York branch of the International Bank of Kurzan. There was a large stipend and the promise of media coverage if she would sing "Casta Diva," and an even larger stipend if she wore the diamond earrings that he had given her. Maddie booked the appearance—it wasn't up to Caroline anymore. Her dresser chose a clingy, black sequined gown with a wide gold belt and Caroline wore the earrings under her long, straight hair.

She and Maddie arrived at the bank together. Caroline was shocked when Oleg Sherepov met them in front of the tall stone edifice on Lexington and ushered them through heavy chrome and glass doors. He had lost his gold earring and acquired an expensive suit. His smile displayed perfect white teeth.

"Can you fucking believe? We own fucking bank," he said, as if he didn't believe it himself. Everything in the entry was gleaming chrome and polished black marble. A piano played somewhere in the lobby. "This for you—from UZI." He handed Caroline a DeBeers jewelry box.

"How exciting," said Maddie. "Open it." Caroline hesitated and Maddie opened it for her with an intake of breath. It contained a dazzling diamond necklace, a perfect match to the earrings. "Put it on," she said. "It's fabulous."

"Maybe later," said Caroline, trying to close the box. She wanted to throw it on the ground but decided not to make a scene.

"No, songbird, now." said Oleg. "UZI wants to see." He pointed at a video camera aimed in their direction.

"I'll help you," said Maddie with a smile to the camera. She fitted it around Caroline's neck.

Caroline held her hair up out of the way and switched from English to Russian. "How is he?" she asked Oleg. "I heard that his surgery was touch and go."

"They cut out his eye," Oleg replied in Russian.

"Will he be at the gala?"

"No, he never leaves his penthouse. They messed up his brain. They might as well have cut off his balls. I don't understand how you lose an eye and your dick stops working. Especially UZI's dick. He doesn't like women any more..."

Maddie was taking forever to fasten the complicated clasp while Caroline was forced to listen to the man who had once terrorized her. She drowned him out with mental music. She made him grow a bulbous, red nose and metamorphose into a clown—a comedic villain in the libretto of her life. She set his monologue to music as he went on about how UZI wasn't the man he used to be and how the sight of blood made him squeamish. She was grateful that Maddie couldn't understand a word of Russian.

"There we are," said Maddie standing back to admire the sparkling necklace. "It's stunning."

The penthouse elevator opened. Caroline stepped in. "Shall we go up?" she said in English. Maddie followed.

"He kept his word to you," said Oleg in Russian. "The poor fool thinks he loves you."

"I don't care what he thinks," she replied in English. UZI had opened that first door for her at La Scala, but she owed him nothing. If the fanged serpent that had defiled her was dead, then justice had been served. She pushed the button to close the door in Oleg's face.

Once the two women were alone, she felt the necklace tighten around her throat. She clawed at it. "I can't breathe," she fumbled with the clasp. "I don't want this damn thing. Take it off, now!"

"I won't do any such thing," said Maddie. "You want to be a diva, then learn to act like one. If a Russian billionaire gives you priceless jewels, you wear them as if you expect to be showered in diamonds every day. And who is he anyway—this mysterious benefactor? Wasn't he the gangster who abducted you? And now he's giving you diamonds? I think I should meet him."

"I forbid it," Caroline pulled on the necklace, trying to break it. "You must never meet him. He's a monster, a killer."

"He doesn't scare me," said Maddie. "And it's time to tell the true story of your life. You owe that to your fans. Sharing a secret like this makes them feel closer to you. A glimpse into the cause of your pain will make them love you even more."

"I'm not ready to share it." Caroline rubbed her neck, realizing that the necklace wasn't coming off. "I sing for my fans. I give them my best every time. Isn't that enough?"

"Sorry, but it's not. People want to know all about you and they will dig up whatever you think that you have buried. It's better that I tell the story of your abduction than UZI—because at some point, he will. Some enterprising reporter will get to him. When that happens, you need the fans already on your side."

Maddie smiled. "Don't look so glum. It's called 'getting ahead of the narrative.' From now on, that will be part of your everyday life. Opera is as political as any other human institution."

"But I've barely recovered. This is happening too fast. I can't get my head around it."

"Fame does that to people. Luckily, I'm here to coach you through it." Maddie smiled. "Case in point: When this elevator opens, you won't be met by adoring fans but by reporters, agents, patrons, and the wealthy vultures of cruel society all primed to tear you to pieces for profit and pleasure. You'd better spread your wings and fly out of here talons-first like an eagle, or they'll eat you alive."

"I don't know if I can do this." Caroline said as Maddie retouched her make-up for her. The elevator dinged. The door slid open.

"Yes, you can. Step into character. Become Norma," said Maddie, and Caroline did.

****

The ride from the Domodedovo Airport to the luxury National Hotel in downtown Moscow was a slow crawl through bumper-to-bumper traffic wrapped in a cloud of petrol fumes. Caroline gazed out at the grimy streets lined by strip clubs, bars and dirty shop windows with nothing in them. How had she ever seen these streets as glorious—imagining them alive with troikas, prancing horses and ghost bells? Even the prostitutes that hovered in doorways looked exhausted. They stared at the hotel limousine with hungry eyes.

The National Hotel was luxurious in every way. Her suite was outfitted just as Maddy had specified with a large window that overlooked Teatralnaya Square and the Bolshoi Theater.

The theater itself was a shambles, a dank, crumbling building long overdue for remodeling. Nevertheless, the mood of the cast was ebullient. A number of soloists from the Pushkin Theater also sang at the Bolshoi and they greeted Caroline as an old friend with flowers and boxes of Red October chocolate. She had once declared this amiable company as her family. Now she stepped into the character of Violetta from *La Bohème* and acted as if she were delighted to see them. As long as she stayed in character—talking, laughing, telling silly jokes—she could fend off the dark matter that crept in on her from all sides. In truth, they seemed less alive to her than the photographs in Baba's chocolate tin.

Life bubbled around her backstage in the usual hive of activity while she went through the necessary motions. There were costume fittings, vocal exercises and stage walk-throughs. Everything was rushed with only one day to rehearse. She had to know where to stand and how the scenery moved on the old stage. There were no video monitors on the set like in European and American theaters. She would have to keep an eye on the conductor, a skill she had mastered at the Pushkin.

The director was concerned. She was a last minute substitution from America and the cast spoke only Russian. She reassured him in Russian that she knew what to do. She proved it during the dress rehearsal. She could call up the passions of Norma and weave a spell over an audience without feeling a thing herself. It was a technique that she had perfected in several languages.

"This is thrilling. You were marvelous," said Maddie, hugging Caroline after the first night's performance that ended in standing ovations and six curtain calls. "The Bolshoi Theater is a dream come true for me."

Caroline stayed at the cast party just long enough to greet the Mayor of Moscow as an old friend and do pre-arranged interviews, then she and Baba were escorted back to their suite at the National. Caroline showered and dried her hair. She joined Baba for tea and chocolate.

"This is what I always wanted—to sing at the Bolshoi," said Caroline. "But Maddie is happier about it than I am. What is wrong with me? I don't feel anything."

"You had everyone fooled," said Baba. "The audience was in tears."

"But not me—not real tears, anyway. I haven't cried since the night I ran away from Kurzan. I haven't laughed either. I left half of me behind in that snowy field—with Peter. What should I do?"

"Go look for it," said Baba. "Maybe it's still there."

****

On the morning of her second day in Moscow, Caroline slipped out of the hotel alone, walked across the square and into Teatralnaya Metro. As she rode the long, fast escalator deep into the bowels of the city, she realized that the country of her soul had gone flat. The sounds and smells of the Metro seemed far away, as if they were avoiding her senses. Nothing was in color anymore—just shades of sepia and gray. She felt drained of color, inside and out.

She caught the Green-Line train that was packed with families, picnics and pets. *It must be a nice day. I didn't notice.* From Kolomeno Station, she crossed under the traffic jam on Andropovsky Boulevard by way of the pedestrian tunnel and entered Kolomeno Park through the ancient Gates of Muscovy.

She was hoping to see how Peter was doing, even if only from afar. She had read articles about Petrosyan Kaminsky's mysterious heir but he had yet to grant any interviews. He must be grappling with the tremendous changes in his life and also with his conscience. He had killed. That must weigh heavily on his soul.

It was cool under the tall oaks that lined the path. The lush park sprawled down a gentle slope to the riverbank. The bleached stone skeletons of once-great churches arched skyward above the trees. Insects hummed, children laughed, and dogs barked. Women strolled in cotton dresses, flirting with men in shirtsleeves. Fall seemed far away and winter snow implausible. With so much happiness all around, some of it must be hers. *All the laughter and smiling faces. Why can't I feel anything?*

Caroline climbed a steep bank to the forested bluff that would lead her through an open field to Kurzan Monastery—the same field she had crossed on the snowy night that she had run away from Kurzan. She crested the hill and stopped in surprise. Instead of an empty meadow, apple trees had been planted in tidy rows that stretched from the base of the bluff to the Moscow River. In their midst rose the pristine whitewashed walls of Kurzan Monastery. The five star-studded blue domes of the restored Church of the Kurzan Goddess gleamed above a flower-filled courtyard.

Caroline followed the footpath that zig-zagged down to the orchard and joined a wider track connecting the road from Kolomeno Park to the open gate of the monastery. A long line of pilgrims waited to enter the church. Some sat on benches with open bibles, others lounged on the grassy lawn or walked among the flowers. Children chased clucking hens across the footpath in front of her. In the distance, nuns herded a flock of bleating goats.

She saw Pavel Pavlov playing chess with his elderly friends in the shade of an oak tree. Gogol rested at his feet. The old colonel didn't see her but the dog raised his head and sniffed the air. He gave Caroline one "woof" and a tail wag before falling back to sleep.

Wind rustled the leaves of the young apple trees. They rippled around her like waves of silver in the sun. She whispered lines from *Norma* to the shimmering boughs:

> *"Pure Goddess, whose silver covers*
> *These sacred ancient plants,*
> *We turn to your lovely face,*
> *Unclouded and without veil..."*

"Come daughter..." said the wind at her ear. " Come into my temple..."

"I hear you, Holy Mother," said Caroline. She raised her hand against the glare of the sun and entered the courtyard, expecting to wait in line with the other pilgrims. No one was there. She crossed the yard and climbed the steps to discover that the Church of the Kurzan Goddess that had been crowded a few minutes before was empty.

She entered the vestibule with its musky scent of incense and tallow and stepped onto the polished stone floor. Her footsteps echoed off the vaulted ceiling, soaring murals and mosaics. Colored light from stained glass windows danced at her feet. The reconstruction of this temple was a work of love as well as art.

Candles burned in every niche of the church though the air was cool, unmoving and smelled of myrrh. She recognized the familiar pink glow from a niche that shone brighter than the others. She followed the light into an alcove and stood before the perfectly restored Virgin of Kurzan.

"It's a miracle," she said, crossing herself in the Russian way.

"Yes, a miracle," said Maria Pavlova, standing beside her. "You have come back to us, dear child. I see that your grandmother raised you in the Orthodox Church."

"Yes Mother Superior," Caroline kissed the hand of Maria Pavlova. "There is an old White Russian church in Seattle. It's where I learned to sing." She gazed up at the icon. "The Virgin of Kurzan looks new. When I held the icon in my hands, it was a ruined block of wood."

"We had it restored by the master-painters at Goritsy."

"The faces look exactly the way I imagined them. How is that possible?"

"The artists claim that a true icon, like this one, paints itself. They only lend their hands and paint brushes and work in a state of deep meditation. We also conducted a chemical analysis and discovered centuries-old hemoglobin soaked into the wood."

"The blood of your pagan ancestors?"

"Quite possibly. Apparently, our relations have lived in this area for at least a thousand years, probably much longer. The bluff above the river is made up of layer-upon-layer of our bones. After a windstorm, you can find skulls and vertebrae that have become exposed."

"So Peter is not a blank slate after all." Caroline smiled.

"Not at all. It just took him a while to believe."

"He must be glad to have family around him. I've always thought that's why he stayed," said Caroline.

"And friends. Even the old partisans from Little Rodinko, the ones who wanted to hang him, have been to visit. They came when the icon was re-consecrated by the Metropolit of Moscow. They are more convinced than ever that Peter is a saint."

"She spoke to me, you know." Caroline stepped closer to the Virgin of Kurzan. "The icon spoke to me. I never told anyone, but she warned me when UZI was about to harm me. After that, she lifted my soul to safety whenever UZI tormented me. She kept me from feeling any pain. I still feel nothing. I believe that she has kept a part of my soul. Now I want her to release it and set me free. Does that sound strange?"

"I have no answer. Icons are portals for the soul. I do know that a wounded soul is not something that the mind can heal," said Maria Pavlova. "I must go prepare for mass but stay as long as you need. I'm glad to have you among us again." She kissed Caroline's cheek.

When the mother superior had gone, Caroline prayed: "Thank you, Holy Mother. You saved me from pain when I couldn't bear it. Now I ask you to release me from this suspended state. Help me to shed the darkness I carry so that I can feel joy and see color again. Please send this penitent back into the world as a whole person and not just pieces of myself."

"Breathe, penitent…" A warm wind gusted through the church. The candles flickered and burned brighter. Caroline inhaled a full, deep breath and blew it out with all the force of her powerful lungs. The darkness that had clung to her insides like bits of tar broke loose and escaped through her mouth in a swarm of tiny black beetles. They buzzed furiously, popped like bubbles and vanished.

Caroline was flushed clean.

Chapter Fifty-four

GREEN APPLES

Kurzan, June 22, 1999

Caroline stepped from the cool shade of the church into brilliant sunshine. The pilgrims had returned and the courtyard was awash in color. She strolled among the beds of peonies with pink, white and orange flowers—smelling their sweet scent. Bees gathered pollen from petunias, violets, snapdragons and borders of purple and white elysium. She feasted her senses on the riotous colors of nature's pallet. It was as if a mad artist had painted the world in vibrant color while she was in the church praying. "It's beautiful," she exclaimed.

"Yes, it is," said Peter."

She turned to find him standing behind her every inch as handsome as she remembered. He wore a dirty apron over a white short-sleeved shirt and jeans. "Peter! How wonderful!" she exclaimed, stepping toward him.

His sun-browned hands were callused working man's hands. He smelled of sweat and compost. He had mud on his boots and a gardening trowel in his hand. "I heard you sing at the Bolshoi last night," he said, smiling. "Like I always said, you are Norma."

"Why didn't you come see me backstage?" She shielded her eyes from the sun and to hide the joy she felt at seeing him. Her emotions were flooding back into her, filling all the empty spaces they had abandoned like the pieces of a Chinese puzzle snapping into place. Being a sentient creature again would take some getting used to. So would being close to Peter again.

"It's not like in the good old days at the Blue Moon Tavern. These days my security needs to talk to your security, and you get the gist."

"Ah yes, the Blue Moon." Caroline smiled. "I'm not allowed to sing jazz anymore. My voice is insured for five million dollars now. Isn't that something?"

"I'm not surprised. The opera world is a big business like any other," said Peter. "Come, walk with me." They came to a wheelbarrow loaded with well-used garden tools. Peter left his apron and boots on it, changing into sandals. "Too bad I don't have a clean shirt," he said, wiping his hands on a dirty towel.

"I don't care," she answered, relishing the sight, the smell, and the sound of him. She wanted to kiss his roughened hands and bare toes. She watched him scrunch up his face and knew that he wanted the same.

"Speaking of business," she said, "I've read about the Denis Stone Foundation. How exciting to have the resources to make a difference in the world. You are the right person to do it."

"I'm trying to close down all the illegal Kaminsky businesses without starting a war. I don't know if it's possible. Petrosyan had his fingers in a lot of nasty pies."

"Are you going to run your foundation from Moscow?"

"For now, at least, while I'm getting to know my Russian family." Peter sighed. "Eventually, I will have to move back to the states. I have a castle in New York City, or so I'm told."

"Petrosyan Towers—it's beautiful, a castle in the sky. I have an apartment with Baba a few blocks from there."

"You'll have to come visit me when I'm in New York." Peter looked around the courtyard. "Where is your security? I can't believe that they let you out alone?"

"It was foolish of me to sneak out. I should get back to the National Hotel before alarms go off."

"Wait," said Peter. "I'll drive you, or rather Ruslan will drive. I'll ride with you."

"I don't know about driving." She frowned. "The traffic is dreadful. It'll take hours to get into Moscow by car but twenty minutes by Metro."

"We'll go on the train together. Come on—like old times." He guided her through the gate and into the orchard. "This is my shortcut when I want to sneak away without the Chechens." The trees were barely shoulder height. Some had rudimentary green apples.

"When can you eat the fruit?" she asked, touching a tiny apple, marveling at its cool, smooth skin and green color.

"It takes years to get a good harvest," he said. "Eventually the fruit from the orchard will support the monastery. That is Pavel's plan, anyway."

"The Colonel always has a plan." She smiled at the earthly sounds of buzzing insects and scolding birds. The air smelled of sweet cut grass and pine.

"And what about you?" said Peter. "Your plans have worked out well. You always said that you would sing in the great opera houses of the world. You are living your dream, aren't you?"

"I've achieved the fame that I wanted. I never imagined how restrictive it could be." Caroline scowled at the thought of her pending theater contracts, obligations for public appearances and interviews, her vocal training, strict diet and exercise regimen. "I've given up on the idea of happiness. There isn't enough time in my schedule."

"And I got the fortune I never wanted and the family I didn't know I had. I didn't plan for either one." Peter sighed. "On the bright side, I am far too busy to waste time feeling sorry for myself."

He gave her a sidewise glance and she laughed at how ridiculous she had sounded. After all, she had deliberately chosen to overload herself with work. "Sorry, I sounded like an ass."

"A bit of a diva, yes." They both laughed.

A gust of wind rustled the leaves into silver waves again that rippled beneath a cerulean blue sky. Side-by-side, they followed the footpath up the hill and into the shade of Kolomeno Forest amongst second growth birch, larch, and poplars. Above the younger trees soared the ancient Siberian white pines, the kedr trees of the sacred circle. They caught the breeze and swayed.

"Did you know that kedr trees don't burn?" said Peter. "That's why these are so much taller than the rest of the forest. They survived the orchard fire of 1928."

"I didn't know that," said Caroline, looking up at the familiar silhouettes of the trees. She imagined the Virgin of Kurzan swinging on a high branch reflecting the sun. "There is so much that I don't know."

Chapter Fifty-five

TEATRALNAYA SQUARE

Moscow, June 22, 1999

Peter boarded the Green-line train at Kolomeno Metro Station behind Caroline. She took a seat and he stood over her holding the handrail in a protective stance. "Just like the old days," she shouted above the roar of the accelerating train.

The car was redolent of Russian summer and farmers hauling fresh produce into the city to sell. They covered the floor with burlap bags of onions and potatoes still coated with moist compost. A little girl held a basket of kittens and clung to her grandmother's arm. A chicken clucked somewhere in the car.

No one spoke over the noise of the train. Passengers either read a book or gazed vacantly into space like Caroline was doing. Peter took the time to stare at her and try to reconcile his confusion. This was the moment he had dreamed of. She was here with him body and soul and her love for him was palpable. His body's response to her nearness was unchanged, nearly unbearable, and his love rekindled. Yet the woman who sat before him was a stranger.

The Caroline he knew had been loose-limbed and braless, free in her movements and careless with her clothes. She should be chattering with the farmers and playing with the kittens—embarrassing him in front of strangers. This new version of her was a bit frightening—a neatly-dressed woman in a tailored linen suit with a Hermes scarf and sunglasses. She sat primly, ankles crossed, hands folded. When she smiled at him, her mouth was asymmetric with thickening along her jawline on one side. He tried to imagine this woman naked in his bed, pressing her breasts against his chest and stroking him the way she did every morning in his dreams. He might have to wear pajamas.

Both Detective Pashkina and Martina Kay had warned him that Caroline would never be the same after her ordeal. He had envisioned her coming back to him as a wounded, frightened creature on the verge of madness. He'd imagined that someday he would be called upon in his role of a physician to save her from herself. Her raw emotionality and volatile nature would eventually be her downfall. He would save her with logic.

Instead she had matured into a successful and self-possessed beauty who had found the courage to return to Kurzan on her own to seek him out. He rubbed at the ache in his chest, tears burning his eyes. *What courage!* The two women had asked if he would want her back, if his love was strong enough. Looking at her profile silhouetted against the window, he knew that the answer was 'yes.'

It was a short walk from Teatralnaya Metro to the National Hotel. Caroline spotted Baba and Maddie in the dining room when they passed the window. Baba saw Peter and waved enthusiastically, beckoning him to come join them.

"I told Maddie not to worry," said Baba as Peter bent down to kiss her cheek. "I knew that Caroline would be with you."

"I'm Maddie Bear, Caroline's agent," said a tall, strawberry blond with bobbed hair and freckles. She extended her hand to Peter. "I know who you are. You're the mysterious Dr. Peter Stone."

"Not so mysterious," said Peter taking a seat while a waiter poured coffee. "I'm rather dull, actually. I spend all day with maps, ledgers and spreadsheets. When I get tired of that, I dig holes in the garden."

"Don't be so modest," said Caroline, wrapping her left arm through his right arm and pressing her breast against him until it was all that he could think of. "Peter has started a new foundation named after his father—the Denis Stone Foundation. They have already rebuilt Kurzan Monastery. It's glorious. You should see what they've done."

"And the icon?" asked Baba. "The Virgin of Kurzan?"

"Completely restored. That and the Church of the Kurzan Goddess. You should take the car and visit Maria Pavlova and Pavel," said Caroline. "Or, I have a better idea." She turned to her agent. "Maddie, can you give Peter five promo tickets for tonight's performance?" She turned to Peter. "I know you came last night…"

"I'll come again," said Peter, covering Caroline's smooth hand with his callused one. "And again."

She beamed at him. "You smell so good," she said, wrinkling her nose.

"So do you," said Peter. The magnetic force that had pushed them apart suddenly reversed polarity. She clung to his arm with her head on his shoulder, as if she wanted to crawl into his heart. He kissed her hair and the world dissolved around them leaving only Peter and the woman he loved.

"I'm so glad to see those two together again," said Baba standing up from the table. "Come on Maddie. Let's leave them alone. Who said there aren't happy endings?"

"I've never seen Caroline happy before," said Maddie as she left with Baba. "She looks positively angelic—like she should sing operettas. And he's gorgeous."

Peter barely noticed that they had gone. He and Caroline were in their own universe, spiraling toward a collision that neither of them could stop. Did he want to stop it?

"Maybe we should talk this through," he said.

"Talk?" Caroline was on her feet. She took his hand and pulled him out of his chair with surprising strength. "Good God, no! I have a suite and four hours before show time."

He followed her to the elevators and to her suite with its flowers and fruit and picture window on Teatralnaya Square. All the way across the room Caroline was unbuttoning her suit, discarding her scarf and shoes. He discarded his sandals, shirt and jeans.

By the time they fell into bed, she had become the woman that he had known and loved for as long as he could remember.

Chapter Fifty-six

THE NEW BOOK OF MIRACLES

Kurzan Convent, Moscow, Russia, Anno Domini 2000

The following letter from Mother Superior Maria Pavlova to Patriarch Alexei II was written in December 2000 and entered into the *New Book of Miracles.*

Greetings to His Holiness Alexei II, Patriarch of Moscow and all Russia,

On the occasion of the second year anniversary of the re-consecration of the Church of the Kurzan Goddess and the third anniversary of the return of our holy icon, the Virgin of Kurzan, I send you greetings.

It has been my honor to serve as Mother Superior during the rebuilding of Kurzan Monastery and the restoration of our community of Kolomeno. As you may know, I was born in Kolomeno Settlement nearly one-hundred years ago. I will soon join my brother, Pavel Pavlov, and his granddaughter, Tanya Pavlova, who rest peaceably side-by-side in the cemetery overlooking the Moscow River.

Only by the grace of God most high have I been granted time beyond my years to bear witness to the healing of this land once thought irredeemable. This land has endured the most cruel desecration with the murder of monks, fire and destruction, the imprisonment and abuse of children, and the theft of holy relics including the Virgin of Kurzan. The misery and decay of human depravity had leeched into the very earth and poisoned every living thing that tried to grow here. The fields that had once been orchards and gardens were barren, strewn with the rusting waste of over seventy years of Soviet oppression. During that time, God was exiled from our lives, if not our hearts.

The night that the Virgin of Kurzan came back to us three years ago was only the first of many miracles. Within hours of the icon's return, all of Russia seemed to know and pilgrims began to arrive. They lined up outside of the ruined Church of the Kurzan Goddess and prayed for redemption and healing before a battered wooden remnant—all that remained of the great icon. They brought with them the weight of their many sorrows and left with a lighter step.

And so began the *New Book of Miracles* which is kept in the Church of the Kurzan Goddess and entered into daily. Strangely, the original Book of Miracles that had been missing since the destruction of Kurzan by the CHEKA in 1928 was discovered sitting alone in a briefcase at the entrance to Kolomeno Park. Because of its great age and some water damage, it is now preserved under glass in a climate-controlled display at the Kurzan Library.

Since then, the land has healed. The monastery was rebuilt by the community with financial assistance from the Denis Stone Foundation. The Virgin of Kurzan was restored and many other icons were returned to the Church of the Kurzan Goddess. Gardens are flourishing once again and a young orchard will soon produce a surplus of apples.

The first marriage in seventy-five years was performed by Bishop Seraphimov who joined my grandson, Peter Denisovich Kaminsky Stone, to Caroline Mikhaelovna Lukhinova Luke in holy matrimony. The following summer, he baptized my great granddaughter, Maria Carolina Stone, and her twin brother, Dennis Pavel Stone. Their births have healed my heart.

In spite of my happiness, all is not perfect within our walls. I mention this because the icon will not remain within my purview much longer. Its notoriety is growing. My successor will be called upon to resolve the problem of foreign visitors who come not to pray but to rationalize. They seek to discover and control what they call the icon's magical properties. More than one visiting professor has asked to take wood samples for scientific analysis, a request that was flatly refused but attempted none-the-less.

Other heretical groups have offered great sums of money to be left alone in the church at night. They were also refused. A church from California wished to sponsor the icon on a world tour. I told them that the icon does not travel.

The bishop suggested sealing the icon behind glass with an alarm of some kind. I declined that suggestion. I believe that the icon will defend against any confinement that separates it from the pilgrims. What happens if or when it does strike out? We have already treated a few burnt fingers, but the icon is capable of much worse. What will be the legal liability of the church if someone is seriously frightened or injured? Could there be an international incident? What will happen if the government decides to override my authority and move it to a museum, as has been suggested by the Hermitage Museum and Tretyakov Gallery? They each have large, well-guarded icon collections, but neither has experience with an immutable entity of unknown power like the Virgin of Kurzan.

I leave these earthly concerns to you and my worthy successor as I prepare to join my Holy Father in the Kingdom of Heaven and to sit at the right hand of Jesus Christ, Our Savior. I am now and forever your faithful servant and a devoted child of the Lord my God,

– Maria Artyumovna Pavlova
Mother Superior
Kurzan